A CENTURY
OF STORIES
NEW HANOVER COUNTY PUBLIC LIBRARY
1906-2006

THE
Young
WIDOW

THE

Young

WIDOW

CASSANDRA CHAN

St. Martin's Minotaur
New York

www.minotaurbooks.com

Library of Congress Cataloging-in-Publication Data

Chan, Cassandra.
    The young widow / by Cassandra Chan.—1st St. Martin's Minotaur ed.
        p. cm.
    ISBN 0-312-33748-5
    EAN 978-0-312-33748-3
    1. Police—Great Britain—Fiction. 2. Private investigators—Great Britain—Fiction. 3. Remarried people—Fiction. 4. Poisoning—Fiction. 5. Widows—Fiction. I. Title.

PS3603.H35556Y68 2005
813'.6—dc22

                                                                2004065376

First Edition: August 2005

10 9 8 7 6 5 4 3 2 1

To Doe, the best mother an aspiring writer ever had.
This is for you, with love and heartfelt thanks
for making everything possible.

ACKNOWLEDGMENTS

I wrote this all by myself and the following people are only guilty of having liked it enough to want to share it with the general public. Thanks are due to the late Kathleen Jordan, who first made it possible for Bethancourt to see the light of day; to Jennifer Jackson, who overlooked my total inarticulateness in our first conversation and went on to sell the book anyway; to Kelley Ragland, who "got" what it was all about and worked to make it better; to Carly Einstein, who has very patiently guided me through the whole publishing process; and to Bill Bumgarner, whose help with my computer enabled the book to actually get written.

THE
Young
WIDOW

CHAPTER

1

*A*nnette Berowne had a sweet, heart-shaped face. She had honey-blond hair and wide brown eyes. She was not beautiful, and certainly not glamorous, but only Phillip Bethancourt noticed that. Everyone else was blinded by the charm of her manner, by a certain ethereal quality mixed with an earthy femininity.

On the evening of the day that Scotland Yard was consulted in the matter of her husband's death, Phillip Bethancourt lay in bed listening to the steady beat of the rain on the windowpanes and admiring the white, lissome form beside him. Marla Tate, one of England's top fashion models, was dozing, passion sated, her coppery hair like a halo on the pillow, her jade-green eyes hidden behind closed lids. Her long legs were entangled with Bethancourt's but her torso had twisted away from him, giving an excellent view of her small, perfectly shaped breasts.

A hush lay over the large bedroom, and with the waning daylight the room had grown dim, letting shadows pool in the corners. In one of them, Cerberus, Bethancourt's large Borzoi hound, lay on his side, fast asleep, adding to the drowsy atmosphere.

Bethancourt was just reaching out a finger to touch one copper curl when he was interrupted by the faint but unmistakable chimes of the ship's clock in the living room. It was striking the hour. It was striking six o'clock.

"Hell," said Bethancourt softly, and his hand descended not on Marla's hair but on her shoulder, shaking her awake.

The languid serenity of the bedroom was shattered as Marla came to full consciousness with a jerk and demanded the time while Bethancourt groped on the nightstand for his glasses, and Cerberus shot to his feet, ears pricked.

"Six o'clock," Bethancourt answered, rolling out of bed and donning a heavy silk dressing gown. "We're supposed to be meeting Jack at this very moment."

"Bloody hell," said Marla.

Detective Sergeant Jack Gibbons was ready to leave his office on time—an unusual occurrence. He sat behind his desk with his Burberry over his arm and his briefcase close to hand, waiting rather anxiously while he wondered if Bethancourt or more work would come to occupy him first.

He had changed his shirt in the men's room and substituted a tweed jacket past its best years for the sweater he had been wearing. Still, he looked all right, he thought, examining himself in the small shaving mirror he kept in his desk for those times when he seemed hardly able to go home at all and needed some sprucing up before interviewing a witness. Reflected back at him was a man of medium height, a little stocky in build, with reddish-brown hair cut short and fierce blue eyes. He looked exactly like what he was: a young, off-duty policeman, but he managed to convince himself otherwise.

The contest between Bethancourt and work was won resoundingly when the phone rang. Gibbons glared at it, but ignoring it never entered his mind. With a sigh, he picked up the receiver.

"Stop by my office on your way out, Sergeant," said Detective Chief Inspector Carmichael's gravelly voice.

"Yes, sir," replied Gibbons respectfully, masking entirely the irritation he felt. "I was just going now, sir."

"Fine, fine. I won't keep you long."

Gibbons sincerely hoped not. It was not often that he left the Yard at anything approaching a reasonable hour and normally he did not begrudge it. His promotion from constable to sergeant had come swiftly, inspiring some to refer to his meteoric rise in the CID, and he wanted to make inspector in as short an order. To that end, he worked long and hard, but with nothing much on his plate at the moment, he felt he deserved a night on the town.

Detective Chief Inspector Wallace Carmichael was looking over a case file spread out across his desk when Gibbons arrived. He had lit an inferior cigar and removed his jacket and he raised bushy white eyebrows as he looked up at his sergeant, noting the change of clothes.

"Got something on tonight, then, Sergeant?" he asked.

"Yes, sir," returned Gibbons. He liked Carmichael, who gave a man every chance to shine, and who was always fair. "Phillip Bethancourt's giving a party tonight at the Oxford and Cambridge Club. A friend of ours has just made partner at Lincoln's Inn."

"Well, I won't keep you," said Carmichael, digging out a second file from beneath the papers scattered over his desk. "We're starting a new case tomorrow down in Surrey. Here's a copy of the case file for you to look over. I'm going down tomorrow morning for a briefing with the chief constable and you can meet me afterward. Say about ten-thirty."

"Yes, sir," said Gibbons, taking the file and stuffing it under his arm. "I'll read it over tonight."

"Go on, then. Enjoy your party."

"Thank you, sir."

When Gibbons returned to his office, he found it occupied by a tall, fair young man with horn-rimmed glasses, immaculately dressed in a silk Armani suit. He was accompanied and utterly eclipsed by a slender woman of undeniable beauty and elegance. She was perched on the edge of Gibbons's desk in a pose reminiscent of one she had lately displayed in a well-known fashion magazine. They were both perfectly composed, neither displaying the slightest hint of the frantic half-hour of preparation that had preceded their appearance.

"There you are," growled Gibbons. "Hello, Marla. I thought you were meeting us there."

"Last minute change in plans," responded Bethancourt, who was leaning comfortably back in Gibbons's desk chair with his long legs crossed at the ankle. "Marla wanted to make sure you were coming."

Gibbons was considerably surprised at this statement. Marla loathed her boyfriend's detective hobby and held the view, not unreasonably, that Gibbons was largely to blame for Bethancourt's involvement in the investigations of various violent deaths. As a result, she was usually less than eager to include Gibbons in their plans.

But she seemed perfectly happy to see him now. The false and brilliant smile that had decorated so many magazine pages flashed across her face and she leaned forward to kiss his cheek, leaving a waft of spicy perfume in her wake.

"I wanted to be sure you'd be there to meet Carol," she said.

"Carol?"

Bethancourt looked amused. "Marla," he said, "has formed the idea that if you could be interested in something other than your work, she might be privy to fewer conversations about murder. I have to admit that if anything is likely to distract you from your career, Carol is certainly a good candidate."

Marla scowled at him. "Don't be silly. I just thought they would like each other, is all. And this seemed the perfect opportunity," she added, turning back to Gibbons. "A party, where the two of you can get on or not as you please."

"Well, that's awfully kind of you," said Gibbons, reflecting that most of the women Marla knew were models, certainly an attractive group. He picked up his briefcase and shoved the file into it. "And I'm ready to go whenever you like—I've just got back from saying good night to the D.C.I."

"Then let's be off," said Bethancourt, rising. "The taxi is waiting downstairs."

There was impromptu dancing after dinner and Marla was in her element. Bethancourt watched with a half-smile on his lips as Giles Porter clasped her far too tightly and waltzed her about the floor. She would expect Bethancourt to assert his rights eventually, but he had half an hour now when he might slip away unnoticed. He lit a cigarette and went off in search of Gibbons, who had disappeared some little while before.

Bethancourt found his friend in the hush of the library, drinking black coffee and poring over a file open on the table before him. No hint of the party penetrated here; all was quiet and well-ordered.

"You're not supposed to have drinks in here," said Bethancourt, strolling over.

Gibbons looked up. "I had more wine than I meant to at dinner," he said, "and I've got to get this stuff into my head tonight."

"I throw splendid parties," said Bethancourt, self-satisfied. He pulled out a chair and dropped into it. "Is that the new case?"

Gibbons sat back and smiled. "How did you know there was one?" he asked.

"You came back from Carmichael's office with a file," answered Bethancourt, shrugging. He took a moment to settle himself into the chair, at last finding the epitome of comfort. "So what is it?"

"The Berowne case."

"Berowne—that sounds familiar."

"Of course it does. He was Geoffrey Berowne of Berowne Biscuits, although he retired a couple of years ago."

"Oh, yes. I remember reading about it." The memory, however, appeared to be elusive, for Bethancourt paused and then said doubtfully, "Poisoned, was he?"

"That's right." Gibbons searched among his papers and selected a report. "Lilies of the valley."

"What do you mean, 'lilies of the valley'?"

"It's what he was poisoned with. I'd never heard of it either."

Bethancourt regarded his friend with a severe eye. "You can't poison people with flowers, Jack. At least, not that kind of flower."

"Yes, you can," retorted Gibbons.

"Nonsense." Bethancourt rose and began to wander down the length of the library, peering into the bays. "There's a section here somewhere," he muttered. "Ah, there." He disappeared into one of the bays and emerged in a moment with a book open in his hands. He turned the pages as he walked back to the table and then paused as he found the entry he wanted.

"Well, I guess you can," he admitted. "It's evidently quite toxic."

"So forensics said," replied Gibbons sarcastically.

"It says here that even the water the cut flowers have been standing in will kill you."

"That's how they think it happened," said Gibbons. "He was having his elevenses, and someone tipped a bit of poisoned water into it."

"It must have tasted awful."

"Must have. But his sister-in-law said he always gulped things down. A coffee cup evidently only held a couple of swallows for him. He'd have it down before the taste registered."

"And it's quick acting," said Bethancourt, who was still reading.

"Just so."

Bethancourt closed the book thoughtfully and sat down. "A

spouse is always the first suspect," he said. "Is there some reason Mrs. Berowne can't have dosed the poor devil?"

"None at all," replied Gibbons cheerfully. "In fact, she behaved quite suspiciously that morning. Everyone, including herself, testified that she was not a great walker and drove everywhere, yet on the morning her husband was murdered, she decided to walk to the village and took twice as long as she should have getting there."

"There you are then," said Bethancourt. Disappointment showed in his eyes. "You'll just be gathering evidence and pushing it along to the attorneys."

Bethancourt was never interested in Gibbons's more mundane cases; forensic science held no charm for him, nor did the violent world of habitual criminals. He was intrigued by the people in a murder case, by what might drive an otherwise ordinary person to murder, and by the deductive process that led to the singling out of that person from the rest. A straightforward wife-poisons-husband case was not one he would spend two minutes thinking about.

Gibbons grinned at him. "It might be a bit more complicated than that," he said. "After all, there's got to be some reason the Surrey CID called in the Yard."

Bethancourt was surprised. "It didn't happen in London?"

"No, he was killed on his estate in Surrey. If it's not the wife, there are certainly plenty of other suspects." He pulled a single sheet from amongst the others. "There's Berowne's sister-in-law from his first marriage who was living in the house; there's his son and daughter-in-law, living in a separate house on the estate; not to mention the cook, chauffeur, gardener, and housekeeper. None of them have alibis."

"And did they all stand to gain from his death?"

"More or less. I was just looking over the terms of the will. The servants all get minor bequests and the bulk of his millions go to the widow for her lifetime." He frowned and reached for his coffee. "It's rather complicated. There's a sum left absolutely to her, but most of it will be inherited upon her death by Berowne's grandson, aged five at the moment. The real estate is also left to him, to be administered by the widow until he comes of age." He scratched his head. "That's odd."

"What's that?"

"Wait—I'm sorting it out. There's a provision here that both Mrs. Berowne and the sister-in-law are to be allowed to live in the house until they die or wish to leave. And—" he consulted a second sheet "—yes, Berowne's son and daughter-in-law are also to be allowed to live in the second house on the estate until their deaths. So even when young Edwin does come of age, he can't kick anyone out and he can't even live in his own house unless he wants to share it with his step-grandmother and his great aunt, with his parents looking on from across the garden."

"My," said Bethancourt. "They must all hate each other like poison."

Gibbons raised an eyebrow. "And how do you work that out?"

"Well, isn't it obvious?" replied Bethancourt. "If the estate was a bastion of brotherly love, he'd just leave it to whomever he liked and assume they'd take care of the others. Instead, what he's tried to do is ensure that no one will be kicked out of their home once he's dead. Clearly that means he was worried that someone would be booted out."

Gibbons considered. "I hadn't thought of it like that," he admitted.

"But what's most interesting is that the son isn't mentioned at all."

"Oh, yes, he is," said Gibbons. "He inherits his father's shares in Berowne Biscuits, and it mentions that nothing more is left to him now because of his interest in the company and the amount settled on him at the time of his son's birth. There's also, if you want to know, a bequest of a hundred thousand pounds to Madeleine Wellman—that's the sister-in-law—and another of the same amount to his daughter-in-law."

Bethancourt shrugged this away. "That's nothing," he said. "People often leave bequests to their favorite relatives. My grandfather did to me, which made my sister furious. Well, it might turn out to be an interesting case at that. You've no idea why the Yard's been asked to lend a hand?"

Gibbons shook his head. "Perhaps they think it's the son," he suggested. "He's taken Berowne Biscuits over from his father and the offices are in London. If they found this murder connecting up with another crime here, they might want us in on it. Anyway, I'll find out tomorrow. I'm meeting Carmichael in Guildford after he's seen the chief constable."

"Are you?" asked Bethancourt. His hazel eyes were bright behind his glasses. "You wouldn't want a lift down, would you?"

Gibbons smiled. "I thought you might offer," he said.

"You can fill me in on the rest then," said Bethancourt, rising rather reluctantly. "Right now, I had better get back before Marla notices I'm gone."

"All right." Gibbons turned over the report on the will and gave his attention to the next item. Then he looked up. "Phillip," he called, "you won't be late, will you? I've got to be in Guildford at ten-thirty."

Bethancourt waved a hand airily. "Don't worry," he said.

Gibbons did not feel reassured; Bethancourt was nearly always late.

CHAPTER

2

D etective Chief Inspector Wallace Carmichael of New Scotland Yard sat in the chief constable's office in Guildford the next morning with an impassive expression on his face. He was an older man, growing heavier as he grew older, with thick gray hair and bushy white eyebrows. Seated around him were Edward Gorringe, the chief constable of Surrey, Divisional Commander Andrews, and Inspector Curry, who was Andrews's dogsbody. Andrews and Curry between them had gone over the basic facts of the case, the real problem of which seemed to be that both senior men had known the Berownes, had socialized with them, and were now understandably reluctant to accuse one of the family of murder.

"Particularly since there's no evidence," Andrews had said. "Mrs. Berowne is the obvious suspect—she's the wife, her husband was wealthy, and she's thirty years younger. But any one of them could have done it, and you can't imagine how difficult it is to grill people with whom you dined last week. The whole thing is a nightmare."

Carmichael sighed. He did not like this case. He was of the old school of detectives, who had worked his way up from uniformed constable to his present exalted position. He had never been very comfortable with wealthy, powerful people; after all, the majority of homicides did not occur within their ranks. There were men at the Yard who specialized in sensitive cases, but they were otherwise occupied, and Carmichael was an experienced, well-seasoned detective; the powers that be had decided that he could handle it. He knew he could, but he still didn't like it.

"So I'm rather afraid," Gorringe was saying apologetically, "when the question of this rumor came up, I rather jumped at the chance to hand things over to you. Not that I believe it," he added, "but it'll have to be looked into all the same, and that's out of my jurisdiction."

"What rumor?" asked Carmichael, turning over a page of the case file.

"It's there," said Curry. "That last statement. Actually, it took us a hell of a long time to dig it out—nobody wanted to repeat it to policemen known to be friendly with the Berownes. You see how our hands are tied."

"Yes, of course," said Carmichael. "But the rumor?"

"It started with Mrs. Langston—an old cat if ever there was one," said Andrews.

"Quite a coincidence, really," said Gorringe. "This Mrs. Langston only moved to Peaslake a year or so ago. Previously, she had lived in Kent, in Hawkhurst, I think. Anyway, it was the same town that Mrs. Berowne had come from, where she had been married to William Burton who died a couple of years before she married Geoff Berowne. That's common knowledge. What Mrs. Langston supplied was the fact that William Burton was an elderly man and that at the time of his death, there were rumors in the town that Mrs. Burton had killed him for his money. He was a well-to-do man, you see."

Carmichael digested this in silence, not liking it very much.

"Well, we can certainly check into that," he said. "Tell me, you all know Mrs. Berowne. Do you think she's guilty?"

There was dead silence. No one looked at him.

The pause was becoming awkward when at last the chief constable sighed. "I've always liked Mrs. Berowne very much," he said slowly. "She's a charming woman and I thought she and her husband were a very affectionate couple. I find it difficult to believe she murdered him. But neither can I discount it."

Carmichael wasn't about to discount it either, although he could see evidence was going to be hard to come by. Andrews had said as much, apologizing for handing Carmichael a probably unsolvable case. "There's nothing to get hold of, you see," he had said. "Lilies of the valley bloom all over the estate. Any one of them could have picked some, put the water from the vase into a bottle, and tipped it into the coffeepot. We've got nothing to say it was more likely this person than that."

Carmichael emerged slowly from the lift, the case file in one hand and his raincoat in the other. He spotted Gibbons lounging on a bench against the far wall of the lobby, reading a local paper. Somehow the sight of his sergeant cheered Carmichael up. He had a high opinion of Gibbons's talent and abilities, and it was a relief at his age to have a sergeant who could be depended on to follow things up properly and not miss anything along the way. He had not, many years ago, been too sure about the idea of university-educated policemen, but if ever there was justification for the notion, Gibbons was it.

He crossed the lobby briskly.

"Good morning, sir." Gibbons folded the paper and set it aside. "How was your meeting?"

Carmichael snorted. "The case is a mess," he said. He handed

Gibbons the case file and began struggling into his raincoat. "How was the train ride down?"

"Well, actually, sir, I caught a lift."

"A lift?" Carmichael paused in adjusting his collar.

"Yes, sir. Phillip Bethancourt brought me down."

"Did he indeed?" Carmichael turned to peer out the glass doors into the car park, his eyes fixing accurately on the gray Jaguar and the tall, slender young man beside it, standing bareheaded in the drizzle and smoking a cigarette.

"I told him," said Gibbons, "that you probably wouldn't want him along when we went to the Berownes', but he said he'd wait anyway. I think, sir, he's curious as to why we're being given the case at all." Gibbons looked up hopefully, for he was at least as curious as Bethancourt, but Carmichael was staring outside and thinking.

Bethancourt's father had been to school with the chief commissioner and word had come down that, when it wasn't inconvenient, Bethancourt was to be allowed to look on during investigations. His father evidently cherished hopes that this would inspire his son to join the force, but these hopes had not thus far borne fruit. Mostly Carmichael hadn't minded. Bethancourt kept discreetly in the background and had even been quite helpful once or twice. And he came from a wealthy family, like the Berownes. Perhaps he would understand these people better than Carmichael or his middle-class sergeant ever could.

"Tell him he can come," said Carmichael abruptly. He shrugged off the raincoat he had just donned. "We'll go down to the canteen and run over the case file briefly. I could use a cup of coffee anyway."

"Yes, sir," said Gibbons, surprised. He rose from the bench and went out in the rain to collect his friend.

୬ ୬ ୬

13

Peaslake was some miles from Guildford. Gibbons drove the police Rover capably through the rain, while Carmichael puffed on a cigar and read over Mrs. Berowne's statement for a third time. Bethancourt followed them in the Jaguar.

"Is this the turnoff, sir?" asked Gibbons.

Carmichael lifted the case file and glanced at the ordinance survey map underneath. "That's right." He gazed out the windscreen while Gibbons negotiated the right-hand turn, and then asked, "Were you and Bethancourt roommates at Oxford?"

"Oh, no, sir," said Gibbons, rather surprised. "He was at Merton." Silence greeted this information, so Gibbons added, "I was at St. Johns. The buildings aren't even adjacent."

"But you were close? Read the same subject, perhaps?" It had suddenly occurred to Carmichael to wonder how his brilliant, ambitious, hard-working sergeant had become such close friends with a man who, while brilliant in his own way, was anything but ambitious and hard-working. Lazy was a better adjective for Bethancourt.

"No, sir," answered Gibbons, glancing in the rearview mirror to make sure the Jaguar was still in sight. "Phillip read classics. We didn't really know each other very well then. We became friends in London, a year or so after we came down."

"Oh," said Carmichael, not much enlightened.

"We happened to run into each other during the Hopkins case," explained Gibbons. "You remember it, sir?"

"Certainly, Sergeant. You were very clever over it, as I recall."

Gibbons said nothing, merely nodding appreciation of this accolade. In fact, it had been his chance meeting with Bethancourt in a pub that had produced the clever idea which led to the case's solution. It had also resulted in Bethancourt's devouring interest in murder cases and had cemented the firm friendship between the two men. Sometimes, thought Gibbons, fortune smiled on you when you were least expecting it.

"So what's our line on this case, sir?" he asked.

Carmichael snorted. "The wife, of course," he answered. "It's usually the spouse, and if you want my private opinion, Gibbons, the real reason Surrey CID called us in is because they couldn't find enough evidence for an arrest." He sighed. "Let's hope we have better luck."

"Yes, sir." Gibbons slackened his speed as they approached a town. "Where to now, sir?"

"This must be Peaslake," said Carmichael, referring to the map. "We go straight through."

They drove through the town—still referred to as "the village" by the inhabitants, but grown considerably beyond that in recent years—and came out again into the country. A mile or so out of the town, they turned off onto a narrow, winding country road with large houses set well back from the street and screened by trees and hedges. After another mile or so, a high redbrick wall sprang up on their right, and they followed its curve for some ways until both road and wall straightened out, and an opening appeared in the red brick marked by granite pillars with wrought-iron gates standing open.

"This is it," said Carmichael, peering at a stone plaque set into the wall beside the gates. "Hurtwood Hall," he read, and grunted. "Well, that's certainly descriptive."

Gibbons turned into the drive, which was overhung on either side by large plane trees. The lane curved gently, leading them on, out from the trees, and ending in a sweeping circle before the house. This was a huge, redbrick Victorian monstrosity and Carmichael found himself thinking that if he had amassed a fortune, he would never by any chance spend it on a residence like this. Gibbons drew the car up to one side of the drive, and the gray Jaguar came to halt just behind it. Bethancourt got out and joined them, peering upward at the house through the fine rain.

"What on earth do you think they do with all the old servants' quarters?" he asked.

"It's pretty awful, isn't it?" said Gibbons in a low voice.

They climbed the steps to the front door, which was opened, after a little delay, by a middle-aged woman in a blue cleaning smock. She ushered them in, saying Mrs. Berowne was expecting them. "If you'll just come this way," she said. Her voice was low, and she avoided meeting their eyes, as if their presence made her nervous.

Carmichael smiled genially. "Would you be Mrs. Mary Simmons?" he asked pleasantly.

"Yes, sir."

"You live in, don't you?"

She shot him an anxious glance, as if this interest in her was somehow menacing. "Yes, sir," she answered, and motioned with relief toward a large drawing room. "In here, please, sirs. I'll just tell Mrs. Berowne you're here."

She beat a hasty retreat while Carmichael was saying thank you.

The decor of the room was unexpectedly pleasant and tasteful. Before the somewhat ornate mantelpiece were drawn up two comfortable-looking armchairs, patterned in a very faded medieval forest brocade. A little beyond them were gathered two more armchairs, a sofa, and a love seat in a bold flower pattern, all grouped about a deep green carpet and an oaken coffee table. The effect was cozy, and quite homey.

For all that, the house had a curiously empty feel to it. It had been built to house a large Victorian family with at least a dozen servants, and something in the silence of the room proclaimed that four women were not enough to fill it. It had the air of a home after all the children had left.

The three men divested themselves of their raincoats and settled themselves on the sofa and armchairs. Gibbons produced a notebook and pencil, while Bethancourt examined the coffee table. Carmichael leaned back in the very comfortable sofa and took in his surroundings with a sharp eye.

Then Annette Berowne came into the room.

16

She had an air about her that drew all their eyes and kept them. There was a peculiar kind of grace to her movements; she seemed to drift, rather than walk, into the room, and though her heart-shaped face was serious, there was an indefinable expression in her eyes that seemed to welcome them.

"Hello," she said, and gave them a smile that warmed her brown eyes and made dimples flash in her cheeks. "I'm Annette Berowne."

She came forward and offered Carmichael a small hand with rose-tipped nails, delicate but firm in its touch.

"Detective Chief Inspector Carmichael, ma'am," he answered. "This is Detective Sergeant Gibbons, and our colleague, Phillip Bethancourt."

She shook hands with all of them and then sank, rather than sat, into a chintz-covered chair and turned melting brown eyes expectantly toward Carmichael, who smiled neutrally at her.

The effect she had on the three men facing her was varied. All three were aware that she was their first suspect in the murder of her husband, yet there was a kittenish quality to her that made thinking of her as a murderer difficult. Carmichael firmly reminded himself that poison was a woman's weapon and tried to order his thoughts, which were unaccountably in disarray.

Gibbons arranged his notebook with great care and inspected his pencil point, all the time intensely aware of the woman seated to his left. She was not, he felt, at all what he had thought she would be. He had rather been expecting the kind of woman his grandmother called a "floozie," but that did not describe Annette Berowne in the least. He noticed that beneath her welcoming expression she looked tired, with dark smudges under her eyes and a slightly strained quality to her marvelous smile. Unexpectedly, he felt a pang of sympathy for her. He glanced at Bethancourt to see what his friend thought of her.

Bethancourt alone noticed that she was not beautiful and thought what a pity that was. She was not plump, but neither was she possessed of the kind of figure obtained by rigorous dieting and even more rigorous exercise. There was a fullness about her hips and abdomen, offset by the generous swelling of her breast. Bethancourt's standards, exemplified by Marla Tate, were high, and this woman did not meet them. Yet he was quite unable to look away from her, which said much about the feminine mystique she embodied. He thought that if she had possessed beauty as well, she would have been phenomenal.

He felt Gibbons's gaze on him, and shifted to meet his eyes, giving a slight shrug to indicate he didn't know what to make of Annette Berowne either.

"First, Mrs. Berowne," said Carmichael in his gravelly voice, "let me offer our condolences on your loss. I understand that this is a very sad and difficult time for you, but I'm afraid we must ask you to go over your evidence once more."

"Thank you," she said. "Daniel—that is, Commander Andrews explained that you would need to ask me things." She kept her eyes fixed on Carmichael, as if he were a difficult schoolmaster who might at any moment produce a question she could not answer. Carmichael had an irritating impulse to soothe her fears.

"If you could just tell us, ma'am, about the day of the murder."

She nodded compliance. "It was a beautiful day," she said in her soft voice. "The first nice one in ever so long. There were some errands I wanted to run in the village and, once I was ready to go, I went into Geoffrey's study to let him know. I asked him if he wanted to come with me, but he had some papers to go over and said no. Kitty came in with his midmorning coffee just as I was leaving and we went out together. I told her where I was going and she asked me to pick up a tin of pears."

"Kitty is your cook?" asked Carmichael.

"Yes." She nodded, and a lock of dark blond hair fell over her cheek. "Katherine Whitcomb—she's our old cook's niece."

"You said she brought in Mr. Berowne's midmorning coffee? Do you know what time this was?"

"He always had his coffee at eleven," she answered. "I checked my watch as I left the house, and it was a minute or so past eleven then."

"Now you said you asked Mr. Berowne if he would go to the village with you." Carmichael's tone was ruminative and gentle. "Yet you knew he was just about to have his elevenses."

"Oh," she said, "I told him I'd wait if he wanted to come. It would only have been twenty minutes or so."

Carmichael nodded. "Now, I want to ask you about the tray. Did you—incidentally, didn't you often take it in to your husband yourself?"

"Usually, if I was in the house," she agreed.

"But you didn't that day?"

She looked a little helpless. "No," she said. "Daniel Andrews asked about that as well, but there wasn't any particular reason. I just didn't. I was in my room changing, and looking forward to going out, and once I was ready, I just ran down to the study. I didn't think of the coffee and I didn't forget it either."

"I understand," said Carmichael soothingly, sounding as if he really did. "Did you notice the tray when Miss Whitcomb brought it in?"

"Not particularly," she said. "I think it seemed just as usual. The same coffeepot and everything, I mean."

"Could you describe how it was usually set out?" asked Carmichael.

"Oh, certainly." She smiled at him, apparently pleased at being asked a question she could answer definitively, and the dimples flashed in her cheeks. "It was always exactly the same," she continued. "A plain cup and saucer, the Rockingham coffeepot, and a little plate of biscuits. Oh, and a napkin."

"No cream or sugar?" asked Carmichael.

"No, he never took any."

"And the tray seemed as usual to you that day?"

"I think so," she answered. "Certainly I noticed nothing out of the ordinary."

"Did Miss Whitcomb pour a cup of coffee for Mr. Berowne?"

"Oh, no." She shook her head. "She just set it down on the table. He liked to let it cool a few minutes, so that he wouldn't burn his tongue gulping it down." Her smile this time was sad. "He drank nearly everything that way, all in one swallow, except for port and cognac."

"Very well," said Carmichael, going on to the next matter. "Now, as you left the study, you told Miss Whitcomb you were going into the village and asked if she needed anything?"

"Yes, that's right. At first she said no, but then she changed her mind and asked for the tinned pears. I told her I'd pick them up and then I left."

"I understand you had decided to walk to the village." Carmichael said it evenly, but she did not seem alarmed.

"Yes," she said. "I usually drive, but it was such a lovely day, I decided to walk. I felt I wanted some fresh air, you see. So I left the estate by the back gate and took the footpath across the fields. I was halfway there when I suddenly thought that I hadn't seen my library card in my wallet while I was checking my money. It was the whole reason for the trip, you see," she added confidingly. "The library rang that morning to say a book on roses I'd been wanting had come in. Anyway, I stopped and checked, and the card wasn't there. So I started back for it, wondering where I could have left it, and at last I remembered seeing it on the bureau and sticking it in my pocket. I was more than halfway back to the estate by then, and I thought of getting the car. But I decided not to. It was still a beautiful day, you see."

Carmichael smiled back at her. "Yes, I see," he said. "So you arrived in the village at about what time?"

"Just before noon, I think," she replied. "I didn't actually look at my watch, you know." She was frowning a little, her eyes downcast, as if remembering something unpleasant or sad. But in the next moment the mood was gone as swiftly as it had come, and she lifted her eyes and smiled ruefully. "There was a point when the day seemed just a little bit less lovely and I was wondering if I'd ever get there and I looked at my watch and it said ten minutes before the hour. But then I came over the top of the hill and there I was."

"That's a very clear account, Mrs. Berowne," said Carmichael. "I know this is a painful time for you and I'm sorry, but I must ask: was your marriage a happy one?"

She looked thoroughly startled, as if it were impossible that he should not already know. "Yes," she said at last, in a low voice. "We were very happy together. Very happy indeed." She caught her breath and bit her lip to hold back sudden tears.

"He was your second husband, was he not?" asked Carmichael gently.

Again she looked surprised. "No," she replied, a little uneasily. "Geoffrey was my third husband."

It was their turn to be startled. "I'm very sorry, Mrs. Berowne," said Carmichael. "I was only told you had been married before, and I'm afraid I assumed . . . you seem rather young to have been married three times."

She smiled at that and raised her chin a little. "I was nineteen when I married Eric Threadgood," she said, almost wistfully.

"That was your first husband?" said Carmichael encouragingly.

"Yes. We met when I got a job as secretary to his brother-in-law." She smiled, a little deprecatingly. "I'm afraid I wasn't a very good secretary, so it's just as well that Eric came along." She sighed. "We'd been married almost five years when he died."

"I'm sorry to hear that," said Carmichael, a little formally. "How did he die?"

She hugged her arms to her body. "In a skiing accident—in

21

Switzerland. He was a very active man for his age—skiing, sailing, golf. In a way, I wasn't really the best wife for him. I've never been very good at sports, and I get horribly seasick."

"You had no children?"

She shook her head, sighing a little. "No—we meant to, but I didn't get pregnant right away and, well, I think really Eric was less interested than I was. He'd worked hard all his life and what he really wanted was to have fun."

Carmichael raised a bushy eyebrow. "He was retired, then?"

"Oh, yes. He was fifty-five when we married—he had taken an early retirement."

"I see," said Carmichael evenly, but what he was really seeing was a pattern. Three husbands much older and wealthier than herself, and three deaths. "And your second husband was William Burton?"

She hesitated and raised her eyes to his, a question hovering in their depths. But then she seemed to think better of it and simply replied, "Yes. I met him in Switzerland shortly before Eric's death. He was very kind to me. We travelled back to England together and were married two months later."

"How long did your marriage to him last?"

The brown eyes were sad and wistful. "Two years," she answered. "Bill wasn't in the best of health when I married him, but I didn't realize quite how bad it was. For the last six months, he was very ill indeed, and the doctor prepared me for the idea that he would die. It was still somehow a surprise when it happened, though."

"It always is," murmured Carmichael sympathetically, but his blue eyes were shrewd. "You married Geoffrey Berowne soon afterward?"

"Well, about eighteen months later, yes."

"I see," said Carmichael again. "Now, Mrs. Berowne, I have just a few other questions. Were you aware of any enemies your husband might have had?"

She shook her head. "None," she said firmly. "He was very well liked and looked up to in the community, Chief Inspector. He was a very kindly man—I can't believe he gave anyone cause to hate him."

"I understand," said Carmichael, almost casually, "that there had been some business disagreements between he and his son."

"Oh." She seemed a little startled. "Well, yes, I suppose there had been. But nothing—I mean—Paul would never hurt Geoffrey. I'm sure he had great respect for his father, even if they did disagree from time to time."

"Well, thank you, Mrs. Berowne." Carmichael beamed at her with his best put-the-suspect-at-ease smile. "You've been uncommonly helpful. Now what we'd like to do is interview the rest of the household and then have a look at the study, if that's all right with you." His tone was positively avuncular.

She blossomed under the smile. "Of course, anything you'd like. Maddie is upstairs in her rooms and Kitty's in the kitchen, naturally. I think Mrs. Simmons is in the dining room at the moment."

Carmichael appeared to think these choices over, though Gibbons knew he had long ago decided what to do. "Perhaps," he said, "my colleagues could talk to Miss Whitcomb, while I see Miss Wellman."

"Certainly." She rose at once, drifting up out of the chair and smoothing her skirt. "If you'll come with me, I'll show you where everything is."

She led the way across the room, and paused abruptly by the door, turning to look up at Carmichael. She hesitated, and took a step closer to him.

"Chief Inspector," she said, "tell me: do you think—well—" She paused, biting her lip, and then went on in an even lower voice, "Will you be able to find who did it?"

Carmichael was unexpectedly touched. "I'm sure we will, Mrs. Berowne," he said, carried away by the moment, although in fact he was not sure of anything of the kind.

Bethancourt, viewing this tableau with a neutral eye, had a sudden moment of doubt as to her guilt. He glanced at Gibbons to see what he thought, but his friend did not look his way; his attention was fixed on Annette Berowne. Bethancourt frowned. He had noticed during the interview how she had spoken to Carmichael and had several times included Gibbons in her glance, but never himself. Was he being ignored because he was not a policeman? Or because she instinctively knew her charm had failed to move him?

CHAPTER

3

itty Whitcomb was a great surprise. In view of the conventional way in which the Berowne household seemed to be run, both men had envisioned "Miss Katharine Whitcomb, cook" as a middle-aged or elderly woman of unattractive mien and generous proportions. What they found was a young woman of about twenty-five with a shining cap of dark hair and a fresh, clear complexion. As for being overweight, there was not an extra pound on her slender frame. This they had ample opportunity to observe, since she was clad in a bright yellow spandex unitard which clung to every line and curve of her body, with a close-fitting T-shirt pulled over the top. A traditional white chef's apron covered the front of this remarkable outfit.

She was standing at a counter in the vast kitchen, turning over pieces of lamb in a large earthenware bowl. She looked up as they introduced themselves, displaying a countenance which exuded common sense. She waved them to seats at a large kitchen table.

"I expect you want the whole story again?" she said, slapping a piece of plastic wrap over the bowl.

"We'd like to go over it, yes," answered Gibbons, as he and Bethancourt settled themselves at the table and exchanged looks.

She wiped her hands, but made no move to join them at the table and be properly interviewed. Instead, she reached over to flick the switch on an electric kettle. "I do the coffee every day he's at home," she said. "That day was no different."

She opened a cupboard and began to assemble mugs and plates on a large tray.

"I set up the usual: coffeepot, cup and saucer, plate with two digestive biscuits, and a napkin, which he never touched."

She opened the refrigerator and removed a bag of coffee, some of which she spooned into a filter. She swung back to the refrigerator, turning on the balls of her feet. They watched the ripple of her slender leg muscles in silence.

"Most days," she continued, replacing the coffee and taking out a container of cream, "Mrs. Berowne came down just before eleven and took the tray up. That day she didn't, so I took it up myself."

She turned again, giving them an excellent view of firm, rounded buttocks, and produced scones from an old-fashioned bread box.

"Mrs. Berowne was in the study with Mr. Berowne when I came in. I put the tray on the table and she told me that she was going into the village and did I want anything. At no time did she go near the tray. I said I didn't want anything and we left the room together. Then I remembered Miss Wellman had been asking for tinned pears the other day and I'd forgotten to pick any up."

She seized the boiling kettle and began to pour the water through the filter into the coffeepot.

"Mrs. Berowne said she'd get them and I said thank you. She went out the side door and I came back here. By twelve-fifteen, I had lunch well in hand, so I went back to get the tray. Sometimes

26

Mr. Berowne brings it down himself, but not if he's gotten involved. I knocked and opened the door and saw at once that something had happened."

She set the kettle down and replaced the lid on the coffeepot with a firm hand. She lifted the tray and brought it to the table where they sat.

"He had his back to the door, of course," she continued, pouring out, "but he was sprawled in his chair—half out of it, actually. So I ran over, but as soon as I saw his face, I knew it was no good."

She set a mug in front of Gibbons and one in front of Bethancourt. "Help yourself to scones," she said. "I make them myself."

Both men, who had assumed she was preparing the tray for someone else, were rather taken aback.

"It was very kind of you to go to all this trouble," said Bethancourt.

"Very kind," echoed Gibbons. "You really didn't need to bother."

She looked surprised. "Everybody eats in a kitchen," she said and, taking her own mug of coffee, moved to sit between them, tucking one yellow leg up beside her on the chair. "Where was I? Oh, yes. I tried to feel for a pulse, but, quite frankly, I've only the vaguest idea where one is and I mightn't have found it if it had been there. I couldn't help thinking he was dead, and it rather unnerved me." Her matter-of-fact tone faltered for a moment, but in the next instant she had collected herself and continued, "Anyway, I rang 999 and then went up to tell Miss Wellman what had happened. Then I went out front to wait for the ambulance."

Finding a corpse had clearly disturbed her, but she showed no emotion about the death itself.

"You don't seem very grieved," said Gibbons carefully.

Kitty looked surprised. "It's been over a month," she pointed out. "I was upset at the time, of course, and sad to see him go, but it's not as if we were close."

27

"This is delicious coffee," put in Bethancourt, reaching to butter a scone.

She grinned, her eyes twinkling mischievously. "Naturally," she replied. "They don't pay me for nothing, you know."

Bethancourt grinned back and took a large bite of scone. "Did Mr. Berowne take it this strong?" he asked around the mouthful.

"Yes. Oh, I see what you're getting at. Well, I don't know what the poison would have tasted like, but if this would have masked the taste, then it did."

"Did Miss Wellman seem surprised when you told her?" asked Gibbons.

"Quite," she answered. "In fact, she thought I must have made a mistake and hurried down to see if she could do anything. Of course, at the time I assumed he'd had a heart attack or something like that. And I forgot to say—" here her tone sharpened, "—there is absolutely no possibility whatsoever that anything but coffee and hot water got into that pot in this kitchen."

"It does seem more likely," answered Gibbons diplomatically, "that the poison was introduced in the study."

She nodded and sipped her coffee.

"Now I understand," continued Gibbons, "that Fatima Sathay, the daily help, was in the kitchen during this period?"

"Fatima *was* our daily help," said Kitty wryly. "She's only seventeen, and her parents made her quit when the news came out about the murder. Poor Mrs. Simmons is working herself to the bone to get everything done herself."

"But Miss Sathay was here on the day of the murder?"

"That's right," she answered. "Fatima was polishing the silver that morning. She'd brought it all down and was here at this table the entire time. She was at it when I took the tray up and she was still here when I went up and found him. She couldn't possibly have left without my seeing her."

Which also, reflected Gibbons, gave Kitty herself the next best thing to an alibi. It was barely possible that she had re-entered the study after Annette had left the house, but by Fatima's account Kitty had been gone for less than five minutes.

"How long have you worked for the Berownes?" continued Gibbons.

"Two years," she answered. "Almost two and a half."

"Could you give me your impression of your employers?"

"That's easy enough," she said readily. "Mr. Berowne could be a very generous man and a very pleasant one, but he was definitely the king of his castle. He seemed, to me, to be very fond of Mrs. Berowne, and she of him. If she married him for his money, he was certainly getting value for it."

"But it seemed a happy marriage? For both of them?"

"I certainly would have said so."

"What about Miss Wellman?"

"She's a bit eccentric, and she's got a sharp tongue, but she's all right, really. I think she and Mr. Berowne got along quite happily until he remarried. She can't stand Mrs. Berowne, and she makes no secret of it. Mrs. Paul doesn't like her any better, but she doesn't say so in so many words. Mr. Berowne was very fond of her, too."

"That would be Marion Berowne, the daughter-in-law? And what about Paul Berowne?"

She shrugged. "He didn't get on with his father. Or his wife, for that matter. And he's the only man I've ever seen who isn't taken with Mrs. Berowne. But that's probably prejudice—he wouldn't like any woman who married his father."

Gibbons looked slightly uncomfortable. "So in your opinion, all men find Mrs. Berowne attractive?"

"Sure. Didn't you?"

"She has a certain allure," admitted Bethancourt, finishing his scone. "What do women think of her?"

"Just the opposite," said Kitty frankly. "All men fall in love with her; all women hate her. She doesn't need them and she shows it."

"You, too?" asked Gibbons.

Kitty frowned, considering. "I can't say I like her," she answered, "but, on the other hand, she's easy enough to work for. And, of course, she's different with me because she does need me—she can't cook for beans. Miss Wellman usually takes over on my night off."

"Do they still eat together, Miss Wellman and Mrs. Berowne?" asked Bethancourt. "I mean since Mr. Berowne's death?"

She laughed, displaying even white teeth. "Lord, no," she said. "The very next day, Miss Wellman came to me and said she'd have a tray in her sitting room for all her meals. I told her fine, but she'd have to come down and get it. Mrs. Berowne still eats in the dining room."

"How about breakfast that morning?" asked Gibbons. "Did everyone seem just as usual?"

"I'm not in the dining room much in the morning," she answered. "But everything seemed much the same. Mr. Paul came in late, looking bit hungover, but that's not unknown."

"Mr. Paul?" questioned Gibbons. "I thought he and his family lived in a separate house."

"Oh, they do," she said, "but Mr. Paul usually comes in to breakfast. Before Mr. Berowne retired, they used to breakfast together every morning and then go up to town together. Now Mr. Paul comes round most mornings to keep his father up to date with things. And Mr. Berowne still went up to the office twice a week or so."

"Liked to keep a finger in the pie, so to speak?" suggested Gibbons.

"That's right."

"And I suppose Mr. Paul rather resented not being left on his own to handle things?"

She shrugged. "There were arguments. I don't know how serious any of them were—I don't know much about business."

Gibbons leaned back, cradling his coffee cup. "Let's go back to that morning for a moment. Were you surprised to hear that Mrs. Berowne intended to walk to the village?"

"I didn't know she did," said Kitty ruefully, "not then. She only told me she was going, and I assumed she meant to drive."

"But you saw her leave by the side door?"

"Yes, but she would have done if she was going to the garage in any case. It wasn't until Mr. Paul said her car was still in the garage that I realized she must have gone on foot."

"Did that surprise you?"

Kitty spread her hands. "I suppose it did, but at that point everything was so topsy-turvy, I don't expect I would have had much reaction if Mr. Paul had said she'd gone by magic carpet. But it was certainly unusual. Mrs. Berowne likes to walk in the garden, but otherwise she's not much for exercise. There are whole parts of the grounds that she's never even seen."

"You haven't said," said Bethancourt, "if you think she killed him."

She raised an eyebrow at him. "Not my place, is it?" she said. "Besides, I really don't know. I wouldn't have said any of them could have committed murder. But I'd have been wrong. One of them did."

Mrs. Berowne had shown Carmichael upstairs to a separate sitting room, part of a suite originally meant for honored houseguests. It was a very lived-in room, arranged to be comfortable rather than elegant. The mantelpiece was crowded with framed photographs, and a television stood openly and unashamedly in one corner. Beside it was a radio which was presently playing a selection of classical music.

Maddie Wellman sat in a chair by the fire, knitting a sweater in deep blue wool. She had a long face, rather horsey, with sharp gray eyes and a long, thin nose. She had curly, iron-gray hair cut short, and a spare, square-shouldered frame.

She raised an eyebrow when Carmichael introduced himself and said, "Scotland Yard, eh? What's the matter? That ass Gorringe not have enough courage to arrest her himself?"

Carmichael was startled. "The investigation isn't complete yet," he said neutrally and she snorted, her eyes dropping once again to her knitting. "May I sit down?" he asked.

She nodded and indicated the other chair drawn up to the fireplace, facing her own. Carmichael settled himself, regarding her with shrewd blue eyes. A no-nonsense sort of person, he decided, with, clearly, a sharp tongue. He fancied he had met her sort before: bluff and honest, and probably a terrible liar. Most noticeable, however, was the fact that she seemed in no way grief-stricken.

"Were you fond of your brother-in-law, Miss Wellman?" Carmichael asked.

"I grew to be," she answered. "I can't say I cared much for him in the beginning."

"Why was that?"

"No very good reason," she replied. "Mostly because he was like the vast majority of men—hugely aware of his own rights and pretty vague about anyone else's."

"You felt he was inconsiderate of your rights?"

She looked surprised. "Not at all. I don't suppose I had any, really. None to speak of, anyhow. No, I was thinking of my sister—not that she ever minded. As I said, I didn't think much of her choice at the start, although I did realize she was the sort of person who needed marriage to be happy."

"You never married yourself?" asked Carmichael.

She shot him a penetrating glance. "I was not more attractive in my youth, Chief Inspector, than I am now. Just less wrinkles, is all. Here." She rose, setting aside her knitting, and picked out a silver-framed photograph from those on the mantel. She handed it to him and resumed her seat.

It was a black-and-white print showing two girls in their early twenties. From the style of their summer frocks, Carmichael dated it to just after the war. The taller of the two girls was clearly Maddie Wellman; she was right in saying she had changed very little. Her curly hair was longer and there was an air of girlish awkwardness about her, but her features were clearly recognizable.

"You will forgive me for pointing out that not all wives are great beauties," said Carmichael.

"Oh, yes, they are," she contradicted him. "No man has ever married a woman he didn't think was beautiful. He may be aware that she doesn't look like Elizabeth Taylor, it may be purely an inner beauty, recognizable only to himself. But he always thinks she's beautiful in some way, and I never had any inner beauty, either. The other girl in the picture," she added, "was my sister, Gwenda."

Carmichael turned his attention back to the photograph, interested to see Berowne's first wife. She looked tiny beside Miss Wellman. She, too, was dark-haired, but otherwise there was not the slightest resemblance. This girl was round-faced, with a sweet smile and large, gentle, dark eyes.

"She looked like our mother," said Miss Wellman. "I took after Father—in more ways than looks."

"You were very fond of her?" asked Carmichael.

"Oh, yes. Everyone was." Miss Wellman looked up, staring into the fire. "She was one of those rare creatures. She had the true gift of happiness and everyone she came into contact with gleaned a little of it. She was a very gentle person, but she could always smooth things over. She liked doing it, it was easy for her." She sighed and turned back to her knitting. "It would have been much better if I could have died instead of her. Then Geoffrey would still be alive, and still happily married—because their marriage was a happy one, odd as that always seemed to me. And he would certainly have been on better terms with Paul."

"You think Gwenda would have smoothed out their business differences?"

She hesitated for a moment. "Oh, yes," she said, a trifle too casually. "She was good at things like that."

So, thought Carmichael, they had differences outside of business, too. But all he said was, "How long ago did your sister die?"

"Nearly eight years ago now. I came to live here a few years before that, when my arthritis started acting up and I had to give up teaching. I wasn't too sure about it really, but Gwenda was quite firm that I should come and, actually, it worked out very well. When she died, Geoffrey made a point of asking me to stay on, so I did. We'd gotten used to each other by then, you see. It wasn't the same without Gwenda, but we got on all right."

"Until he remarried?" suggested Carmichael gently, but she was not to be drawn out. She gave him an amused glance.

"It didn't make a great deal of difference to me," she said. "Beyond that I didn't like to see Geoffrey making a fool of himself and that I had to put up with Annette at mealtimes. Geoffrey always insisted on family meals."

"So you didn't resent Mrs. Berowne?"

"Don't be silly, Chief Inspector. Of course I resented her. Any fool could see that. I probably would have resented any woman who tried to take my sister's place. I also might have got over that if she hadn't been such a conniving little twit. Annette has never thought of anybody but herself in her whole life."

Carmichael frowned at this; Annette had not struck him as a conniver, and he wondered if her undeniable charm had affected his judgment.

"Did you feel that she treated Mr. Berowne badly?"

"It depends on what you mean by that," she replied, giving him a wry glance. "She kept up the illusion she was in love with him, billed and cooed over him and all that, but that's about all she did. Kitty and I still run the house between us."

"So you feel she didn't take on the responsibilities she should have?" Carmichael tried to keep his tone neutral, but she shot him a sharp glance.

"There was more than that," she said tartly. "But I don't suppose you'd believe me if I told you. She's already got you wrapped around her finger, too."

Carmichael deeply resented this. "Nonsense, Miss Wellman—" he began.

"Let me put it this way," she interrupted. "Geoffrey was a kindly, deeply religious, and generous man. He could also be totally unreasonable and he wasn't beyond cracking the whip to make things come out the way he wanted. Annette played on his beliefs, took advantage of his generosity, and supported his whip-cracking in order to drive wedges between him and his family."

"If she went to all that trouble to keep him to herself, it hardly makes sense that she would murder him," Carmichael pointed out.

Miss Wellman snorted. "Nonsense. He wasn't any good to her once she'd won the game. None of us realized that, of course," she added. "Foolish of us, but then one doesn't suspect people one actually knows are murderers, even the most unpleasant people."

"No one ever suspects that," Carmichael told her. "Now, if we could just go over the day of the murder. You went down to breakfast with the rest of the family?"

"Yes. I was down first, I usually am. It was a fairly ordinary morning. Geoffrey and Paul were discussing business, and Annette was reading a magazine. I left when I'd finished eating and came back here. Kitty came up to go over a few household details, and then I spent the rest of the morning at the desk there, writing letters. I did get up once to open the window, but I didn't notice anyone out there besides our gardener. It was some time after noon when Kitty came up and said she'd found Geoff dead in his study. I didn't believe her—Geoffrey always enjoyed excellent health. I got downstairs as quickly as I could and went in to him, but it was no use. I've had some first-aid training and it was clear to me he was dead." For the first time, her gray eyes looked rather bleak. "So I went out to wait for the doctor. I had no idea, of course, that it was anything but a sudden heart attack."

"Of course not." Carmichael had watched her carefully, but she had made this statement too many times before for him to tell whether there was deception in any part of it. He smiled at her. "I'm almost done, Miss Wellman. I'd just like to ask you about the business differences Mr. Berowne was having with his son. Am I right in assuming they arose after Mr. Berowne had retired?"

"Certainly," she answered. "Before that, Geoffrey ran the company and Paul followed whatever he said. No problem there."

"Who was in the right in most of these disagreements?"

"Depends on what you mean by 'right,' " she said. She paused, peering intently at her knitting, and counting under her breath. Then the click of the needles resumed and she looked back at him. "Geoffrey was very clever about business and investments, so, from the point of view of profits, he was certainly right. On the other hand, it was unreasonable of him to blame Paul for not having the same cleverness. It was also rather unreasonable of him to give Paul the business and then not let him run it."

"But surely," said Carmichael, "if Mr. Berowne was so knowledgeable about such matters, it was unreasonable of Mr. Paul Berowne not to take his advice."

"Oh, he did take advice. No, it wasn't as simple as that, Chief Inspector." She thought for a moment. "Here's an example: some other little biscuit company wasn't doing very well and Paul wanted to take it over. He asked Geoffrey, who said he was a fool if he didn't. So Paul put in a takeover bid. I'm not sure what happened next, but at any rate, things didn't go as planned. Paul did acquire the company in the end, but it cost far more than he had thought, at which point Geoffrey made a terrific fuss and told him he was an idiot for buying at that price."

"I see," said Carmichael.

"However," she said sharply, "if you think Paul killed him because Geoffrey criticized him, you're wrong. My nephew may not be a brilliant businessman, but neither is he vindictive."

"No, I'm sure he isn't," said Carmichael. "He and his father had no disagreements aside from business?"

"No, of course not," she muttered, but once again Carmichael felt she was hiding something.

"Well, thank you very much, Miss Wellman," he said pleasantly, and rose to go.

Mary Simmons was clearly alarmed by the police. Gibbons and Bethancourt cornered her in the dining room where she was waxing the table, but all her replies to their questions were monosyllabic and her eyes flickered between them like the eyes of a mouse confronting two cats.

"I understand you weren't in the house on the day of the murder?" asked Gibbons, smiling to put her at her ease.

"No, sir," she answered, anything but easy in her manner.

"You were at Mr. Paul's house, is that right?"

"Yes, sir."

"And what were you doing there?" asked Gibbons, deciding he had better restrict himself to questions that required more than a yes-or-no answer.

"Cleaning. Their charwoman is off on Wednesdays, and I give the house a thorough going-over."

"Now you arrived just as Mr. Paul was leaving, correct? And by eleven o'clock you were working downstairs in the living room?"

"Yes, sir."

"And where were Mrs. Paul and her son during that time?"

"They was upstairs in the schoolroom, sir. I could hear them playing the piano while I was cleaning."

She repeated this parrot-like, giving them the answer that had been got out of her by the Surrey officers in—so far as Gibbons could tell—exactly the same words, as if any alteration might damn her.

He glanced at Bethancourt; his friend was often good with skittish female witnesses, and he was in fact wearing his most charming smile. It was a pity that Mrs. Simmons did not look up long enough to see it.

"I take it Mr. Paul's charwoman isn't quite up to snuff?" asked Bethancourt genially. "I mean, if you have to give the house a good going-over every week, she can't be doing a very expert job."

"She only comes to help with the daily chores," muttered Mrs. Simmons, her eyes fixed firmly on the table she had been waxing.

"Ah, I see," said Bethancourt. "She just tidies a bit and does the washing up."

Mrs. Simmons nodded silently, and Bethancourt gave his friend an exasperated glance.

Gibbons abandoned the attempt to wring fresh information out of her. It was possible that she had returned to the main house and poisoned her employer, but looking at her Gibbons had to wonder if she would have had the nerve.

"Well, thank you very much, Mrs. Simmons," he said, leading Bethancourt out.

In the hallway they met Carmichael just coming down the stairs, and reported their progress to him.

"Then that's the household done," said Carmichael. "Let's find Mrs. Berowne and have a look at the study."

Annette was found in the writing room, which she had pointed out to them earlier. She came out quietly when they knocked and stood looking up at Carmichael as if he held the answers to all questions. Uncomfortably, he recalled his urge to come to her defense during his interview with Miss Wellman, and he avoided her eyes.

"We'd like to see the study now, Mrs. Berowne," he said.

She nodded. "It's down this way," she said.

The study was at the far end of the house, by the side entrance. It was a long room, with wide windows looking onto a terrace, which in turn led down to the garden. On the wall opposite the windows was a fireplace with a small scalloped table to the right of it. At the farther end of the room stood a large rolltop desk accompanied by a modern desk chair on rollers.

Annette indicated the table beside the fireplace. "This is where the tray was."

Carmichael glanced at it and then at the desk; Berowne's back would have been turned to the table while he was working. His eyes rose to the mantelpiece and encountered a small porcelain vase with a bunch of dead daisies in it.

Annette followed his gaze. "Oh!" she said. "I don't know how that got left there. Only, of course, I told Mrs. Simmons not to bother with this room until Daniel Andrews was sure he was finished with it."

"Please leave them, Mrs. Berowne," said Carmichael as she began to reach for the vase. "Can you tell me who usually provides the flowers for this room?"

She looked bewildered. "Well, no one does. I put some flowers in that vase, but that was more than a week before my husband was killed. Someone must have seen them and instead of just throwing them out, they decided to replace them. Kitty, I suppose, or Maddie."

"You think these are not the original flowers?" asked Carmichael.

"Oh, no." She shook her head. "Mine were lilies of the valley."

She clearly did not see the import of her words—the poison had been described to the family only as "an alkaloid"—but all three men glanced sharply at her and then at the vase.

"Is it Kitty or Miss Wellman who does the flowers in the rest of the house?" asked Carmichael.

"Usually either myself or Maddie. She would probably be the most likely person to have changed these. Or Marion might have brought them over," she added doubtfully.

"Do you remember which flowers were in the vase the day your husband died?"

"Well, it must have been these, mustn't it?" she said. "No one's been in to change them since then."

"But you don't really remember seeing them?"

"Well, no," she answered, frowning in thought. "No, I can't remember one way or another. Is it important?"

"Probably not," said Carmichael cheerfully. "We just like to get to the bottom of any little anomalies."

While this conversation was taking place, Gibbons was looking over the desk. It stood open, revealing neatly organized pigeonholes, an immaculate blotter, and a pen and pencil set. The Surrey CID had already taken and gone over the papers and correspondence Berowne had been working on when he died. They had all seemed to be in order and, so far as anyone could tell, nothing was missing.

Bethancourt had drifted over to the bookcase, which covered half the wall beside the desk, and was idly examining the book spines. Now he moved over and nudged Gibbons.

"Look there," he murmured.

Gibbons looked. Halfway along one of the middle shelves was the same book on poisons that Bethancourt had consulted the evening before, along with two others on forensics and firearms.

Gibbons raised his eyebrows. "That's interesting," he said. He turned. "Sir?"

"Excuse me, Mrs. Berowne," said Carmichael. "Find something?" he asked as he came up to the two younger men. Gibbons nodded a the bookshelves.

"Ah," said Carmichael. One bushy eyebrow rose. "Yes. Gibbons," he added in a low voice, "I think perhaps you should run out to the car and bring in some evidence bags."

"Yes, sir," said Gibbons.

Bethancourt remained behind, still hovering beside the bookcase, but watching Annette Berowne from the corner of his eye. Her manner—even when she had mentioned the lilies of the valley—was perfectly open, and he was involved in trying to work out whether or not that openness was assumed.

Carmichael turned back to Annette, who had retreated discreetly to the doorway.

"Mrs. Berowne," he said, pacing back toward her, "was your husband particularly interested in poisons?"

"Poisons?" she repeated. "No, I don't believe so."

"He seems to have several books on the subject."

"Does he? I never noticed." She frowned thoughtfully. "He certainly never spoke about it. Unless—he was very fond of detective stories. I think they often have poisonings in them." She shivered a little.

"I understand it's an uncomfortable topic," murmured Carmichael soothingly. "I'm very sorry to have to bring it up."

"No, no," she said, her voice low and rather strained. "I understand it's necessary."

Carmichael resisted the urge to pat her arm encouragingly. "All the same," he said, "I'd like to take the books and have a look at them. The vase and flowers as well."

"Anything," she said, waving a hand vaguely. "Anything you like." She drew a deep breath to steady herself and then said in a clear voice, "Please carry on, Chief Inspector. Take away anything you need. If you'll excuse me, I—you see, I haven't been in this room since . . ." She passed a hand over her forehead, disarranging her hair. "That is, if you don't need me, I think I'll go upstairs for just a little while."

"Certainly," said Carmichael. "An excellent idea, Mrs. Berowne. We will be going over to see Mrs. Paul Berowne shortly in any case."

"Thank you, Chief Inspector." She looked up at him gratefully as he held the door for her.

Carmichael closed the door carefully behind her, looking

thoughtful. He caught Bethancourt's eye as he came back to the center of the room, and raised a bushy eyebrow.

"A very confounding woman," he said.

"Yes, sir," said Bethancourt levelly, suddenly aware that Carmichael had felt an intense attraction to Mrs. Berowne and was struggling with it. That was most unusual; Bethancourt had never seen Carmichael in the least flustered by any witness before. It made her, in his mind, an even more intriguing suspect. Although she appeared unaware of it, she must know of the effect she created. The great question was whether or not she had been using it deliberately.

"I can't make out if she's clever or merely lucky," he said.

Carmichael rubbed his chin thoughtfully. "You'd think a clever woman would have come up with a better alibi," he said.

"It seems to be working well enough for her, sir," said Bethancourt dryly.

"Mmm—yes, so it does. I think we'll have to have her walk us to the village and time it." He glanced out the French windows at the fine, steady rain. "Not much chance of it today," he added.

"No, sir," agreed Bethancourt.

Carmichael frowned. "I wonder what's keeping Gibbons," he said.

Gibbons closed the front door behind him and hung his Burberry over the back of a chair. Looking up, he saw Mrs. Berowne just coming into the hall. She looked very pale and her brown eyes were glistening with unshed tears. She did not see Gibbons for a moment and when she did, she drew a startled breath and then dabbed hastily at her eyes with the tips of her fingers.

"Mrs. Berowne?" asked Gibbons, coming forward. "Are you all right?"

"Oh, yes," she answered. "I just felt a trifle faint was all, and now I can't seem to find my handkerchief . . ."

Gibbons produced his own and handed it to her. "Perhaps you should lie down for a few minutes," he said, for she still looked very pale to him.

"Yes," she said, and managed a small smile. "I was just going upstairs. Thank you so much—I'll be fine now."

"You're welcome," replied Gibbons, taking his handkerchief back. He watched as she turned and began to climb the stairs. Then her step faltered and she clutched at the banister. Gibbons dropped the evidence bags as he jumped to steady her.

"It's all right," he said, lowering her to sit on the steps. "Here, put your head down for a moment. That's right—I'll just fetch you a bit of brandy."

He had seen the drinks cabinet earlier in the drawing room. He seized a whisky glass, splashed a couple of fingers of expensive French cognac into it, and returned to the hall.

Mrs. Berowne was still sitting as he had left her. He sank down beside her and put an arm about her shoulders.

"Here we are," he said gently. "Try sitting up now, and have a bit of this. Don't worry, I've got you."

He brought her up slowly and handed her the brandy. She sipped it obediently and then smiled at him.

"You're very kind, Sergeant," she said.

"Not at all," he replied, peering at her face for any sign of returning color. To his relief, he thought he detected a slight improvement. "Is that any better?"

She nodded. "Yes, a bit."

"Have a little more of the cognac before you try standing up," he said.

She did as he suggested, and as he watched her drink, he was suddenly aware that his arm was still about her and she was leaning comfortably against his shoulder. It was certainly odd to find himself in such a cozy position with their prime suspect, and it made him a little uneasy. There was no denying that Annette Berowne inspired a protective feeling in him, which was not at all a helpful thing to feel about someone he was trying to prove guilty of murder.

"There," she said, handing him the glass and making an effort to smile. The dimples flashed again in her cheeks and then disappeared. "I think I'll be all right now."

"I'll just see you upstairs," he said.

He helped her to rise and then took her elbow to escort her up the stairs.

"I don't know what came over me," she confessed. "I thought I was handling everything beautifully, and then suddenly I felt quite faint. It must," her voice quivered, "have been that conversation about poisons."

"Don't think of it now," commanded Gibbons. "I know this is a very difficult time for you, but you must try not to make it any worse than it already is." He cast about for a safe subject. "Didn't you say you were fond of roses? Are there many in your garden here?"

"Oh, yes," she answered. "One corner of our garden has nothing but roses—all different kinds. You must have a look before you leave, if you're interested. We have a very fine gardener. The first Mrs. Berowne loved flowers."

They reached the top of the staircase and she directed him down the corridor to her room. He opened the door for her.

"You'll be all right now?" he asked.

"Yes," she answered. "All I need is to lie down for a little. Thank you so much again, Sergeant—I appreciate your kindness very much." She smiled and squeezed his arm to take the formality from the words. "I'll see you before you go?"

"I expect so," he answered. "Take care of yourself now." He let her close the door on him and then turned and ran downstairs to collect his evidence bags. He did not notice that he was whistling as he walked back to the study.

CHAPTER

$\mathcal{I}$t's getting late," said Carmichael, looking at his watch. "I think we'd better run into the village before we see Marion Berowne or we shan't get any lunch."

The two younger men agreed with this sentiment heartily. They had collected the evidence in the study and stowed it carefully in the boot of the Rover. They had gone back to Miss Wellman, who had emphatically denied replacing the lilies of the valley in the study with daisies. She insisted she had not been in the study in weeks.

Then they had gone out into the rain and eventually run the gardener to ground in a potting shed at the bottom of the garden. If Kitty Whitcomb was something of an anachronism, James McAllister ran truer to form than anyone would have believed possible. He was an ancient, monosyllabic, and curmudgeonly Scotsman. Yes, he had been working in the tulip beds just off the terrace on the morning of the murder. Mr. Berowne had come along quite early and bothered him for some time about a foolish plan to uproot the rhododendrons by Little House. Yes, of course he meant Mr. Paul Berowne, not Mr. Geoffrey. Why should Geoffrey Berowne want to fool with Little House's rhododendrons? Then later he had seen Mrs. Berowne emerge from the house and go off along the path. No, he didn't know what time it was—he didn't wear a watch—other than it was before lunch. He had lunch at one. Asked how he knew when it was time for lunch if he had no watch, he looked scornful and replied that he knew because he was hungry. This statement delighted Bethancourt, who privately resolved to inquire of Kitty at the first opportunity whether or not the old man was really on time for his meal every day.

McAllister apparently had not the least concern that he might be suspected. He had finished with the tulips just before lunch and had returned to the potting shed to clean his tools and see to the tomato seeds. He had not seen Mrs. Berowne return, nor had he seen anyone else until he had gone in for lunch and been faced with the news of his employer's death.

The rain was falling more heavily when they emerged from the potting shed and traced their way back through the gardens and along a path that led to the other side of the estate and the garage. This was the old stable, completely renovated, with a small, attractive apartment in what had once been the hayloft. Here they found Ken Mills, the chauffeur, who was a good-looking young man who looked as if he was no stranger to the weight room at the gym. He had, however, even less to add to the investigation than McAllister. He had seen Mr. Paul leave for work that morning in the BMW, his usual car. Mr. Paul had returned shortly, however, saying that the car seemed to be overheating. On investigation, this turned out to be because the thermostat had gone. It was not a difficult thing to fix, but he had had to go to the dealers in Guildford for the part. He had seen no one else that morning. Mr. Paul had returned shortly after noon to see how the work was coming and was still there when word of the tragedy had come from the house.

It was now almost two and Bethancourt, who was not usually an early riser and who seldom ate breakfast, was nearly starving, and only his gratitude to Carmichael for having let him come at all had prevented him from skipping the chauffeur interview and going in search of lunch. He fervently applauded the chief inspector's plan to eat before seeing Marion Berowne.

They were just starting back to the house when Mills leaned out of his window and called down to them.

"Chief Inspector!" he said. "Kitty's just rung up—she's fair peeved with you. She says your lunch has been ready for close on an hour and if you don't come and eat it at once, she'll put it in the bin."

Carmichael, considerably surprised, thanked him for the message, and they resumed their walk to the house.

"No one said anything about giving us lunch," Carmichael said. "Did they to you, Gibbons?"

"No, sir."

"Those scones were delicious," said Bethancourt dreamily, lengthening his stride.

Kitty met them at the kitchen door, her dark eyes snapping with irritation.

"You'd be Chief Inspector Carmichael," she said. It was an accusation.

Carmichael admitted it.

Her eyes travelled over his figure. "You don't look like you never eat."

"I'm very sorry, Miss Whitcomb," he said. "We weren't aware that you had made lunch for us."

Kitty was unappeased. "What," she demanded, "do you think people have cooks for?"

She did not appear to require an answer. She turned and pointed to the kitchen table, which was set for three. "I've put you there," she said, in a tone that did not bode well for them if they were not seated and eating in the next ten seconds.

They sat.

With brisk efficiency, she brought three pint bottles of Bass from the refrigerator, and then removed a steak and kidney pie from the oven. A basket of towering popovers followed, and lastly she placed a thermos on the table.

"There's coffee in there," she said. "Can you serve yourselves?"

They thanked her and assured her they could.

"All right then." She stripped off her apron. "I'll be in my sitting room if you want anything more—just knock."

The pie was wonderful, the popovers crisp and delicate. While they ate, they brought each other up to date and compared their notes to the reports in the case file.

"What this is missing," said Carmichael, tapping the file, "is a profile of Berowne himself. That's understandable—all the Surrey officers knew him."

"I think we're beginning to get a picture, sir," said Gibbons.

"Yes." Carmichael nodded. "Miss Wellman called him deeply religious—I think perhaps it might be wise to pay a visit to the vicar, just to round out the picture."

"That's a good idea."

Carmichael reached for the thermos. "One more cup of this fine coffee," he said, "and then we'd best be off to the Little House."

Bethancourt knocked on Kitty's door before they left and was told to come in. She was sitting cross-legged in an armchair, a cookbook open in her lap and a pad and a pencil balanced on the arm.

"Lunch was luscious," he said. "We're uncommonly grateful to you."

"I'm glad you liked it," she answered.

"We've put the dishes in the sink," he added.

"Well, thank you, but you really shouldn't have bothered. Clearing up is part of my job."

Bethancourt only smiled. "I wanted to ask you something.

About McAllister," he said, and she looked curious. "I just wondered if he came in to lunch at the same time every day."

"One o'clock on the dot," she said. "Occasionally, if he's in the middle of something, he's a bit late. But he's no trouble—he wants a plain ham sandwich and a packet of crisps every day. Sometimes, if it's cold, he'll have a little soup."

"That's fascinating," said Bethancourt. "There's Jack calling me—I'd better go. Thanks again."

Kitty shook her head as he closed the door. "Daft," she said, and returned to her book.

"No flowers in her sitting room either," Bethancourt reported to the others as he joined them outside.

"Not *now*," said Gibbons.

The side door of the house opened onto the terrace, from which one could either go down into the garden proper or follow a gravel path that led off at an angle between the trees. They chose the latter course, following the path until they came to Little House, which was little only when compared to the main house. This one was much more attractive and was far older—a small, late Georgian manor house.

"This must have been the original house," said Bethancourt, interested. "It's lucky whoever built that Victorian horror didn't just pull this down."

"Probably just a farmhouse here in the beginning," agreed Carmichael. "There are McAllister's rhododendrons," he added. "I see he hasn't started digging them up yet."

"Did you really get the impression he ever intended to?" asked Gibbons and Carmichael chuckled.

Marion Berowne answered the door herself. She was about thirty-five, a tall, well-turned-out woman, who had been very handsome before her face had come to look so strained.

She led them into the drawing room and said, "I must ask you not to speak too loudly—my son is having his nap upstairs." Her voice was pleasantly husky.

"Of course, Mrs. Berowne." Carmichael smiled at her. "Mine are grown now, but I remember how it used to be at nap time."

She smiled back and thanked him, but the smile did not reach her eyes.

"We'd just like to go over the statement you made to Commander Andrews," said Carmichael, settling himself in an armchair.

She made a little gesture. "It was really a perfectly ordinary day," she said. "Paul went over to the main house for breakfast, and Mrs. Simmons came in while I was feeding Edwin in the kitchen. She went up to the schoolroom—she always does that first, so I can have a place to keep Edwin out of her way. When I'd finished in the kitchen, I took Edwin up there, and we were still there when Aunt Maddie rang looking for Paul."

"So your husband did not return here during the morning?"

She flushed. "He came back to call the office, but I didn't see him—I was already up in the schoolroom. I didn't realize he hadn't gone up to Town." He voice was faintly bitter. "I told Maddie he was at the office, but she said no, he'd had car trouble and was probably at the garage."

It struck all her listeners as odd that Paul Berowne should not have told his wife where he was. She was clearly embarrassed by her ignorance, which begged the question of whether Berowne's action had been deliberate.

"Do the schoolroom windows overlook the path to the postern?" asked Carmichael.

She shook her head. "No, I'm afraid not. It's on the other side of the house." She gestured again. "I'm sorry I can't be more help, but, really, I thought it was a perfectly ordinary day until Aunt Maddie rang up."

Carmichael nodded. "We've been told," he said carefully, "that of late there had been some disagreements between your husband and his father over the business. Can you tell us anything about that?"

"Only that they had them," she answered. "I don't really know much about the company itself. Geoffrey still put in an appearance at the office once or twice a week and I know they had a row there once. Paul was quite upset about it—he said the staff would never learn to respect him if Geoffrey was going to tick him off in front of everybody." She paused. "Geoffrey had a bit of a temper at times," she added. "Not violent or anything, but he'd just burst out when anything distressed him."

"Did he ever make threats—even threats he didn't mean?"

"Threats?" She looked puzzled. "I don't think so. He'd just rant a bit, really."

"I see," said Carmichael. "Did your husband get on well with his father outside of business?"

"Yes, of course. Paul's an only child so he and Geoffrey were very close."

"I understood there had been some tension over Mr. Berowne's remarriage."

She smiled ruefully. "It was not generally well-received. Geoffrey was rather hurt; he couldn't understand why the rest of us didn't take to dear, sweet little Annette." Her voice was laden with sarcasm.

"She was unpleasant?" asked Carmichael.

"Oh, no. Not unpleasant. Just doing her sweet little waif act all over the place and keeping a sharp eye out for number one all the while. It wears very thin, that. She nearly drove Aunt Maddie mad by constantly telling her how Geoffrey would like that, or wouldn't like this, just as if Maddie hadn't been living with the man for twelve years. She told Paul she did wish he wouldn't aggravate his father so. And she told everything to Geoffrey in a way that put us all in the worst possible light. I thought, when she first came, that we might be company for each other—we're much of an age. But Annette doesn't care for anyone but Annette. She'll flirt with men, but women are utterly useless to her." She shrugged.

"But did the marriage seem to you to be a happy one?"

She paused, thinking this over. "I suppose it did," she said. "Certainly Geoffrey seemed happy with her."

"And she with him?"

"Well, I never thought, really. Now I can see that obviously she wasn't, but at the time . . . Yes, I guess she seemed happy enough."

"Were you surprised to hear Mrs. Berowne had decided to walk to the village that morning?" asked Carmichael.

Marion gave a short laugh. "Stunned is more like it. Annette never did anything that energetic. We stopped having picnics down by the lake because she never wanted to walk so far. But of course she could never have accounted for her time that morning if she'd driven."

"I see," said Carmichael. "Thank you for being so frank, Mrs. Berowne. There are just a few other questions. Had you been in Mr. Berowne's study in, say, the week before his death?"

"I'm not sure." She frowned thoughtfully. "I might have been—it was an easy place to catch him if you wanted to see him without Annette. I think I took Edwin over to tea with Aunt Maddie the day before, but Geoffrey wouldn't have been in his study then." She paused and then shook her head. "I seem to think I did pop in on Geoffrey one morning, but I can't be sure."

"Can you remember if there were flowers on the mantelpiece when you were there?"

"Flowers?" She looked startled. "I suppose there might have been. If I noticed at the time, I don't remember now."

"You never brought any flowers in yourself?"

"Well, I may have done at some time, but not recently. May I ask why?"

Carmichael smiled. "Just a loose end," he said. "I think that's all for now. We appreciate your help very much."

"Certainly, Chief Inspector. I—oh, dear, I think that's Edwin waking up. Can you let yourselves out? Thank you so much."

The church was an uninspired example of late Perpendicular with a modern and rather garish stained-glass window. Reverend Oakley waved a hand at it with pride.

"That was Geoffrey's Berowne's doing," he said. "The original went in the war, and we just had plain glass until Geoffrey offered to donate the money for a new window." He gazed at it happily. "It came out rather well, don't you think?"

"Splendid," said Carmichael heartily, and even Gibbons, who knew him well, could not detect whether or not he was dissembling. "As you may know, Reverend, any murder investigation starts with the victim. We've come to you hoping you could give us some insight."

Reverend Oakley nodded thoughtfully and motioned them to sit in the pews. He was a short, stout man with what little hair he had left clipped short and rather shrewd eyes.

"He was a good man," he said. "A little old-fashioned in these times, but who of his age isn't? He wasn't sensitive, but he was generous and tried to be kind. I'm not sure what else to say. He'll be sorely missed."

"We've been told that he was deeply religious," said Carmichael.

"Oh, yes." Oakley nodded agreement. "Faith had taken a strong hold of him in his youth—he apparently considered becoming a minister, or so he once told me, but of course his father expected him to take over the family business."

"Would he have made a good minister in your opinion?"

Oakley hesitated, his eyes narrowed in thought. "No," he answered at last. "As I said, he was not a sensitive man and I believe a certain amount of sensitivity is necessary in my job. He had very strong views on right and wrong and was not apt to be very sympathetic to transgressors. He could be rather intolerant. But I feel I am giving you a wrong impression of him. He was, I think, a happy man for the most part, and he was certainly successful. People in his position don't often become introspective and there's no reason why they should."

"We've also been told he had a temper," prompted Carmichael.

"A temper?" Oakley smiled. "More a bit of bluster when anything upset him, I should say. He always calmed down quickly, though he wasn't good at admitting he was in the wrong even when that was true. But then, I don't know many people who are."

"No," agreed Carmichael. "Chagrin and atonement don't usually go hand in hand. Had he been worried lately, do you know?"

"Nothing that he mentioned to me," answered Oakley. He paused and then added, "He did say sometime back that he was concerned over Paul's handling of the company, but that was several months ago. He was planning a lengthy vacation with Mrs. Berowne at the time, and was worried how Paul would do without him."

"But he took the vacation anyway?"

"Yes. I certainly recommended that he do so, and I believe Mrs. Berowne was quite eager for the trip. He liked to please her."

"You seem a shrewd judge of character, Reverend," said Carmichael. "What do you think of Mrs. Berowne?"

Oakley smiled. "I've heard the rumours, of course," he replied. "My own wife thinks Annette killed Geoffrey. But I can't say I agree. I thought Annette was very fond of her husband and she certainly seemed grief-stricken after his death. Annette has always struck me as being just a little unsure of herself and I think being Geoffrey's wife compensated for that."

"Unsure?" Carmichael raised an eyebrow. "I don't think I would have described her that way, Reverend."

"Oh, not outwardly," replied Oakley. "All I'm saying is that I think her outward self-confidence stemmed from being Mrs. Geoffrey Berowne."

"But she's still Mrs. Geoffrey Berowne," said Carmichael.

"Well, yes. But it's not the same."

"No," agreed Carmichael. "Not the same at all."

Fatima Sathay had gotten a job as a receptionist in a local hair salon. She was a doe-eyed Indian girl with a shy smile, very earnest, but nonetheless rather enjoying her role as chief witness. Carmichael was relieved to be interviewing her at work and not in the presence of her parents, whom Commander Andrews had described as "guardian dragons."

"I got to the house at nine that morning," she said, "and went up and made the beds just like always. Then I helped Kitty clear away the breakfast things since Mrs. Simmons was over at Little House. She'd asked me to do the silver, so I brought it all down to the kitchen and got started, thinking I'd do the dusting later."

"And you were still there when Miss Whitcomb took up the coffee tray?" asked Carmichael.

"Yes, sir."

"Did you see her make it up?"

Fatima shook her head. "Not really. I mean, I was mostly looking at the silver. I saw her out of the corner of my eye so to speak, but I couldn't swear that she didn't put anything in it."

"No, naturally not," said Carmichael, although he knew that in fact no poison had been found in the pot, only in the cup. Since they now knew the poison had come from the vase in the study, that went far in ruling Kitty Whitcomb out. She could only have poisoned Berowne if she had reentered the study after seeing Annette leave the house.

"What I'm interested in," continued Carmichael, "is how long Miss Whitcomb was gone. You told Commander Andrews it was less than five minutes."

"That's right," said Fatima, nodding seriously. "I didn't actually notice the time when she went up, but it must have been eleven because that's when Mr. Berowne always had his coffee. And when she came back, Kitty said we deserved some elevenses, too, and we both sat down with a cuppa. I looked at the clock then, so I'd know how long a break I took, and it was just five minutes past."

"And Miss Whitcomb never left the kitchen again, until she went up to fetch the tray?"

"She didn't, sir. She'd have had to walk right past me, and I couldn't have helped but notice."

"That's very good, Miss Sathay," said Carmichael, smiling. "Now I'd just like to have your impressions of the household. Did everyone seem to get on together?"

"Well, I suppose so," she answered. "I didn't really see very much of them, except for Mrs. Simmons and Kitty. Sometimes I'd overhear people talking while I was cleaning, but I never heard any fights. Miss Wellman was a bit sharp with everyone and I don't think she liked Mrs. Berowne much, but I never heard them arguing."

"How about Mr. and Mrs. Berowne?"

"They seemed very fond of each other, sir, for all he's so much older than her. But she didn't seem to mind that. I heard them once," she added, lowering her voice, "when I was in the hall outside their bedroom. It was right in the middle of the afternoon!"

"Is that so?" Carmichael hid a smile at her indignation. Clearly in her seventeen-year-old mind older married people should reserve sex for the nighttime hours. He thanked her and took his leave.

"That pretty well knocks Kitty Whitcomb out of it, don't you think?" asked Gibbons outside.

"Almost certainly," Carmichael agreed. "It's still barely possible that she went back into the study and contrived to pour Berowne a cup of coffee, but I can't see how she would have managed it in the time. She couldn't just march in, pour the coffee, and leave; she'd have to at least speak to him briefly." He sighed. "But of course, Surrey CID never really suspected any of the servants. Andrews and Gorringe are convinced it's one of the family."

Gibbons loosened his tie and took a long, grateful draught of single malt scotch, savouring the smoky aroma the Isle of Isla is so deservedly famous for. He relaxed with a sigh into an overstuffed armchair, propping his feet on one of the five coffee tables in Bethancourt's drawing room. Bethancourt was a wealthy young man, but with eccentric tastes. He was very fond of coffee tables.

The room itself was spacious, with the graceful proportions of a bygone era. The wide windows with their elegant moldings were hung with heavy gold drapes, only a shade different from the gold Aubusson carpet. Both these items had been chosen by Bethancourt's mother, a woman with excellent taste. Bethancourt himself had supplied the rest of the furnishings, which were also excellent individually, but which hardly created a cohesive whole. The five coffee tables were all of differing styles, while the Chesterfield sofa and the four luxurious armchairs were each upholstered in a different pattern. Still, it was a very comfortable room and its owner was very fond of it.

Bethancourt, who had showered and changed, now lounged on the sofa, looking clean and refreshed and sipping his own drink. Cerberus was stretched out underneath his legs, and man and dog looked as if they thought all was right in the world. Gibbons shifted slightly in his chair and set his glass down on a coffee table.

"We made a good start today," said Gibbons, trying to sound optimistic and partly succeeding.

Bethancourt nodded. "We're beginning to get a picture of life at Hurtwood Hall," he agreed.

"A rather contradictory one," said Gibbons. "Everyone loathes Mrs. Berowne and resented Geoffrey for marrying her, and yet the Reverend Oakley claimed Berowne was a happy man."

"He probably was." Bethancourt swirled the dark amber liquid in his glass. "It's like a simmering kettle from which the lid has been removed. Geoffrey Berowne was the lid on his family. He wasn't a sensitive man and probably didn't realize what was boiling away underneath."

"I don't see how you make that out," said Gibbons, reaching for his glass.

"Don't you? Berowne married Annette four years ago and I've no doubt that there was quite a ruckus about it at the time. I also don't doubt that Berowne put his foot down pretty sharply and thereafter everyone walked softly around him and did their best not to give Annette any ammunition to carry to him. Even Maddie Wellman with her sharp tongue would have sense enough to see that if she continued to protest too much it would be she and not Annette that Berowne would see as the cause of the strife, and she'd be out on her ear. Berowne probably believed everything had settled down beautifully."

"Carmichael thinks Maddie was lying about there not being any differences other than business ones between Geoffrey and Paul," said Gibbons.

"That's interesting," said Bethancourt. "Paul's behavior is highly suspicious, after all. His car dies on him and instead of hopping into one of the four other working vehicles on the estate, he decides to forget about work and spend the morning wandering about the grounds communing with nature."

"We're going to see him tomorrow at his offices here," said Gibbons. "And after that I've got an appointment to go down and speak with Dr. Bryan Warren in Kent tomorrow afternoon."

"Who is Dr. Warren?"

"It's that rumor about Mrs. Berowne having killed her previous husband," explained Gibbons. "Dr. Warren was William Burton's personal physician and signed the death certificate. Carmichael talked to the Kent CID when we got back and there was never any kind of investigation into the death of William Burton. He was seventy-two, had been ill for several years, and died of a heart attack."

Bethancourt nodded and reached for his cigarette case. "I'd be more interested to know," he said, "where the rumor started in the first place." He flicked his lighter open, inclining his head to light the cigarette, and then leaned back again, settling his shoulders comfortably against the sofa back. "I mean," he continued, "we have garnered ample evidence today that Annette Berowne possesses the knack of rubbing other women up the wrong way in abundance. Was this just a case of all the old gossips in the village spontaneously saying, 'Mr. Burton's dead. That horrid wife of his must have killed him. She only married him for his money, you know.' Or did someone actually tell someone else something?"

"I see your point," said Gibbons. "But those things are the very devil to winkle out."

"Well, I can't see what you think you're going winkle out of the doctor," retorted Bethancourt. "He's going to tell you that there's not the slightest possible doubt Burton died of natural causes. If there had been, he'd at least have done a postmortem. Even if he's wrong and she pumped Burton full of lilies of the valley day in and day out, he's not going to admit it now."

"Probably not," agreed Gibbons. "But he might, for instance, tell me that the widow was devastated by the idea of an autopsy."

"I suppose so," said Bethancourt unwillingly. His principle interest in Gibbons's cases was the characters of the people involved; things like medical evidence were always by-the-way for him.

There was silence for a moment while Bethancourt smoked thoughtfully and Gibbons drank off half his whisky. "That leaves our prime suspect," he said, frowning at his glass thoughtfully. "What did you think of her, Phillip?"

"Annette Berowne?" Bethancourt wore a contemplative air. "Do you know, I find it very difficult to draw any definite conclusions about her. She's a very suspicious person."

"Good Lord, Phillip, we all know she's a suspect," said Gibbons, exasperated.

"Oh, I don't mean in that sense," replied his friend. "Look at her as if she weren't a suspect. I often do that with people, and while it doesn't tell me whether they're murderers or not, I usually do get an idea of what they're about, so to speak. But where does it lead us in the case of the enigmatic Mrs. Berowne? Either she married Berowne for his money and got her kicks from sowing dissent among the familial ranks, or else she married him for love, or at least for emotional security, and is simply frightfully clumsy at handling people."

"But somehow neither description seems to me to fit her," said Gibbons with a sigh. "I went down there with, I thought, a pretty open mind, but she wasn't any of the things I thought she might be."

Bethancourt cocked his head to one side. "And now?" he asked.

Gibbons spread his hands. "She seems a very unlikely murderer on the face of it." He did not confess the wholly inappropriate desire to protect her that had come over him; he was rather embarrassed about it.

"You were attracted to her." Bethancourt grinned.

Gibbons smiled back at him. "I suppose I was. Certainly she's very attractive, but she's hardly the first good-looking woman I've had to deal with in a case."

"No," said Bethancourt slowly. He drew thoughtfully on his cigarette. "But Annette Berowne is different. Half her charm comes from the fact that she seems unaware of it. And what makes it all so dangerous is that, unlike other women, her manner suggests she's as attracted to you as you are to her."

"You can't think she was flirting with me," said Gibbons, appalled.

"Not at all. I meant 'you' in the general sense, not the particular. Look at the effect she had on poor old Carmichael."

"Carmichael?" asked Gibbons, surprised. "He's not usually very susceptible."

"He was this time. You should have seen him while you were off getting the evidence bags."

Gibbons was smiling. "I never would have guessed," he said. He finished off his drink. "Well, attractive or not, there's got to be some way to prove Annette Berowne innocent or guilty. Why do you think she goes in for older men?"

Bethancourt shrugged. "Any number of reasons," he replied. "Left fatherless as a child, or perhaps abused. The Reverend Oakley said she was insecure, and older men are usually better established than ones her own age."

"True," agreed Gibbons. "And it's not just older men, it's *rich* older men."

"Just so. Of course, if she really is the human equivalent of a black widow spider, the reason for the wealthy part is obvious."

The chime of the doorbell and Cerberus's sharp bark in response interrupted their conversation.

"Good heavens," muttered Bethancourt, hastily checking his watch. "That must be Marla—we're dining with some fashion people tonight."

He leapt to his feet and headed toward the hall, his dog at his heels.

Marla looked magnificent as usual. Bethancourt gazed at her admiringly as she greeted Cerberus, bending to scratch his ears with one perfectly manicured hand. Straightening, she smiled and said, "We're late again."

Bethancourt ignored this in favor of kissing her hello. The kiss lingered for a moment and then he drew back, smiling into her jade-green eyes, and said, "*You're* late."

Her eyes went from languid to sparkling.

"If I'm the only one who's late," she said, "then why aren't you ready to go?"

"But I am ready," protested Bethancourt.

"Oh?" Marla took half a step back and looked eloquently down at his feet, which were clad in slippers.

"I lost track of time," admitted Bethancourt.

"I'm so glad," cooed Marla, leaning into him again, "that a date with me is such a memorable event for you."

Bethancourt laughed. "Nonsense, Marla," he said firmly, turning to usher her down the hall. "You know perfectly well that a date with you is the epitome of any man's dreams, myself not excepted. Let me just get a jacket and change my shoes."

She smiled back at him and then paused, her face falling, as she caught sight of Gibbons, still sitting with his drink in the living room.

"Hello, Marla," he said.

"Hello, Jack," she replied, recapturing her smile. "Phillip, do go finish dressing."

"I am," he answered.

Bethancourt disappeared in the direction of the bedroom and Marla smiled charmingly at Gibbons and inquired what he had been up to that day.

"Nothing much," lied Gibbons, who knew Marla was best kept in the dark about murder investigations. "Paperwork," he added.

"Really?" she said. "How terribly dull for you."

"All part of the job," said Gibbons uncomfortably, aware that she didn't believe a word he was saying. "And what were you doing today? Working?"

"It seems incredible," she said, ignoring his inquiry, "with all the dreadful things going on in the papers, that they keep you sitting at a desk."

"Well, you've got to finish one case before you can start another," explained Gibbons.

"Of course you do," she said. "Phillip," she added, as Bethancourt returned suitably attired, "Jack's just been telling me all about this enthralling new case."

Bethancourt picked up his glass without batting an eye. "Really?" he said. "He told me he'd been working at the office all day."

"Don't be ridiculous," said Marla, suddenly losing patience and glaring at both of them. "Jack never wears a jacket and tie at the office. That's your best interviewing suspects outfit, and you know it."

"Court appearance this morning," said Gibbons promptly. "Just a small case. It didn't take long."

"I'll bet it didn't," muttered Marla, defeated.

"We really ought to be going, Marla," said Bethancourt, draining his drink. "We're going to be half an hour late as it is."

"Are you coming with us, Jack?" asked Marla, flashing him her sweetest smile.

Gibbons had seen that smile plastered over too many magazine pages to have much faith in its sincerity. "I can't," he said. "I have to be up early tomorrow." *Besides,* he added silently to himself, *I probably can't afford wherever you're going.*

They filed out of the flat, Gibbons remaining firm in his refusal to join them, and bade each other good night. Gibbons looked after them for a moment as they made their way down the street in search of a taxi, arms linked, Bethancourt inclining his head to catch what Marla was saying. For a moment, he felt lonely. Then he turned and went off in the opposite direction to wait for the bus.

CHAPTER

Gibbons leaned back against the leather upholstery of the gray Jaguar and let his mind roam over the events of the morning while Bethancourt guided the car down the A21. They had visited the London offices of Berowne Biscuits that morning and had met their final suspect, Paul Berowne. He was a thin, gray-haired man, quiet and sober in manner, with a thin-lipped mouth that gave nothing away and the same strained look in his eyes that his wife had worn. Gibbons knew he was thirty-eight, but he looked much older.

Berowne was very correct in his manner. He received them politely and ordered tea from his secretary. It was at this point that Bethancourt abandoned the policemen and went happily off to help the temporary typist fetch the tea. It was a surprisingly long time in coming.

Nothing Carmichael said during the interview had seemed to disturb Berowne in the least. In a quiet, measured tone, he repeated his original statement: the temperature gauge in his car had come on almost as soon as he had left the estate that morning and he had immediately returned to the garage. Mills had swiftly diagnosed the problem and explained that it would take a little time to put right. Berowne had left him to it and had returned to the house to phone his office.

"You didn't think of taking one of the other cars, or perhaps the train?" asked Carmichael.

"No, I didn't," Berowne replied. "There was nothing of particular importance awaiting me here and I really only enjoy driving the BMW."

After ringing his secretary, he had gone to find McAllister in the garden to speak to him about replacing some rhododendrons with ornamental trees. That done, he had taken a walk around the estate. It had been a beautiful morning and he hadn't wanted to spend it inside. He had returned to the house for another cup of coffee, but had used the kitchen door and therefore had not seen either Mrs. Simmons or his wife. About noon or shortly thereafter, he had returned to the garage to see how Mills was getting on. It was there that Maddie Wellman had found him with the news of his father's death.

"So your walk took nearly three hours," said Carmichael.

Berowne shrugged. "About that, I suppose. I didn't walk the whole time; I sat down by the pond for a while."

"Still, it seems a long time."

"I was thinking things over," replied Berowne, unperturbed. "Ever since I took over from my father here, things have not run smoothly and I've been very worried about it. Lately I've been wondering just what I could do to get things back on track. The answers have not been obvious."

"Ah, yes," said Carmichael. "I understand that you and your father had had several disagreements recently about the business?"

"There were bound to be differences." Berowne sighed and looked tired. "My father had a real flair for business and investments. My grandfather started Berowne Biscuits, but my father made it what it is today. I don't have that flair. I'm reliable and hard-working, but I don't have his genius. Father never understood that his gift was special, that I didn't do things his way because I couldn't."

"Did these disagreements reflect on your relationship at home?"

"Not at all. And they weren't precisely disagreements. My father would discover something I had done, or left undone, and then fly off the handle about it. But he was always right and I admitted that."

"Naturally, you felt some resentment over this treatment?"

"I certainly wished he wouldn't lose his temper so easily," replied Berowne, "but I've been wishing that all my life. If you're implying that I wanted him to stop interfering, you're quite wrong, Chief Inspector. I relied very heavily on my father's advice. In fact," now he looked harassed, "I don't really know how I'm going to manage without it."

"I'm sure things will work out," murmured Carmichael. "Now, Mr. Berowne, I'd just like to ask you about your stepmother."

A look of distaste came into Berowne's eyes. "I know nothing against her, other than the fact that she married my father for his money and tried to alienate him from his family. I don't even know if she was being unfaithful."

"But you suspect it?"

He shrugged in answer and although Carmichael probed, he could draw nothing further from him on the subject.

They had gone on to interview Berowne's secretary and the office manager, both of whom were so discreet that they barely admitted to knowing their employers at all. Bethancourt had done better with the temporary typist, who had been working in the office for almost four months. She gleefully divulged that on the days Geoffrey Berowne had come into the office, everything had been turned upside down and that father and son had usually had a row behind the closed door of Mr. Berowne's office. The last row, however, had taken place in full view of all the secretaries and half the staff and had centered on some investments made by the younger Mr. Berowne. Geoffrey had called his son a fool and had stormed off to lunch. This had occurred the week before the murder. The office as a whole thought Annette Berowne had killed her husband; the temporary typist had never seen Mrs. Berowne herself, but everyone assured her that the woman was a real man-trap and quite horrid.

Gibbons was roused from his thoughts by the realization that the car had slowed almost to a crawl and was edging its way toward the verge.

"Phillip!" he said sharply.

"What? Oh, dear." Bethancourt guided the car back onto the road and accelerated. "I was just looking at the hop fields."

Gibbons sighed and wished, not for the first time, that they could have taken the motorway. Bethancourt was actually a very good driver when he was paying attention. Unfortunately, he was easily distracted and spent a good part of any trip gazing about him at almost anything but the road ahead, slowing as he drew near some interesting feature and then racing on at top speed until something else drew his attention. There were far fewer distractions on the motorways.

Gibbons glanced at the ordinance map in his hands and resigned himself to the fact that they would shortly have to turn off onto a secondary road for some miles. He had better, he decided, give up thinking about the case and turn his attention to Bethancourt's driving.

"I think the turnoff's coming up," he said.

"I see it." Bethancourt shifted down smoothly. "I don't think I've ever taken this road before. Look at that church over there, Jack."

"Splendid," agreed Gibbons, keeping his eyes on the road.

"I'm glad it cleared up," said Bethancourt. "It's nice to get out of London on a day like this."

Gibbons had to admit this was true.

They drove into Hawkhurst without further incident and found the doctor's surgery in a narrow side street. Bethancourt parked the Jaguar at the curb and affixed a lead to Cerberus's collar, but then declined to go in with Gibbons.

"I want some tea," he said. "I'm sure I saw a tea shop back there on the High Street."

Gibbons regarded him good-humoredly. "You want to see if you can find anyone to gossip with," he said.

"That too," agreed Bethancourt with grin. "I'll meet you back here."

Bethancourt chose his tea shop carefully. Hawkhurst boasted two of these establishments, one toward the end of the High Street, next door to a small antique shop, and one more centrally located, close by the post office. He inspected both through the windows. The one by the antique store was carefully countrified, with chintz curtains drawn back from the windows, solid pine tables and chairs, and china teapots. The second was larger and less meticulous in its decor: the tables were formica, the floor linoleum, and tea was served in stainless-steel jugs. The first was patronized by a smattering of people, generally well-off looking, while the second was fairly crammed with the ladies of the village. There were two young mothers seated in the back with their children, shopping parcels on the floor beside them. The front was taken up by middle-aged to elderly women seated at tables in twos and threes.

Bethancourt entered the second shop and selected a table near the older women, all of whom looked him and his dog over carefully without ceasing their conversations. Cerberus stretched out on the floor by his master's feet, yawning and closing his eyes. Bethancourt ordered tea and muffins and settled down to listen to his neighbors' conversation.

The pair on his right were two of the older ladies and were discussing their grandchildren. The three in front of him were apparently avid gardeners. Bethancourt, who had grown up in the country, knew something about gardening, but not enough to enter into the esoteric discussion about peas. He turned back to the grandmothers just as one of them was detailing a near-accident involving a grandchild and a passing car, and how she had told her daughter-in-law several times that the yard ought to be fenced.

"Excuse me," said Bethancourt politely. "I couldn't help overhearing you—is there a lot of traffic around here? Because our oldest is just two."

"Oh, no," said the lady who had spoken. "My son's family lives on a particularly nasty curve, and the house is far too close to the road. It's not a general problem at all."

"I'm relieved to hear it," said Bethancourt.

"Have you taken a house in Hawkhurst, Mr., er . . ."

"Bethancourt. Phillip Bethancourt. No, actually, I'm just starting to look in this area. I haven't even been to the estate agents yet—I thought I'd drive around a bit and get the feel of the place first. It's very lovely around here."

Both ladies agreed that it was lovely and proceeded to point out in detail just what made it so. The gardening club, seeing that contact had been made with the unknown man, abandoned their discussion of peas and joined in. Introductions were made, including the two women on the farther side of the grandmothers.

Bethancourt vouchsafed the information that he and his wife had just had their second child and wished to move out of London. They had been looking in Surrey, which was where his wife was from, but had failed to find just what they wanted. But they had run into a very nice lady there, who had suggested they try Kent. She was from Hawkhurst herself and had mentioned the village.

"Really? I wonder if that could have been Dottie Langston?"

"No," answered Bethancourt. "No, I don't think that was the name."

"Or perhaps Julie Hoving?" suggested someone else.

"No, dear, that was Buckinghamshire she moved to."

"Brown, I think," said Bethancourt tentatively. "Was it Ann Brown? That's not quite right, I know . . ."

Dead silence greeted this suggestion.

"Surely," said the grandmother on his right, "surely you can't mean Annette Berowne?"

Bethancourt beamed at her. "That was it," he said. "I knew Ann Brown wasn't right. Do you know her?"

A chorus of voices broke out all around him. Didn't he know who Annette Berowne was? Didn't he read the papers or listen to the news? Why it was just last week . . .

"Last week?" echoed Bethancourt, looking bewildered. "But what happened?"

"She killed her husband," said Mrs. Evans flatly.

"No!" Bethancourt managed to look appropriately shocked. "Are you sure it's the same woman? She was rather small, brown eyes and light brown hair, almost blond?"

"That's her," said Mrs. Mathews.

"It made all the papers," put in Miss Bascomb. "However did you miss it?"

"Well," Bethancourt smiled deprecatingly, "you know how it is with a new baby in the house . . ."

They did know, but before they could get sidetracked on a subject they knew far more about than he, he asked them if they had really known Annette Berowne. A babel of assents came at him from all sides. What they could tell him about Annette Berowne, or Annette Burton as she was.

"She killed her last husband, too, you know," confided Mrs. Alden.

"No!" exclaimed Bethancourt. "How horrible. Was that here in Hawkhurst?"

They were eager to tell him all about it. They had never liked Annette—from the moment she set foot in Hawkhurst, they had their suspicions. Poor old William Burton had brought her back from that health spa he had gone to in Switzerland. And she actually *lived* in the house with him for two months before they were finally married, although why they had bothered at that point was beyond the ladies. Bethancourt, to whom marrying a woman he had not already slept with was unthinkable, tsked-tsked and shook his head.

"It was after that she began to give herself airs."

"Lady of leisure, that's how she fancied herself."

"We heard she was just a secretary before she married."

"Poor William Burton had his head turned by her, that's a fact."

"Any fool could see she married him for his money."

"Of course she did! When a woman in her twenties marries a man of seventy, there's always a reason—and it isn't the usual one."

"But what happened to Mr. Burton?" asked Bethancourt.

About this the ladies were vaguer. They reluctantly admitted that he had been in poor health and that Annette had helped to nurse him. Then, just as he was getting better, he had suddenly died. The majority of those gathered seemed of the opinion that Annette had poisoned him, but there was one notable dissension. Miss Loomis, a thin, elderly woman with bright, birdlike eyes, said very firmly, "Bosh. Annette didn't have enough brains to poison the cat."

Since Miss Loomis had thus far said hardly anything, merely listening and occasionally raising an eyebrow, Bethancourt was interested.

"So you think she's innocent, Miss Loomis?" he asked.

"Oh, no. I didn't say that."

"Then what do you think happened?" pursued Bethancourt.

Miss Loomis set her teacup down carefully in the center of the saucer. "What no one's told you," she said, "is that William Burton was a diabetic. The district nurse taught Annette to give him his shots. Naturally she explained how important it was to make sure there was no air in the syringe. It wouldn't take much for even Annette to realize that if there were nothing *but* air in the syringe and she injected it into a vein . . . Well, I'm sure you see."

"Oh, yes," said Bethancourt, intrigued. "And there would be no evidence at all."

"None." Miss Loomis smiled at him as if at a bright pupil. Then, having said her piece, she returned her attention to her tea.

"Letitia used to be a nurse herself," said Mrs. Evans.

"That was a long time ago," said Miss Loomis placidly.

"She really should have been a doctor," confided Mrs. Mathews from Bethancourt's other side.

Miss Loomis shook her head. "Girls didn't do things like that in those days," she said, but not as if she minded.

"No, I suppose not," said Bethancourt, looking at her reflectively.

"I hope," said Miss Bascomb, "that all this talk of murder won't put you off Hawkhurst."

"Oh, no," answered Bethancourt. "Not at all. I mean, it's not the sort of thing that happens often."

They agreed with alacrity that it was not and from there the conversation became more general. Bethancourt was interrogated as to his employment, his wife and children, the flat in London, and his birthplace. He was directed to the estate agents and told about several properties he might like to view. Eventually, the ladies began to check the clock and excuse themselves, leaving Bethancourt to follow suit.

He found Gibbons waiting for him in the Jaguar.

"I saw you in the tea shop," said his friend with a grin. "It looked as if you were a big hit."

Bethancourt opened the door and ushered Cerberus into the back seat. "I suppose I was," he answered, sliding into the driver's seat. "How was the doctor?"

"Highly indignant," answered Gibbons. "He gave me a list of all the things that were wrong with William Burton to prove that his death was thoroughly expected."

"The ladies," said Bethancourt, switching on the ignition and letting in the clutch, "say that he was recovering when he was struck down."

"That's true, to a certain extent," replied Gibbons. "He had diabetes, which was playing him up pretty rough, and the doctor thought it was about to carry him off. Then, all at once, it went into remission or whatever these things do—I've got all the technical terms down in my notes—and Burton started looking a bit better. But, as the doctor carefully explained to me, it was all an enormous strain on a body that wasn't functioning too well anyway. Therefore, he was not at all surprised when a heart attack carried the old boy off."

"I see," said Bethancourt thoughtfully.

"I've still got to see the district nurse," said Gibbons. "She lives a bit out of the village—I'll show you the turnoff."

"All right," answered Bethancourt. "I'd like to see her, too."

"I also," continued Gibbons, "interviewed Mrs. Ridge, Burton's longtime housekeeper, who apparently gave notice five minutes after Burton died."

"Did she turn up her nose at the idea of murder as well?"

"Not as emphatically as the doctor," replied Gibbons. "She disliked Annette thoroughly—referred to her as 'that gold-digger'—but says Burton was indeed very ill for a long time and the doctor had prepared her for the idea that he might die at any time. It never occurred to her that anything might be wrong until the rumors started and even now she says that if Annette killed him, she certainly can't make out how. She definitely didn't start the rumors."

"No," said Bethancourt. "No one seems to really have been told anything. And I would be willing to bet that my ladies weren't so sure themselves until they heard about Geoffrey Berowne."

"So you think it's a mare's nest, too."

"Well, I would," admitted Bethancourt, "except for one astute old lady." He repeated his conversation with Miss Loomis.

"We'll ask the nurse about it," said Gibbons. "Still, it's only an idea—nothing at all to back it up."

Bethancourt did not reply.

Miss Donsworth, the district nurse, was a pleasant, efficient woman of about forty. She scoffed at the idea that Annette had murdered William Burton.

"Why should she have?" she demanded. "Mr. Burton was a very ill man and his wife knew it. All she had to do was wait—he couldn't have lasted more than a year."

"But she'd already been nursing him for two," said Bethancourt. "Perhaps she couldn't bear it any longer."

Miss Donsworth shook her head. "I don't think so," she said. "Mrs. Burton was really quite good at nursing—never impatient or anything like that. And, besides, how would she induce a heart attack? It's not so easy to do, you know."

Gibbons outlined Miss Loomis's theory.

"Well!" Miss Donsworth was thoughtful. "Certainly I explained the dangers of injections very carefully to her," she said. "I always do. So it's possible. On the other hand, I don't know if she'd have thought of it. Common sense wasn't her strong point—she was a decent enough nurse, as I said, but you had to explain everything very precisely to her."

"Did you like her?" asked Gibbons.

"Like her?" Miss Donsworth seemed surprised by the question. "She was all right, I suppose. We weren't friends, if that's what you mean."

"Did you think she had married Mr. Burton for his money?" asked Bethancourt.

"Oh, yes," replied the nurse placidly. "She must have, mustn't she? But that's nothing out of the ordinary—women do it all the time."

"Er, yes," said Gibbons, a bit startled by this pronouncement. He glanced at Bethancourt, whose eyebrows were arched over the rims of his glasses. "Well, thank you very much, Miss Donsworth. You've been very helpful."

"Well," said Gibbons as they returned to the car, "that should be a warning to you, Phillip. Be sure to marry a rich woman."

"I suppose I had better," replied Bethancourt, grinning. "It would certainly please my mother—she's a terrible snob at heart."

"What does she think of Marla?" asked Gibbons, settling into his seat and fastening his safety belt.

Bethancourt threw him a look. "She's never met her," he answered. "I'm not that big a fool."

He turned the car in the drive and headed onto the road while Gibbons considered his friend thoughtfully. It had never occurred to him before to wonder how Bethancourt felt about Marla, whether he was at all serious about her. They had been dating for almost a year now, which was as long as Gibbons could remember any other relationship of Bethancourt's lasting. Now that Gibbons thought of it, Bethancourt had always had a girlfriend in tow. He was undeniably attractive to women, although in Gibbons's more objective eyes his friend was not really handsome and was definitely on the skinny side. Still, he had a certain charm which he did not hesitate to use and which kept him supplied with steady female companionship.

Bethancourt seemed to regard women and sex as being in the same category as food and shelter. Gibbons himself did not have the capacity to sustain a relationship that was merely entertaining and which had no deeper meaning. He had persuaded himself into the appropriate feelings on several occasions, but had always fallen short on the time and energy these things required. He supposed he was really rather inexperienced.

Rather abruptly, he asked Bethancourt if he ever contemplated settling down with Marla.

Bethancourt was understandably surprised. "I don't know as I've ever contemplated settling down at all," he replied. "Why?"

"Oh, I don't know," answered Gibbons. "I was just thinking about relationships."

Bethancourt raised a quizzical eyebrow. "You're not trying to tell me you've suddenly fallen for my girlfriend, are you?"

"Don't be daft, Phillip. Marla and I don't even get on."

"I thought not," said Bethancourt, dexterously making a turn while lighting a cigarette. "But one never knows. Then I assume you were thinking about Annette Berowne with her propensity for older men, and you got sidetracked."

"Not exactly," sighed Gibbons, "but I suppose I'd better start thinking about it. At least," he added, brightening, "the idea that she killed William Burton seems washed out."

"Do you really think so?" asked Bethancourt, shooting him an impassive glance.

"Well, I do, really," said Gibbons. "There's no evidence of it at all."

"There's no evidence she killed Geoffrey Berowne, either."

"Well, no, but we do know that he was murdered, whereas William Burton looks to have died of natural causes."

For once Bethancourt stared straight ahead at the road, smoking silently for a moment. "There's a disturbing pattern, though," he said at last. "One could easily see Berowne's death as being a case of overconfidence on her part, having pulled the same thing off so easily twice before. Look at the thing this way, Jack: she's married to Eric Threadgood and getting less and less happy about it. And then, one day on the slopes in Switzerland, she sees a way to get rid of him and keep his money. It's pure impulse, but it comes off beautifully. No one ever suspects anything but an accident. Then there's William Burton. She marries him, thinking perhaps that he'll die quite quickly. But once she sees he's going to hang on for a bit, well, she gets the idea from the nurse for how to do away with him. Pure serendipity. Geoffrey Berowne is a more difficult case, but she's sure of herself now and eventually comes up with a plan."

"Yes, I see the pattern," said Gibbons. "First, a near accident; next a little more deliberate but still leaving her perfectly safe; and then a more elaborate crime. It's the kind of pattern I've seen in criminals before: starting small, almost inadvertently, and then graduating to full-scale criminal activities, a little bigger with every step they take. But Annette Berowne's a bit different. For one thing, if she'd solved her marital and monetary problems with Eric Threadgood's death, why did she marry William Burton?"

"I don't know," said Bethancourt. "It would be interesting to know how well-off Threadgood left her."

"Carmichael's working on that," said Gibbons. "You can come round to the Yard when we get back and see what he's dug up."

"No time," answered Bethancourt with a glance at his watch. "Hell, I didn't realize it had gotten so late." The Jaguar leaped forward.

"Date with Marla?" asked Gibbons.

"You've got Marla on the brain," retorted Bethancourt. "No, it's the fencing club's annual dinner—and I have to dress for it."

"I didn't realize you still fenced," said Gibbons.

"Not in tournaments anymore," said Bethancourt briefly. "Just at the club to keep my hand in. Look here, Jack, the dinner shouldn't run late. I'll drop round your flat afterward and you can tell me what you and Carmichael have deduced."

"All right," said Gibbons. "But you'd better ring first and make sure I'm not still at the Yard."

"Very well," agreed Bethancourt.

Gibbons was regretting these arrangements when he arrived home at ten o'clock, carrying a stuffed potato and a bottle of beer to augment the canteen sandwich he had had for dinner three hours ago. It had been a long day and he was very tired. He stripped off his working clothes and pulled on a plaid flannel robe and a pair of slippers. He sank into an old, much-worn armchair with a sigh and flicked on the television, turning the station to the sports highlights. He was just starting to eat, balancing the potato in its take-away box on his knees, when the doorbell rang.

"Oh, really," he said, and rose to answer it.

Bethancourt appeared cheerful and rather tipsy. He tossed his raincoat onto a chair and sprawled comfortably in the second elderly armchair.

"How was your dinner?" asked Gibbons, picking up his potato.

"Excellent," answered Bethancourt, eyeing the potato with distaste. "Escargot, and cold cream of vegetable soup, and veal medallions with madeira sauce. Raspberry sorbet for pudding. Very nice."

"There's some more beer in the refrigerator," said Gibbons.

Bethancourt put his head on one side. "I don't think that would be at all wise," he said. "I've already had scotch and a good bit of wine, and a brandy. I think adding beer would be asking for trouble."

"There's a bottle of Bells in the cupboard beside the refrigerator," said Gibbons.

"That will do nicely, thank you," said Bethancourt, rising to get it.

He returned with the bottle and two glasses. "In case you feel inclined," he explained, "after you finish your beer and—er—snack."

"This," said Gibbons, indicating the half-eaten potato, "is not a snack. It is the second course of a meal begun with a ham sandwich in the canteen. I admit there was rather more time between courses than I would have liked."

"Well, all I can say is I'm sorry for you," said Bethancourt, resuming his seat and producing his cigarette case. "If that's the kind of food you eat, it's no wonder you're grumpy at the end of the day."

"I'm only tired. I didn't have a nice, relaxing dinner. I was working."

"Well, have a nice, relaxing drink now and tell me all about it," said Bethancourt. He poured two drinks, set one beside Gibbons's chair and leaned back to light his cigarette. He looked, Gibbons thought, abominably comfortable and pleased with life.

Having finished the inside of the potato, Gibbons began tearing off pieces of the skin with his fingers. "Carmichael spent the afternoon talking to Switzerland and looking up Eric Threadgood's will. Threadgood died in a freak skiing accident at fifty-six years of age. Basically, he fell and broke his neck. There were no witnesses, but it was never considered anything but an accident. Annette was also out on the slopes at the time, but it's difficult to see how she could have arranged the accident, especially in view of the fact that she's not a very expert skier and was presumably on the beginner's slope while Threadgood was on the more dangerous runs."

"What about the will?"

Gibbons popped another piece of potato skin into his mouth. "Before his marriage, Threadgood had left all his money to his niece and nephew. After he married, he made a new will dividing it up between them and his wife, unless he and Annette had children, in which case everything went to Annette."

"So she only got a third share?" asked Bethancourt.

"That's right." Gibbons washed the potato skin down with the last of his beer, and reached for the scotch. "It was still enough for her to live on, in a very modest way, if she sold the house he'd bought when they married and his boat. I expect she'd have sold the boat in any case since she didn't like sailing."

"Still," said Bethancourt thoughtfully, "it would mean a cutback in her lifestyle."

"Most definitely," agreed Gibbons. "Threadgood had been spending pretty freely—just a little bit more than he should have. He had to dip into his capital to pay for that boat. So she might have married Burton for the money."

"Still, it puts paid to my theory that she killed Threadgood impulsively, or even by accident," said Bethancourt.

"Well, there's not really any evidence either way," said Gibbons. "Your theory could still be true. And even if Threadgood's death was an accident, his death might have later led her to think how nice it would be if she could get rid of Burton, and from there to how easy it would be. Of course," he added, "even if she's innocent of their deaths, that doesn't mean she didn't kill Berowne."

"No," agreed Bethancourt thoughtfully. But he was now conversely thinking of how it might have been if Annette were innocent. There she would be in Switzerland, having received the shock of her husband's death, and just beginning to realize how much her own life would change in consequence. Whether she had loved her first husband or not, she must surely have enjoyed the difference marriage made in her life. And now that would all be taken away. If she had been fond of Eric Threadgood, the whole situation would have been that much more devastating. And then there would be old William Burton, a kindly man, well-off and taken with her as nearly all men were. So easy to encourage him, and there would be no need to start counting the pennies. True, Burton was going to need a lot of time and care from her, but it wouldn't be for long and she was still young. All in all, Bethancourt decided, it had probably been a hasty decision on her part, but she could not have regretted it too much or she would not have gone through with the wedding.

"She inherited everything from Burton?" he asked.

"Oh, yes," answered Gibbons. "He really hadn't anyone else to leave it to." He sighed. "But, as Carmichael pointed out this evening, it really doesn't matter. He's planning to spend tomorrow looking into Annette's contacts in London and getting hold of her credit card records and such. It's something Surrey CID never did, and it might lead somewhere. Carmichael's thinking is that she must have had some motive for killing her husband beyond that she was bored with him."

"What about the vase and the poison book?" asked Bethancourt.

"Not back from the lab yet. We should hear next week," answered Gibbons. "If they're clean, we're in real trouble because although it's well enough to find motive, other people had motives, too, and what we really need is hard evidence that she did it."

"Cheer up, Jack," said Bethancourt. "If you get motive, you might well be able to elicit a confession."

"Here's to hope," said Gibbons, tossing off the last of his whisky. He did not, however, sound very hopeful.

CHAPTER

armichael sighed and picked up his cigar from the ashtray.

"I do wish," he said, "that Surrey CID would keep their messes to themselves."

"Yes, sir," said Gibbons.

They had been working on the case for a week and had turned up nothing. So far as they could determine, Annette's account of her trips to London agreed exactly with what her credit cards said; there was no large block of time unaccounted for. There were no suspicious calls on her phone records. They had spoken with her friends from before her marriage to Berowne, but none of them had known anything to her discredit. They had gone over the Surrey CID reports minutely, and had spent wearisome hours compiling timetables. But every line of inquiry had simply petered out on them.

Carmichael looked again at the report Gibbons had just handed him.

"It looks like you talked to most of the first-class passengers on that cruise," he said.

"Yes, sir," said Gibbons. There was no hint in his voice of how extremely tedious he had found the task. "I interviewed the crew as well. There were three other couples who shared the Berownes' dinner table and with whom the Berownes spent some time. But they all said they found the Berownes to be a very affectionate couple, despite the age difference between them. Some of the women didn't think much of Geoffrey for going out and getting himself a trophy wife, but none of them thought Annette was in any way unhappy."

Carmichael sighed. He selected a forensics report from among those on his desk and stared at it glumly. Behind him rain pattered gently against the window and the city lights shone through in yellow streaks.

"No fingerprints on the vase," he said. "There were traces of the poison left in it, though. Geoffrey Berowne's and Mary Simmons's prints on the cover of that book—just what you'd expect. They haven't finished doing all the pages, but so far there's nothing but partials."

"About the vase, sir," said Gibbons, "Kitty Whitcomb has remembered seeing it two days before the murder. It was full of fresh lilies of the valley then."

This did not cheer Carmichael as much as his sergeant had hoped. "So the murderer was topping it up," he said. "That makes sense. He or she must have been putting fresh ones in the same water for nearly a week before the murder, to make sure it was strong enough to do the trick."

He leaned back and puffed on his cigar. "If Annette Berowne is a sociopath who has killed three husbands, I'm afraid we're going to have to wait for death number four before we get her," he said discontentedly.

Gibbons was silent for a moment. "Do you believe she is a sociopath, sir?" he asked.

"I don't know what I believe," grunted Carmichael. "But it has occurred to me, Gibbons, that the reason neither we nor Surrey has found anything is because we're looking in the wrong place."

"It's occurred to me, too, sir," admitted Gibbons.

"What do you think of her personally, lad?"

Gibbons hesitated. "If she wasn't his wife," he said slowly, "and wasn't inheriting millions, I'd have to say I think she's innocent. Certainly I've come to doubt the sociopath theory—she doesn't seem to fit that profile at all. She may have killed Berowne, but I don't think she killed the others."

"And if she's not a sociopath, I can't see what possible motive she could have had," said Carmichael. He leaned forward again and rested his cigar in the ashtray. "Let's see—we've gone over everything we could think of, aside from timing her walk to the village."

"I did try, sir," said Gibbons. "Several times."

"Not your fault, lad," said Carmichael, glancing at the rain pattering against the windows. "Well, we might as well be thorough. You can take the walk on the first fine day we have, but otherwise I think it's time to broaden our scope. In nine out of ten cases the spouse is guilty, but this could be the tenth case." He shifted through the case reports. "We'll give everyone else a thorough going-over, including the servants. Surrey didn't do much there—they were convinced from the beginning that it was one of the family."

"The case does have that feel to it, sir," agreed Gibbons.

"I thought so too, but we won't rule anything out. First, however, I think we'll look at Paul Berowne. His behavior on the morning of the murder is just as suspicious as Mrs. Berowne's. We can spend tomorrow looking into Berowne Biscuits before we tackle him directly again. Unless," he added, "it's a fine day, in which case you can go down to Hurtwood Hall and tie up our loose end with Mrs. Berowne."

"They're predicting a clearing trend," said Gibbons rather doubtfully and Carmichael snorted.

"They've been predicting that all week. Well, if you can get down there, try to see if her story about starting back for the library card holds up." He rummaged on his desk for another sheet of paper. "We estimated the walk took her twenty minutes to half an hour longer than it should have, depending on the pace she set."

"Yes, sir," said Gibbons, who had already received these instructions three times before.

"I'll talk to some City people tomorrow and see what they think of Paul Berowne," continued Carmichael. "I can check his finances, too."

"Do you want me to speak to Miss Wellman if I get down there?" asked Gibbons. "You always said she was holding something back about Paul Berowne and his father."

Carmichael considered this, but then shook his head. "No," he said, "I think I'd rather tackle Miss Wellman myself. If nothing turns up tomorrow, I'll go down the next day to draw her out a little. After all, there was nothing preventing her from walking downstairs and poisoning Berowne herself."

"And she did resent him for marrying Annette."

"Just so," agreed Carmichael. "Well, we'll see how we get on tomorrow. You take yourself off now, Gibbons, and get a nice supper and some sleep. We're in for the long haul here, and I don't want you wearing yourself down."

"Thank you, sir," said Gibbons, rising. "I'm sure you're right. If we can just come to a conclusion, no matter how scanty the evidence, we'll have a better chance of solving this."

"Let's hope so, lad. Off you go now."

It was nearly eleven o'clock and the small, exclusive restaurant was beginning to empty out. It was the kind of place that relied on solid worth rather than trendiness to bring in its clientele, and its cozy atmosphere allowed its guests to talk quietly over some of the best food in London. At a table near the back, Gibbons swallowed a spoonful of his lobster bisque and sighed blissfully.

"God, that's good," he said.

"They do it very well here," said Bethancourt, sampling his own soup. "Yes, very good indeed."

"Thank you for this, Phillip," said Gibbons, savoring another spoonful. "I don't think I realized how much I needed to relax. And I haven't had a real meal—much less one like this—in I don't know how long."

"You're welcome," replied Bethancourt. "I take it there've been no new developments?"

"No," said Gibbons glumly. "Not a single bloody thing. Carmichael's talking about widening the investigation. He's going to look at Paul Berowne tomorrow, and go on down the list from there. We haven't looked at the servants at all, for instance."

"The servants aren't a bad idea," said Bethancourt. "After all, their bequests are quite a windfall for them. One of them might have wanted something badly enough to kill for it."

"It's possible," said Gibbons, "but McAllister and Mrs. Simmons have both worked on the estate for donkey's years. It's hard to imagine what would suddenly make them want to leave. And Kitty Whitcomb and Ken Mills, who could easily have a reason to want a change, couldn't have done it."

Bethancourt frowned and leaned back to allow the waiter to collect the soup plates. "I know Kitty's got an alibi," he said, "but I didn't know Mills had."

"Not an alibi, strictly speaking," answered Gibbons. "We've confirmed that he did go straight to the shop for the part for the BMW, and certainly he could have nipped off to the study once he got back, but it would have been risky. Paul Berowne might have returned to the garage at any time to see how the work was coming, and why should Mills take that risk? The next day, when things were back to normal, would have done just as well."

"Still," mused Bethancourt, "I should imagine it takes a good deal to work oneself up to a murder. Having done so, I don't think it would be so easy to put off for another day, as if it were a lunch date or something."

"There is that," agreed Gibbons, but not very hopefully. "I'm still betting it's one of the family. I just wish I knew which one."

"So you think Annette's definitely out of it?" asked Bethancourt.

"I don't know," answered Gibbons. "The more I talk to her, the more I think she could be innocent. But the problem there is that I like her, so I don't trust myself." He sighed. "But then, I'm getting to like them all. Annette is absolutely delightful and the way she looks on the police as if we were the answer to her prayers is very disarming. And Maddie Wellman may be a sharp-tongued old woman, but she's such a character you don't mind it. Kitty—well, it's safe enough to like Kitty, I suppose."

"And what about Marion and Paul Berowne?" asked Bethancourt.

"I've seen less of them," admitted Gibbons. "But I tell you it's a bit unnerving to be talking to Annette and laughing at something she's said, and then to suddenly remember that she may have deliberately poisoned a man, and probably stood there and watched him die. It wouldn't matter so much if we were getting anywhere with the investigation, because then one's focus is narrowed. But we're not getting anywhere and my focus is all over the place."

"It'll all settle down once you get a lead," said Bethancourt consolingly. "You'll jump on it like a hound on a scent, and all your feelings about these people will get stashed in the back seat. It's only because you don't know who to suspect that you're getting muddled now."

But Gibbons's words had made him remember that first day and how he had wondered if Annette Berowne had been deliberately using her charms in an attempt to disarm the police. He wondered again now and wished that he had made more of an effort to accompany his friend on his endless rounds of interviews.

The fish course arrived and Bethancourt inhaled deeply and happily as he picked up his fork.

"So what's on the agenda for tomorrow?" he asked.

"If it ever stops raining, Carmichael wants me to walk Annette over that footpath to the village, and see how the time works out. I'd really rather get started on Paul Berowne, but I suppose there's something to be said for tying up loose ends."

"How would you like a ride down there? I've got nothing on for tomorrow."

"I'd love a ride," answered Gibbons. "I'm not sure about taking you along on the walk, though. It's going to be hard enough to get her to keep her own pace with just me along."

"That's all right," said Bethancourt, reaching to refill his wineglass. "I'd like to have another chat with Kitty."

"The way to a man's heart is through his stomach," said Gibbons, grinning. "She didn't seem like your type, Phillip."

Bethancourt raised his eyebrows. "I wasn't aware," he said, "that I had a type."

"Of course you do." Gibbons's grin widened. "Your type is spectacular and glamorous."

"Kitty is not glamorous," agreed Bethancourt judiciously, in the manner of an art critic remarking on a new artist, "but she could be said to be spectacular in her own way. Her figure, I should say, is up to any man's standards, and although her face is not exactly beautiful, she is very pretty. The pinkness of her cheeks, I am sure, owes nothing to cosmetics."

"Don't be pompous," said Gibbons, laughing. "And, anyway, she's not stunning, which is generally how you seem to prefer women."

"I only said I wanted to talk with her," retorted Bethancourt.

"Believe it or not, I have been known to hold conversations with downright unattractive people of both sexes."

"I'm sure you have," said Gibbons, still grinning. "Never mind."

Bethancourt was awakened the next morning by the telephone. Thinking it might be Gibbons with a change in the program, he imprudently answered it and instead heard the well-bred, unwelcome tones of his sister.

"Phillip?" she said. "How like you to still be abed at this hour."

Bethancourt pulled the clock from the nightstand and held it six inches in front of his newly opened, still blinking eyes. It appeared to be eight o'clock.

"It is like me," he agreed, and closed his eyes.

"Well, I did wait till I got to Town to ring you," she continued.

"Town?" repeated Bethancourt, his eyes flying open once again. "You're in Town?"

"That's what I'm trying to explain," she said patiently. "I've had the most frightful morning, what with Clara breaking an ankle and the dogs getting into Mrs. Garvin's garden—I nearly missed my train. However, it's all right now, since I've found you in."

"It is?" asked Bethancourt doubtfully.

"Yes, indeed," she replied decisively. "I want you to look after Denis for an hour or two."

Bethancourt called to mind the fact that he was due to pick Gibbons up in two hours to aid in a murder investigation. It did not seem a very appropriate activity for a boy of five. "I really don't think—" he began.

"You really must help me out today, Phillip," she said firmly. "I'm at my wit's end. We'll just get a taxi and be round in twenty minutes. You're a darling, Phillip."

"Margaret—" said Bethancourt, but she had rung off. "Oh, Lord," he groaned, and propped himself up on the pillows.

He knew from past experience that he was probably doomed to baby-sit his nephew. Margaret, four years his senior, was like a steamroller once she got started, and no excuse he put forward would be tolerated. Even as children, they had not got on well, and their differing personalities as adults had done nothing to bring them closer. Margaret led a very busy, well-arranged life, doing a great deal of work for various charities whilst running an immaculate household. Bethancourt was essentially lazy and had never won an argument with her. His only chance, he realized, of avoiding the plans she had made for him was to leave the flat before she arrived. And if he did that, he would be hearing from his mother in no time at all, and the incident would be repeated down through the years as evidence of his irresponsibility.

While he was cleaning his teeth, it occurred to him that the presence of his nephew might not actually spell disaster. There was no real reason he shouldn't take the boy along and let him play in the kitchen while he was talking to Kitty. Denis might even provide an easy excuse to visit Marion Berowne again. Her son, he recollected, was near Denis's age.

When Margaret Sinclair-Firthing arrived at her brother's flat, she found him drinking coffee. He had showered and shaved, but was still clothed in an elegant silk dressing gown embroidered with cattails. Margaret recognized it as one she had given him for Christmas two years ago.

"I'm glad you still like that," she said, kissing his cheek.

"I certainly do," responded Bethancourt. He was not lying; he might feel that his sister had many flaws, but there was no denying she had excellent taste.

There was a strong family resemblance between them. Like her brother, Margaret was tall and slender with a delicately shaped nose, a firm jaw, and thick, straight hair just a shade lighter than Bethancourt's. Her eyes were blue rather than hazel and there was no humor in them whatsoever. She was beautifully turned out in a periwinkle silk suit.

Her son was a skinny, tow-headed child with his mother's blue eyes.

"Hello, Uncle Phillip," he said, as a politely brought-up child should, and then abandoned his relative in favor of the said relative's dog. "Cerberus!"

"Denis," said his mother, "you're going to get all over dog hair."

"He's going to anyway, if he's spending the day with me," pointed out Bethancourt.

"I expect so." Margaret sighed and cast a disapproving glance at the dog. "Better you than me," she added, brightening.

"So you pointed out when you gave him to me," said Bethancourt dryly.

"Good heavens," said Margaret, coming into the living room. "You've got another coffee table."

"Rather a nice one, don't you think?" said Bethancourt.

"It's very nice, but you have four others," she answered. "Most people have one at maximum."

"Really? How odd."

"Don't be sarcastic, Phillip." She looked about the room. "There is absolutely *no* cohesion in this room," she said severely. "You really should have had a decorator in."

"I like it the way it is."

"You might like it just as well if it looked nice."

Bethancourt gave up. "What charity is it today, Margaret?" he asked, lighting a cigarette.

"Orphans," she answered succinctly. "And then I'm lunching with Sir Rodney and Mrs. Chilton. I should be done by one-thirty or two."

"Rosemary Chilton? Is she Sir Rodney's latest?" asked Bethancourt, who much enjoyed twitting his sister about her aristocratic friends. There was nothing Margaret loved so much as a title, even those belonging to people who were less than admirable. "Good gracious, at the rate he's going, he'll have run through the entire charity committee by midsummer."

Margaret frowned at him. "I don't know and I don't want to know," she answered firmly. "What Sir Rodney does in his private life is no concern of mine—or yours."

"If Rodney didn't want people to gossip about his private life, he should leave other men's wives alone," retorted Bethancourt. "He's a toad, Margaret, and you think so yourself."

"Sir Rodney is the guiding force behind a very worthwhile cause," said Margaret primly.

"Ah," said Bethancourt, suddenly enlightened. "I see. That diatribe you spouted off about him last month was only a reaction to his chatting you up."

"It was no such thing," snapped Margaret, her outrage merely confirming her brother's hypothesis. "I was merely distressed about Claire Lyndhurst, who, after all, should have known better."

"Well, at least Frasier Lyndhurst never found out about it," said Bethancourt. "It could have been worse."

Margaret's only reply was frosty silence and Bethancourt relented. "So what time did you say you'd be done?" he asked.

"One-thirty or two."

"I have to drive Jack Gibbons down to Surrey," said Bethancourt firmly. "I can take Denis with me, but I don't know when I shall be back."

A gleam appeared in Margaret's eyes. "But that works out wonderfully," she said quickly. "I was going to do some shopping after lunch. I'll ring you when I'm done to see if you're back—around four or five?"

"I suppose—" began Bethancourt.

"Now, Denis," she continued, turning away from her brother, "you be a good boy and mind your uncle."

"Yes, Mummy."

"And, Phillip, make sure you don't forget to give him some lunch. Oh, and here—" she handed Bethancourt a canvas bag. "There are some of his toys in here. All right, darling, give me a kiss. You have a nice time with your uncle. And thank you, Phillip. You've saved my life."

Left alone together, man and boy stared at each other for a long moment. Cerberus panted happily. Then, "I've got to dress," said Bethancourt, stubbing out his cigarette. "Then we'll go for a drive in the country."

"I just came in from the country," said Denis.

"I can't help that," answered Bethancourt. "Anyway, this will be different country and you can ride in the back with Cerberus."

He fled to his bedroom.

Gibbons was incredulous.

"You can't be serious, Phillip," he said.

"Shh. You'll make him feel unwanted and then he'll have to spend his adult life in therapy working it out."

"But, Phillip—"

"He'll develop a complex about policemen," warned Bethancourt. "It'll be all right, Jack," he added. "I'll slip round the back with him and Cerberus. Kitty won't mind."

The drive down was principally marked by the fact that there was barely enough room in the back seat for both boy and dog, a situation which was aggravated by Cerberus's objection to acting as a roadway for Denis's toy lorry. He was far too well bred a dog to bark or even growl at a diminutive member of his master's family, especially not when he outweighed him. He pushed.

"Hey! Cerberus!"

"What is going on back there?" demanded Bethancourt. "Jack, can't you cope with a small boy and a dog?"

Gibbons obligingly twisted around in his seat. "What's wrong, Denis? Oh, dear." Gibbons tried to reach into the back, but was somewhat hampered by his safety belt. "Move, Cerberus. Over, boy. Here, Denis, sit up."

"My lorry!"

"What lorry? Oh, I see."

The lorry proved to be elusive. Gibbons swore and released the belt.

"Watch it, Jack!" said Bethancourt, grabbing for the gear shift. "You almost knocked her out of gear. What on earth are you doing?"

"Getting the damn lorry," said Gibbons in a muffled voice.

"Don't swear, Jack. Denis is only five."

"All settled now," said Gibbons, righting himself and refastening the safety belt.

"Good," said Bethancourt.

"Vroom!' said Denis. "Vroo—Cerberus!"

"Denis," said Bethancourt, "don't yell at the dog. His hearing is roughly a million times better than yours, so that actually he could hear you perfectly well if you spoke in a whisper."

"Oomph!" replied Denis. Then, in a strangled voice, "Uncle Phillip!"

"What is it now?" said Bethancourt sharply. "Jack . . ."

"Oh, dear," said Gibbons, twisting round again.

"Jack, watch the gear shift!"

"I can't see Denis at all."

"What?" Bethancourt immediately slackened speed and began to pull over. "The windows were closed . . ."

"Cerberus is lying on him," explained Gibbons, reaching to release his belt again.

"Christ, Jack!" said Bethancourt, swerving back onto the road.

"Don't swear, Phillip. Denis is only five. Cerberus, move!" Gibbons tugged on the dog's collar. Unwillingly, Cerberus shifted, revealing Denis still clutching his toy. "Good boy," said Gibbons, although whether to dog or child was not clear. "There you go, Denis. Cerberus, stay."

"Say thank you to Mr. Gibbons," said Bethancourt.

"Thank you, Mr. Gibbons."

Peace reigned for several moments. Then Denis, recovered, again attempted to pretend Cerberus's flank was a motorway. This time, the dog had had enough. He gave up trying to control the situation, since every time he gained the upper hand, Gibbons made him relinquish it. Clearly the thing to do was to escape altogether. He tried to bolt into the front seat.

Since both bucket seats were fully occupied by grown men who were not prepared to have 110 pounds of dog in their laps, this maneuver was not entirely successful.

"Bloody hell!" exclaimed Bethancourt, stamping on the clutch as the shift was knocked out of gear and a plumy tail blinded him.

"Mmpf!" agreed Gibbons, whose abdomen had taken most of the impact of the Borzoi's leap and who now found his arms unexpectedly full of dog and his face full of fur.

"Ooh, Uncle Phillip," came from the back seat as the Jaguar swerved sharply and then came to an abrupt and sharp stop, its nose in a hedge. Bethancourt switched off the engine and fumbled for the break, at present buried beneath his dog.

"Off, Cerberus," Gibbons was saying feebly, but the big dog had insufficient room to turn.

Bethancourt pulled up the brake with a jerk and flung out of the car, slamming the door behind him. In a moment, he appeared at the passenger door and opened it, ordering the dog out. Cerberus climbed off Gibbons's lap with a guilty air. Gibbons followed, wiping stray hairs from his face.

"Denis," said Bethancourt, in a remarkably controlled voice, "get back on your side of the seat. And put that filthy lorry away." He flipped up the passenger seat, and reintroduced Cerberus into the back. Gibbons got back in while Bethancourt walked around the car to the driver's side.

"Now, he said, resuming his own seat, "Cerberus, you will lie down and stay that way. You, Denis, will refrain from upsetting him with that toy. It is not polite to bore other people—or, in this case, dog—with your own interests when they do not care for them. Is that all clear?"

"Yes, Uncle Phillip."

Cerberus wagged his tail.

"Then I will try to get the car out of the hedge."

This he proceeded to do with some dexterity, and the rest of the trip was relatively quiet, marred only by a threat of car sickness just as they were arriving at their destination.

Kitty Whitcomb was considerably surprised, upon responding to a knock on the kitchen door, to find the step filled with a man she barely knew, an exceptionally large dog, and a small boy.

"Hello," said Bethancourt brightly. "Remember me?"

"Phillip Bethancourt," she answered readily. She let her eye rove over the rest of the assemblage. "I know you said there might be more questions, but I must say this is the most bizarre interview technique I've ever heard of."

"This is my nephew, Denis Sinclair-Firthing," said Bethancourt. "Denis, Miss Whitcomb."

"How do you do?" responded Denis politely.

"Very well, thank you," said Kitty solemnly, shaking hands.

"And this is Cerberus."

Kitty stretched out a hand, which must have smelled interesting, because Cerberus promptly licked it. Kitty smiled.

"Well," she said, "come on in then."

"Denis," said Bethancourt, leading the way. "I think it might be permissible for you to play with your lorry on the table here." He raised an inquiring eyebrow at Kitty.

"Certainly," she said. "Are Chief Inspector Carmichael and Sergeant Gibbons with you?" she asked while he settled the boy at the table.

"Sergeant Gibbons is with Mrs. Berowne," he replied.

She nodded. "We're having lunch at one-fifteen today," she said pointedly.

"Splendid," said Bethancourt, beaming at her. "I haven't forgotten how wonderful your cooking is."

She smiled back. "I've just made some coffee," she said.

"Thank you," said Bethancourt, who felt that he needed something after the events of the morning.

"And how about you, Denis?" she asked. "Do you like hot chocolate?"

Denis's eyes got very round. "Oh, yes, please," he said.

"All right, then."

She poured Bethancourt's coffee, which he sipped gratefully while he watched her prepare the hot chocolate. She had abandoned the yellow unitard today for a pair of black leggings and an oversized shirt with the sleeves rolled above the elbows; it was curiously alluring.

"So what's the big question today?" she asked, turning and leaning back against the counter while she waited for the milk to heat.

"I don't have one," said Bethancourt rather regretfully. "Just a lot of little ones. The Paul Berownes, for instance. It struck me as odd that he didn't tell his wife he was still here that morning."

Kitty's eyes drifted to Denis, who was happily pushing his lorry across the vast expanse of the table. "I see," she said.

"Not at all," replied Bethancourt. "It's just a coincidence, possibly a fortunate one, but a coincidence nonetheless."

Kitty merely raised her eyebrows; she did not believe him. "I don't think their marriage is a very happy one," she answered. "They almost got divorced a while back, before I came here, or so my aunt told me. I don't know why they didn't."

"Your aunt worked here before you, didn't she?"

"That's right. She recommended me for the job when she retired and I was glad to take it. I love cooking, but restaurant work was wearing me out."

Bethancourt sipped his coffee contemplatively. "I'd like to meet your aunt sometime," he said.

"That's easy enough. She lives in the village here." Kitty turned back to the milk, pouring it into a mug and mixing it up with the chocolate and sugar.

"To return to the Paul Berownes," said Bethancourt. "How do they get through the evenings if they're so unhappy? Does he stay late at the office, or lock himself in his study? Or come over here? Denis, say thank you."

"Thank you, Miss Whitcomb," said Denis, clutching the mug eagerly. "Thanks awfully."

"You're welcome," she said, smiling at him. "I put in extra sugar."

"It's awfully good," he said. "Much better than Mrs. Clancy's."

"I'm very flattered." She sank into the chair beside Bethancourt, drawing her legs up onto the seat. "Mr. Paul does all those things," she said. "Plus he spends a good deal of time at the pub."

"Is he over here very often?"

"Not on his own," she replied. "Only once every week or two, he comes and spends the evening with Miss Wellman. Sunday, of course, was family dinner day, and they all came over then."

"I see," said Bethancourt. "He only came to visit his aunt. That doesn't sound like he was particularly close to his father."

"No," said Kitty slowly, "he wasn't. I believe they were closer before Mr. Berowne's marriage, though."

"You didn't see much of Paul yourself, then?"

"No." She caught his meaning and grinned impudently at him. "No," she repeated. "I wasn't having an affair with him. Not my type."

Bethancourt grinned back. "Would you tell me if you were?" he asked.

She shrugged. "Probably. I wouldn't shield a murderer, no matter who it was."

"I believe you," said Bethancourt. "You don't know if he was having an affair with anyone else?"

"Not that I've heard. And I truly don't think he is—unless it's someone down at the pub and that's not likely. He spends too much time here in Peaslake to be seeing anyone in London."

"I see. So if Mr. Paul drowns his marital woes at the pub, what does his wife do?"

Kitty shrugged. "She takes care of Edwin, mostly."

"And in the evenings, when Edwin's in bed?"

"Well, she can't leave the child alone," said Kitty practically. "I don't really know how she spends her time—it's not like I'm in the house with her."

"I'm going to play with my stamps now," announced Denis.

"Stamps?" said Bethancourt curiously.

Denis nodded. He dove into his canvas bag and produced a pad of cheap writing paper, an ink pad, and a plastic case containing two dozen small, square rubber stamps. These he dumped unceremoniously onto the table, stirring them around a bit until he found the one he wanted. He dabbed it on the ink pad and then pressed it carefully on the paper while Bethancourt watched, fascinated.

"It's a fish," he said.

"I'm going to make a row of them," announced Denis, and proceeded to do so.

"I never had anything like that when I was a kid," said Bethancourt.

Kitty laughed at him. "Haven't you ever seen them before?" she asked.

Bethancourt shook his head. He was picking up the stamps one by one and examining the pictures carved on them. "These are great," he said.

"For all ages, apparently," said Kitty dryly.

"I'm sorry," said Bethancourt, abandoning the stamps. "Where were we?"

"The Paul Berownes," she answered.

"Oh. Well, I can't think of any more questions about them," said Bethancourt. "Let's go on to someone else. How about Maddie? We all know how little she likes Annette. So what does she do with her time?"

Kitty smiled. "Oh, Maddie keeps herself busy. There's the Women's Institute and the church, and she has quite a coterie of friends. At least once a week, she's out to dinner or lunch. And she likes the telly. If she hasn't any plans, she's usually in her sitting room after dinner watching a program."

"She sounds awfully active for a woman with crippling arthritis," said Bethancourt.

"It's not *crippling*," corrected Kitty. "It just makes her move slowly. And I guess it can be pretty painful sometimes. She has good days and bad days—she always came down to meals when Mr. Berowne was alive, but if her arthritis was acting up, she'd spend the rest of the day in her room, reading or watching the telly."

Bethancourt's answer was interrupted by a sharp buzz from the intercom on the wall.

"Speak of the devil—that must be Maddie now," Kitty said, rising to answer it. "Hello? Maddie?"

"Could you come and get Edwin, dear?" The voice from the box was tinny, but Bethancourt thought he detected a note of exhaustion in it. "I'm afraid I'm done in."

"Of course," answered Kitty. "I'll be right up." She turned to Bethancourt. "I'll be back. Maddie's baby-sitting, but her arthritis is bad today and I told her I'd take over if it got to be too much. Help yourself to more coffee if you like."

She trotted out and as soon as the sound of her steps had faded, Bethancourt rose and went to the door of her sitting room. It was quite large and once, in the grand old days, would have been the servants' hall. Now it was sparsely but comfortably furnished with a couple of armchairs, a large bookcase filled mostly with cookbooks, and a desk with a large diary lying open beside a laptop computer. At the farther end was a stationary bicycle and an assortment of weights, as well as a television set up so that it could be watched from the bicycle. There was another door in the right-hand wall, probably once the housekeeper's office, but now, Bethancourt was willing to bet, fitted out as Kitty's bedroom.

"Uncle Phillip?"

Bethancourt swung round, startled in spite of himself. "Yes, Denis?"

"What are you doing?"

Bethancourt reflected on the merits of explaining how an invasion of privacy was sometimes justified, and decided against it. "Just looking around," he answered. "It's a funny old house, isn't it? Let's go back and look at those stamps of yours. How are the fish coming?"

"I've finished with them," said Denis. "I'm doing clowns now."

Kitty, returning with Edwin Berowne in tow, found uncle and nephew quietly creating modern art at the table.

"Edwin," she said, "this is Denis Sinclair-Firthing."

The two boys assessed each other silently.

"Say how do you do, Denis," prompted Bethancourt. "Edwin here is your host."

"Hello," said Denis. "Do you want to see my stamps?"

"All right," said Edwin politely.

The stamps, however, were soon eclipsed by the toy lorry. From the capacious canvas bag, a small race car was produced and there was soon some kind of race going on beneath the table. Cerberus, much-tried, moved with dignity to a spot by the door.

"Well, where were we?" asked Kitty, sitting down.

"Maddie," answered Bethancourt. "How was her arthritis the day of the murder?"

Kitty frowned, thinking back. "I don't know," she said. "She didn't complain about it, so I expect it wasn't one of her bad days."

"Had she any plans to go out that day, do you know?"

"It was Wednesday, so she'd have the Women's Institute that night. I don't know of anything else, but she wouldn't necessarily have told me unless she was going to miss a meal. She wasn't dressed for anything when I went up to tell her about Mr. Berowne."

"Kitty," interrupted Edwin from the floor, where the race seemed to have come to its conclusion. "Can I show Denis the piano? He says he can play, too."

"All right," agreed Kitty. "But don't make a mess in there. And, Denis, put those cars and the stamps away before you go."

Denis complied with this command with some help from his uncle, and then trailed out after his new friend with the canvas bag over his shoulder.

Kitty had turned thoughtful, gazing after the boys with an uncertain look in her eyes.

"Is it certain," she asked, "that one of the family killed Mr. Berowne? I mean, the gates are always left open except at night. Couldn't someone else have come in?"

"It would have to be someone else who knew his habits," answered Bethancourt. "Someone who knew he was usually in his study in the mornings, and knew that he had coffee brought in at eleven."

Kitty shook her head. "No, that's not likely, is it?" she said. "Just wishful thinking on my part. It's been so awkward here lately, you see. Maddie's convinced Annette did it, and I suppose the rest of us think the same, but we're not sure. Ken Mills and I usually go for a run early in the mornings, and I've caught myself wondering about him. I know he's wondered about me."

"But you have an alibi," said Bethancourt.

"Yes, but Ken doesn't know that. I mean, he hasn't been running round checking times and talking to Fatima. He can't be sure."

"And you can't be sure about him." Bethancourt spread his hands. "I wish I could reassure you. Mills is far from being our chief suspect, but he did have the opportunity, so he can't be ruled out altogether."

Kitty sighed and started to reply, but then her eye caught the clock. She sprang out of her chair as if propelled. "I've got to start lunch," she said. "And you'd better check on those boys."

"True." Bethancourt rose and Cerberus, too, got to his feet and shook himself. Kitty eyed him.

"I think you'd better stay down here, my lad," she said. "I'm not sure Mrs. Berowne would appreciate your magnificent fur all over her parlor carpet."

"Fair enough," said Bethancourt. He patted the dog's head. "Stay, Cerberus," he said. "You mind Kitty."

Cerberus looked at him reproachfully and, with an enormous sigh, laid back down.

"There," said Bethancourt. "Now, where is this piano?"

Kitty explained and Bethancourt went off. But when he reached the parlor, it was quite empty. The piano was closed and the music stood neatly on its rack. Bethancourt bent to look at it and found it to be a Beethoven sonata, quite beyond the capabilities of two little boys. He glanced around, becoming more convinced every moment that the boys had never been here. He checked the drawing room next door, but it was empty and also in pristine condition. Hastily, he retraced his steps to the kitchen.

"Kitty," he said, "they're not there."

"Not there?" She swung around, alarm spreading over her face.

"I don't think they ever were," said Bethancourt. "Is there another piano?"

"No—oh, Lord, yes, of course there is." She laid down the knife she was holding and made for the door. "There's one at Little House— that's probably where Edwin meant to go all along. At least, I hope so."

Bethancourt followed her through the length of the house, past the infamous study and out through the side door. Once off the terrace, they broke into a run along the little path that led them past the gardens and under the shelter of the budding trees. Above, the clouds were rolling in, gunmetal gray and threatening. Cerberus broke into a canter and ran ahead of them.

"There's no real danger, is there?" panted Bethancourt. "I mean, they wouldn't have left the estate?"

Kitty shook her head. "No. But there's the pond or the brook. Oh, they must be at Little House."

Cerberus was waiting for them on the doorstep. The door was closed, but not locked and in a moment they were inside. There was no sound of a piano. Kitty raced up the stairs with Bethancourt at her heels.

"Thank God," said Bethancourt. From an open door at the end of the corridor he could hear the boys' voices.

"Well, there you are," said Kitty as they rounded the doorjamb.

The schoolroom was large and open, remarkably bare of furniture. At one end stood a baby grand and beside it was a collection of various-sized children's chairs and desks, an upright blackboard and, beyond them, an easy chair and table. At the opposite end the wall was covered with bookshelves and cabinets, the latter of which were arrayed with a jumble of stuffed animals, sporting equipment, and open volumes of the *Encyclopedia Britannica*.

The two boys were playing with a veritable army of small toy soldiers spread out in the middle of the floor. They looked up, surprised at their elders' entrance, but neither Kitty nor Bethancourt scolded them. They had, after all, asked permission to go and play the piano and they could not really be blamed for the fact that the adults had had a different piano in mind.

"Well, I've got to get back," said Kitty.

"I'll look after them," said Bethancourt. "They might as well finish their game here, and I'll bring them back for lunch."

Kitty nodded. "All right," she said. "Thanks."

"Uncle Phillip," said Denis. "Cerberus is standing on the soldiers."

"Sorry," said Bethancourt. "Cerberus, come."

Cerberus came to heel whilst his master wandered about the room, idly inspecting some of the toys and books. He ended up by the piano and sat on the bench for a few moments, looking over the music displayed and taking note of the portable tape deck that sat beside the music stand. It was, he saw, one of those which could record tapes as well as play them.

The boys were still fully occupied with their game. Bethancourt patted his dog and removed himself to the easy chair, leaning back comfortably while Cerberus lay down at his feet. He lit a cigarette and glanced out of the window. Above the trees, the sky was very dark and, even as he watched, the first heavy raindrops splattered against the window. He hoped it was going to blow over before he had to take the boys back for lunch. He hadn't brought an umbrella, and Denis's raincoat was in the Jaguar. He could imagine what his sister would have to say about that oversight.

He turned his attention to the apparently fierce battle being conducted on the carpet. The soldiers were a mismatched lot, representing as they did everything from Napoleonic calvary to modern-day commandoes. He reflected that Edwin must have a passion for the things; even Denis didn't have this many. A horrible thought crossed his mind and looked around for his nephew's canvas bag. It had been pushed into a corner and looked considerably depleted.

He cleared his throat diffidently. "Denis," he said, "are all these soldiers Edwin's?"

Denis, in the process of advancing his toy lorry—now apparently a tank—looked up. "Oh, no," he answered. "Some of them are mine."

"I see," said his uncle nervously. "I don't suppose all the ones on your side are yours and vice-versa?"

"No," Denis replied, looking puzzled. "We divided them up."

"We had to," explained Edwin, "so both sides would be even."

"And what," asked Bethancourt, "gave you the idea that battles are ever even? Oh, never mind," he added, as both boys merely looked confused. "Carry on." He glanced at his watch, estimating the maximum amount of time he could allow the game to continue before he would have to stop it and get down to the complicated business of trying to sort out which soldiers were whose.

The rain was really pelting down now, running in broad rivers down the panes of glass. Bethancourt leaned back and relaxed again. He couldn't possibly walk the boys back through this. If it didn't let up before one, he would just have to forage for lunch here. He felt a pang as he thought of Kitty's cooking.

One o'clock was drawing near when he heard footsteps in the hall and Marion Berowne appeared. The strained look was even more apparent in her face, and dark circles beneath her eyes indicated sleepless nights. But she greeted him pleasantly.

"Hello," she said, smiling. "Kitty told me you were baby-sitting."

"Hello, Mummy," said Edwin, sitting up.

"Hello, darling."

"Denis," said Bethancourt, "say hello to Mrs. Berowne. This is my nephew, Denis Sinclair-Firthing."

Marion looked startled. She replied automatically to Denis's greeting and then looked at Bethancourt with new eyes.

"Sinclair-Firthing?" she said, her eyes travelling over his face. "Not Margaret Sinclair-Firthing?"

"That's her," agreed Bethancourt. "Mrs. Arthur. Do you know her?"

Marion laughed. "I've just been having a meeting with her," she answered.

"Really?" Bethancourt raised his eyebrows. "What a coincidence. The orphans' charity?"

"That's right. My first mother-in-law did a great deal of charity work and I got involved in a small way through her. I don't do as much since I had Edwin, but I like to keep up with the orphans. I was one myself, you see."

"I didn't know," said Bethancourt. "It must have been rather awful."

She shrugged. "You can't miss what you've never had," she answered. "My parents died when I was very young. My grandparents took me over, but they didn't want me—they were done with children. By the time my grandfather died and my grandmother had to go to a home, I was too old to be adopted, but too young to be on my own. So I finished up in the orphanage."

"I'm sorry," said Bethancourt. "It must have been very difficult after having your own home."

"Yes and no," she answered. "It's true that the orphanage wasn't a very nice place, but there was a matron there who was very attentive to me, and, as one of the older children, I got to take care of the younger ones quite often. In a way, it was the first time I'd ever felt wanted or needed. I think we all need a bit of that, don't you?"

"Of course," answered Bethancourt. "It's a natural part of the human condition."

She smiled deprecatingly. "I'm sorry," she said. "I don't usually go on about it, but I'm afraid these meetings always bring my own experiences to mind."

"Not at all. I found it quite interesting," said Bethancourt truthfully.

"Well," she said, pushing back a lock of damp hair, "I'd better get out of these wet things. Would you mind keeping watch a few minutes longer?"

"Of course I will. Only," he added, indicating the soldiers, "I'm afraid I'm not much good at it."

Marion reviewed the game with a practiced eye. Then she sighed. "They've mixed them up thoroughly, haven't they?" she said.

"Thoroughly," agreed Bethancourt. "It's rather a pity there seem to be so many duplicates."

"Yes," she said. "Well, let me change and then we can sort it all out."

Happy to be relieved of sole responsibility, Bethancourt sat back in the armchair and lit another cigarette. Marion rejoined him in a few minutes, now clad in a royal-blue jumper and a pair of gray slacks, with her hair tied back. Somehow she looked younger in these more casual clothes.

"By the way," she said as they knelt together on the carpet, "I told Kitty I'd keep the boys here for lunch if that's all right with you."

"That would be splendid," replied Bethancourt. "I was wondering how I'd get Denis back in this downpour."

"All right, Edwin, Denis," said Marion, "here are three identical ones. Two of them are Edwin's. Which one is yours, Denis?" This took some discussion and Marion turned back to Bethancourt. "I didn't know whether you'd rather stay here or go back to the house for lunch, so I told Kitty you'd ring if you weren't going to eat there. Kitty's rather a martinet about meal times," she added.

"I know," said Bethancourt with feeling. "If you truly don't mind keeping Denis for me, I think I should go back and check in with Sergeant Gibbons."

"I don't mind at all," she answered. "It'll be nice to have a playmate for Edwin. No, no, boys," she said to the children, who had divided up the three identical soldiers and gone off in search of more interesting pursuits. "You mixed them up and now you have to help unmix them. Don't you know that generals have to look after their casualties once the battle's over?"

Bethancourt helped to sort out the rest of the soldiers and then, borrowing an umbrella from Marion, made his way back along the soggy path to the main house. He wondered if Gibbons had managed to finish his walk before the rain began.

CHAPTER

7

Gibbons had not managed it. He had had his doubts before they even started, but Annette had seemed quite eager for the outing, insisting that they would have plenty of time before the storm broke.

So they set out under the gray skies, Gibbons carrying an umbrella in one hand while his other arm was taken by Annette. He had not offered it—he was not of a generation which thought of such things—but she slipped her hand around his elbow quite naturally as they left the house. It was just another instance of her complete comfort in the presence of the police and it added to his growing conviction that she was innocent. He checked his watch as they made their way down the terrace steps, Annette pointing out the different beds of flowers to him. He kept her on this topic for a while, trying to tactfully discover if her horticultural knowledge was great enough to encompass the lethal quality of lilies of the valley, but gave it up in the end. After all, even if she knew nothing about plants, she could easily have read about the poison in her husband's book.

As they left the estate and started up the narrow path through the woods, Annette gave a little sigh of contentment and smiled up at him.

"I hadn't realized how much I've missed having someone to walk with," she said. "I remember, after William died, I felt the same way. Before those last few months, we used to walk around the garden together in the afternoons, and our pace always matched so perfectly."

"I hope I'm matching your pace now," said Gibbons, a little anxiously. "It wouldn't do at all for you to go quicker than you did that morning."

"No, no, you're fine," she said, with a reassuring squeeze of his arm. "Not quite like William, because he really couldn't walk any faster, but you're letting me lead, so to speak."

"That's good," said Gibbons. "It sounds like you enjoyed those walks."

"Oh, yes." She sighed a little and was silent for several steps. "Although I'm afraid my second marriage was rather a mistake," she said at last. "Eric's death hit me very hard—harder than I realized at the time. William was so kind and helpful, and I'm afraid I let things go too far before I even knew what I was doing." She looked up at him with questioning eyes. "Do you understand what I mean?" she asked.

Gibbons hesitated. "I'm not sure," he said. "Are you trying to say that you, well, grew emotionally dependent on him without knowing it?"

"Yes." She nodded, satisfied. "That's it exactly."

"How did you meet him?"

"At the ski lodge. He was staying there, too."

"At the ski lodge?" echoed Gibbons, astounded. "But I thought he was in ill health."

"Oh, he wasn't skiing." She smiled at the notion. "He was on his way home from a clinic in Berne. Some friends of his had rented a chalet nearby and he had stopped to visit them. They hadn't room to put him up, so he took a room at the lodge. We used to spend the afternoons together while everyone else was skiing. We enjoyed each other's company very much, but of course most of my attention was taken up with Eric."

Whose attention, thought Gibbons, was probably wholly on his skiing. He did not voice the thought, however, and asked instead, "So William was there for some time?"

"Not really, no," she answered. "It was only three or four days. He was due to leave the day Eric had his accident, but canceled his plans and stayed to take care of things. I really wasn't much good at the time. William dealt with the undertakers and arranged to have Eric shipped back to England. He travelled back with me and stayed for the funeral. Then he persuaded me to come back to Kent with him until I could decide what to do next."

"And you stayed there and married him."

"Yes. You see how it was. I was so crushed when Eric died I really barely noticed William. And then, when it was all over and I finally came out from under, there was William and I had already got used to depending on him. And he wanted me to marry him." She sighed. "I knew he was very ill, of course."

"Was it a relief when he died?" asked Gibbons gently.

"I suppose it was in some ways," she answered. "It was a relief not to see him suffering anymore, and I was rather exhausted from nursing toward the end. But," she added, lifting her chin, "it wasn't at all a relief to be left alone again. I hate being alone; I'm just no good at it. And I can't see," she said, almost fiercely, "that there's anything wrong with that. People are *meant* to be together."

"It's certainly the happiest state of affairs," said Gibbons, who had not previously considered whether or not it was. "But I sometimes wonder if people were meant to be happy."

"I've wondered the same thing," she said in a faltering voice.

"I'm sorry," said Gibbons. "That was a dreadful thing to say under the circumstances."

"No, no," she said, smiling up at him. "It's true whatever the circumstances. Don't feel badly."

She squeezed his arm with the hand that rested in the crook of his elbow and he smiled back at her.

The path had widened and leveled off, and they had come out from beneath the trees. A stone wall ran along their left, separating the footpath from a wide meadow sparsely dotted with sheep. To their right was another meadow, unfenced and hedged in by the trees. It was undeniably a pretty spot, but Gibbons was made uneasy by the look of the low, swiftly moving clouds.

"I wonder if we shouldn't turn back," he said. "It's looking very threatening."

"Oh, I think it will be all right," she said, adjusting her grip on his arm. "We're almost halfway there now."

Gibbons acquiesced only because if they were halfway to the village, it would do no good to turn back. He checked his watch; they had been walking for almost twenty minutes.

"It was just about here," said Annette, "that I remembered about my library card and stopped to check my purse."

It was said quite casually and Gibbons felt a pang of doubt assail him. The footpath here ran quite straight with the meadows stretching out on either side and the trees rising beyond them. He could not see how any part of it was distinguishable from any other and somehow he felt she had picked the spot at random.

He was distracted in the next moment, however, by the first big raindrops.

"Oh, dear," said Annette. "I'm afraid you were right."

Gibbons stopped and opened the umbrella, holding it mostly over Annette. They continued on, but as the rain pounded down and the footpath began to turn to mud beneath their feet, it became clear that they needed shelter. Gibbons, wiping the water from his eyes, looked around without much hope. He was just deciding that the nearer trees would be the best they could do when he spotted a cattle shelter off to the left.

"Look," he said, pointing. "Do you think you can make it across the meadow?"

She nodded, clearly relieved. "I think there's a stile just ahead," she said.

He helped her over it and they began to run toward the shelter. It stood back against the trees, putting the width of the meadow between it and them. The ground was very uneven, and their progress was not swift as they stumbled along, Gibbons trying to support Annette and keep the umbrella over her simultaneously.

At last they made it, collapsing against the back of the shelter and laughing, exhilarated by their effort and filled with a sense of the ludicrous at their bedraggled appearance.

"Oh, dear," gasped Annette, pushing at her hair which, despite Gibbons's best efforts with the umbrella, had become rather wet. "I must look frightful."

"Not at all," said Gibbons, who was brushing his own hair with his hand in the hopes that he could deflect the water from running down his collar. But he glanced at her and the sight made him smile. "Only a little damp," he said.

Having got her hair out of her face, Annette began dabbing at her eyes. "Has my mascara run?" she asked and raised her face to his.

He looked down at her and with a wet finger gently wiped away a brown smudge from beneath one brown eye.

"There," he said. "That's fine, now."

He had leaned close to her and from out of nowhere an impulse rose in him to close the gap and kiss her. Appalled at himself, he stepped back abruptly and began to shake the rain out of the umbrella vigorously. Thus occupied, he did not hear her little sigh of disappointment.

Damn, he thought to himself, stealing another glance at her as she attempted to wring the water out of her hair. The first woman he had felt drawn to in some time, and she would have to be a suspect in a murder case he was investigating. They got on so well together that if she had been anyone else he would be suggesting they have dinner some night at this very moment. As it was, he would have to watch his step and hope that they would still be on speaking terms once the case was over. Very often even the innocent were only too happy to see the back of the police as soon as they could. Gibbons grimaced at his fate.

Annette leaned back against the shelter and stuck out one foot, surveying her shoe sadly.

"I think it's done for," she said.

"Mine, too," said Gibbons, leaning back beside her. "We should have worn galoshes."

"Yes. Oh my, look at it come down."

The cattle shelter was not very deep, but they were lucky in having the wind at the back of it. They stood companionably, watching the rain fall, pointing out some feature to each from time to time, but otherwise keeping silent.

At last the first torrent passed away, leaving a steady but much lighter rainfall. Both of them were becoming increasingly uncomfortable in their damp clothes and wet shoes, and they agreed that they had better start back. They picked their way across the meadow, soaking the hem of Annette's skirt and Gibbons's trousers to the knees. A sense of the ludicrous again overwhelmed them as they regained the footpath, now a mixture of mud and stones, and they began to giggle as they stumbled along. Annette had taken Gibbons's arm again, nestled up against his right side so that they could both crowd under the umbrella. It was a pleasant sensation. As he walked through the rain and mud, putting the final touches on the ruin of his nearly new shoes, with all thoughts of detective worked banished from his mind by the absurdity of the situation, Gibbons was very happy indeed.

Bethancourt was happy, too. Kitty had made omelets for lunch: creamy, wonderful omelets with sliced almonds, still-firm mushrooms, and little bits of bacon. She had added white wine and cream to the eggs and the slightest hint of tarragon. They were delicious and were accompanied by a green salad, buttery popovers, and a dry white wine.

Bethancourt ate with his bare feet stretched toward the fireplace, where his shoes and socks were drying, with Kitty seated opposite him. She watched him with an amused smile, having finished her own meal.

"You're very fond of food, aren't you?" she asked.

Bethancourt nodded and swallowed a mouthful of omelet. "I'm fond of this kind of food," he said.

Kitty's smile broadened. "And can you cook, yourself?" she asked.

"Some things," answered Bethancourt.

They were interrupted by Miss Wellman returning with her tray. She and Bethancourt had been introduced earlier when she had come in for her lunch, and Bethancourt had taken to her immediately. Now she cast a sharp look at him and said, "I didn't know the police were still here. Eating us out of house and home, aren't you?"

Bethancourt grinned as he finished off the last of his omelet. "It's the reason we came back," he said. "So that we could have another of Kitty's meals."

Miss Wellman smiled unexpectedly. "She is a wonderful cook, isn't she?" she said. "You're a treasure, Kitty. I don't know how I'll bear it if I have to move to that horrible lodge."

"Do you think you will?" asked Kitty, clearing the dishes off the tray.

"I don't know." Miss Wellman's sharp gray eyes glanced at Bethancourt. "If the police don't shake a leg and arrest Annette, I may have to. Being a thorn in her side has its moments, but I'm not sure I'd fancy it down through the years. Good Lord," she added, "what an uncommonly beautiful dog!"

Cerberus, hearing Kitty moving about, had come out from his place beneath the table. This room was simply crammed with good smells and thus far he had not benefited from any of them.

"His name's Cerberus," said Bethancourt as Miss Wellman held out her hands and Cerberus sniffed politely.

"Now that's an idea," said Miss Wellman, burying her hand in the fur behind Cerberus's ears. The dog's tail waved gently. "I'll get a dog. Annette ought to hate that—she's very timid with animals. I'll get an Irish wolfhound. A big one," she added, as if they came in smaller sizes. Kitty giggled, apparently at the thought of Annette Berowne facing a dog as large as a small pony.

"Have you ever had a dog?" asked Bethancourt, who could not help but be concerned over the welfare of an animal purchased solely for its annoyance value.

"Not since I came here to live," answered Miss Wellman. "Geoffrey was allergic, you see. When Gwenda married him, she had a nice little beagle, but she soon had to turn him over to me. There's no reason not to get one now, however. I'd rather like to have a dog again."

"There's certainly plenty of room on the estate for a big dog to run," said Bethancourt.

"You'd better be sure he doesn't get into the garden," warned Kitty. "McAllister would have your head."

"That's true," agreed Miss Wellman. "I'd have to watch him."

"Once he was trained," said Bethancourt, "it would probably be easy enough to keep him out."

The conversation turned to the merits of various methods of dog training. They were just discussing the books of Barbara Woodhouse and the indignity of screeching "walkies!" in a high-pitched voice, when Gibbons and Annette made their appearance.

They came in dripping and grinning rather foolishly like people who know they are a mess, but have given up trying to do anything about it.

"I'm very sorry, Kitty," began Annette in placating tones, "but we—oh!" This last was in the nature of a shriek and was directed at Cerberus, who had roused himself from leaning against Miss Wellman's side and turned round to view the newcomers.

"It's all right, Annette," said Miss Wellman sharply. "It's only a dog."

"Yes, of course," said Annette weakly.

"He's very gentle," said Gibbons.

"He won't bother you," said Bethancourt quickly. "Cerberus, come. Down, lad."

"Anyway," said Annette, eyeing the dog, but addressing herself to Kitty, "we stopped to wait out the worst of the storm and I'm afraid it's made us rather late. I am sorry, Kitty."

"That's all right," said Kitty. "I'll do the omelets while you change."

Gibbons, having shed his dripping coat, had sat down in a chair and was stripping off his shoes and socks.

"I'm terribly sorry, Mr. Gibbons," said Annette. "I'm afraid I don't have anything you could change into."

"He could have one of Geoffrey's dressing gowns," said Miss Wellman. There was a hint of malice in her tone and Bethancourt glanced at her sharply.

"Yes, of course," said Annette, with only the faintest hesitation. "I should have thought of that. Do come up with me, Mr. Gibbons, and I'll show you."

"Well, perhaps I'd better," said Gibbons cheerfully. "I'm afraid my trousers are soaked through."

They started out, but Annette hesitated, and then turned back.

"Kitty," she said firmly, "Mr. Gibbons will eat with me in the dining room."

"Certainly, Mrs. Berowne," answered Kitty, but her eyebrows had risen.

Miss Wellman snorted.

Annette ignored this and turned and led Gibbons out.

Miss Wellman rose. "I'd better be getting back upstairs," she said. "Good-bye, Mr. Bethancourt."

Bethancourt nodded and murmured good-bye, but she paused at the door. "Good-bye to you, too, Cerberus," she said, her eyes twinkling. "Yes, I think an Irish wolfhound will be just the thing."

"Well," said Bethancourt after she had gone, "I suppose I should go and collect Denis." He glancing out the window and sighed. "His feet will get soaked and Margaret will kill me."

"You can drive over, you know," said Kitty from the stove. "You just take the road to the garage and go round from there."

Bethancourt brightened. "I hadn't realized that," he said. "Very well, I'm off to face the elements. Thank you again for the lovely lunch, Kitty."

"You're welcome."

"Oh, and I forgot to ask you—which pub is it that Paul Berowne's so fond of?"

She smiled at him. "Thinking of getting a drink?" she asked.

"Well, perhaps," he replied, smiling back. "Not today, because I have to get Denis back, but I was thinking of coming round tomorrow or the day after."

"Make it the day after," she said, "and I'll take you. I have Sunday evenings off."

Bethancourt was a little surprised, but not displeased. "Sunday, then," he said. He hesitated. "Perhaps I could take you to dinner? I don't know if there's any place here you'd like to go?"

"There's the Brittany," she said. "I think you'd enjoy that."

"I'm sure I shall," answered Bethancourt. "Sunday at eight? I'll see you then. Come, Cerberus."

Bethancourt was worried. When he had wondered about Annette Berowne's designs the night before, it had never occurred to him to wonder whether or not Gibbons was succumbing to them. He wondered now. The expression on his friend's face when he had come in from the rain, and the length of time he had spent over lunch spoke of far more than the liking Gibbons had confessed to. The temptation to eavesdrop on the conversation in the dining room had been severe, and Bethancourt privately admitted that only the presence of Kitty had prevented him from giving in.

He lit a cigarette as he guided the Jaguar down the drive, and cast a sidelong glance at Gibbons, who was frowning down at his still-wet shoes.

"I think they're done for," observed Bethancourt heartlessly.

"Yes," said Gibbons sadly, struggling to kick the shoes off, "I expect they are."

"Annette seemed very pleased to see you this morning," said Bethancourt conversationally.

"Did she? Well, she was eager to time that walk."

"She kept you a long time over lunch, too," said Bethancourt. "Did you learn anything interesting?"

"Not really." Gibbons sighed. "It was just ordinary chitchat. She spoke a bit about Geoffrey, but nothing that helped the case any."

"I think she likes you."

Gibbons looked a little startled, as if this was not something he had considered before. "Do you?" he said slowly. "Well, I guess I like her, too." He reddened as he remembered the moment in the rain when he had wanted to kiss her. Would have, too, had she been anyone but who she was. He cursed his luck again.

Bethancourt had seen the flush, and it worried him more than ever. To his eye, Gibbons appeared to be developing an infatuation for his prime suspect. That he did not seem to realize it only made things worse.

They were silent for a moment. Bethancourt turned out of the gates onto the narrow road, and then suggested diffidently, "You don't suppose she's deliberately trying to make you like her, do you? If she's guilty, I mean."

Gibbons was surprised. "Good God, no," he replied sharply. He looked thoughtful for a moment, and then shook his head. "No, I really don't think so. She hasn't been at all forward or anything like that. We just happen to get on together."

It might, thought Bethancourt, be perfectly true. But he was still uneasy. Gibbons had given the idea less than a minute's thought.

"Well—" Bethancourt broke off and stamped on the brake as a rabbit sprang into their path. The short stop threw the back seat into chaos as Cerberus half-slid onto the floor, Denis fell on top of him, and toy soldiers and rubber stamps spread themselves liberally over the carpet. The toy lorry sped under the passenger seat and shot out between Gibbons's feet.

"Everyone all right?" asked Bethancourt.

"Yes, Uncle Phillip," said Denis, pushing himself off the dog and back onto the seat.

"Here," said Gibbons, handing him the lorry. "Oh, dear—I'll help you pick them up, Denis."

"I'd better stop," said Bethancourt, pulling over.

"No, it's all right," said Gibbons, who had assumed a sort of contortionist's position and was now wedged firmly between the two front seats. "You can't help anyway unless you want to crouch out in the rain. Here, Denis, I'll hand you the stamps and you put them back in their case. That's right."

"Thank you, Mr. Gibbons."

"If you're sure, Jack," said Bethancourt, letting the car idle and trying to glance into the back, his view of which was effectively blocked by Gibbons's shoulders.

"Oh, yes," said Gibbons in a muffled voice. "We're managing splendidly."

Bethancourt acquiesced and eased the car forward gently. He took the next curve slowly, careful not to upset Gibbons's precarious balance, and continued on toward the A-road back to Town. The rain fell steadily, drumming against the car's top, running in tiny rivers where the wipers pushed it to the edges of the windscreen. For once Bethancourt's driving was stable as he mulled over what had been said. The sound of Gibbons and Denis counting toy soldiers came from the back seat.

"There," said Gibbons at last. "You'd better close the bag now, Denis. Umph." He grunted as he wriggled his shoulders out from between the seats and twisted around back to a sitting position.

"Travelling with children is exhausting," he murmured. "I'd better rethink the three kids I was going to have."

"At least you found out while there was still time," responded Bethancourt automatically.

Gibbons was silent for a moment. Then he asked in a different tone, "Have you ever thought about having children, Phillip?"

Bethancourt glanced at his friend, jerked out of his own thoughts by the seriousness of the question. "I always thought," he said dryly, "that I would get married first."

"Well, yes," said Gibbons impatiently. "But have you ever thought about whether or not you'd like a family someday?"

Bethancourt rubbed his chin thoughtfully. "Not really," he said. "I suppose I assumed I'd have a family at some point—I mean, nearly everyone does."

Gibbons sighed. "I haven't really given it much thought myself," he said. "But . . . I think I *would* like a family. I mean, I think I'm the sort of person that would be happiest with a family."

Since Gibbons had previously always viewed himself as the sort of person who would be happiest if he made chief inspector before thirty-five, Bethancourt was understandably startled.

"What's brought this on?" he asked.

"Oh, I don't know," said Gibbons vaguely.

Bethancourt thought he knew, but he firmly repressed the urge to say anything. He had already tried to put Gibbons on his guard and failed. Instead, he announced, "I've got a date on Sunday. Kitty's going to take me to the pub where Paul Berowne regularly drowns his sorrows."

"I knew you fancied her," replied Gibbons genially.

"Not at all," said Bethancourt. "This is strictly detective work. Have you got a date?"

"A date?" Gibbons looked confused.

"To try your walk again," explained Bethancourt.

"Oh! I said I'd ring and perhaps we could try tomorrow, weather permitting. I've got to check with Carmichael first, anyway, and see how he wants to schedule it in. What sorrows in particular does Paul Berowne want to drown?"

"He has an unhappy marriage," said Bethancourt. "Kitty's going to find out all about it from her aunt."

"I don't see how that gives him a motive for murdering his father," said Gibbons.

"Well, no—"

"Uncle Phillip," Denis interrupted from the back, "Edwin and I made a tape of our playing. Can we listen to it, please?"

"Er," said Bethancourt, momentarily caught off guard. "Of course, Denis," he added, recovering. "Mr. Gibbons and I would love it. Plug it in, Jack."

Gibbons raised his eyebrows, but obliged and in a moment the tinny sound of two little boys thumping away at a piano emerged. What, exactly, they were playing could not be determined.

"Splendid, Denis," said Bethancourt heartily.

"Turn it up, Uncle Phillip—the good part's coming."

Bethancourt shot an apologetic look at Gibbons and twisted the volume control resignedly.

"I meant to mention the tape recorder in the schoolroom," he shouted to his friend.

"What you should have done," muttered Gibbons, "was confiscate all the cassettes."

"Sports clothes," snarled Marla. "Ralph Lauren. *Polo*, for God's sake."

Bethancourt smiled at the telephone. "When's the shoot?" he asked.

"Monday," she answered. "Phillip, you absolutely must teach me to ride tomorrow."

Bethancourt's grin widened. Last year, Marla had been involved in a fashion shoot on a country estate. Someone had been persuaded to lend their Arabian stud to the proceedings and all had gone smoothly until the photographer suggested that Marla should be photographed actually mounted on the stallion. Marla, who until that day had never been nearer a horse than the sidelines at a polo match, nevertheless agreed, used as she was to the whims of photographers. The stud's knowledgeable groom boosted her up, where she did her best to pose as desired and to look as if she knew what she was doing, despite the fact that the ground looked rather farther away than she had counted on. The stallion, who knew an inexperienced rider when one was on his back, and who took a dim view of riders in general, decided he had had enough. He was prevented from bolting by his groom's firm hand on his lead, but that was not an insurmountable problem. He bucked. Marla somersaulted out of the saddle, describing a beautiful arc through the air, and landed solidly on the ground which such a short time ago had seemed so far away. Her subsequent bruises had forced her to withdraw from a lucrative swimsuit and an even more lucrative lingerie shoot in the next week and a half. Needless to say, the incident had had a negative effect on Marla's attitude toward horses.

"It's rather a big job to learn to ride in one day," said Bethancourt, who was an excellent rider and an enthusiastic polo player—a sport which he enjoyed out of all proportion to his ability to play it. "But I will do my best."

"We'd better get an early start," said Marla gloomily. "Tomorrow's the only time we've got because I'm flying out to Ireland on Sunday afternoon, so as to be able to start shooting at dawn on Monday."

"All right," said Bethancourt. "Early it is. Don't worry, Marla, it will be fine. Really. What made you agree to it in the first place?"

"My agents didn't tell me horses were going to be involved," said Marla. "And, well, I can't really afford to turn down Lauren, especially not when there's a rumor going round that they might be looking for a new Lauren girl."

"I see," said Bethancourt.

"It's probably not true," she added despondently. "It's probably just a rumor started by people who want to force models onto horses."

"A conspiracy," said Bethancourt solemnly.

CHAPTER

8

*S*aturday dawned bright and clear. Carmichael was used to having to work weekends, yet he still felt a pang as he looked out on the morning and prepared to say good-bye to his wife. Dottie Carmichael was now fifty-three, with graying hair and a thickening waistline, but he still loved her very much. Lately he had begun to feel that there had been too many mornings like this, too many weekends cancelled, too many dinners missed. He had a sudden temptation to send Gibbons on to Hurtwood Hall alone; there was, after all, very little to be followed up on and Gibbons was quite capable of handling it all himself.

But of course that wouldn't do. It wouldn't be right and anyway, even if he gave in to temptation, he would only spend the day worrying about how his sergeant was getting on.

Dottie, picking up on his mood, laughed at him from across the breakfast table.

"Look at you," she chided gently, "so gloomy and all because you have to work on a Saturday. As if you weren't accustomed to it after all these years."

"That's just it," he answered. "These days I'm beginning to feel I've worked enough Saturdays. Sundays, too, for that matter."

"So that's it," she said. "You're seeing your retirement on the horizon. Well, dear, I'm afraid there's a few more miles to go before you get there."

He chuckled and took her hand. "Not too many, though," he said.

"Certainly not as many as there were," she agreed.

Carmichael sobered. "I expect it's also this case," he said. "I don't like it, Dottie. There's not a chance of proving anything. Our only option is to worm a confession out of someone and at the moment I haven't any idea who to start with."

"Everybody draws a bad card sometimes," she said. "You'll do your best, just as always." She put her head to one side and considered him. "Are you certain it's not the widow that's troubling you?"

"In what way?" Carmichael knew of one way in which Annette Berowne troubled him a good deal and he suspected Dottie knew it, too, but she would never broach that subject openly.

"Because intellectually you think she's guilty, but your instincts say she's not. That's not usual for you—normally the two go hand in hand."

"You could be right," he said thoughtfully.

She squeezed his hand and released it. "There's Sergeant Gibbons driving up, dear. You shouldn't keep him waiting."

Thus preoccupied with his wife's insight, Carmichael replied automatically to Gibbons's greeting and they rode the first few miles in silence. Rousing himself at last, Carmichael glanced over at his sergeant and said, "Sorry, lad. I was thinking over something." His eye ran over the younger man's figure. "Is that a new jacket?"

"Yes, sir," said Gibbons. "I thought my old tweed was looking a bit worn, so I stopped last night on my way home and bought a new one."

"Well, it's very nice. Looks fine on you."

"Thank you, sir."

Carmichael sighed and shifted in his seat. "We'll just do the best we can today, Sergeant. I'll start on the servants with Miss Wellman and see if I can't trick something about Paul Berowne out of her. God knows what I got from the City and his finances yesterday wasn't much help."

"No, sir," agreed Gibbons. "Is there anything you want me to cover with Mrs. Berowne?"

"You can ask her about the servants. You've already spoken with her about Paul Berowne, I believe."

"Yes," said Gibbons, "the other day, when I was getting her to talk about her life at Hurtwood Hall. I was really trying for more about her husband, but we covered the rest of the family pretty well."

"Well, get whatever you can, lad. Paul Berowne is far too composed for us to have another go at him without some kind of edge."

Annette opened the door to them herself. She seemed rather subdued and a slight puffiness around her eyes revealed she had been crying. But she greeted them with a smile that lit up her brown eyes and gave her hand to Carmichael.

"It's so nice to see you again, Chief Inspector," she said. "Will you be coming with Sergeant Gibbons and me?"

Carmichael shook her hand heartily and gave it back to her. "I'm afraid not," he answered. "I must speak with Miss Wellman again."

"Well, we'll miss you," she said simply. "Shall I show you up to Maddie?"

"No, no. I can find my own way. You and the sergeant had best be off while the weather holds."

"But it's a lovely day," she protested. Her eyes twinkled at Gibbons. "We won't be needing your umbrella today, Sergeant."

"No, ma'am."

"Then we'll leave you to it, Chief Inspector."

She gave him a warm parting smile and then led the way down the hall to the side door by the study.

"I'm so glad you've come," she said as Gibbons held the door for her. "I needed a distraction today. And I'm sure this sounds silly to you, but timing my walk makes me feel as though I'm helping to find Geoffrey's murderer. It's the only thing I can do at all."

"We very much appreciate it," said Gibbons as she linked her arm in his and strolled across the terrace.

Gibbons had convinced himself the evening before that his unexpected desire to kiss Annette had been nothing more than a normal reaction to spending time with a very attractive woman, and he was surprised now to find that he, too, was looking forward to their outing. He shrugged the thought away; it was only natural, after all, to enjoy a pretty woman's company. Gibbons was not very practiced at lying to himself—there had never been much need before—but he was turning out, if only he had known it, to be rather good at it.

"Did something upset you this morning?" he asked. "You seemed rather down when we arrived."

Her face darkened at once. "Oh, it was nothing," she said, but her voice was unsteady. "Maddie said some very unkind things this morning. She's got rather a sharp tongue, but, well . . ." She trailed off, but then drew a breath and said, "I never realized how much she disliked me. Geoffrey always said to pay her no mind, that it was just her way, that she was curmudgeonly. I thought, now that he's gone, that perhaps I should make more of an effort. After all, she must be grieving, too, and I've paid no attention to that. But she was quite, well, vicious. I didn't understand," she added in a low voice, "that she'd been taking her meals in her room to avoid me."

"I'm sorry," said Gibbons. "It must be terribly lonely for you here."

"Yes . . ." Her voice caught and she bit her lip, but in the next moment she raised her head and said firmly, "There's no use in going on about it. You're my distraction, Mr. Gibbons. Tell me an amusing story."

Gibbons smiled. "How about a bit of detective work instead?" he said. "Today I'm interested in anything you can tell me about the people who work here."

She looked up at him, surprised. "But surely none of them would . . ."

"Why do you say that, Mrs. Berowne?" asked Gibbons alertly. "Do you think you know who killed your husband?"

"No." She shook her head quickly. "Not that. But I guess I assumed it must have been Paul or Maddie." There was pleading in her eyes. "But I've thought and thought and I can't see *why* they would have done it."

Neither could Gibbons. As far as he could see, if anyone was going to be murdered at Hurtwood Hall, it should have been Annette herself.

"That's what we're trying to find out," he said gently. "And it doesn't do to eliminate people just because they weren't as close to the victim as others. That's why we need to look into the servants."

"Yes, of course. I see that." She tucked her hand more securely into the crook of his elbow. "Well, I don't know how much I can tell you. All the servants were here when I married Geoffrey, except for Kitty. We had Janet then—rather a motherly old soul. Kitty's actually a better cook."

"But what do you know about Kitty personally?" asked Gibbons.

"Let's see. I know she went to cooking school in Paris and then came back here and got a job in a restaurant in London. Apparently they thought very well of her, but she didn't like the life. So when Janet retired, she recommended Kitty and we were happy to have her. It worked out well all round."

For the first time, Gibbons felt a slight annoyance with Annette. "What about boyfriends?" he asked patiently. "Or hobbies?"

"Well, she must have a boyfriend," said Annette. "She's very pretty. But I'm afraid I don't know anything about that. It doesn't seem polite, somehow, to pry into people's personal lives."

"No," agreed Gibbons, "but unfortunately it's my job. What about any of the others?"

But Annette knew very little about any of them. Mrs. Simmons was a widow who had worked for the Berownes ever since Geoffrey had first bought Hurtwood Hall. Her husband had been alive then, but after he had died, she had sold her house and moved into the old servants' quarters on the top floor. Berowne had had them renovated for her. McAllister, too, was an old employee, hired by the first Mrs. Berowne at what Berowne had always said was an exorbitant salary. Ken Mills had been hired more recently, just a few months before Annette's marriage. She believed he was saving up for his own garage.

They could see the village ahead by the time Gibbons thought he had pulled all the information he could from her, and he glanced at his watch as they came into the High Street. It had taken them just over forty minutes to walk the two miles, which left twenty minutes unaccounted for on the day of the murder.

"Shall we have some tea before we start back?" asked Annette. "The walk has made me quite thirsty."

"Of course," said Gibbons. "I'm thirsty, too."

Annette seemed unaware of the hostile looks they encountered at the tea shop, but Gibbons fumed inwardly at them. He escorted her to a table in the corner and held out a chair facing the wall for her. If she hadn't noticed, he was determined that the outing shouldn't be spoiled for her.

"Now on the way back," he said, taking the seat opposite her, "I want you to tell me when we reach the point where you turned back for your library card and also where it was you realized you'd had it after all."

She nodded. "I can do that." She folded her hands on the table and smiled at him. "You've been asking all the questions," she said. "Do you mind if I ask you one?"

"Not at all," answered Gibbons, although he was instantly wary. There was no denying that they got on well together and, if she were the murderer, she might feel they had established enough of a relationship for him to answer questions about the investigation. If she could discover who, besides herself, was their prime suspect, she might then be able to "remember" something or manufacture some kind of evidence to encourage their beliefs. It was something he had known to happen before.

"What made you want to become a detective?" she said. "I mean, it seems an interesting job, but there's also so much unpleasantness attached to it."

Gibbons was totally disarmed. He smiled back at her. "But I think it's one worth doing," he answered. "You get a real sense of satisfaction, of accomplishment, every time you close a case. And I didn't want a desk job, which is what most work comes down to these days. Even as a detective," he added, thinking of the piles of paperwork from his last case residing at this moment on his desk at the Yard, "there's a fair amount of that. But most of the time, you're out investigating, interviewing people, putting the pieces together."

"But what attracted you to it in the beginning?" She was sincerely interested; he could tell that and was rather flattered.

"Well, I suppose it was a natural option for me," he said. "My uncle was a policeman in the uniformed branch and my grandfather was a village constable. So when I came down from Oxford, I thought it wouldn't hurt to enroll in the police academy, just to see how I liked it. And I did like it. I expect I have a certain bent for this kind of thing, and on the practical side, it's a good career with plenty of room for advancement."

Their tea arrived and Annette stirred sugar and milk into hers, a thoughtful expression on her face. "So you don't mind the unpleasant parts?" she asked. "You don't worry about becoming, well, hardened I guess is the word."

Into Gibbons's mind sprang some of the more callous jokes that were current around the Yard and he flushed a little, remembering how he had laughed at them and even repeated them. "I expect a certain amount of hardening is unavoidable," he said honestly. "But it's no worse than being, say, a doctor. You have to find a way to cope with horror. And if you truly believe you're making a difference, then it's worth it."

She sighed a little. "You seem so sure of yourself," she said. "You're in charge of your life. I wish I was more like that. Lately, since Geoffrey died, I've begun to think that I've never really done much to make of my life what I wanted. I've sort of stumbled across things or people that I thought would make me happy, but if they hadn't happened along, I'd still just be waiting."

"It's never too late to start," said Gibbons. "But you have to think things out and decide what you want to accomplish. And just after a tragedy isn't really the best time for clear thinking."

"I suppose not," she agreed, a little wistfully. "And I haven't the least notion what I might like to do anyway. Except . . ."

"Yes?"

"Well, I have thought that I would like to have children. I've always been a little envious of Marion with Edwin."

"Why didn't you and Geoffrey have kids?"

"Geoffrey didn't want any. He was fifty-eight when we married, and he felt very strongly that it would be wrong to bring a child into the world when he couldn't hope to be a real father to it. He thought a child needed both its parents and of course he might have died while any child of ours was still quite young. I suppose I agreed with him in principle, but even before he was killed, I had begun to wonder if I had been a little too ready to fall in with his plans." She shrugged and smiled. "But you know how it is when you're in love—nothing seems like an obstacle. What about you, Mr. Gibbons? Have you ever thought of having a family?"

It was the very thing he had brought up to Bethancourt the day before, but it rang no bells in his mind now.

"Yes," he said. "I do want a family someday. But of course I need to get a little further in my career before I can afford to support one." He smiled sheepishly. "One always thinks of getting married and having children as something that comes naturally, something that will just happen. I've only recently realized that nothing happens unless you work at it."

She laughed. "No, we're both perfect examples of that, aren't we? If having children were inevitable, I ought to have half a dozen by now."

Gibbon started to reply when his eye was caught by the clock.

"Good Lord," he said. "We've been sitting here for over half an hour." He smiled at her. "It's been very pleasant, but I'm sure Chief Inspector Carmichael is wondering what's happened to me. Are you ready to start back?"

"Oh, of course." She rose with a little flurry. "I should have thought."

"Just let me pay for the tea," said Gibbons.

Outside, as she took his arm, she reached up and kissed his cheek.

"Thank you," she said. "That's the best half-hour I've spent since this horrible business started. It was very kind of you."

Gibbons had long since forgotten his resolve to keep up his guard. He smiled back at her and squeezed her hand where it lay on his arm. "I enjoyed it, too," he said.

Maddie Wellman was not at all pleased with any part of the investigation which did not focus on Annette Berowne, and she said so with considerable force. Carmichael eyed her meditatively. She was not knitting today and from time to time would rub fretfully at her knees and hands; obviously, her arthritis was troubling her. He wished he could have come at a better time, but there was no help for it.

"Think of this, Miss Wellman," he said. "Suppose we did arrest Mrs. Berowne and it came to trial. Would you like her to be acquitted just because I hadn't discovered that Kitty Whitcomb was desperate for money and that Geoffrey Berowne had refused to advance her any?"

"Bosh," said Maddie, but rather feebly. She sighed deeply. "Well, I expect you'll do what you like anyway, so we may as well get this over with. Kitty Whitcomb doesn't need any money because she's paid a handsome salary and does not gamble or collect expensive knickknacks. Her one and only interest is cooking, aside from an obsession with her health."

"She's a hypochondriac?" asked Carmichael, considerably surprised.

"No, no." Maddie waved an impatient hand. "She's up before dawn every morning to go jogging and she's got a panoply of exercise equipment in her room that she's always fooling with." A gleam appeared in her gray eyes. "I drive her mad by telling her that it's all in the genes and that her mother was fat and so was her aunt."

Carmichael smiled. "What about boyfriends?"

"There's Ken Mills. There was another one for a few months—I don't remember his name—but that broke up and I rather think she and Ken have taken up again." Maddie frowned. "I'm not entirely certain whether it's just for convenience sake now. I'm inclined to think so. They seem very friendly, but not lover-like the way they once were. And I did hear that Ken was seen in the local with another girl some little while ago."

"And what about Mr. Mills?" asked Carmichael. "Aside from his affair with Kitty, that is."

"He wants his own garage," she answered promptly. "That's why he took the job here. It's a good salary and gives him an opportunity to save up. He makes a bit extra down at the local garage when they're busy and he's not wanted here. It was really rather silly to keep him on after Geoffrey retired and didn't need a driver full-time anymore, but Geoffrey didn't like to let him go. He said that in a few more years Ken would have saved up enough to start his business and he'd leave then in any case. Geoffrey was like that; he liked to help people."

"And what do you know about this new girlfriend?"

"Nothing. I just overheard Mira telling Kitty about it. I assume she's some local girl."

"Who is Mira?" asked Carmichael.

"Mira Fellows. She runs the local pub. She and Kitty are great friends."

Carmichael made a note of that. "I asked you the other day," he said, "about close friends of Mrs. Berowne."

"And I told you she didn't have any. If you're going to dredge up a bosom friend now, I shan't believe you."

"No." Carmichael smiled. "Not that. But what about your own friends?"

Maddie laughed. "Checking up on me now, too, are you? Very well."

She rattled off a list of names and addresses, which Carmichael duly took down, though her amused reaction to his question did not lead him to expect much to come of it.

"Let's go on with the servants then," he said when she was done. "Take Mrs. Simmons next."

Maddie's eyebrows rose. "But surely she's accounted for," she protested. "She was at Little House listening to Marion and Edwin play the piano."

"In a different room," said Carmichael. "That's not a very strong alibi and you know it. Besides, I like to be impartial."

"Oh, very well. Far be it from me to impugn your impartiality." She rubbed at her knuckles. "Mary Simmons is a rather sad creature," she said. "Her husband beat her and nothing Gwenda nor I could ever say would make her leave the brute. I think, really, that's why she took the job here to start with—Gwenda wanted someone who would stay until after dinner and that meant Mrs. Simmons wouldn't have to face her husband until late in the evening. Not," she added blackly, "that that seemed to matter to him. In any case, he died seven or eight years back and she couldn't wait to get out of that house, even though it was hers now. Too many bad memories, I suppose. Geoffrey suggested that she could live in the old servant's quarters upstairs and had a couple of the rooms done up for her. She was very happy with the arrangement; she felt secure on the estate. He also saw to the selling of her house in the village. If you think she would have poisoned him, you're mad."

"I didn't say I thought so," said Carmichael mildly. "Does she have any children?"

"Three, I believe, but they all live elsewhere." She narrowed her eyes at him. "Doing well, as Mrs. Simmons tells it. And if they hadn't been, Geoffrey would have helped them if she'd asked."

Carmichael grinned at her. "I understand the point," he said. "That just leaves McAllister."

Maddie hooted. "He's an old crank," she said. "I can't tell you much about him—McAllister keeps himself to himself. Gwenda found him someplace when they first bought Hurtwood and had the gardener's cottage fixed up for him."

"Really? I didn't realize he lived on the estate."

"Oh, yes. It's away on the west side of the grounds, built up against the wall. But I can't tell you what he does there. For all I know, he has homosexual orgies every night."

"Is he homosexual?"

"I haven't the least idea. He was single when Gwenda hired him and he's stayed single ever since, but that doesn't mean he wasn't married earlier in life."

"I see. I'll speak to him later. One more thing: it's been suggested that Annette Berowne might have been having an affair. Is that true?"

Maddie considered this for several moments before reluctantly shaking her head. "No," she said. "I'm sure it's not. I would love to believe it, but I can't see how she would have managed it. She didn't leave the estate regularly, not even on the days when Geoffrey went in to the office. And I think I would have known if something like that had been going on. She may be a gold digger, but she was a faithful one."

"Well, thank you very much for your help," said Carmichael, rising. "I think that's it—unless you'd care to tell me what the trouble was between Geoffrey Berowne and his son?"

He'd caught her off-guard, as he'd meant to, and she dropped her eyes, rubbing again at her hands.

"I've already told you," she muttered. "Geoffrey thought Paul wasn't running the business right."

"Yes, but there was something else."

"I don't know where you got that idea," she replied spiritedly, recovering herself. "It's true that they weren't as close as they had been before Annette came traipsing into our lives, but that was hardly Paul's fault."

"It was perfectly clear when I spoke to Mr. Berowne that he resented his father," said Carmichael, "and not just because he was a better businessman." He softened his tone. "I'll find out in the end," he said. "And if it truly didn't have anything to do with this business, it would be better to tell me now."

"There's nothing to tell," she replied stubbornly.

Carmichael sighed. "Very well," he said. "You know where to reach me if you change your mind."

She stopped him at the door.

"By the way," she asked, "have you brought the blond with you?"

"Bethancourt?" asked Carmichael, surprised. "No, he's not with us today. Why do you ask?"

"Oh, no reason. I liked him, was all. I liked the way he looked at Annette."

"The way he looked at her?" echoed Carmichael, mystified.

"Yes," she said. "One can see it in his eyes. He's not taken with her at all, and that's very rare in a man."

Bethancourt lay in bed, staring wakefully into the darkness, with Marla nestled against his side, her long legs tangled with his. He had had a pleasant day. It is always pleasing to the male ego, in this day and age, when a man can demonstrate to a woman his indisputable superiority in an endeavour, no matter how trivial. The day had started with Bethancourt cantering the gelding around the ring and taking him over a few jumps, so as to disperse with his initial friskiness before putting Marla up on him. The look in Marla's eyes as he returned to her was, Bethancourt imagined, much like the look Guinevere must have given Lancelot after he had finished jousting for her honor. And the lesson that followed had gone well. Marla had not, of course, learned to ride, but she had picked up the basic concepts and he had taught her a few tricks which, if they did nothing else, served to boost her confidence. That, Bethancourt judged, was what she truly needed, and the news that stallions kept for stud were not typical of the equine race in general further served to calm her fears.

After the riding lesson, there had been long, hot baths, dinner at a favorite restaurant, and a friend's lavish birthday party. All in all, Bethancourt had not given more than a passing thought to the Berowne case all day. But he was thinking about it now. A message from Gibbons had been waiting for him when he came home, detailing the results of his walk with Annette in a tone of voice which alarmed his friend very much.

"Annette Berowne may be out of it," Gibbons had announced in joyful tones. "The timing of the walk works out perfectly with her story. I'll tell you about it tomorrow."

Now Bethancourt lay in the dark, thinking of Annette Berowne. He had initially applauded Carmichael's determination to investigate other suspects, but it now occurred to him that the moving force behind this decision must have been Gibbons's reports. He had been responsible for most of the interviews with Annette, and while he would never deliberately suppress evidence, might not his feelings have influenced him? It was possible that he had taken her word where Carmichael might have challenged it. If that were true, and if it ever came to light, Gibbons's career would be over.

Bethancourt shifted slightly. Perhaps, he thought, he was overreacting. Perhaps Annette was indeed innocent and everything would be all right. He didn't much like the idea of her as Gibbons's girlfriend, or—God forbid—his wife, but so long as she was innocent, he could accept it. Except that even if she were innocent, he could still not believe she was seriously interested in Gibbons. He simply could not imagine Annette putting up with the kind of neglect Gibbons's career would require. Far more likely that she was merely using Gibbons to keep close to the investigation.

And what, thought Bethancourt in alarm, if no one were ever arrested for the murder? He had known cases before where the police were virtually certain of a criminal's identity, and yet were unable to make an arrest. If that attitude were to prevail about Annette Berowne, Gibbons's attachment to her would not go down at all well at New Scotland Yard. There might even be suspicions that Gibbons had prevented an arrest from being made. Bethancourt almost groaned aloud.

"Marla," he whispered, "are you asleep?"

He felt her stir down the length of his side.

"No," she answered, although she almost had been. "What is it?"

"Would you fall for a man who had no men friends?"

"No," she answered promptly. "There's always something wrong with people like that."

"Women as well as men?" asked Bethancourt, not very clearly, but she seemed to understand him. She nodded.

"Of course. What brought this to mind?"

"Well, I'm rather worried about Jack."

"Jack?" She lifted her head from his chest. She might have known murder was involved. She was well aware how obsessive Bethancourt could become about his mystery cases, but heretofore they had not intruded into time spent in the bedroom. This seemed to mark a new stage and she definitely did not like it.

"I think he's found someone he fancies," confided Bethancourt.

"Oh." Marla was appeased. "A woman with no women friends?"

"That's right. And I think she's rather calculating, too. She's very charming—"

Marla's head came back off his chest. "Is she beautiful?"

"No," answered Bethancourt without hesitation and this seemed to reassure her. "She's not beautiful at all, but I doubt Jack's noticed that. And it doesn't matter, because she has this—allure, I suppose is the best way to describe it."

"Like Abbie," said Marla.

"Who?"

"Abbie Waite—you've met her. She's not even pretty, really, but you never notice, her personality comes through so strongly. Even in photographs."

"Rather like that," Bethancourt admitted. "Only in this case, the personality is geared to pander to the male ego, rather than being admirable in itself."

Marla stirred languidly. "I shouldn't have thought that would be Jack's thing," she said.

"I suppose all men are somewhat susceptible," said Bethancourt, remembering his own feelings earlier in the day while looking down at Marla from horseback.

"Nobody's immune," agreed Marla, "but I still would have expected Jack to fall for a more modern type. A career woman, who would have something interesting to tell him at the end of the day."

"I think you're right," said Bethancourt, rather impressed with her accurate summing up of the tastes of a man she had never paid much attention to. "But I also think that somewhere deep down, Jack has a fantasy of a nice little woman waiting at home like his mother did."

"With six children, she didn't have much choice."

"I suppose not," agreed Bethancourt.

"Well," said Marla, settling herself more comfortably, "there's nothing you can do. It's no good telling people the light of their lives are perfectly dreadful and all wrong for them. It just puts their backs up. They have to find out for themselves."

"All too true," agreed Bethancourt. *But,* he added to himself, *what if Annette's a murderess as well as the wrong person?*

Marla shifted against him again, sliding her hand down the length of his belly while she drew herself up until her lips could reach his. Bethancourt turned to her and forgot his worries for the moment.

"I don't think she did it, Phillip," said Gibbons on the phone the next morning. "I timed the walk and there's twenty minutes unaccounted for. That tallies exactly with the time it took her to start back for her library card, and then turn round again once she realized she had it—I timed that, too. And twenty minutes is rather long for slipping some poisoned water into a coffeepot."

Things always looked bleakest at night. This morning Bethancourt had reminded himself that Gibbons was no fool and that, if he thought Annette was innocent, she very likely was. He still thought his friend was heading for a broken heart, but that, after all, was not disastrous. It happened to nearly everyone sooner or later.

Nevertheless, the absolution of Annette on such flimsy evidence made him uneasy. "It could have taken twenty minutes," he said. "We know she left the house and she might have waited to make sure McAllister was out of the way before she went back in again."

"She wouldn't even have seen him down there where the tulips are," argued Gibbons. "No, I know there's no proof as yet, but I really believe we can cross her off."

Bethancourt forbore to mention that if McAllister could see her, she could certainly see him if she looked in the right direction.

"Well, that's good then," he said lamely. "Are you going back down there again today?"

"No," answered Gibbons. "I'm off to interview Mrs. Simmons's children. It's rather pointless, really, but Carmichael wants everyone eliminated. I rang to see if you wanted to come."

"I don't think so," said Bethancourt. "I've got things to take care of here and then I'm running down to see Kitty this evening."

"All right then," said Gibbons cheerfully. "I'll let you know if I turn anything up. God, but it's good to have at least one suspect cleared."

"What did Carmichael say when you told him?"

"Not much really. He did say he'd ruled out the idea of her having an affair, but he didn't find out anything more about Paul Berowne. I think he was disappointed with that—he's certain there's something there. He's going to start digging for it in earnest on Monday, starting with the office staff and going round to the vicar."

"He's very likely right," said Bethancourt. "Well, I'll ring you tomorrow and tell you what I find out at the pub tonight."

"Right-ho. Talk to you then."

Bethancourt hung up the receiver, determined about one thing. Whether there was evidence to back it up or not, he had to find out for sure whether Annette Berowne was guilty or innocent. At the moment, he was not at all sure which answer would be best for his friend.

He had known Gibbons well for several years now and had seen him through the acquiring and subsequent loss of three or four girl-friends, but he had never seen him in this kind of stew over a woman before. Gibbons's previous liaisons had been casual affairs, begun usually with a burst of enthusiasm quickly subsumed by his devotion to his work. He had not seemed to care much when things ended; on one occasion he had admitted to Bethancourt that he was relieved. Only once had he been truly upset by the end of a relationship and had complained bitterly of Lisa's lack of understanding about the hours that his job entailed. Bethancourt had forbore to point out that Lisa's objections had not been to the hours, but to the fact that she never crossed Gibbons's mind during them. Well, he thought wryly, that was one complaint Annette Berowne couldn't make.

Bethancourt tried to turn his attention to other matters, but he could not concentrate. He told himself that there was nothing he could do until the evening, but it made no difference; he could not settle to anything. Finally he gave up the unequal struggle and spent an hour outlining the facts of the case on his computer. When it was finished he stared fruitlessly at what he had done for another half-hour before abandoning it in disgust and venturing out to take Cer-berus across the Thames for a long walk in Battersea Park.

When he returned, he was still so anxious to get on with the eve-ning that he showered, shaved, and dressed and was ready to go well before time. He left anyway, arriving at the servants' entrance to Hurtwood Hall a full fifteen minutes early. If Kitty Whitcomb had only known how unheard-of an occurrence this was, she would have been flattered.

She had dressed up for the occasion in a leather miniskirt and a close-fitting twin set trimmed with satin. Bethancourt gazed at her admiringly.

"You look lovely," he said. "Shall we go?"

The restaurant she had chosen was in Guildford, a small, intimate place with candlelit tables and snowy linen. Kitty appeared to be well-known here; she was greeted effusively by the maitre d', kissed by the waiter, and assured that Anton would be out to see her as soon as he could manage it.

Bethancourt settled himself in his chair, lit a cigarette, and raised his eyebrows. "Do you come here every night you have off?" he asked.

"It's amazing how you do that," Kitty said, eyeing him.

"Do what?"

"Manage to get so comfortable," she answered, surprising him. "You did it in my kitchen, too. You just seem to settle in, as if you were as comfortable as you would be at home."

"I am comfortable."

Kitty abruptly returned to his original question. "I do come here fairly often," she said. "I also used to date the chef."

"Anton?"

"Anton."

Bethancourt considered. "You seem to be on very friendly terms."

"We are. Why shouldn't we be?"

"Well, I don't know. I've often wondered why, when people break up, they so often never want to see each other again. After all, they presumably had something in common to begin with."

"I know it happens that way sometimes," she agreed, "but it never made any sense to me. I'm still friends with all of my old boyfriends."

Bethancourt was smiling at her, his eyes twinkling behind his glasses. "My," he said, "you're almost aggressively practical, aren't you?"

She didn't like that; she shrugged and said, "Practical, certainly. I don't know about aggressive."

They were interrupted by the waiter who had brought the wine list and stood holding it, hesitating between them.

"The gentleman's paying, Mark," said Kitty, indicating that the list should be given to Bethancourt.

"Thank you," he said, "but I think you're probably a better judge of wine than I am. You take it. And," he added as the waiter departed, "don't stint. I can afford one splendid night out."

"I'll take you at your word," she warned.

"By all means, do. In fact, you can order the entire meal if you like. I'm sure you know Anton's cooking better than I do, too."

She shot him a curious glance, but merely said, "Very well," and returned her attention to the wine list.

The ordering taken care of, the wine brought and approved, Kitty propped her elbow on the table, rested her chin on the heels of her hands, and said, "So what exactly do you have to do with the police?"

Bethancourt had no intention of impugning Scotland Yard's honor by revealing his true status. Discretion, in this case, was definitely the better part of valor.

"Consultant," he answered. "But actually, I don't get called in very often, mostly just when they want a new slant on things."

"And what do you do when you're not consulting?"

"Try to look after my investments," said Bethancourt deprecatingly.

Kitty's eyebrows rose and her eyes ran over his clothes, as if trying to gauge their worth.

"So what you're really saying is that you're independently wealthy."

"You could put it that way, depending on your definition of wealthy."

"But then why Scotland Yard?"

"Because I enjoy it," he answered. "Most of the time, anyway," he added, thinking of the wrinkle that had been introduced to this case.

The same thing had apparently occurred to Kitty, for she said slowly, "I rather thought you and Sergeant Gibbons were friends."

"We are. We've grown quite close over the years."

"He was at the estate yesterday," said Kitty. "I didn't see him, but Mrs. Berowne was all flushed and happy when she got back from her walk with him. She hasn't looked like that since the murder."

Bethancourt sighed. "I know," he said. "I don't know what will come of that—nothing good, I'm afraid."

"You don't like her."

"Not at all," he said. "I like her fine, if she's not a murderer."

"But you're not attracted to her," said Kitty. "Maddie pointed that out to me yesterday."

"Well, no," admitted Bethancourt. "I expect it's because I like independent women. Mrs. Berowne is more the let-me-understand-you type."

Kitty sipped at her wine. "She could be innocent," she said, as if considering a new and troublesome idea. "I haven't told you yet what I found out from my aunt. I had to drag it out of her—she's the loyal retainer type and doesn't approve of gossip—but I got it in the end. And it does rather give Mr. Paul a motive."

Bethancourt settled his glasses more firmly on his nose. "I'm all ears," he said.

"It was about five years ago," began Kitty. "Paul and Marion had been married for three years or so and they weren't very happy. At least, Mr. Paul wasn't. He'd been having an affair with some woman in Town and wanted a divorce. According to Aunt Janet, Marion was devastated. She'd had a miscarriage the year before and was just beginning to come out from under the depression when Paul told her he wanted a divorce. Mr. Berowne—Geoffrey, that is—didn't approve of divorce and insisted that they go to counseling. That didn't go too well and the divorce probably would have happened, but then Marion found out she was pregnant again."

"And Geoffrey wasn't about to let her wander off with his grandchild."

"It was more than that." Kitty took a sip of wine, holding it in her mouth for a moment before swallowing. "Geoffrey didn't approve of divorce, but he was dead set against it if there were children involved. Marion held out for a while, hoping Paul would come around, but when he didn't, she went to Geoffrey and told him everything. They hadn't told him about Paul's affair before, and when he found out that Paul was still seeing this other woman and had been all along, he was really furious. He always had a bit of a temper, but it was usually one big flash and it was over. This time, he stayed angry. Maddie tried to calm him down, but she's not much good as a peacemaker and just ended up having a fight with him herself. Geoffrey laid down the law to Paul. He said if Paul didn't drop this other woman and do his duty by Marion, he'd disinherit him and kick him out of Berowne Biscuits."

Bethancourt frowned. "But I thought he had already settled a large sum on Paul when Paul married."

"No, I don't think so," said Kitty slowly. "I think it was just a nice start—the big money came from the promotion and raise he gave Paul later on. Geoffrey raised Paul's salary to match his own."

"I see," said Bethancourt. "I take it Paul caved in to his father's threats then?"

"Not right away. He did leave the estate, and my aunt thinks he was looking for another job, but didn't find one. In any case, he came back after about five months or so and accepted his father's terms. Geoffrey apparently tried to make it up to him, but Aunt Janet says it was never the same between them after that. They'd been close before, but since that time there was a kind of wall between them."

"Isn't that interesting?" mused Bethancourt. "And about a year later, Geoffrey marries Annette. Yes, I can see why he wasn't prepared to put up with much guff about her."

"But don't you see the motive this gives Paul?" asked Kitty. "If he had found another lover, it would be the same thing all over again unless Geoffrey was out of the way."

"You said you didn't think he was having an affair."

"I didn't," she answered. "But I could have been wrong."

"Even if he wasn't," said Bethancourt, "he could have just been so fed up that he would have done anything to get out. Yes, Kitty, this definitely constitutes a lead. I, as well as Chief Inspector Carmichael and Sergeant Gibbons, am very grateful to you. Do you know who the other woman was?"

Kitty grinned. "I thought you'd ask that," she said. "Aunt Janet didn't remember her name, but she thought it was either Amy or Ann, and her last name began with an 'S'. She was a solicitor acting for some firm Berowne Biscuits was taking over, that's how she and Mr. Paul met."

"That's certainly enough to go on," said Bethancourt, jotting the information down in the back of his address book. "Here, let me have your aunt's address, too—I'm sure Carmichael will want to talk with her."

Kitty gave it readily enough, but added, "She mightn't admit it all to him. And, by the way, I would appreciate it if my name wasn't mentioned when they talk to Maddie and the Berownes. Maddie will probably fire me if she finds out I sent this investigation in any direction but straight at Mrs. Berowne."

Their starters arrived then, putting off any further discussion of murder in favor of one about food. Bethancourt eyed Kitty speculatively as they ate. In this atmosphere, she sparkled and he found himself more attracted to her than he had expected.

It was a very enjoyable dinner. The food was excellent and Anton, when at last he appeared, was a pleasant addition. Bethancourt, who enjoyed dining out, was almost reluctant to leave the restaurant and move on to Paul Berowne's favorite pub.

CHAPTER

9

An hour before closing on a Sunday night, the pub was quiet. There was a group of regulars huddled at the far end of the bar and a young couple installed at one of the tables against the wall, but that was all.

It was an old pub, dark and small, with low ceilings and odd nooks and crannies stretching out at the back. A young, auburn-haired woman was perched on a stool behind the bar, reading the evening paper; she looked up as they came in and smiled.

"Kit!" she said, and then her eyes travelled over Bethancourt, assessing him. She and Kitty exchanged a look Bethancourt could not read.

"This is Phillip Bethancourt," said Kitty, sliding onto a barstool. "Phillip, Mira Fellows."

"What can I get you?" asked Mira, stowing away her paper and rising.

"We've already had brandies at Anton's," said Kitty. "I think I'll stick with that."

"Me, too," said Bethancourt. "And let me buy you something."

"Thanks."

Mira produced the drinks, pulled a half-pint for herself, and settled opposite them, resting her elbows comfortably on the dull wood of the bar. Blue eyes regarded Bethancourt with both humor and intelligence, and she exchanged another glance with Kitty, which this time Bethancourt interpreted as approval of himself, whether of his appearance or his trustworthiness he did not know.

"So," said Mira, "you want to hear about Paul Berowne."

"That's right," said Bethancourt. "Anything you can tell me."

"There's not much to tell really." She shrugged and sipped her beer. "He comes in three or four nights a week, but keeps to himself." She jerked her head over her shoulder. "There's a table in the back where he always sits and usually he's got a book or some papers. On busy nights when it's crowded, he joins the regulars there at the bar, but he doesn't say much."

Bethancourt considered this singularly unhelpful statement while he lit a cigarette. Mira was watching him; there was more she hadn't told him yet.

"So he doesn't talk to anyone here?" he asked.

"Not about the kind of things you want to know." Mira spread her hands. "He chats to me sometimes on quiet nights when he comes up for his drinks. We talk about films, or the book he's reading, or local gossip. A few times, when he's been particularly down and maybe had a few too many, he's told me how worried he is about his work and how inadequate he feels. But nothing more personal than that, nothing about his family." She hesitated. "He strikes me as a deeply unhappy man," she summed up. "From what he's said to me, he doesn't think much of himself and I have the impression that he only goes on because he hasn't the strength of mind to kill himself. But if he hated his father, or had some other reason to wish him dead, he never told me about it."

"Mira!"

Two of the men at the far end of the bar raised their empty pint glasses.

"Coming," she said, and pushed herself away from the bar. "I'll be right back."

Bethancourt watched her as she walked back to her other customers. So Paul Berowne had found that his own self-worth had been the price of his father's bargain and, having lost that, he had had no will left to reject it again. It was not the portrait of a man bent on murder, but Bethancourt still felt that Mira was holding something back. When she returned to them, he asked, "Do you like him?"

Mira, whose expression had been remarkably open and frank before, now dropped her eyes and shifted her elbows on the bar.

"I suppose I do," she answered unwillingly.

"She feels sorry for him," put in Kitty disapprovingly. "Deep down, Mira's a softie. You should see her collection of stray cats."

Mira shrugged this away impatiently. "Paul's a sad person," she said. "Naturally I feel sorry for him."

Bethancourt glanced at Kitty, who was leaning over the bar.

"Well, go on, Mira," she said. "God knows it's taking long enough."

"Not everybody is as cold as you about these things," retorted Mira. "Some of us have feelings."

Kitty groaned and rolled her eyes and Bethancourt was suddenly enlightened.

"You slept with him," he said to Mira.

She flashed him a startled glance. "You're bloody quick, aren't you?"

"I have my moments of perception," said Bethancourt. He turned reproachfully to Kitty. "You told me Paul Berowne wasn't having an affair."

"One night isn't an affair," retorted Kitty. "And since I knew he was spending so much time here, I figured he wasn't seeing anyone."

"Anyone *else*, you mean," corrected Bethancourt. He turned back to Mira. "When did this happen?"

Mira was hugging her elbows, but this time she met his eyes. "About a fortnight before the murder. It had been a busy night and I had just finished pushing everyone out when I realized Paul was still back in his corner. I thought maybe he'd had too much to drink and was having trouble standing up, but when I went back he wasn't drunk. He just looked utterly miserable, so I told him to stay put and I'd bring him another one and we'd have a good talk. And, well, one thing led to another."

Kitty was shaking her head over her friend's deplorable lapse. "Only you could go from pity directly to passion," she said.

"It's not as if he's unattractive, Kitty," said Mira. "And by the time we got to that, I'd had a few drinks myself."

"And he never tried it on again?" asked Bethancourt.

"He couldn't very well after he'd insulted her," said Kitty. "Tell him, Mira."

"He came in the next night," said Mira, "and took me aside to explain that he hoped I wouldn't take last night the wrong way, and would I please not tell anyone. I was rather offended. I mean, it was he who made the first move and if he thought it was such a terrible mistake, then he should have thought twice. And as for thinking I would blurt it all out to everyone in the pub, well, it was just insulting."

"But you did tell Kitty," pointed out Bethancourt.

"Well, I'd already told her," said Mira defensively, "and she was the only one. I made it perfectly clear it wasn't to go further."

"You have to admit it was offensive," said Kitty.

"Quite," said Bethancourt. "I do admit it. Did he come in again after that?"

"Not for more than a week," said Mira slowly. "In fact, it was the night before the murder that he came back and apologized."

"Ah," said Bethancourt, watching her. "And that led back to the bedroom, did it?"

Mira was staring at the countertop while Kitty sipped her brandy and confidently waited for her friend to deny this.

"Well . . ." began Mira, and then trailed off.

"Mira!" exclaimed Kitty. "You didn't!"

"He's really rather sweet, Kitty," said Mira. "And awfully good in bed."

Kitty groaned. "You have a genius," she said, "for choosing losers. Sexually skillful ones, no doubt, but losers nonetheless."

"Paul's not a loser," said Mira, "just unhappy."

"Mira, the man could be a murderer."

"Well, I didn't know that," said Mira defensively. "I thought Annette Berowne had done it. You said she had."

"So you've seen him since the murder," said Bethancourt.

"Oh, God," said Kitty.

Mira nodded. "He didn't come in for over a week after it happened," she said, "but he's been in several times since then, and he's spent the night, which he didn't before." She hesitated, and took a deep swallow of her beer. "Look," she continued, "the reason I'm telling you this is because of something he said the day of the murder. I didn't think anything of it at the time, but when Kitty rang and said it wasn't certain Mrs. Berowne was the killer, well, I got worried."

"The day of the murder?" asked Bethancourt, surprised. "He was here then? At what time?"

"He rang early and woke me up," said Mira. "He wanted to come round at once, but I told him to give me an hour. So I guess it would have been about half nine when he got here."

"And how long did he stay?"

"Not long. Less than an hour, because I had to start preparing to open."

Bethancourt breathed again. He had been fearing that Paul Berowne, on the verge of becoming the prime suspect, was about to be given an alibi.

"He wasn't," he asked delicately, "here to continue the activities of the night before?"

Mira flushed. "No," she answered. "He came because he was afraid he'd been seen leaving then. Ken Mills had been in that night with Patty Dobson—I told you about that, Kitty—and she lives at the other end of town. Apparently when Paul left here, Ken was just coming back from seeing Patty home. Paul dodged him, but he thought Ken might have seen him anyway and he wanted to warn me that it all might be coming out. I was worried for him, but he seemed calm enough about it and just said, 'It had to come to an end sometime. This is as good a time as any.' I thought then that he meant our affair and was just being fatalistic. But now, well, it's occurred to me he could have been referring to his situation with his father and that he'd decided to end it."

The look in her eyes appealed to him to tell her she was wrong, but Bethancourt did not see it. He was thinking rapidly, seeing how it all might have come about. Paul Berowne, unquestionably a beaten man, well-mired in one of life's deeper morasses, suddenly found not, perhaps, hope or love, but at least a reminder that life could be different. It might well have been enough to ignite all the passions the man had kept bottled inside him for so many years. And just at this opportune moment, he would have noticed the lilies of the valley Annette had placed in her husband's study. He must have known what they could do, and had carefully replaced them when they withered to strengthen the poison in the water. Whether his course had been unalterable at that point, Bethancourt was not sure, but then had come the fear of discovery, the knowledge of what Geoffrey would do if Ken Mills were not discreet enough. The obvious solution was to kill his father before he could learn of it.

It was an enormous motive, one equal to the millions Annette Berowne had inherited along with her freedom. For the first time, Bethancourt began to see a glimmer of hope in the case.

Bethancourt was buoyant as he escorted Kitty back to the car and drove the short distance to the estate. They were laughing as they drove up the drive and followed the curve to the offshoot that led to the servants' entrance. The Jaguar's headlamps swept the front of the house as they passed and Bethancourt's laughter died. Parked off to one side, he had seen a police Rover.

"What is it?" asked Kitty, who apparently had not noticed the car.

"Nothing," answered Bethancourt, pulling up into the little paved space outside the kitchen door.

"Do you want to come in and have some coffee?" she asked. "I think you probably should."

Bethancourt agreed automatically, so preoccupied with Gibbons's presence here that he did not notice the look in her eyes. It was possible, of course, that something had happened, that both Carmichael and Gibbons were in the house, attending to a new development in the case. But Bethancourt did not believe it. When the police arrived late in the evening in the pursuit of their duties, there was normally a blaze of light and noise. He had seen only a single light in the windows of the drawing room, and the house was quiet. And he could think all too easily of another explanation for Gibbons's presence here. In all his worrying, it had somehow not occurred to him that Gibbons might have taken things so far. The thought depressed him.

His thoughts were so far away that he was taken by surprise when they entered the kitchen and Kitty pressed against him, running a finger down his shoulder, and asked playfully, "Do you really want coffee?"

Bethancourt looked down at her, not unaware of the irony of the situation. Here he had been fretting over Gibbons's possible indiscretions and now he was offered the opportunity to commit one himself. Kitty, however, was not a suspect, and he was not a police officer. But neither was he a free man.

"Oh, Kitty," he said regretfully, "I really, truly never meant to mislead you. I already have a girlfriend, you see."

"Well, I wasn't asking to try out for the part," she retorted, drawing back a little. "Besides, I already knew that. I asked Sergeant Gibbons."

"Oh." Bethancourt was surprised.

"But it was worth asking anyway," she continued. "Not everyone is faithful all the time."

Bethancourt's surprise had turned to amusement. "So what you're saying," he said, "is that you would like to use me for sex."

She was delighted with the phrase; her eyes sparkled and she chuckled, leaning into him again. "Exactly," she agreed. "I don't suppose you would care to . . . ?"

Bethancourt knew he had no business accepting such an invitation and on any other night he would have refused. In fact, he began to say that he really had to be getting back to London, when he suddenly had a vision of exactly what he would be going back to: a night spent pacing his flat and gnawing over the problem of Gibbons and Annette Berowne.

His mind warred with temptation while Kitty pressed herself against him, smiling up into his face as she reached out to touch his cheek.

"I really shouldn't," he said rather weakly.

"Of course not," she murmured, sliding her hands behind his head to bend his face down to hers. Her lips touched his lingeringly and Bethancourt found that somehow his arms were around her. It was not until several minutes later, however, that he realized he had given up the struggle.

Gibbons had returned to London late that day. At the close of the first really nice weekend of spring, thousands of other people were also on the road to Town, and he muttered imprecations at them as he nudged the police Rover through the traffic. When he finally arrived back in his neighborhood, it took him an additional hour to find a parking space, even one several blocks from his flat.

But his sunny mood returned as he entered his flat, stripping off his working clothes and heading for the shower. True, Mrs. Simmons's children seemed above reproach and he had garnered nothing that would give their mother a motive for murdering her employer, but he hadn't really expected to. And they had made at least one step forward in exonerating Annette—which was, if only he had admitted it to himself, the only step he really cared about. It remained, of course, to clear her name, but he was certain that too would come.

Emerging from the shower, he thought of ringing Bethancourt before he remembered that his friend would by this time be off to take Kitty Whitcomb to dinner. Gibbons grinned. He didn't really expect Bethancourt to learn anything useful and he didn't think Bethancourt expected it, either; this was merely a good excuse to take a pretty girl out while Marla was away. Left to himself for the evening, he pulled on a T-shirt and jeans and sallied forth to collect some Indian take-away for his supper.

He watched television as he ate, choosing a program he had seen once before and liked. Unfortunately, he had no idea of how the plot had progressed since he had first seen it weeks ago and found himself merely confused. He watched until the end nevertheless and it was not until he rose to clear the table afterward that he noticed there was a message on his answering phone. There had been nothing when he came in, and he cursed himself for not checking it again on his return from the Indian restaurant. If Carmichael was looking for him urgently, he would not be pleased.

But it was Annette Berowne's voice that greeted him when he pressed the play button. She sounded distressed and unsure of herself.

"I'm sorry to bother you at home. It's just I felt I couldn't wait—

oh, but probably it would be better if I had. I wanted to know . . . If you do come in, could you ring me?"

Gibbons rang back at once and she answered on the first ring.

"Oh, it is you," she said, and he thought she sounded tearful. "I'm sorry. I shouldn't have rung you. It's not the kind of thing to discuss on the phone . . ."

"Has something happened?"

"Yes. Oh, nothing really to do with my husband's death, but I couldn't think who else to call."

"What is it? What can I do?"

"Nothing. I can't talk about it over the phone, that's why I said I shouldn't have rung. I just wasn't thinking—"

"Do you want me to come down?"

Annette hesitated. "No," she answered. "That's too much to ask of you."

"Nonsense," said Gibbons. "I'd be very happy to come if you want to see me. It's not a long drive."

Again she hesitated and then, almost in a whisper, she said, "If you truly shouldn't mind . . ."

"I don't mind at all," said Gibbons firmly. "I'll leave straightaway."

He rang off, grabbed a jacket and the keys to the Rover, and fairly sprinted the distance back to the car.

When he arrived at Hurtwood Hall, Annette opened the door to him herself. Her heart-shaped face was tear-streaked and she clutched a handkerchief in one hand, although she seemed composed at the moment.

"Thank you so much for coming," she said softly, closing the door behind him. "It was very good of you to humor me so."

"Not at all," said Gibbons. "I told you I didn't mind in the least."

She led the way into the drawing room, but did not sit. Instead she paced down and back and then stopped a few feet from him. She examined her handkerchief carefully as she said, "There's a dinner party tonight. Lilian Danforth is giving it; she and her husband are probably our closest friends down here."

Gibbons, a little puzzled, said nothing and she continued.

"I only found out about it because Maddie was going and I was a little surprised I hadn't been invited. I don't know if I would have gone—Geoffrey hasn't been dead very long, after all, but I thought it odd that Lilian hadn't rung me anyway. I said so to Maddie and she said—" her voice faltered, but she raised her chin and went on, "she said that everyone thought I had killed Geoffrey and there was talk that I had killed Bill Burton, too." She looked at him directly, her eyes dark pools of anguish. "I knew the police suspected me— it's your job, after all. But that everyone else thought—Tell me, Jack. Is it true?"

"Well," temporized Gibbons, "there's bound to be—"

"Just tell me!"

Her plea was so impassioned that Gibbons could not help but respond to it.

"Yes," he said, "it is."

She turned away from him and began sobbing, clutching the back of a chair with white knuckles.

"Not everyone believes it," said Gibbons. "Reverend Oakley doesn't. And neither do I."

He stepped toward her and touched her arm. She turned to him readily, burying her head on his shoulder and weeping unrestrainedly. Gibbons wrapped his arms about her and stroked her hair.

"There's bound to be rumors like that," he said. "Murder cases are the very worst for that kind of thing. But it will pass, I promise you. Once we've solved the case—"

"But will you?" Her voice was muffled against his shoulder. "Daniel Andrews couldn't. And they'll all think I did it, they think so already."

"Spouses are always suspect," said Gibbons. "And we will solve it.

We've already made progress and it's only been a couple of weeks. Give us a little time."

She nodded and sniffed, her sobs seeming to lessen. Without thinking, Gibbons planted a kiss on her head and with that action became abruptly aware of her body against his, of her hand on his chest.

She looked up and gave him a tremulous smile; his own was no less shaken in reply. He found he was holding his breath.

"Thank you," she said, reaching up to kiss his cheek.

Time seemed to have slowed to a crawl. Her kiss landed close by the corner of his mouth and he followed the impulse to turn his head just that little bit so that their lips met while alarms sounded in his brain.

She responded to his kiss, shifting against him and in that moment, when his emotions washed over him in a flood of desire, he drew back abruptly, horrified at what he had been about to do, and put her from him. He was shaking violently.

"I'm sorry," he stammered. "I can't do this. It's wrong."

She stood back from him, rejected, her brown eyes hurt and confused.

"I didn't mean—" she began and stopped herself. "You've been such a comfort. I didn't expect that you would . . ." Her voice trailed off and her eyes fell from his. "It was just the moment," she said more clearly. "I didn't mean it to lead to anything, either."

Gibbons found his breathing was still ragged, though he was reassured by her words. "I'm sorry," he said again. "I think I'd better go."

She nodded and followed him toward the door. She seemed so desolate that he paused.

"You were right," he said. "It was just the moment. I'll be back to see you later and in the meantime you must try to keep up your spirits. Just remember that things will come right in the end."

"I will," she said. "Thank you." She stood aside while he opened the door and then asked hesitantly, "I know that under the circumstances we couldn't possibly, well, you know. But you didn't stop because you think I killed him, did you?"

The last phrase was almost a whisper.

"God, no," said Gibbons fervently, but he knew as he turned away that there was only one way he could prove the truth of his words to her and unless he did so the suspicion would remain between them.

He heard the door close behind him as he walked to the Rover, his footsteps crunching in the gravel of the drive. He fumbled the keys into the ignition, his hands still trembling, and wondered what madness had come over him. He had wanted women before, but never like that. Even now, his heart raced at the memory of Annette in his arms and a part of him wished he had not remembered his duty, wished he had been drunk or had any excuse to forget and make love to her. The terrifying thing was he knew, if he had had such an excuse, he would have made use of it. It would destroy the case—any evidence he uncovered would be nullified by the fact that he wanted to exonerate his lover—and with the case would go his career. They would probably sack him, and even if they didn't, he would never rise beyond sergeant. Yet there was a corner of his mind that whispered that no one need ever find out, and it was not stilled by even the horrifying picture of being cross-examined in court as to his relationship with the widow of a murdered man.

He let in the clutch too abruptly and the tires spun briefly as he shot away from the house, racing down the drive.

CHAPTER

ethancourt was awakened in the dark before dawn by Kitty's movements in the bedroom. He blinked and stretched.

"What time is it?" he asked.

Kitty turned from the closet and smiled at him. "Nearly six," she answered. "I'm just getting ready to go for my run. There's coffee in the kitchen."

"I could use a cup," he said, propping himself up on the pillows. "When will you be back?"

"By seven."

Bethancourt considered. "I should probably leave before that," he said. "I have to get back to London and report to Jack before he leaves for the Yard."

Kitty nodded and sat on the edge of the bed to put on her shoes. "There's fresh towels in the bathroom," she said. "And the coffee will keep warm." She tied the laces efficiently and then leaned over to kiss him. "It was a lovely night," she said.

"It was," he agreed. "I don't know when I'll be back, but I'm sure I'll see you again in the next day or two."

"All right."

She rose, waved good-bye from the doorway, and was gone.

From the kitchen windows, Bethancourt could detect a glimmering in the eastern sky. He poured himself a cup of coffee, savoring the aroma, and took a deep draft before lighting a cigarette. In the cold light of morning—what there was of it—he was inclined to feel ashamed of himself. He wondered if he had been drunker the night before than he had believed himself to be, but shook the thought away impatiently. Drunkenness was no excuse for doing something he had acknowledged at the time was wrong, but had gone ahead with anyway.

He sighed and rubbed his face, feeling the stubble on his cheek. Nothing, he reflected, looked very good at this time of day. Even what he had learned about Paul Berowne did not seem very exciting now. It was not, after all, proof of anything, though no doubt Gibbons would take it as further evidence of Annette's innocence.

That thought depressed Bethancourt further. He drank deeply from his coffee cup and tried to shake off his mood. Perhaps he was wrong about Gibbons, he thought stoutly, perhaps there had been a perfectly legitimate reason for his visit last night. Bethancourt did not believe it, but he repeated the idea firmly to himself as he stubbed out his cigarette and drained his cup. Yes, and what he had discovered about Paul Berowne might well lead to the solution of the case. As for himself, he would simply have to try to be less self-indulgent in the future.

This positive attitude lasted him out to the car, but rapidly vanished as he swung the Jaguar onto the main drive and glanced uneasily toward the front of the house, half-afraid the Rover would still be there. But it was gone and he heaved a sigh of relief, lighting a cigarette and blowing out the smoke in a great stream as he sped toward London.

Gibbons had been up half the night in an agony of self-doubt, an emotion which hitherto had been completely unknown to him. By morning, however, he had calmed himself. He could no longer deny that he had feelings for Annette, but he could deny their depth, and he had reasoned his way to a truce with himself, not realizing how uneasy a truce it was. It was only natural that he should feel for her, so lonely in her grief, wrongly accused of her husband's murder and already convicted in the court of public opinion, striving so valiantly to bear it all. Circumstances had combined last night to cause him to overreact, but there was no reason to fear it would happen a second time. The thing to do was to put it firmly out of his mind and concentrate on solving the case. Once that was done, he would be free to explore exactly what Annette had come to mean to him.

And yet the look in her eyes when she had asked if he believed her a murderer continued to haunt him. He found himself dwelling on it when he did not mean to, and wishing he had found some way to reassure her.

The ringing of the telephone interrupted his thoughts. In his turmoil, he had completely forgotten Bethancourt's promise to ring him with the results of the night's investigations, and he was almost surprised to hear his friend's voice.

"You're up early," he said.

"I wanted to catch you before you left," said Bethancourt. "I found out more than I ever expected last night."

"About Paul Berowne?" asked Gibbons, rather taken aback.

"Yes. Mind, there's no proof of anything, but it does give him a solid motive."

As Gibbons listened to his friend's recital, the last of his introspection vanished and he grew increasingly excited.

"Good work, Phillip," he said. "I have to confess, I never really thought your date with Kitty would lead to anything, and I couldn't have been more wrong."

"What will you do now?" asked Bethancourt.

"That's up to Carmichael. I'll ring him at once—he's going to be furious that no one told us about this before now."

"Well, it was several years ago," said Bethancourt. "I don't suppose anyone realized it would be important. Especially since no one knew he was having another affair."

"One could look at it like that," said Gibbons, who clearly did not. "In any case, I imagine the first thing to do will be to find the woman Berowne had the affair with."

"Carmichael won't pull Paul Berowne in for questioning at once, then?"

"I wouldn't think so," answered Gibbons, "but, as I say, I'll have to check."

"Well, let me know what happens," said Bethancourt.

"Of course I will. I'll ring you when I know what the program is. And thank you, Phillip—you've done very well for us."

Gibbons rang off and dialed Carmichael's home number, but found that the chief inspector had already left for the Yard. It was an old habit of Carmichael's, when a case wasn't going well, to get to the office early. Gibbons hastily swallowed the last of his coffee and left for New Scotland Yard.

Carmichael had spent his Sunday investigating Maddie Wellman. He had spoken to the headmistress at the school where she had once taught and had interviewed her friends and her bank manager. He had failed to uncover a motive, and it still seemed to him that if Maddie was going to murder anyone, it would have been Annette Berowne rather than her husband.

He was deeply unhappy with the case and saw fewer possibilities of solving it every day. It was frustrating Gibbons as well; just look at the way the lad had jumped to the conclusion that Annette Berowne must be innocent because it wouldn't have taken her twenty minutes to poison the coffee. Obviously Gibbons was as anxious as his superior to make any headway at all, since normally he would never take such a leap of faith in a case. Carmichael hadn't liked to disillusion him about how little progress this represented and had received his sergeant's news neutrally.

Well, he told himself, at least he had done what he could to eliminate the peripheral characters and it now seemed very unlikely that any of the Berowne employees had committed the murder. That still left them with four solid suspects: Annette Berowne, still chief among them by virtue of her status as spouse and main legatee; her stepson Paul, who had been at odds with his father and who stood to gain complete control of Berowne Biscuits upon his father's death; his wife, Marion, a less likely suspect since she and Geoffrey had been on good terms, but still a legatee; and Maddie Wellman, who had deeply resented Geoffrey's remarriage and who was now set up for life without having to bend to her brother-in-law's will.

He was just contemplating the impossibility of ever arresting any of these people when Gibbons burst into his office, his blue eyes alight.

"I've got something, sir," he said eagerly. "Or, rather Phillip Bethancourt has."

Carmichael was surprised. "Bethancourt?"

"Yes, sir. He took Kitty Whitcomb to the local pub last night to ask questions about Paul Berowne."

Carmichael frowned. "I thought you had looked into the pub, Sergeant," he said.

"I did, sir. I spoke to the barmaid and to a group of regulars, but they all reported that Paul Berowne, although he came in often, always kept to himself at a corner table in the back." Gibbons grinned. "I should have gone with Kitty, sir, but I have to admit it never occurred to me. And it wasn't just the pub. Kitty had been speaking to her aunt, who was the cook at the Berownes before her, and dredged up some old gossip."

"Let's have it then." Gibbons's enthusiasm was infectious, but Carmichael remained cautious. By the end of Gibbons's tale, however, he was feeling more optimistic. It was nothing like proof, but it did give Berowne a far more solid motive than the one he had been assigned before.

"Surrey CID should have told us this," said Carmichael, disgruntled. "They must have known. And they might have winkled out for themselves that Berowne was having an affair. It was happening on their patch, after all, and they'd know best how to get it out of the locals."

"They mightn't have known all the details, sir," said Gibbons. "If they didn't know it was Geoffrey who put an end to his son's affair, it wouldn't seem very pertinent. I'm sure Geoffrey would have put the best face on all of it. He probably told people Paul changed his mind about the divorce when he realized Marion was pregnant."

"And they were so concerned with Annette Berowne, I expect they never investigated anyone else very seriously," admitted Carmichael. "Still, I'm going to have words with them about it. In the meantime, I'll want to talk to Mira Fellows myself. And I'll look in on the old cook while I'm down there, although she's hardly likely to tell me more—or even as much—as she told her niece. You get on to finding this Amy or Ann, Gibbons, but be discreet about it. I don't want Paul Berowne put on the alert. Whatever you do, don't ring up Berowne Biscuits for the information."

"No, sir. No need in any case. Kitty said she was acting for a firm Berowne Biscuits acquired about five years ago. It should be simple enough to find out which company that was and who represented them in the negotiations."

Carmichael paused to beam at his sergeant. He had had many

men under him in the past who would have had to have that line of inquiry spelled out for them, and he was pleased to have his high opinion of Gibbons confirmed.

"That's good thinking, lad," he said. "I'm off now—ring me on the mobile when you've got something."

"Yes, sir," said Gibbons.

"And, Gibbons—thank Bethancourt for me when you speak to him."

"I will, sir."

It did not take long for Gibbons to look through the public records of mergers and acquisitions and find the occasion, five years ago, when Berowne Biscuits had acquired Taylor's Toffees. It was, he hastily ascertained, the only acquisition Berowne had made that year, and he went on to search out the solicitor's firm that had acted for Taylor's during the negotiations. This took a little more work, but eventually he tracked it down and then it was a simple matter to obtain a list of the firm's employees. There were several women, but only one whose name corresponded to Janet Whitcomb's memory: Amy Sullivan.

He rang up the firm and was connected to Miss Sullivan after only a slight delay. He identified himself and asked, "Were you the solicitor acting for Taylor's Toffees when they were acquired by Berowne Biscuits about five years ago?"

There was a pause before she answered. "That's right," she said at last. "But if you're looking for any information about the acquisition, you would have to go through Mr. Steiner."

"I'm not actually interested in the acquisition itself," answered Gibbons. "I'm looking for the woman who dated Paul Berowne at that time. Was that you, Miss Sullivan?"

From her reaction, the source of his interest was not a surprise to her.

"Yes," she said at once, in a low voice. "That was me."

"Then I need to speak with you, Miss Sullivan," said Gibbons. "Will you be in your office for the next half-hour or so?"

"Oh!" she said, flustered. "No, that wouldn't be—I mean, I'd rather come to you. I could take an early lunch, if noon would do?"

Gibbons glanced at the clock; it was 11:15. "That would be fine," he answered. "I'm at New Scotland Yard; just ask for Detective Sergeant Gibbons at the desk."

From her quick acceptance of his interest in her personal life, Gibbons assumed Amy Sullivan had read about the Berowne murder in the papers. When she arrived, he was expecting a flood of questions about Paul Berowne's present status as a possible murderer and was prepared to parry them. But in the event, she seemed determined to avoid the topic altogether.

"Look here," she said, setting down her briefcase and sliding into the chair Gibbons held for her, "I want you to know I didn't realize Paul Berowne was married when it all started."

Gibbons took his own seat and considered her. Marion Berowne struck him as being far more attractive than Amy Sullivan, although Miss Sullivan was unquestionably better turned out in a very smart suit. Her face lacked the elegance of Marion's bone structure and beneath the well-tailored clothing her figure was less well-proportioned.

"I mean," she went on, "Paul and I were working together quite closely for a time and he was always available to have a drink after we were done or to get some dinner—never a mention of having to get home to his wife. Naturally, I assumed he was single."

"So you're saying he deceived you," said Gibbons.

"No, no." She had flyaway hair and now she pushed distractedly at her bangs. "I can't say that. It just never occurred to him that I didn't know. He was very apologetic when it came out, but of course by then it was too late."

"You were already in love with him."

She sighed. "Yes."

Gibbons eyed her. He found it interesting that even five years later, she was still determined not to be viewed as a home wrecker. But her guilty feelings were not why they were here.

"At some point," he said, "Mr. Berowne must have suggested he get a divorce so you could marry."

"That's right." She nodded.

"But, in fact, he didn't."

"Well, no, but it isn't what it sounds like. He meant to. He really did."

"Then what happened?"

She related the same story he had already heard: how Marion Berowne had objected and how Geoffrey had attempted to bring his son to heel.

"So Paul left Berowne's and moved in with me," she explained. "He didn't file for divorce right away because we both agreed that he should get a new job first." She sighed heavily. "Only he couldn't seem to find one."

Paul Berowne had energetically pursued job opportunities at first. He had never thought it would be a problem and his first port of call had been to the presidents of companies with whom he had dealt in his capacity as vice president of Berowne Biscuits. They had all been very tactful, but they had also been well aware of who the guiding genius at Berowne's really was and one by one they had politely declined to offer Paul the kind of position he was looking for. Paul had apparently believed it was fear of his father that motivated them and had gone boldly off to new pastures.

But the only jobs he found were in middle management, which marked a considerable descent from the giddy heights he was used to. At first he had rejected such jobs with disdain until, bit by bit, he began to realize it was the best he could do, that his former position with Berowne Biscuits had not reflected his own worth at all, but only his father's desires. And the knowledge changed him.

"When I first met him," said Amy reflectively, "he was full of confidence, a man in charge of a leading company, and very sure of himself. He wasn't perfect, and he was, for example, deeply distressed by the failure of his marriage, but that didn't really alter his view of himself and his world. Only it turned out it was his father's world and when Paul left it, he also left behind who he was."

"So he went back."

"Not exactly." She hesitated, avoiding his eye, and then said reluctantly, "I guess I sent him back."

"Really?" The interest in Gibbons's voice was keen. "You broke up with him?"

"I—yes, I don't suppose there's any other way to put it. But it's not what it sounds like."

Gibbons reflected that nothing was what it sounded like with Miss Sullivan.

"It was a bit awkward from the start," she explained, "having him move in with me. The flat I had then was small and it was hard to find room for his things and, well, we seemed to get in each other's way a lot. I think he felt it more than I did; he'd never lived in a place where he didn't have his own bathroom and dressing room and study and God knows what all else. In the beginning we didn't worry about it since we planned to move to a bigger place as soon as Paul got a new job—we even had our eye on a flat in Mayfair for a while. But after the first couple of months, well, it became clear that the situation was going to be less temporary than we'd thought."

"But that can't have been the end of it," said Gibbons. "I don't believe you threw him out just because the flat was a bit crowded."

"No, of course not." She was indignant at the suggestion. "I did try to be sympathetic and supportive, but he began closing me out.

In the end, he wasn't even looking for another job and he didn't want to discuss it. He started drinking a good deal and then there were rows." She gestured. "He just wasn't the same man I'd fallen in love with. In fact, no one could be more different. He was creeping round the flat almost as if he were afraid of me and we hardly ever made love anymore. I finally told him I didn't think it was working out."

"And how did he take it?"

"Very quietly, actually. I was surprised. He said he'd been thinking the same thing, only he hadn't had the courage to say anything. I went to a girlfriend's that night and the next afternoon he rang and said he'd spoken to his wife and he'd be moving back with her as soon as he was packed up." She spread her hands. "I never spoke to him again."

Carmichael had finished with Mira Fellows and Janet Whitcomb, neither of whom had added anything to the information Gibbons had brought in that morning. Nevertheless, Carmichael did not consider the time wasted. He had nailed down a few points and made absolutely certain that Paul Berowne had left Mira in plenty of time to return to the estate and poison his father.

That finished, Carmichael had returned to Hurtwood Hall and now stood in the garden, eyeing the tulip beds. These were planted around the edge of the terrace and the gardener, McAllister, had been working here on the morning of the murder. Carmichael was bothered by the fact that he could not place Paul Berowne anywhere near the study at the appropriate time. Berowne had spoken to McAllister here, but that had been earlier, long before Geoffrey Berowne had been served his coffee. But there was a gap between the time Paul Berowne had left Mira and the time he had arrived back at the garage to check on his car. McAllister said he had seen Mrs. Berowne leave the house which, if she was innocent, had been just after eleven. If that were the case, and Paul Berowne had arrived after her departure, how could McAllister not have seen him?

The most obvious explanation was that McAllister had moved round to the other end of the terrace. The side door could still be seen from here, but only if one made an effort. Carmichael knelt down in the damp grass and fixed his attention on the flower bed. No, from this angle, one probably wouldn't notice someone emerging from the house.

Carmichael went in search of the gardener, whom he finally found in the kitchen garden, tending the early lettuces. He did not look pleased to see the detective.

"I just need a bit of clarification," said Carmichael genially. "You said Mr. Paul Berowne spoke to you that morning while you were working in the tulip beds. Just where in the tulip beds would that have been?"

McAllister did not look up. "By the fountain."

"The fountain?" echoed Carmichael, puzzled. He had seen no fountain in the area.

McAllister nodded curtly.

"I see," said Carmichael, thinking it out. "So there are tulips other than those around the terrace. You started with this other bed that morning?"

"That's right."

"And about how long would that have taken you?"

"Don't know."

Carmichael sighed. "Perhaps you'd better show me where they are."

McAllister glared. "And if I do," he said, "who's going to tend to these lettuces, eh?"

"I imagine you could continue with that later," said Carmichael, losing patience. "This is a case of murder, Mr. McAllister, and my investigation takes precedence over gardening concerns. If you find them too distracting, we can always continue this discussion down at the nick."

This threat had less impact than Carmichael had hoped. McAllister merely snorted and said, "And if we do, it'll be damned difficult to see the bloody fountain from there."

But he rose and led the way out of the kitchen garden, making his way at a good pace along the winding paths of the garden proper until they reached a small rectangular plot surrounded by hedges. A large fountain stood in the center, solidly covered with cherubic angels and dolphins. There was a seat in an alcove of the hedge from which one could admire this monstrosity and gravel paths led from the bench to the fountain. Splashed in the angles were the tulips, but the beds were nowhere near as large as the long one that ran around the terrace. Mentally, Carmichael calculated that McAllister must have worked for less than half the time he had spent on the larger bed.

"So you started here first thing that morning?" he asked.

"Not first thing," admitted McAllister. "I just saw to a few things in the potting shed first."

"How long had you been here when Mr. Berowne came by?"

McAllister considered. "Not long," he answered.

It was like pulling teeth, thought Carmichael. "Where exactly were you?"

"I was mulching this one here."

"And had you done any of the others yet?"

"No."

"So it would have been about nine o'clock."

"If you say so." McAllister shrugged.

"And you went from here to the terrace?"

McAllister grunted an affirmative.

"Very well, let's go along there then."

The gardener sighed in an exaggerated manner and started off for the terrace. When they arrived, he indicated the end of the terrace farthest from the side door as the place he had started.

"Did you bring all the mulch up with you to begin with?" asked Carmichael. "Or did you have to go back for it?"

"I used what was left from the fountain beds. Then I got some more."

"And that lasted you until you finished?"

"No. I had to fetch more."

Gradually, Carmichael began to make a tentative timeline from McAllister's grudging replies. He had come up to the terrace probably about nine-thirty or a bit after and had run out of mulch perhaps an hour later. In any case, he had been halfway done when he had left to replenish his stock, and he had seen Mrs. Berowne leaving the house shortly after his return, probably not more than fifteen minutes later.

Carmichael stood in the spot McAllister had estimated as being near the place where he had stopped work and gazed up at the door. It was still far enough away from this point that people might have passed without McAllister noticing.

"How sure are you that no one used that door after Mrs. Berowne left?" he asked.

"I'm not sure," said McAllister. "I've told you all that before. I was working, not following the comings and goings of everybody else. They've got a right to use their own back door, haven't they? I'd not have noticed unless they made a lot of noise."

"But you did notice Mrs. Berowne," said Carmichael. "Why was that? Was she making a noise?"

"Not her."

"So why did you notice her?"

McAllister relented. "I expect I just happened to look up as she came out. I think I'd just finished a bag of mulch and was looking round for another one."

"So if one of the others—say Ken Mills—said he had entered the house this way, you wouldn't say he was lying?"

"No," said McAllister, exasperatedly. "I wouldn't, because I wouldn't know if he had or not."

"All right," said Carmichael. "Thank you very much, Mr. McAllister. You can get back to your lettuces now."

McAllister snorted and headed off at once.

"It's shaping up nicely, lad," said Carmichael, setting aside the notes Gibbons had made of his interview with Amy Sullivan. "God knows it's a whacking great motive."

"It is that," agreed Gibbons. "Do you want to bring Berowne in for questioning now?"

Carmichael glanced at the clock and considered. It had taken him longer than he had planned on down at Peaslake and it was now late afternoon. "He might be tired now and easier to break," said Carmichael. "It's a psychological edge, grabbing a man just as he thinks he's done for the day and can go home. But, no. I won't be any fresher than he is and this is important. I don't want to cock it up because I've already had a long day and have missed my supper. We'll wait until morning."

"Yes, sir," said Gibbons, relieved that he was not going to be kept at his post until all hours of the night, but careful not to show it. Showing one's superiors that you were eager to go home was not the way to advance in the police.

"In fact," said Carmichael, "you can have a nice lie-in tomorrow."

"I can?" said Gibbons, startled.

"Yes. I'll ring you in the morning once I've brought Berowne in and you can run down to Hurtwood Hall and talk to Maddie Wellman and Marion Berowne. Check out one of the cars tonight when you leave, and you can start straight from your place in the morning."

"I'll do that," said Gibbons. "Anything special you're hoping to get from the women, sir?"

Carmichael rubbed his chin. "It's too much to hope for any confirmation from either of them," he said, "but get what you can. In particular, find out if either of them suspected he was sleeping with Mira Fellows. I'd also like to be sure that this is what Maddie Wellman was keeping back from me. I'd rather like to tackle her myself, but there's no help for it. If I went down to talk to her, she'd be on the phone to her nephew before I was well out the door."

"Yes, sir," said Gibbons. "I'll do my best."

"I know you will, Sergeant. Come straight back here when you're done and you can give me the high sign if you've anything urgent to report. I doubt you will have," he added. "It's a long shot that they'll tell you anything at all, but it's got to be tried."

CHAPTER

11

The King's Head and Eight Bells was Bethancourt's local pub and Gibbons found him there that evening,
ensconced in a corner with the *Guardian* and a pint
of bitter, his dog stretched out beside his feet. He looked, from the
doorway, abominably comfortable and at ease, but his face was
worried when he raised his eyes from the paper and saw Gibbons
approaching.

"What's up?" he asked. "Is there a fly in the ointment?"

"No, no," Gibbons hastened to reassure him. "Everything's tick-
ing along like clockwork."

Bethancourt let out a long-drawn breath and reached for a cigarette.

"You really shouldn't do that to me, Jack," he said. "I thought for
sure you'd found out Paul Berowne had an ironclad alibi when you
said you hadn't brought him in for questioning."

"The wheels of justice grind slowly," said Gibbons, bending to
pet Cerberus. "Carmichael wanted to come at him fresh, and it was

late this afternoon when he got back from talking to Mira Fellows. We're bringing Berowne in first thing in the morning. Just let me get a drink and I'll tell you all about it."

Gibbons returned shortly and settled himself opposite his friend, taking a long draft of his beer and leaning back with a sigh.

"It's looking very good, Phillip," he said, "and it's all due to you. Carmichael said to pass along his thanks."

"I was lucky," answered Bethancourt. "If Kitty hadn't taken to me, I never would have found it out. So it's all standing up?"

"Perfectly," Gibbons assured him. "I talked to Amy Sullivan to-day—that's the lady Berowne had the affair with—and she bears out everything Kitty told you. Mira came through with the chief and confirmed that Berowne left the pub that morning no later than ten-forty, giving him plenty of time to poison his father and get to the garage by noon. The only thing that's not ideal is that Carmichael couldn't get McAllister to place Berowne at the scene. On the other hand, McAllister is rock-solid on the fact that anybody could have come or gone and he wouldn't necessarily have noticed them. And anyway, I've high hopes Carmichael will wrangle a con-fession out of Berowne tomorrow. Berowne doesn't strike me as a hardened man; I'm sure he must bear a terrible burden of guilt for what he's done."

"And it is a bloody strong motive," sighed Bethancourt.

"It is that." Gibbons paused, considering his friend. "What would you have done, Phillip?"

"Done?" asked Bethancourt, puzzled.

"You're a rich man. What would you have done if your father threatened to cut you off?"

"It would be an idle threat at this point," mused Bethancourt. "The money from my portfolio is mine absolutely. But imagining, for the moment, that it was not . . ." He smoked thoughtfully and then shook his head. "It's silly to speculate. My father is not Geof-frey Berowne, and surely the relationship between father and son had just as much to do with the outcome as the threat itself. And even if that were not so, with Paul Berowne's example staring me in the face, I could hardly say I would choose as he did."

"No, of course not. It's just, well, my father has never had anything to give me besides his good opinion. I'd do a lot to keep that, but if I lost it, I wouldn't be out on the street."

"Oh, I imagine it was more than just the money," said Bethancourt. "Remember, Paul Berowne was living entirely in his father's world—his home was his father's home, his job was his father's job. A man defines himself, in a sense, by where he lives and what he does for a living. When Paul left, it was more than just money he left behind."

Amy Sullivan had said much the same thing, and Gibbons nodded. "Anyway," he said, "I'm to go down to Hurtwood Hall in the morning to talk with Maddie Wellman and Marion Berowne. Did you want to come? I can't imagine Carmichael would make any objections if you did."

"I'll come," said Bethancourt. "I take it there are no other leads at the moment? You never did tell me how the interviews with Mrs. Simmons's children went."

Gibbons waved a hand. "Nothing there. I admit, Phillip, that I was beginning to wonder where to look next when you rang this morning."

"And what about Mrs. Berowne?" asked Bethancourt. "What were you up to at Hurtwood Hall last night?"

Gibbons froze and his shocked silence told Bethancourt all he needed to know. His heart sank.

"Nothing," said Gibbons. "Just a bit of hand-holding."

"I see," said Bethancourt as neutrally as he could, knowing it was a mistake to have asked. The atmosphere between them was suddenly charged with tension.

"And what do you mean by that?" demanded Gibbons.

"Nothing at all," said Bethancourt, striving for an even tone. "Your hand-holding is none of my business."

But Gibbons's own guilt over what had so nearly occurred the night before had already put him on the defensive.

"For God's sake, Phillip," he burst out, "I don't know what you're implying. Surely you don't think I would be mad enough to start an affair with Annette."

"What does that matter?" retorted Bethancourt. "Do you think if lust was at the bottom of this I would be so concerned? Having sex doesn't mean you're in love and abstinence most assuredly doesn't mean you're not."

"Sex matters to most people," said Gibbons hotly. "It would certainly matter to the prosecuting attorney."

"I don't give a damn about the prosecuting attorney," said Bethancourt. "It's you I'm worried about."

"I see," said Gibbons coldly. "You still think she did it, even with what you uncovered about Berowne last night."

"I don't know if she did or not," answered Bethancourt. "But her motive remains just as strong as Paul Berowne's and there's no proof either way. And I have to say her actions strike me as suspicious." He regretted the words as soon as they left his mouth, but it was too late.

"What actions?" demanded Gibbons incredulously.

"Never mind," muttered Bethancourt.

But Gibbons was too intelligent not to work it out for himself. His blue eyes were frigid pools as he glared at his friend.

"So you think she's deliberately set out to ensnare me in order to make certain she's not arrested for murder. God, how ludicrous! Is it so impossible for you to believe that a pretty woman might be attracted to me?"

"Of course not," said Bethancourt. He had gone too far and knew it. "Look, Jack, I didn't mean to say that. I just think getting involved with a suspect is a bad idea, that's all."

"I'm not involved with her," Gibbons fairly shouted. "How often do I have to tell you? Yes, I'm attracted to her, but that means nothing and it is certainly not affecting my view of this case."

"All right," said Bethancourt wearily. "I don't want to be having this conversation. All I did was ask what you were doing there last night—it was you who flew off the handle."

"Only after you implied you believed I was sleeping with her."

"I didn't mean to."

Gibbons relapsed into silent fuming while Bethancourt drank off the rest of his beer and silently rose to fetch another from the bar. Gibbons's outburst had merely served to convince him that his friend was indeed deeply involved with Annette Berowne. The fact that he refused to admit it only made it worse, and far more dangerous. And his angry denial that he might have slept with Annette assured Bethancourt that he had thought of doing so, and not in some abstract fantasy. At some point, Bethancourt was sure, Gibbons had nearly taken the step that would lead to his downfall.

He brought two pints back to the table and said, "Look, Jack, I'm sorry. I didn't mean to imply that there was anything wrong with Annette, or that your mind wasn't on the case."

Gibbons rubbed his face. "I know you think I'm inexperienced with women," he said, "and maybe I am, at least compared with you. But I'm not stupid enough not to know when I'm being made use of. Annette and I get on together, that's all."

"You know I don't think you're stupid, not in any way at all," said Bethancourt.

There was an awkward silence. Gibbons broke it by sighing and saying, "In any case, it may all be over after Carmichael has a go at Berowne tomorrow. I've seen him crack tougher nuts than he."

Bethancourt raised his glass. "Let's drink to the chief inspector's success then," he said.

The conversation languished thereafter and when Bethancourt

suggested they move on and get some dinner, Gibbons refused the invitation, saying he had better get home.

Bethancourt cursed himself for a fool. He had known better than to interfere, but his concern for his friend had overridden his good sense. He had hoped, he supposed, that Gibbons would tell all, thereby allowing Bethancourt to judge how deliberate Annette's effort to get Gibbons into her bed had been. Despite what had been discovered about Paul Berowne, Bethancourt remained deeply suspicious of Annette.

He told himself as he lay in bed that night that he was overreacting; just because Gibbons looked to be chucking his much-beloved career away on this woman didn't mean she was guilty of murder. Paul Berowne was the chief suspect now, and with good reason. Probably he would confess tomorrow, and it would all be over.

Nevertheless, it was some time before he fell asleep.

Bethancourt was not sure that Gibbons would still want him along in the morning, but the detective rang shortly before ten to say he was starting for Surrey, and did Bethancourt still want to come?

"Of course I do," said Bethancourt. "Is Berowne at the Yard then?"

"Yes—Carmichael just rang me to say I could start. We'll take the Rover, if you don't mind, since I've already got it here."

"Fine. It will be fun to be chauffeured for a change."

But Gibbons was uncharacteristically silent on the trip down, driving steadily with his attention on the road.

"Thinking about what's happening back at the Yard?" asked Bethancourt finally.

Gibbons colored, which proved to Bethancourt he had been thinking nothing of the kind, and answered, "No. I was thinking about Maddie Wellman and Marion Berowne. I'm a little nervous, actually."

Bethancourt raised his eyebrows. "Why?" he asked. "You've interviewed dozens of witnesses before—why should these two make you nervous?"

"Because Carmichael would rather have done these himself," answered Gibbons. "God knows it's going to be delicate work, and I've not really taken this kind of thing on before. I'm just trying to think how Carmichael would have gone about it."

"You'll be brilliant," said Bethancourt with assurance. "Don't underestimate yourself. You're very good at your job."

"I suppose," said Gibbons, still worried. "Well, we're almost there now—time to screw my courage to the sticking point."

"I was a fool," said Marion Berowne bitterly. "I thought that since we had once been happy together, we could be happy again if only he would give up that woman. I thought it was my depression over the miscarriage that had driven him away, and with a new baby, things would be different." She gave a humorless laugh. "I couldn't have been more wrong."

She had not denied the story when it was presented to her, nor even asked why they should dredge it up. Instead, their questions had immediately plunged her into a gloom in which she seemed not to care what they asked.

"Then the reconciliation wasn't a success?" asked Gibbons.

"God, no. He never forgave me for not letting him go. Even Edwin—Paul seemed to resent him instead of caring for him." She drew a deep and ragged breath. "I've spent years regretting that I went to Geoffrey—but I was so sure then that we could be happy again."

"And yet you've stayed married?"

"What other choice was there? And there's not been much reason to fight for a divorce again. Paul and I have organized our lives so that there's very little time we have to spend together. What would be different if we divorced? I'd move into the main house, no doubt, but that's not very appealing with Annette there. I'm sure Paul thought the same."

"Then you were unaware," asked Gibbons gently, "that your husband had begun another affair?"

She was startled, and stared blankly at him for a moment.

"I don't think he was," she said shakily.

"We have testimony to that effect," said Gibbons.

"But he—oh, God."

Abruptly she broke down, leaning over the arm of the sofa with her face buried in her hands. Her crying was silent, but her shoulders shook with its force.

"Here." Bethancourt rose from his chair and seated himself beside her, slipping an arm about her and proffering his handkerchief. "We know it must be a shock," he said soothingly, "especially after the terrible experience you had before. Did you still love him after all, then?"

The handkerchief obscured her face, but she nodded ashamedly.

"I'd given up any hope," she said haltingly, the tears still running down her cheeks. "I knew it would never be good between us again. But I did still care."

Bethancourt patted her back.

"It's—it's not the same woman, is it?" she whispered and then hunched her shoulders as if she could not bear the answer.

"No," answered Gibbons, "not the same."

She let out her breath in a long, tremulous sigh and blew her nose.

"That's it," said Bethancourt. "Try to bear up."

"But," she gasped, "how will I ever face him tonight? I can't—I simply can't."

"That may not be a problem," said Gibbons slowly.

She looked at him questioningly, not understanding.

"Chief Inspector Carmichael has taken him in for questioning at New Scotland Yard," said Gibbons. "I don't know if he will be released tonight or not."

She couldn't grasp what he was telling her.

"Why?" she asked.

"You must see," said Bethancourt gently, "that this gives him a motive for murder."

She stared wildly at them. "But I thought Annette killed Geoffrey."

Gibbons bristled, but kept his voice calm. "There is some reason to believe Mrs. Berowne is innocent," he said.

"But I'm sure Paul wouldn't have hurt his father," she protested, tears filling her eyes again. "He wouldn't do something like that."

"Nothing's certain yet," said Gibbons. "You never suspected then that your husband might be guilty?"

She shook her head wildly. "No. I'm sure he isn't. He can't be."

There was clearly no more she could tell them, and they took their leave as soon as they could without seeming callous.

"I hope Miss Wellman doesn't cry," grumbled Gibbons as they made their way toward the main house. "I hate it when witnesses break down in tears."

"Oh, I don't think Maddie Wellman is the type to weep on your shoulder," said Bethancourt. "She's made of sterner stuff."

"Let's hope she'll be more helpful," said Gibbons. "I haven't got anything so far that you didn't already tell me. It would be nice if we could uncover an extra bit for Carmichael to spring on Berowne."

Mrs. Simmons opened the door to them and guided them up to Maddie's sitting room. Bethancourt wondered where Annette was, but was pleased that Gibbons did not ask.

"Back again, eh?" said Maddie as they came in. "I suppose you'll expect another meal."

"Not today, Miss Wellman," said Gibbons cheerfully. "I have orders from Chief Inspector Carmichael to speak to you and get back to Town as quick as I can."

"Then you'd better be at it," she answered. "Here, Mr. Bethancourt, pull up another chair for yourself. That one there will do. So what have you come about today?"

"Chief Inspector Carmichael," began Gibbons, "was wondering why you hadn't told him that Geoffrey Berowne had prevented his son's divorce."

"Why should I? It's ancient history." She dismissed the subject with a wave of her hand.

"So you don't feel that Paul bore his father any resentment for his actions?"

"Of course not. Paul acknowledged that it was his duty to try to reconcile with Marion in light of the baby on the way, and so it was."

"So you maintain that the reconciliation was effective?"

"Of course it was."

"Then why are they still so unhappy?" asked Gibbons mildly.

"They're not," she snapped.

"Really? Marion Berowne seems to feel quite differently. I haven't spoken with Paul yet, but he looks an unhappy man to me."

Being caught out did not seem to phase her in the least. "Marion likes to dramatize things," she said. "Every marriage has its rough spots."

"So that would, in your opinion, explain the affair Paul Berowne has been having? A rough spot in his marriage?"

She colored. "An affair? He can't have been."

"But he was, Miss Wellman."

"Not that Sullivan woman again?"

"No. We've spoken to Miss Sullivan, and she's not seen him since their breakup six years ago."

"It was all her fault, you know. She set her cap for him the minute they met." Maddie seemed almost eager to serve up the old news and steer their attention away from the present. "But he gave her up, you know, of his own accord."

"Yes. But only after his father threatened to disinherit him and fire him from his job."

"Geoffrey never did that!"

Her voice was shrill, her eyes giving away the lie.

"Two people say that he did," said Gibbons relentlessly. "Perhaps you'd like to correct us? Give us your version of events?"

She was sullen and did not answer at once. Then, "No," she said, "I wouldn't. Get out of here, both of you. Get out now. And you can tell your chief inspector the only way he'll speak to me again is down at the station with my solicitor present."

"Miss Wellman," began Gibbons persuasively, but she cut him off. "Get out!" she repeated.

There was nothing they could do but go.

"Hell," said Gibbons as they reached the top of the stairs. "I bloody well mucked that up."

"I can't see what else you could have done," said Bethancourt. "She was bound to be upset when you started pointing the finger at her beloved nephew."

Gibbons ran a harassed hand over his hair and grimaced. "The D.C.I. wouldn't have got himself tossed. And he's not going to be best pleased that I did."

Bethancourt considered briefly and decided against pointing out that Carmichael's forty years' experience gave him an authority that could not hope to be matched by a sergeant still in his twenties. Instead, he said thoughtfully, "Do you know, she was nearly frantic to shift your suspicions away from Paul."

"As you said, he's her beloved nephew." Gibbons gave him a sharp look. "You can't mean you think she knew he did it."

"No," answered Bethancourt. "She would have been prepared for this line of questioning in that case. But I was thinking it possible she had killed Geoffrey herself, knowing everyone would suspect Annette."

"Leave it to you to resurrect another suspect just as we're narrowing them down," grumbled Gibbons. "Still, I take your point. If

Carmichael brought her in and hammered it into her that he was going to charge Paul, she might break down and confess."

"Only if she did it," said Bethancourt. "Well, what now? Back to Town?"

"No," said Gibbons slowly, starting down the stairs. "I think we ought to try Mrs. Simmons."

Mrs. Simmons, however, was as taciturn as usual, replying only in monosyllables. She sat before them in the writing room like a frightened bird, her eyes darting around as if in search of escape. It did not matter how gentle Gibbons was with her, nor how tactfully he phrased his questions, she would do no more than agree with the story he sketched out. Bethancourt, taking pity on her and thinking she might be more at ease without both of them hovering over her, excused himself and waited out the rest of the interview in the hall.

He was standing there, leaning up against the wall and smoking, when Annette came down the stairs.

She looked very small and forlorn and for an instant, before she was aware of him, he felt a pang of pity for her. Then her head turned and she drew in a sharp breath, startled.

"Why, Mr. Bethancourt," she said, continuing down the stairs to meet him. "I didn't know you were here."

"I came down with Sergeant Gibbons," he replied, motioning toward the closed door of the writing room. "He's just speaking with Mrs. Simmons. I expect," he added, smiling, "he'll want you next."

She flushed, but her expression was eager.

"Has there been a development?"

"In a manner of speaking," said Bethancourt. "I think it would be best if you spoke to Jack—I really haven't any business being here at all, but this case has rather drawn me in."

"Oh, but I'm sure you're being a great help," she said, her eyes travelling to the writing room door as if willing it to open. "And we all appreciate it very much," she added, returning her attention to him.

"My contribution has been pretty minimal," he said. "But how are you? Are you bearing up under it all?"

Annette sighed. "It's been difficult," she said in a low voice, and her eyes strayed again to the implacably closed door.

Bethancourt studied her, groping for some clue as to what had occurred between she and Gibbons in her manner, but could discern nothing.

"Is Mrs. Simmons being helpful?" she asked. "She's awfully reserved, you know."

"It's why I came out," admitted Bethancourt. "I thought she might be more comfortable without both of us there."

"Perhaps," Annette agreed doubtfully. "It was kind of you to think of it."

Her eyes were back on him, but her whole being was focused on the writing room. On Gibbons's presence there, wondered Bethancourt, or on what Mrs. Simmons might be saying?

Yet when the door finally opened, she flinched back, coloring again and looking up through her lashes as Gibbons emerged.

He smiled warmly as he saw her, his eyes softening from their fierce concentration.

"I was just coming to speak with you," he said.

Her answering smile was a little uncertain, as if she feared a rebuff. "Mr. Bethancourt says there's been a development?" she asked hopefully.

"Yes," affirmed Gibbons. "If we could sit down somewhere . . ."

"Of course. Come into the drawing room."

She led the way back down the hall and into the room where they had first met her, settling herself on the couch and looking expectantly at Gibbons.

He sat beside her and, Bethancourt was almost sure, started to take her hand. Instead he stopped himself and turned the gesture into reaching for his notebook.

"This will be difficult for you to hear," he said gently, "and I want to stress that we're still far from making a case, but Chief Inspector Carmichael has brought Paul Berowne in for questioning."

"Paul?" she repeated doubtfully. "But I can't believe that Paul . . ."

"Tell me, Annette," continued Gibbons, "were you aware that a couple of years before your own marriage, Paul and Marion had wanted to divorce?"

"Yes, I knew," she said, a little bewildered by the change in subject.

"Did you know that it was Geoffrey who stopped them?"

"Of course," she replied. "He told me about it himself. But I don't see what that has to do with his death. It was years ago."

Gibbons frowned a little. "I'll explain," he said, "but first tell me what Geoffrey said."

"He told me Paul had been seeing another woman in London," she answered willingly enough, "and wanted a divorce. Marion was very upset—she hadn't realized what was going on—and for that alone, Geoffrey thought Paul ought to give the marriage another chance. Then it turned out that Marion was pregnant with Edwin and, well, I've told you how Geoffrey felt about children needing both parents. He eventually persuaded Paul to go to counseling and was very pleased when Paul and Marion patched things up, although he thought Paul rather resented his interference. But it all turned out well in the end."

Gibbons was frowning, clearly confounded by her answer. "Geoffrey didn't tell you how he had persuaded Paul to return?" he asked.

"Well, I suppose there were a lot of rows," she admitted.

"He didn't tell you that he had cut Paul off, fired him from his job, and was going to disinherit him?" asked Gibbons sharply.

Annette looked horrified. "No, Geoffrey would never do that."

"I'm afraid he did," answered Gibbons. "He was very determined that Paul should fulfill his responsibilities."

Annette bit her lip. "I know he didn't believe in divorce," she said in a small voice. "He did have strong opinions and a bit of a temper. Are you sure he didn't just say those things while he was angry?"

"I don't know," said Gibbons. "Perhaps that's how it was. But Paul did take him seriously. He left home for a time and as I understand it, Geoffrey did cut off his allowance."

Annette sighed and shook her head. "Geoffrey must have let his temper get the better of him. And if Paul took him at his word, I'm sure Geoffrey would have felt obliged to carry his threats out. But he would have relented in the end, I'm sure of that."

Neither Gibbons nor Bethancourt thought so, but there was no point in poisoning her husband's memory for her. They acquiesced with murmurs of agreement.

"Still," she said, "I can't see what it has to do with Geoffrey's murder. It seems a little odd to me that you think Paul would have waited all this time to take his revenge."

"Not revenge," said Gibbons. "Think—what would happen if Paul fell in love again?"

Her brown eyes went wide as realization struck. "And—was he in love?" she asked in a low voice.

"He was having an affair," said Gibbons. This time he did reach out and pat her shoulder. "We'll see what he has to say for himself. This may yet all blow over—there's still very little to build a case on. But now I want you to think very carefully. Did you never suspect Paul might be guilty?"

"I suppose I've thought that of everyone at one time or another," she said, "but only because I knew it had to be one of us. No, I never really believed it could be Paul. Although," she added slowly, "I have thought how odd it was that Paul didn't go into work that morning. I remember another time, last year, when something went wrong with his car and he made a big fuss about being late for work. He finally took one of the other cars and Geoffrey said how silly he was to be so attached to the BMW."

"I see," said Gibbons. "But even though you thought that odd, you never seriously considered it might be Paul?"

"No," she said a little bitterly. "After all, it's just as odd that I should walk to the village instead of driving."

"Now, we've been over all that, Annette," said Gibbons kindly. "You mustn't torture yourself with it. You've been very helpful. We'll just have a word with Kitty, and then I'm afraid I've got to get back to London. But I'll let you know how things go."

Once again Bethancourt was left feeling confounded with Annette Berowne as they took their leave of her and made their way to the kitchen. If she was in love with Gibbons, she had shown very little sign of it to his mind, and yet she had seemed very sincere when she had declared she had never considered her stepson a serious suspect. Perhaps, he thought to himself, he had got it all wrong. Perhaps she did not care for Gibbons, had no intention of seducing him, and was innocent of murder as well. It was a happy thought, but one which he could not bring himself to place much confidence in.

The interview room was bare and clinical, a room for facts, although Carmichael had heard more fabrications than facts here in his thirty-six years with the Yard.

He set the tape recorder going and regarded the man who had become his prime suspect with shrewd eyes. Paul Berowne was not a fool; he knew that his summons here boded ill for him, and yet he had not demanded a solicitor and Carmichael wondered why. He sat quietly on the opposite side of the table, his hands still in his lap, and watched Carmichael expectantly. If he was nervous, he did not show it.

"I'd like to go over the morning of the murder again," began Carmichael. "You said, I believe, that you took a walk?"

"Yes," answered Paul.

"Did you remain on the estate the entire time?"

"Yes."

"You did not, for instance, walk into the village? Perhaps stop at the pub?"

The ghost of a smile touched Berowne's lips. "You've spoken to Mira," he said quietly. Deep in his eyes was surprise. Not, thought Carmichael, surprise at the betrayal, for he had expected that, but surprise at how, even thus prepared, it still hurt.

"Yes," agreed Carmichael, "we have. Her story of the morning differs from yours at several points, Mr. Berowne."

"I think," answered Berowne dryly, "you can easily see why. However, there's no point in trying to cover things up. I did lie to you, Chief Inspector. Whatever Mira's told you is the truth."

"I would still like to have your version."

"Very well." Now that he had been discovered, Berowne seemed impatient. "The morning began just as I told you. Once I had phoned the office, I also phoned Mira and asked if I could come by. She wasn't awake yet and said to give her an hour to pull herself together. So," his lips quirked in a sardonic smile, "I took a walk around the estate. I must have gotten to the pub at about half nine, perhaps a little after."

"And what was the reason for your visit?"

"You know. I had gone to bed with Mira the night before and I was afraid Ken Mills, our chauffeur, had seen me leaving. I wanted to let Mira know so that she wouldn't be at a loss if it suddenly became common knowledge."

"Was this an affair of long standing?"

"No. We had slept together once before, that's all."

Carmichael's blue eyes were intent. "So your chief concern that morning was that Mira Fellows should not be taken unawares by gossip."

"That's right. Once I'd spoken to her, I returned to the estate to see how Mills was coming with the car. I was there when Maddie rang down with the news about my father."

His tone was perfectly normal, even disinterested and his eyes gave nothing away.

"Weren't you just the least bit worried about how your father would take the news of your affair?" asked Carmichael.

Paul Berowne regarded him gravely for a long moment. "Why should I have been?" he asked quietly.

"You would do far better, Mr. Berowne," said Carmichael severely, "to stop playing games with me and answer as forthrightly as you can. I ask you again, did you not fear your father's reaction to the news that you had been having an affair?"

Berowne let his eyes drop and moved restlessly in his chair. "I rather hoped he wouldn't find out," he said. "Mills certainly wouldn't go to him with it—he's not that sort of man. And it was perfectly possible that I had been mistaken and Mills hadn't seen me at all."

This was not a forthright answer, but Carmichael chose to ignore the fact. "Yet you were concerned enough to warn Miss Fellows."

"It wouldn't have been right not to."

"And if you were not mistaken, and the news became common knowledge in the village, did you really think your father wouldn't hear of it?"

"In that case, I suppose he eventually would."

"And what do you think he would have done then?"

Berowne shrugged.

"Did you have any reason to believe his reaction would be any different than it was the last time you committed adultery?"

Berowne flinched at the bald words and paled, but he did not lose his composure. "No," he answered.

"So what did you plan to do, Mr. Berowne, when he did find out and you lost your job and were disinherited?"

"I had no plans."

"Perhaps because you had taken steps to ensure you wouldn't need any?"

"No," said Berowne flatly.

"Surely facing all that again must have been a rather galling prospect."

A faint, humorless smile touched Berowne's lips. "I'm long past feeling galled by anything, Chief Inspector."

"Really? Even murder?"

Berowne started to reply and then closed his mouth tightly in a thin line.

"Let's see." Carmichael consulted the papers on the table before him. "It was six years ago, wasn't it, that you left your wife and moved in with Amy Sullivan? How long was it before you returned?"

"Five months."

"And why did you come back, Mr. Berowne?"

"Because I discovered Amy and I were not well-suited and I began to believe I had acted hastily."

"Ah, so it wasn't because you couldn't find another job."

"No."

His voice was very low and Carmichael knew he was lying.

"What was wrong with Miss Sullivan?" he asked conversationally.

"Nothing was wrong with her. She and I just didn't get on when we had to be together all the time, that's all."

"So you thought you might as well return to your wife, whom you no longer loved. That's a rather exceptional attitude, Mr. Berowne."

Berowne hesitated. "It seemed the right thing to do," he said. "Having been disappointed a second time in love, it didn't seem worthwhile to go on looking. And I was fond of Marion."

"Of course. Earlier you mentioned your walk around the estate. Do you know very much about plants and trees?"

Berowne, though obviously relieved at the change of subject, nevertheless found it difficult to change gears so abruptly.

"I know something," he said. "I'm not an expert like McAllister but I know a bit."

"How about flowers, Mr. Berowne? Do you know much about them?"

"I know most of the ones that grow on the estate. I suppose, if McAllister suddenly gave notice, I could keep them pruned and alive if I had to." He was clearly at a loss as to Carmichael's purpose and spread his hands. "Are you suggesting, Chief Inspector, that five years ago I should have become a gardener?"

"Of course not, Mr. Berowne. I was merely interested in your horticultural knowledge. Are you fond, for instance, of lilies of the valley?"

Berowne seemed honestly bewildered by this question, and if he was dissembling, Carmichael could not tell.

"They're very pretty," he answered rather helplessly.

Carmichael leaned back in his chair. "Our neighbors," he said conversationally, "planted some oleander last year. That's pretty, too. Have you ever seen it?"

"Yes," answered Berowne. "We haven't any on the estate, but I've seen it elsewhere. It is, as you say, very attractive."

Carmichael was shaking his head. "Their cat got into it, though."

"Did it? We've never had a problem with pets—my father was allergic and we never had any."

"Ah, so then likely you wouldn't know."

"Know what?"

"That oleander is poisonous. The cat died."

There was a long pause. Berowne watched his interrogator warily.

"No," he said softly at last, "I didn't know."

"So your knowledge of plants and flowers doesn't reach to which ones are poisonous and which aren't?"

"No, it doesn't."

"I wouldn't like to have you in the garden, then. You might plant the lettuce next some nightshade."

"I know about that, of course," said Berowne impatiently. "Everyone knows about that one. It's been used in dozens of mystery stories."

"So it has," agreed Carmichael, who never read the genre. "Your father was fond of mysteries, I believe."

"Yes, he was. I like them, too, or I used to do. He and I used to share them."

There was something terribly sad in Berowne's tone.

"But not of late?" suggested Carmichael gently. "Not in the last five years or so?"

Berowne only shook his head.

"How did you feel," asked Carmichael, "when your father tried to end your relationship with Amy Sullivan?"

"I was angry, of course." But his tone was utterly devoid of emotion. "And hurt. I didn't realize until then that I'd never stood up for myself before. There were so many times I wanted something different, but I always went along with what he suggested. Not because he forced me, but because his suggestions were always sensible and it seemed unreasonable to object. I was . . . shocked, I suppose is the word, to see what happened when I refused."

"So you made up your mind to do without him."

"I suppose." He straightened and met Carmichael's eyes. "But it has nothing to do with this case, Chief Inspector. The two situations are completely different. I wanted to divorce my wife and marry Amy Sullivan, or I thought I did. I gave in to weakness and slept with Mira twice, but there was no question of marriage. Mira isn't in love with me and she wouldn't have me if I offered. My father could hardly threaten to disinherit me if I didn't break it off with Mira when there was nothing to break off to begin with."

"It's true that you'd only slept with her twice before your father was murdered," agreed Carmichael, "and I suppose that hardly constitutes a full-blown affair. But that's changed since he died, hasn't it? You've spent many nights with her since then. You can hardly expect me to believe your desire for her company would have dissipated had your father lived." Berowne only shook his head in reply.

"Let's move on," said Carmichael, leaning back in his chair. "Miss Fellows says you left her at about ten-thirty, perhaps a few minutes later. Would you agree with that?"

"Yes, I expect that's about right."

"And yet it was nearly noon when you returned to the garage. I doubt it took you an hour and a half to walk back to the estate, Mr. Berowne."

"No, of course not. I was a little upset after I spoke to Mira and I didn't want Mills to see anything was wrong. So I stopped at the house and got a cup of coffee before going on to the garage, just as I told you I had."

"Ah, so that bit was true as well, was it?"

"I didn't actually lie, Chief Inspector," said Berowne. "I simply omitted any mention of my visit to Mira. Everything else occurred exactly as I told you."

"I see," said Carmichael, pretending to consult his notes, although Paul Berowne's earlier statement was engraved on his memory. "Yes, you said your wife had already gone upstairs with Edwin, and you heard Mrs. Simmons hoovering in the living room, which was why neither of them saw you. But you didn't mention the time. It was a long cup of coffee, Mr. Berowne. By the account you're giving me now, you sat over that cup for nearly an hour."

"As I said, I was upset."

"Why? Did you and Miss Fellows argue?"

"No, nothing like that."

"You were upset, perhaps, at the idea that you couldn't see her again and that, in fact, it would be wise if you were to abandon your habit of spending the evenings at the pub altogether?"

Berowne said nothing at first and then, in a moment, he nodded.

"And surely you must have been at least a little concerned that these precautions were coming too late, that your father might find out about it all in any case?"

This time Berowne refused to reply at all.

"And if he did, what could be done? You'd already failed out on your own; it's hardly likely it would be any different this time. You'd truly backed yourself into a corner. I don't imagine you would have killed him if you had seen any other way out."

"I didn't kill him."

"I think you did, Mr. Berowne. I think you sat over your coffee until you'd worked yourself up to it and then you went to the study and poisoned his coffee. Or perhaps I'm wrong. Perhaps you thought of all this on your walk back from the village, and went straight to your father's study. And then you had the coffee to calm yourself down before you had to face Mills."

Berowne was staring down at his hands and made no reply.

CHAPTER

12

"loody hell!" shouted Gibbons.

He was alone in his office at the end of a very long day, having just left an equally weary and frustrated Carmichael. Paul Berowne had not confessed.

The most harrowing experiences of Berowne's personal life had been probed to their depths and at this point the man was an emotional wreck, but he still insisted he had not killed his father. In the afternoon, as the interrogation had become ever more torturous, he had finally asked for his solicitor, but even with the man present they had kept at it until well past dinnertime. Carmichael had given up then, telling Gibbons he would speak to Berowne again in the morning, but that there was little hope of a confession then and after that they would have no choice but to let him go.

Gibbons kicked viciously at the legs of his desk and swore again. He was certain Berowne was guilty; he was the only suspect whose situation had recently changed—all the rest of them had been putting up with their unhappy circumstances for years. And yet, he had also been certain that Berowne was essentially a weak man who would crack under Carmichael's expert interrogation. He didn't like the thought that his judgment of the man had been so wrong.

Caught up in the tension of the day-long interrogation, he had not realized until now how much he had been looking forward to reporting to Annette tonight that it was over, they had their man, and no one would any longer believe her guilty of murdering her husband. Now he would have to tell her that all their efforts had failed.

It never entered his head that he would not go and prepare her for Berowne's release in the morning, although he would not have considered such a thing in another case. He would, he decided, go home and shower before he drove down.

"What on earth's wrong with you, Phillip?" demanded Marla exasperatedly. "You haven't heard a word I've been saying."

They were in a taxi on the way to a charity ball and Marla was in a very testy mood. Attendance at the ball was mandatory for Bethancourt because it was one of his sister's charities and he would never have heard the end of it if he had not appeared. Previously he had avoided taking Marla to such affairs, since he did not look forward to the reception she would receive from Margaret, but he had known he could not avoid the meeting indefinitely.

Marla, although she would rather have died than admit it, was nervous at the thought of meeting the Sinclair-Firthings. To ameliorate this, she was splendidly dressed in green satin and Bethancourt had been extremely complimentary. But now he seemed distracted and was clearly paying her no attention at all.

"I did hear you," replied Bethancourt automatically. "You said it rained nearly all the time you were in Ireland."

"But you aren't thinking about it," said Marla, unappeased. "What *are* you thinking about?"

"Jack and his new lady-love. I think he's truly head over heels."

"What of it? They'll go out for a while, she'll throw him over, and it will be done. God knows it's not pleasant, but it's hardly earth-shattering. It happens all the time."

There was nothing else Bethancourt could say without referring to the murder investigation, whose existence he had thus far managed to keep from her. Even if he was going to tell her about it, now, when she was tense, was hardly an opportune moment.

"Quite right," he said. "I don't know why it's got me down this way."

"We're here," announced Marla, dropping the subject abruptly. "Do try to pull yourself together, Phillip."

Bethancourt succeeded in this tolerably well, although the evening was difficult. Marla was not pleased with the reception given her by Margaret, which was exquisitely polite and lacking in any warmth whatsoever. Fashion models did not belong to the social strata to which Margaret aspired. Arthur Sinclair-Firthing was more admiring and Marla exerted all her charms on him, which did not go unnoticed by Margaret. Before they had been there an hour, Bethancourt had a headache.

"I do hope, Phillip," said Margaret acidly as he guided her around the dance floor, "that you are planning to take her with you when you leave. I don't want to have to detach Arthur from her myself."

Bethancourt glanced over to where Marla and Arthur were dancing, admittedly closer than was strictly necessary.

"I'll take care of it," he murmured. "I'll collect her after this dance."

"Good."

"I don't see Marion Berowne here," said Bethancourt. "Isn't she on the committee?"

"Yes, but there's been a death in her family—" Margaret cut herself off and looked at him suspiciously. "Which you know perfectly well," she continued, blue eyes narrowing. "I thought it odd when

Denis said you'd taken him to the Berownes, but I didn't take the time to put two and two together. This is one of those cases you're meddling in, isn't it?"

"My friend Jack Gibbons is working on it, yes."

"My God, Phillip, and you dragged my five-year-old son into the middle of it? What on earth possessed you?"

"He was hardly in the middle of anything," protested Bethancourt. "He spent the day playing soldiers with Edwin, who, I should have thought, is a perfectly acceptable playmate."

"And who was watching them while you were grilling suspects?"

"Jack was grilling suspects, not me," answered Bethancourt, not entirely truthfully. "I stayed with Denis."

The music ended before she could reply, and Bethancourt gratefully led her off the floor. Marla was making her way toward the ladies' room, so he returned his sister to her husband and melted away into the crowd.

"You dance beautifully, Phillip," said Rosemary Chilton. "I only wish Dick would do as well. He's perfectly happy to come along, but he won't step a foot on the dance floor."

Rosemary Chilton, reflected Bethancourt, was also on the committee, in addition to being an inveterate gossip.

"Then won't you let me?" he responded, offering his hand.

She accepted with a smile.

"It's a wonderful evening," said Bethancourt, clasping her firmly about the waist and falling into step with the music. "You've all surpassed yourselves."

"It has come off rather well, hasn't it?" agreed Rosemary. "Though it's been a madhouse in the last fortnight. Poor Marion Berowne broke down completely and suddenly couldn't do anything."

"Really?" asked Bethancourt. "Where is she tonight? I haven't seen her."

"Oh, my dear, she isn't here. We've hardly seen her for the last two weeks. Nancy Clarendon may say what she likes, but I think it's that miserable husband of hers."

"Has she a miserable husband? I don't think I've met him."

"Perfectly dreadful man," Rosemary assured him. "Not unattractive, mind you, but the way he treats her, well!"

Bethancourt pretended to be aghast. "He doesn't beat her, does he?"

"Oh, no, nothing of that sort," said Rosemary. "But when Marion was pregnant, he went off and had an affair and even tried to divorce her before the baby was born."

"Presumably he came to his senses before the blessed event?" asked Bethancourt, curious as to how the affair had been seen from the outside.

"The way I heard it, Paul only went back to poor Marion because his father threatened to cut him off without a penny if he didn't."

"But why would she want him back on those terms?"

Rosemary shrugged. "Hormones, probably—she was pregnant after all."

"But surely that's all water under the bridge by now."

"It would be if they'd ever made it up properly. Marion tries to put the best face possible on it, but when she does manage to drag him out to affairs like this, they barely speak to each other. He could at least pretend—it's so terribly obvious to everyone."

"There's no excuse for bad manners," agreed Bethancourt. "But surely she could have come tonight without him?"

But something else had caught Rosemary's attention. She stiffened suddenly in his arms and stared daggers at someone past his left shoulder. Bethancourt turned his head and saw Marla dancing with Sir Rodney Randolph. He smiled to himself. Randolph, darkly handsome and very charming, was notorious for having affairs with other men's wives and for successfully conducting several of these affairs simultaneously. Bethancourt did not like him, but he felt Marla was perfectly safe from his blandishments. She would not know of his reputation, but she dealt regularly with the attentions of men who were looking for trophies and was not likely to mistake Randolph's intentions.

Rosemary Chilton was another matter. Bethancourt had been joking the other morning when he had suggested to his sister that Rosemary might be Randolph's latest conquest, but now his words came home to roost. From the look on her face, it was quite obviously true, and if looks could kill, Marla would have ceased living in the last few seconds.

"I see Rodney has found my girlfriend," he said.

"Oh, did she come with you?" said Rosemary with a strained effort to be casual. "She's very pretty."

"I think so," said Bethancourt. "Lucky for me that Rodney's not her type. She's a model, you know, and sees all too much of perfect looks like his." He grinned. "That's why she's dating me."

Rosemary relaxed a little, though not entirely. Knowing that Randolph's charms would fail with Marla was not the same as knowing he wasn't trying. But she smiled back at him and said, "Are you fishing for compliments, Phillip? I wouldn't have thought it of you."

"Not at all," protested Bethancourt. "And just to prove it, I'll return to our previous topic of conversation. If I can remember what it was."

"Marion Berowne," supplied Rosemary. "You were asking why she wasn't here tonight. Nancy Clarendon says it's delayed shock over that business with her father-in-law, though Marion was simply a trooper right after it happened."

"Her father-in-law? Has he forbidden her to go to balls like Cinderella's stepmother?"

Rosemary giggled. "No, hush, it's not funny at all. The man was murdered."

"What?" Bethancourt appeared surprised. "Oh, Lord, of course.

The Geoffrey Berowne case. I've seen it in the papers, but I never connected it with Marion Berowne. Stupid of me."

"They say the wife did it," confided Rosemary.

"Really?" said Bethancourt. "From what you've been telling me, I should have thought the son was a good candidate."

"You really shouldn't make fun," said Rosemary, giggling again. "It's quite serious. And just because a man's a rotten husband doesn't mean he's a murderer."

Which, thought Bethancourt, was quite true.

He recaptured Marla from Randolph as the dance ended and found her in need of refreshment.

"I need a drink," she declared. "And to sit down. My feet are killing me."

"In those shoes, no wonder," said Bethancourt sympathetically. "Go on into the next room and I'll fetch the drinks."

But when he brought her champagne, he found her surrounded by half a dozen men and it was all he could do to push through and deliver her glass. She showed no immediate desire to be rescued, so he slipped away to find a quiet corner in which to telephone Gibbons.

"Quite the belle of the ball."

Bethancourt, emerging from the crowd, turned and saw Randolph beside him.

"It does seem that way," he agreed blandly.

Randolph turned away from his contemplation of Marla and scanned the crowd. "Have you seen Margaret?" he asked. "I was looking for her."

"Not since the last dance," answered Bethancourt and was about to excuse himself when Randolph continued, "She's a fine-looking woman, your sister."

His tone was that of a man admiring his possession, both smug and fond. If Bethancourt had not known better, he would have assumed Randolph and Margaret were sleeping together, and he was correspondingly infuriated.

"As her brother, you'll have to excuse me from commenting," he said coolly. "Speaking of looking for people, Rosemary was asking for you a little while ago. I think that's her, over there."

Randolph looked suddenly a little uncomfortable, and Bethancourt smiled and slipped away on his errand.

He found some quiet in the building's lobby and dialed Gibbons's number on his mobile phone. His friend's description of the day's interrogation had been abbreviated since he had rung while Bethancourt was dressing for the ball, and Bethancourt was eager for more details. But although it was now past eleven, Gibbons did not answer his phone.

Gibbons, showered and changed and fed, had taken out a police Rover and driven down to Hurtwood Hall. He had by no means forgotten the events of two nights ago, but he was so distracted by the bad news he had to deliver that he never thought of how his arrival there, at this time of night, might be misinterpreted.

Annette smiled warmly at him, her brown eyes alight, and reached out to touch his arm as she ushered him in.

"I'm so glad you came," she said.

"I wanted to give you what news there is," he answered.

"Of course," she said. "Come and sit down."

But her smile did not fade as she led the way down the hall to a little sitting room. She had obviously been spending the evening here: a television in the corner was tuned to a game show and a half-finished drink stood on an end table beside an armchair. She used the remote to flick off the television while he sat on the love seat opposite the chair, unsure of how to begin.

"Would you like a drink?" she asked.

"That would be wonderful," said Gibbons.

She turned to the drinks cabinet and then gave a little laugh. "How funny," she said, turning back. "I don't know what you like."

"Scotch, if you've got it."

"Of course we do."

"I'm afraid the news isn't good," said Gibbons, taking the plunge. "I'm sorry, Annette. We weren't able to get a confession from Paul. He'll be released in the morning."

Her face sobered as she handed him his drink and, picking up her own glass from the end table, sat beside him.

"Do you still believe he did it, then?" she asked.

"Yes." Gibbons took a swallow of the whisky and felt some of the tension ease out of his muscles. "But it means digging for more evidence—we can't make a case as things stand."

She looked troubled. "I've been thinking, since you left this morning, that you must be right," she said slowly. "Paul meant so much to Geoffrey that I hate to believe he would have hurt him, but all day I've been remembering the arguments they had. I always saw them from Geoffrey's point of view. Even when he was furious with Paul, Geoffrey always loved him, and it never occurred to me that Paul might not feel the same. But now, thinking back on the look in his eyes, on some of what he said, I think I was wrong."

"It isn't pleasant to see beneath people's masks," said Gibbons. "I'm sorry you had to be put through this."

"It hasn't been any more pleasant for you," she said. "You must have had an awful day. You look so tired."

"It was a bit grueling," admitted Gibbons, swallowing more of his Scotch. "But it's my job, after all."

"Well, at least you can relax now," she said. "Here, I'll top up your drink."

Gibbons let her, although he knew he was going to be driving back to London shortly. He could not resist the comfortable languor that was stealing over him.

"There," she said, handing the glass back to him.

"Thanks." He smiled at her. "You're taking it very well," he said.

"I'm afraid I wasn't so restrained. I'd been so looking forward to giving you good news for a change."

Her answering smile was warm and she reached out to lay the back of her hand against his cheek.

With a shock, Gibbons realized she believed because he had come himself, rather than phoning, he was there to pick up where they had left off two nights ago. He cursed himself for a fool.

Setting his drink aside, he captured her hand and said, as gently as he could, "Annette, no. I didn't come for this."

She reddened at once, snatching her hand away, the hurt and embarrassment plain to be seen in her eyes.

"No, of course not. I'm sorry."

She rose and turned away from him and he stared at her back, not knowing how to put things right.

"Annette," he said at last, "it's not that I don't care for you. I do, very much."

"I know," she answered, facing him again and trying for a smile that did not quite succeed. "It's all right."

But in her eyes he saw the same doubt he had seen two nights ago, when she had asked if he believed in her innocence.

"I don't think you know what you're asking of me," he said, desperate to make her understand.

"I'm not," she said. "Please. It was just a misunderstanding. I'm very grateful you came to tell me about Paul. It was very good of you."

He stared at her for a long moment, and then, not knowing what else he could say, he accepted her effort to put the conversation back on a normal footing.

"Not at all," he said, and rose. "I'd better be getting back."

"Yes, it's getting very late. Thank you again for coming."

Gibbons left her at the door with a polite good night, and walked slowly across the gravel drive to his car, his thoughts in turmoil. She didn't seem to understand his position at all, but of course she had been badly hurt and couldn't be thinking clearly. And he had no choice but to leave her with her trust in him broken, because the price of her trust was too high. It would come right in the end, after they'd solved the case.

He leaned his forehead against the cool roof of the car. He didn't really believe it would come right. Once her innocence had been proven in open court, he could never prove he believed in it now. And if he didn't love her enough to demonstrate it now, she would never accept it later. She would always wonder at his motives, would never be sure the feeling he offered her was genuine.

He was shaking as he strode back and rang the bell a second time. Annette, when she opened the door, looked surprised. But before she could say anything, he reached out and took her in his arms, searching out her lips with his own. She responded eagerly, pressing against him and wrapping her arms about his neck.

"I love you," he said. "Nothing else matters."

"I love you, too," she said.

Dottie Carmichael took one look at her husband's face and knew it had been a bad day.

"I've kept some supper warm for you," she said. "You get yourself a beer while I serve it up."

Carmichael did not feel very hungry, but experience had taught him Dottie's opinion of a canteen sandwich for supper, so he acquiesced with a smile.

"That's good of you, dear. I'm fair worn out."

He got a bottle from the refrigerator and settled himself at the kitchen table while she bustled about the stove.

"I thought we would crack it today," said Carmichael, pouring the beer into the glass set ready for him. "It all seemed set to me."

"Paul Berowne? Did you bring him in for questioning today?"

"That we did."

Dottie set a plate of stew and some bread before him on the little kitchen table and then sat down opposite him with her tea. Carmichael speared a piece of carrot and frowned at it.

"I thought he'd confess," he said. "I've told you about him, Dottie—he's always struck me as a weak man. I believed from the beginning that if he was guilty and we could bring any pressure at all to bear on him, he'd break down."

"You're a good judge of character," said Dottie. "As you should be, after all these years. You're not often mistaken about people."

"No," agreed Carmichael, eating the carrot.

"But he didn't confess?"

"No. And is that because I was wrong in my judgment of him, or because he truly isn't guilty?"

"I don't know, dear. What evidence was there against him?"

Carmichael told her what Bethancourt had discovered and described his interview with Berowne in detail.

"I was right in part, at least," he concluded. "Berowne isn't arrogant at all. So many rich men are, and that was what I expected of him before we met. And when I heard about his past, it only confirmed the impression I'd had of him."

Dottie was thoughtful. "But he's an intelligent man?" she asked.

"Oh, yes."

"Then surely he could see you hadn't really any evidence against him. Perhaps, having made this bid for freedom, he's grown a little more backbone. Enough, at least, to hold out against you."

"I can't say he showed much evidence of backbone today," said Carmichael. "It was all very harrowing, and he appeared truly agonized about having the whole story dredged up and gone over with a fine-toothed comb. I would have said all the spirit had been beaten out of the man long ago. But if that's so, then why didn't he confess?"

"You think he's innocent," said Dottie.

"I don't know what to think."

"Well, who else do you suspect?"

Carmichael sighed. "All of them," he answered. "I'm almost certain it wasn't one of the servants, but any of the family might have done it. Next to Berowne, the widow's got the best motive. On the other hand, Gibbons's instincts are telling him that she's innocent, and why should I act on my own instinct and ignore his?"

"Because," said Dottie, smiling, "you've more than twice the experience that he has. Sergeant Gibbons is still a very young man, and didn't you tell me Mrs. Berowne was an attractive woman?"

"I don't think Gibbons would be swayed by that."

"Young men are idealistic," said Dottie. "They don't like to think that pretty women could be murderers, not if they've got another suspect who will do just as well."

Carmichael laughed, his spirits suddenly lifting. "I don't know if Paul Berowne murdered his father or not," he said, "but I do know I couldn't get on without you, Dottie. Let's go to bed and I'll see what it all looks like after a good night's sleep."

"You are impossible!" fumed Marla. "I can't believe you've been sneaking around for the past fortnight and *lying* to me about it."

"I haven't been lying," said Bethancourt mildly, though inwardly he was cursing his luck. "I just didn't bring it up. You know you loathe talking about murder investigations."

"I hate your sneaking around behind my back even more!"

The Berowne murder had naturally been a chief topic of speculation at the ball, but how exactly Marla had divined his own involvement, Bethancourt was not sure. She was furious, though, and he had ushered her out as quickly as he could, if not as quietly as he would have wished.

"I do wish you wouldn't refer to it as 'sneaking,'" he said. "I have not been sneaking. I have not broken any dates with you. I did not refuse to spend Saturday teaching you to ride. In fact, I have spent exactly as much time with you as I would have had there been no case."

"Yes, but you were thinking about it all the time."

"Obviously not. If I had been, you would have noticed."

"I did notice—" Marla broke off and stood stock-still, her jade eyes widening. "Jack's girlfriend!" she exclaimed. "*That's* what you're so worried about. She's involved in the case."

"The prime suspect, in fact."

Marla's mercurial temper swung abruptly out of the red.

"And do you believe she did it?"

"I don't know whether she did or not. That's the trouble."

"But . . ." Marla frowned. "Isn't dating a murderess going to be terrible for his career?"

Bethancourt shot her a humorless grin. "Death for his career," he affirmed.

"But he's always been so keen on his work. Or," she added dubiously, "does he imagine he can keep it secret?"

"He's a fool if he does," said Bethancourt bitterly. "The man has no idea of discretion. He went down there the other evening and left an unmarked police car parked out front."

Marla giggled. "He didn't really?"

"Yes, he did. And it's not funny."

"It is, rather."

Bethancourt ignored this. "It could be even worse if she's innocent," he said grimly. "Can you imagine what a barrister for the defense would make of an investigating officer who was in love with his prime suspect and ended up arresting someone else?"

"Dear God," breathed Marla, "it could make the front page of the tabloids."

"Almost guaranteed to," agreed Bethancourt glumly.

Marla put her head to one side and considered. "But if she's guilty, as you seem to think, it would work in his favor. Arresting the woman he loves is certain proof of his belief of her guilt. In fact, the defense wouldn't dare bring it up at all and there would be no point in the prosecution bringing it in."

"Public humiliation would be averted," agreed Bethancourt. "But it would still ruin his career—Scotland Yard frowns on its officers becoming involved with murder suspects. The only hope is to get it all wrapped up quickly before things get out of hand. Which doesn't look like happening. They pulled in the murdered man's son today, but Carmichael failed to get a confession out of him."

"Well, naturally," said Marla. "Why should the man confess if there's the slightest chance he could get off? *I* wouldn't."

"You'd be surprised how many people do, though," said Bethancourt reflectively.

"Well, they're idiots, that's all. So, has he slept with her yet?"

"Who, Jack? No, I think not, but it's only a matter of time."

"That's all right then," said Marla. "They can't fire him for thinking about it. He's just got to keep himself under control. Phillip, why are we walking? There were plenty of taxis back there and my feet hurt."

"Of course," said Bethancourt, who had not hailed a taxi at once upon emerging from the hall because he knew Marla would have refused to share it with him, thereby giving him no chance to calm her down. "I wasn't thinking. I'll get one now."

Gibbons awoke from a sound sleep and was instantly alarmed. He hadn't meant to sleep at all, but after a long day, two drinks, and making love twice, he had dropped off in spite of himself. A glance at the clock reassured him: it was not yet 3:30 A.M. There was still plenty of time to slip out quietly.

Annette was asleep beside him, curled up like a kitten, but she stirred and woke when he eased out of the bed. He smiled down at her.

"I was trying not to wake you," he said.

"Where are you going?" she asked sleepily.

"I have to leave," he said regretfully. "I must be back in London before morning and we can't risk anyone seeing me go."

"I know," she said. "But I wish you weren't going."

"So do I."

She sat up to watch him dress. "Will I see you tomorrow?"

"I don't know," he answered. "I don't think I had better come down unless Carmichael sends me. But I'll ring you."

"Good. Kiss me good-bye, then."

Gibbons grinned. "I always meant to."

He kissed her lingeringly, but broke it off before the kiss could turn into anything else, knowing he absolutely had to leave. He closed the bedroom door silently behind him and felt his way down the stairs in the dark. He let himself out the front door and took a deep breath of the chill night air. It had been foolish, he realized, to leave the car in so conspicuous a spot. Maddie Wellman's rooms were at the back of the house, but what about Mrs. Simmons? Well, with any luck she had stayed asleep. The next time, he must remember to park down by the gate and walk to the house from there.

It was that thought that stopped him cold, the full realization of what he had done washing over him. He had told Annette that nothing but love mattered, only now he found that it did. He sat in the car limply, staring at the steering wheel. He should go to Carmichael, confess everything, and ask to be taken off the case. But that would end his career as surely as being found out would. They wouldn't fire him, but any hope he might have of promotion would be gone forever, and he had worked hard to ensure that he would rise in the ranks as quickly as possible. He could not quite face the fact that he had just thrown all that away.

The Rover's engine made a terrific noise in the quiet of the night as he started it up, and it seemed to him that the crunch of the gravel beneath the wheels was enough to wake the entire neighborhood. He left the headlamps off and glanced uneasily back at the house as he started down the drive, but the windows remained dark.

CHAPTER

13

"Where on earth have you been, lad?"

Carmichael's voice was more surprised than angry, but Gibbons flinched nonetheless. He had never been late to the office before—at least, not while there was a case on—and felt it keenly.

"I'm sorry, sir," he said, rather stiffly. "There's no excuse; I simply overslept."

Carmichael eyed his sergeant, who looked hollow-eyed and defeated. He had seen Gibbons looking better after spending most of the night at work, and said so.

"Yes, sir. I just couldn't seem to get to sleep."

And that, of course, thought Carmichael, was the problem. Gibbons hadn't been doing anything constructive with his sleepless hours, only going over their failure to wring a confession from Paul Berowne.

"Well, I've just been going over the statements again," said

Carmichael, dismissing the subject. "I want to have another hard look at our other suspects."

Gibbons was startled. "You think Paul Berowne is innocent, then?" he asked.

Carmichael leaned back thoughtfully and rubbed at his upper lip. "I haven't given up on him," he replied, "but there's no denying that yesterday has put doubts in my mind. You'll go on with Berowne, lad, while I see what I can dig up about the others. I spoke to him this morning before we released him, but he hadn't anything more to say. I tried to find out if he had ever suspected his wife of having an affair, especially of late, but he merely claimed he wouldn't know whether or not she had been. He thought not."

"Even if she had," said Gibbons doubtfully, "it wouldn't give her much motive. I mean, she hadn't as much to lose as her husband."

"Well, I don't know," mused Carmichael. "That bequest would come in handy if she was in love with a poor man. In any case, it's a place to start. I'll be looking at Maddie Wellman, too." He turned back to the statement on his desk. "Now both Mrs. Simmons and Berowne claim to have heard the piano being played upstairs in the schoolroom at about eleven, but Mrs. Simmons was hoovering from time to time, which would have drowned out the sound."

"Yes," said Gibbons. "I remember."

"Berowne is certain that he heard the piano when he came in, and later the hoover, but he has no idea how long he had been in the house when the hoover started. When I asked this morning, he couldn't remember if he heard the piano in the intervals when the hoover was off. So I want you to have a word with Mrs. Simmons today, Gibbons." Carmichael flicked his finger at the report. "This is all rather vague, really. Find out if she was running the hoover for any length of time—it would have taken Marion Berowne at least twenty minutes and probably half an hour to run over to the main house and get back again. And find out if she heard anything that might have been Berowne coming in or leaving—or whether there was an extra coffee cup used."

"Yes, sir."

"I want you to talk to Mira Fellows again, too," said Carmichael. "Get her to remember everything she can about Paul Berowne's visit that morning and see if there's anything we've missed there. I'm going to talk with Commander Andrews and Chief Constable Gorringe again. They both knew the family well, and I want their thoughts on Maddie Wellman." He snorted. "It's the least they can do for me, having saddled me with this mess."

Gibbons smiled. "Yes, sir. Do you have any angle on Miss Wellman?"

"She's a more difficult nut to crack," admitted Carmichael. "It's always been perfectly possible that she came downstairs, had a chat with Geoffrey, and poisoned his coffee. In fact, you'll remember that Mrs. Berowne thought it most likely that Miss Wellman had replaced the flowers in the study."

"But what would have been her motive?" asked Gibbons. "Frankly, sir, it's always seemed to me that if Miss Wellman were going to murder anyone, it would have been Annette."

Carmichael grinned at him. "I've always thought the same," he agreed. "But people's minds work in mysterious ways. As much as she disliked Mrs. Berowne, she may have felt even greater resentment of Geoffrey for bringing Annette into the house to begin with. You said she seemed honestly surprised that Paul Berowne was having an affair?"

"It looked that way to me, sir."

"Then it's probably true—Miss Wellman isn't good at subterfuge. But Paul may well have spoken to her about the impossibility of his situation with his wife, how he felt it was even worse lately. In addition, there may have been quite a small thing—something Geoffrey said or did—that caused her to reach the end of her tether. It's certainly not impossible that a person would snap after putting up with a bad situation for four years."

"True," agreed Gibbons.

"And we'll have another look at Annette Berowne," said Carmichael. Gibbons's heart fell into his toes and he flushed, but Carmichael did not seem to notice. "After all, her motive remains just as strong as Berowne's, and far stronger than either Maddie Wellman's or Marion Berowne's. Well, let's get on with it, lad. I'll drop you at the pub on my way to the chief constable's office."

The day was as gray as Gibbons's spirits. He failed to get anything more from Mira Fellows than had his cohorts, and it was past eleven o'clock when he finally gave it up and began his walk along the footpath to the estate. The clouds had rolled in, but the rain was holding off, and he walked briskly in an effort to make it to shelter before the rain started. He had only, he thought, to make it as far as Little House, as Mrs. Simmons would be working there as she had on the day of the murder.

He had come halfway and without thinking he looked toward the cattle shelter that he and Annette had taken shelter in and was surprised to see someone sitting there. Gibbons stopped and stared.

It was a heavyset man in his fifties seated on the edge of the feed trough and eating what looked like a muffin. A dog sat beside him, ears pricked and watchful eyes fastened on the sheep in the meadow.

It was a long shot, thought Gibbons, as he climbed over the stile and began to make his way across the meadow. The odds that this man had been here on the Wednesday Geoffrey Berowne was killed were next to nothing, but it wouldn't do to ignore him. Probably the interview would take just long enough to let the rain start.

The man, noting Gibbons's progress, came out to meet him, muffin in hand and sheepdog at his heels.

"Can I help you?" he called when they were within a few yards of each other.

Gibbons pulled out his ID and introduced himself, earning a surprised look from the man.

"Don't meet many Scotland Yard detectives in my sheep meadows," he said. "I'm Harry Denford."

"These are your sheep then?" asked Gibbons.

Denford nodded, looking quizzical. "There some problem with them?"

"No, no," said Gibbons. "Not at all. I was just wondering if you happened to look in on them at about this time on the fourteenth."

"If it were a Wednesday, I did," said Denford. "I come round every Wednesday morning to make sure all's well. And then I have my elevenses before I go on," he added, gesturing with the half-eaten muffin.

Gibbons's heart leapt at this matter-of-fact utterance. He had plodded across the meadow because it was his job to interrogate anyone in the area, but he had not really expected anything to come of it.

"Did you happen to see anybody walking by on the footpath that Wednesday?" asked Gibbons eagerly.

Denford frowned thoughtfully. "Don't get many people up here as a rule," he said, "but I did see some folk one day. Now whether it was that Wednesday or not, I can't be sure." He considered a moment and then went on. "It were a fair bit ago, maybe as much as a month."

"So you've seen no one in the last two or three weeks?" said Gibbons, trying to sort this out.

"No. As I said, not many people come by this way. But this day—and a nice, bright day it was, too—it might have been Victoria Station."

"Really? How many people passed by?"

"Well, only two," admitted Denford. "First I saw Mr. Berowne, coming from the village."

"That would be Paul Berowne? You know him, then?"

"I've seen him in the pub of an evening," said Denford. "I don't know if he saw me, since I was in among the sheep and didn't notice him till he was passing. I waved, but he didn't look my way."

No, thought Gibbons, Paul Berowne would have been thoroughly preoccupied, whether he was on his way to murder his father, or merely reflecting on his interview with Mira.

"What time was this?"

Denford looked doubtful. "After ten," he said, "since that's when I got up here. And before eleven, because that's when I sit down to have my snack."

"Very well," said Gibbons. "And the next person to come by?"

"That would have been a lady," answered Denford. "A pretty thing, she was. I was sitting down by then, so it would have been after eleven—no, I'm wrong. That was the day I found the dead lamb. I had to look for it, so I was late getting to my snack. It must have been at least eleven-thirty when the lady came by."

Gibbons nodded, jotting it all down in his notebook. "And which direction was she going?"

"Toward the village."

Gibbons looked up, startled. "Just toward the village? You didn't see her turn around and start back toward the estate?"

"No. Why would she?"

Gibbons was confounded. He turned to look at the footpath, which ran straight here and could therefore be seen from this vantage for a considerable distance in either direction. He remembered

223

distinctly the spot where Annette had said she turned back; it was barely thirty yards from the stile and well within view from where he stood now.

"So she just walked past on her way to the village?" he asked. "She didn't stop or anything?"

Denford was looking curious. "Not that I saw," he answered. "I was sitting over there, eating my scone and enjoying the day when I saw her walking along. She was pretty and I watched her go past until she got to the bend over that way."

Gibbons did not know what to think. He did not believe Annette was lying, and yet Denford had not seen her.

"Right about there," he said, pointing, "the lady claims she remembered forgetting something back at the house and turned back. About ten minutes later she found she had it after all, and turned round again and made for the village. Would you have seen her if she did that?"

Denford rubbed his chin. "Probably," he said, "but I can't be sure. It's not like I was watching for her and I don't recall exactly where she was when I noticed her."

It was a shock, just as he had thought he was on the verge of confirming Annette's story in every particular, to have her alibi dissolve before his eyes. Gibbons was bitterly disappointed. He took down Denford's address and phone number and proceeded on his way.

When he reached the spot where Annette had turned back, he paused to survey the area. Over by the shelter, Denford was plain to be seen, packing a thermos back in his haversack in preparation for leaving. Ahead, toward the estate, the trees which would have hidden Annette from his view were still some distance away. Perhaps Denford had simply not noticed her until she had come into view the second time.

Gibbons was extremely sorry he had noticed Denford at all. He remained firm in his belief that Annette's story was true, but there was no question that Denford's evidence hurt her alibi rather than helped it, and he was dreading having to tell Carmichael about it. He knew what it would look like to the chief inspector. He would, he told himself, have to do his best to emphasize Denford's inability to be sure he would have seen Annette had she done as she said. But he was uncomfortable about it nonetheless.

He made it to Little House before the rain, and could hear the hoover as he came up to the door. His watch said eleven-twenty-five, which tallied with what they knew so far of the morning of the murder. Rather than knocking, he lounged against the doorjamb and waited for the noise to stop, which it did in another ten minutes. Of course, he had no way of knowing when Mrs. Simmons had started.

She opened the door to him when he knocked and immediately looked nervous. Gibbons sighed inwardly. No matter how un-threatening he tried to appear, his mere presence seemed to frighten this timid woman and it made getting information out of her very awkward.

"Good morning, Mrs. Simmons," he said, smiling. "How are you today?"

She did not meet his eyes.

"Mrs. Berowne's upstairs," she muttered.

"That's good," said Gibbons, coming into the hall and letting her close the door behind him. "But I just want a word with you, first, if you wouldn't mind."

She nodded and stood waiting, head bowed, for whatever questions he chose to rain down upon her. Gibbons sighed again.

"I only want to get some times clear," he said. "Perhaps we could sit down?"

She led him silently into the living room and obediently perched on the edge of a chair. It looked like she was ready to flee at a moment's notice.

"I'd like to go over the day of the murder again," said Gibbons.

"You said you arrived as Mr. Paul was leaving, and Mrs. Marion and Edwin were in the kitchen. Is that right?"

She nodded.

"You cleaned the schoolroom," continued Gibbons, "and then came downstairs. What did you do next?"

"I cleared up the breakfast things," she answered. "Just as usual. Then I did Mr. Paul's study and the dining room after that. Then I came in here."

"And that's when you heard the piano from upstairs?"

"Yes." She nodded, her eyes firmly on her hands folded in her lap. "It was just eleven, because I'd heard the grandfather clock striking as I was coming in."

"But you didn't hear Mr. Berowne come in the kitchen door? It would have been about the same time, perhaps a few minutes later."

She looked frightened that she couldn't give him the answer he wanted. "You can't hear much from the kitchen in the living room," she said. "It's at the opposite end of the house. I'd only hear if there was shouting."

"I see," said Gibbons soothingly. "You're doing very well, Mrs. Simmons—this is just the kind of information I need. So you didn't hear anything that might have been Mr. Paul coming in or moving around? No? Very well. Now about when did you start hoovering?"

She seemed somewhat reassured. "When I came in."

"So about eleven," mused Gibbons. "And how long did it take you to finish hoovering in here?"

She looked helpless. "I don't know," she said.

"I think I heard you hoovering when I came up," said Gibbons encouragingly. "That would have been eleven-thirty or so. Did you start at about eleven today?"

"Yes."

"And when you stopped, you heard the piano again?"

"Yes. While I was working in here, too."

"But, Mrs. Simmons," said Gibbons, "if you had the hoover going, how could you hear the piano?"

"I have to turn it off," she said defensively. "I do the carpet, and then I have to adjust it for the floors. And I have to stop and move the furniture to get under it."

"I see," said Gibbons. "I didn't understand before." He thought it over, noting the position of the chairs and tables. It seemed unlikely that Mrs. Simmons could have been hoovering continuously for more than fifteen minutes—not long enough for Marion Berowne to get to the study and back.

"That's very clear, then," he continued. "Now you said you cleaned up the breakfast dishes in the kitchen. When was the next time you went in there?"

"After I'd finished the living room. Around noon it must have been."

"And was everything just as you'd left it?"

"I think so. I didn't notice anything different."

"Not, say, a dirty coffee cup?"

"No, sir. The dishes were all put away in the washer, like I'd left them."

It didn't really prove anything, thought Gibbons. Berowne might have put the empty cup in the washer on his way out, rather than leaving it sitting in the sink or on the counter. And by this account, Mrs. Simmons would have been hoovering when Berowne left for the garage, and could not possibly have heard him.

After the antics of the night before, Bethancourt rose late the next morning. He was surprised not to find a message from Gibbons waiting on the answer phone, but he prudently waited until Marla had left before ringing his friend. But New Scotland Yard informed him that Detective Sergeant Gibbons was out of the office.

Bethancourt rang off and frowned at the phone. He had not spoken to Gibbons since his friend's brief call the evening before when he had rung to say Paul Berowne had not confessed. They had had no opportunity to compare thoughts on this development and it struck Bethancourt as peculiar that Gibbons had made no effort to get in touch with him since. Neither, he recollected, had Gibbons been at home late last night and for that Bethancourt could think of only two explanations: there had been another development in the case, or Gibbons had been with Annette Berowne.

And if there had been a new development, it was surely odd that Gibbons had not found two minutes to ring his dogsbody and let him know.

"I'm making too much out of this," said Bethancourt to his dog. "Let's get you brushed."

Cerberus merely wagged his tail and stood obediently while Bethancourt sat on the edge of a coffee table and began removing clouds of lose fur.

"Probably," he said, "poor Jack was too depressed to ring. From the moment I told him about Paul Berowne, he was counting on a confession. So was I, if it comes to that, but Jack has a lot more riding on this. He very likely went to bed early last night—people often sleep a good deal when they're depressed—and with nothing new to report, he didn't bother ringing this morning."

Cerberus panted happily.

"You think that's right, don't you, lad? Of course it is. Still, it leaves us with the problem of who did murder Geoffrey Berowne, if it wasn't his son. It's a pity I'm not a dog. I could have had a quick sniff around that study and known at once if anyone besides Annette and Kitty had been there that morning. Easiest, of course, for Maddie Wellman to sneak in, but if she did it, why didn't she provide herself with at least a partial alibi? A nice, long phone call to a friend would have done the trick."

Annette, he thought, had provided herself with an alibi, or as good a one as she could get if she were guilty. Marion Berowne had an alibi of sorts as well, though nothing that couldn't be easily broken. But Bethancourt had always thought it a very odd coincidence that Annette Berowne, if she was innocent, had chosen to put lilies of the valley in her husband's study. In that case, the murderer could not have planned to kill Berowne before he or she noticed the flowers there. And whoever it was would have had to have known that lilies of the valley were deadly, certainly an arcane bit of information. That led back to Paul Berowne, who had shared an interest in mystery stories with his father and who might have looked at Geoffrey's books on poison, or even been told the fact by Geoffrey himself while discussing mysteries.

"That's a thought," said Bethancourt aloud. "I wonder if there have been any mystery books written that use lilies of the valley as the murder weapon. It's worth checking out."

Who else might have known about the flowers? There was McAllister, who very likely knew all kinds of odd things about plants. Maddie Wellman and Marion Berowne were more of a stretch; neither of them were horticulture experts and it was difficult to see how else they might have come by the knowledge. If they had been planning Geoffrey's murder, they might have read his books on poison, but it was asking too much to believe that, just as they had hit upon their method, Annette would innocently provide it. But of course Annette could have read the books too, and selected lilies of the valley on purpose. She might have planned it months before and been waiting for spring and the blossoming of the flowers.

Gibbons had not kept in contact with Bethancourt because of a feeling he knew to be ridiculous and yet could not put out of his mind. It seemed to him that anyone as perceptive as Bethancourt, and who knew him so well, would take one look at him and know he had become Annette Berowne's lover the night before. But by the end of the day the depth of his guilt had engendered a desire to confess, and even to be scolded. Bethancourt, he knew, would disapprove and probably be quite sharp with him, and he went almost eagerly to face him.

In the event, Bethancourt was neither sharp nor particularly observant. His first look at Gibbons apparently did nothing more than remind him of the hour.

"Jack! Good Lord," he said when he opened the door to the detective. "What's the time?"

"Nearly seven," answered Gibbons, surprised.

"And I've never walked Cerberus," exclaimed Bethancourt, running a harassed hand through his already disheveled hair.

Gibbons looked down at the dog who gazed back at him mournfully.

"You don't mind, do you, Jack?" continued Bethancourt, pulling on a jacket and grabbing the dog lead. "We don't have to go all the way to Battersea Park if you're tired."

"I am tired," said Gibbons, following his friend out. "What have you been so busy with?"

"The Internet," answered Bethancourt, turning down the street toward the embankment. "I've spent all day looking for a mystery novel in which someone is poisoned with lilies of the valley. I've gone the rounds of the chat rooms, posted queries to newsgroups and bookstores, and spent the rest of the time plowing through synopses."

Gibbons was beginning to feel alarmed. "You didn't mention the Berowne case, did you?"

Bethancourt shot him a withering glance. "What do you take me for?" he asked. "I posted one of those 'Need help with title' queries—you know, where someone remembers something about a book they've read, but can't think of the title."

"Oh," said Gibbons, reassured. "I see. You pretended you already knew of such a book. But why?"

They had reached the embankment gardens and Bethancourt bent to unclip the lead from Cerberus's collar, freeing him to inspect the trees. The Thames was iron-gray beneath the cloudy skies and a brisk wind came off the water. Bethancourt huddled against a tree to light a cigarette.

"It's one way Paul Berowne could have known about the fatal properties of lilies of the valley," he said, straightening. "We know Annette put them there originally, so the murderer must have seen them and thought what a wonderful opportunity it was. That means he or she already knew they were poisonous, which is an odd bit of knowledge to have. I mean, neither of us knew it."

"True," said Gibbons. "But any of them could have read about it in that book in the study."

"Yes, but why should they? People don't normally browse through books on poison for light reading. They use them to look things up, like whether or not the last mystery they read was based on a reasonable premise."

"So you're saying that only someone who read mysteries could have done it?" Gibbons looked thoughtful. "There aren't any on Maddie Wellman's shelves, but I don't know about Marion Berowne."

"Nothing that definite," admitted Bethancourt. "I just thought that if there was such a book, we might be able to prove Paul Berowne had read it."

"That's good," said Gibbons, "because Carmichael has spent all day investigating the two women. Not," he added, "that we've turned up much, beyond that it would have been exceptionally easy for Miss Wellman, and rather difficult for Mrs. Berowne." It was not quite deliberate, but somehow he did not mention his interview with Harry Denford.

"Difficult?"

"Mrs. Simmons never ran the hoover continuously for more than about fifteen minutes," explained Gibbons. "And when she wasn't running it, she could hear the piano from upstairs. Marion

Berowne couldn't have made it to the study and back in that time."

Bethancourt gave him an odd look. "But the piano's no alibi anymore," he said. "Didn't you realize that?"

"No. Why should I?"

"That horrible tape that Denis and Edwin made of their playing," answered Bethancourt. "You can't have forgotten. We had to listen to it for half the trip to London."

"Of course I haven't forgot—" began Gibbons, grimacing, and then he broke off. "Oh," he said. "Of course."

"After the boys were done playing," said Bethancourt, "there was more—obviously something they had recorded over. It might have been an adult and a child playing 'Chopsticks.' But in any case, the mere fact of the tape itself means Marion Berowne didn't have to be there for Mrs. Simmons to hear the piano playing. She might have recorded herself and Edwin at any time and set the tape to play back while she ran over to the Hall."

"You're right," said Gibbons, shaking his head at himself. "I should have realized that as soon as I heard that horrible tape. But I just never thought."

"It doesn't mean she's guilty," said Bethancourt. "No one else has an alibi either."

"No, but it's something I ought to point out to Carmichael," said Gibbons. He sighed. "I'm just not sure how I'm going to explain how I came to let you bring your nephew along on a murder investigation."

"Don't," said Bethancourt, flicking his cigarette into the street. "My sister knows Marion Berowne—it's not unreasonable that Denis might have gone to play with Edwin in the normal way of things."

Gibbons agreed gloomily. It seemed to him that every time he turned around, there was something else about this case he had to keep from his superior.

"It's really not very pertinent how we found out," pointed out Bethancourt, noticing his friend's low spirits.

"No, of course it's not," Gibbons agreed, sighing.

Bethancourt eyed him and his suspicions of his friend's activities the night before returned to him unbidden. Gibbons stood beside him, hands jammed into his pockets, his eyes following Cerberus's movements along the green. But Bethancourt did not think he was really seeing the dog.

There was a long pause.

"You look like you could use a drink," said Bethancourt at last. "Come along to the pub and I'll buy you one."

"All right," said Gibbons.

Bethancourt called to his dog who came obediently to heel and they strolled along Cheyne Walk until they reached the King's Head and Eight Bells. There was a fair amount of custom at this time of the evening, but Gibbons found an unoccupied table in one corner while Bethancourt fetched the whiskies from the bar. A group of young women there admired Cerberus enthusiastically but Bethancourt, once he had collected the drinks, detached his dog and himself and came grinning back to the table.

"I think they fancied you," said Gibbons, smiling.

"It's always nice to be appreciated," said Bethancourt. "Isn't that right, Cerberus? Cheers."

Gibbons raised his glass and drank, but then found himself unable to either pick up their conversation about the case or introduce the subject of Annette. He stole a glance at Bethancourt, who was watching him with a worried air, and hastily looked away again.

"Do you want to talk about it?" asked Bethancourt, who still hoped, though without much optimism, that his suspicions were wrong.

"I don't know what talking would solve," responded Gibbons.

"But, yes, I suppose I do. I spoke with Annette last night. I—we're in love with each other, Phillip."

It was what Bethancourt had been dreading, and he understood the implication at once. It was on the tip of his tongue to say, "If she cared anything about you at all, she'd have put you off," but he swallowed the words. Who was it that had told them Annette never thought of anyone but herself? Whoever it had been, Bethancourt heartily agreed with them.

"Ah," he said. "Then that makes it all the more important we close the case quickly."

Gibbons laughed humorlessly. "Aren't you going to say 'I told you so'?"

"No," said Bethancourt firmly, "I'm not. Look here, Jack, it's not as bad as all that. Undeniably, you've got an awkward situation on your hands, but that's only because the case is ongoing. As soon as we solve it, you and Annette will be perfectly free to do whatever you like. And we're getting closer all the time. I'm sure it won't be long now."

"I hope you're right. She's so wonderful, Phillip. I've never known a woman like her before. I still can't believe she loves me."

Bethancourt listened to his friend go on in this vein, sharply curbing the caustic remarks that sprang to his mind. He was rather relieved when Gibbons refused his offer of dinner and took off to have an early night.

It was ten o'clock and Gibbons had just settled down in bed with a book when the doorbell rang. His first thought was of Bethancourt, and he wondered, as he rose and pulled on a dressing gown, why his friend had come round instead of ringing. But when he opened the door, Annette stood there.

Her smile was glorious and her soft eyes beamed at him.

Gibbons was so startled that for a moment he said nothing and only stared at her. Then he swept her into his arms and hugged her tight.

"Annette!" he exclaimed. "I never expected it would be you. I rang earlier, but Mrs. Simmons said you'd gone out."

"I've been having dinner with an old friend," said Annette. "A very old friend—he was quite surprised when I rang him up this afternoon and asked if he'd dine with me. I thought of him," she explained, "because he lives in London. I left after we'd finished dinner, but who's to say I mightn't have had a nightcap?" She chuckled, pleased with herself. "I could have had two nightcaps," she added, "which gives us at least two hours, I should think."

Gibbons laughed delightedly and kissed her.

"You were wonderful to think of it," he said. "Here, let me get you something."

Her arms tightened about his neck. "I don't want anything," she said. "Only you."

The Carmichaels were sitting in their armchairs beside the fireplace, though the spring evening was too warm for any fire. Dottie had put on the television when they had come in after supper, but neither of them was watching the program. Carmichael had the Berowne case file open on his knee and Dottie was dealing out a game of patience on the little table by her chair while she listened to him wrestling with his problem.

"It seems to be coming back round to the widow," said Carmichael, "but I don't see how we'll ever prove it. Commander Andrews as much as told me today that he and his lads had come to the same conclusion."

Dottie snorted. "So, since there wasn't any proof, they handed it over to you?"

"That's about the size of it," agreed Carmichael with a rueful shake of the head. "Although, to give them their due, they felt their friendship with Mrs. Berowne might have been coloring their reactions. They were all so fond of her that they couldn't quite bring themselves to believe she'd done it in the absence of any proof."

"And now what does this Andrews say?"

"He thinks it must be Paul Berowne," admitted Carmichael. "He was quite excited with what we'd uncovered about him. But of course he doesn't know about the sheepfarmer—Gibbons only got that after I'd talked with Andrews." He grimaced. "It's so close to being proof positive that Mrs. Berowne lied about her movements that day, and yet it just misses. This farmer—Denford's his name—admits it's possible he just didn't notice Mrs. Berowne when she first came into view. He doesn't think it likely, but it's possible. And it is possible, Dottie. I went back up there with Gibbons after he'd reported in, and that meadow's pretty wide. It's a fair distance from the far side of it to the path. If you happened to be looking toward the village, you might not notice someone coming along from the opposite direction. You'd have to catch the movement out of the corner of your eye, so to speak."

"Well, was he looking off toward the village?" asked Dottie, ever practical.

Carmichael shrugged. "He doesn't know. How should he?"

Dottie tapped her cards against her chin. "So you've got the son, with both opportunity and motive, and now the wife with both as well."

"She's always had both," said Carmichael. "Don't forget that it was very unusual for her to walk to the village."

"So will you bring her in for questioning?"

Carmichael took out a cigar and removed its wrapper thoughtfully.

"Not just yet," he answered at last. "I'll wait a day or two more and hope something else turns up. After all, we don't really have any more on her than we did to begin with. I do wish that farmer could be more positive."

He looked very downcast and Dottie bit her lip, but could think of nothing encouraging to say. This looked like being one of the few cases in her husband's career that would end in failure. They had lived through the others and they would live through this, but it was never good.

Bethancourt spent the evening pummeling his brain for some kind of lead to follow, though he was well aware that any lead, however slim, would already have been pounced on by Gibbons and Carmichael. And following leads was not really his strength; when he had been helpful in previous investigations, it had usually been through insight into the characters of the people involved. That was what interested him primarily, but he found he no longer cared who had killed Geoffrey Berowne so long as it could be proved in short order and save Gibbons from the noose that he was rapidly weaving for himself.

Near midnight he decided that sleep would prove impossible and took Cerberus out for a hopefully exhausting walk across the Albert Bridge to Battersea. It was more than an hour later when he returned, but his brain was still buzzing uselessly. He hesitated and then rang Marla, who was luckily at home and still awake.

"I've just got in from a nightclub, actually," she said. "What are you doing?"

"Nothing," he answered. "Could I come round?"

"Yes, I think that might be nice."

"Good. I'll be there in half a tick."

Marla was blessedly understanding. She had caught his mood

over the phone and said nothing at all when she opened the door to him, only gathering him into her arms eagerly, and, after an hour or two of urgent and arduous passion, Bethancourt at last fell asleep at her side.

CHAPTER

14

Gibbons woke early the next morning, his hazy mind still full of the night before. For two hours he and Annette had made love and talked of inconsequential things, and the only blight on his pleasure was her necessary departure. That and the guilt that was hammering at his conscience. The guilt made him rise at once, although he could have had another hour's sleep, and push off for the Yard after a single cup of coffee. He was there well before Carmichael, and so took the call that came in from Maddie Wellman.

He had not spoken to her since she had ordered him out of her room and he tried now to inject a conciliatory note into his voice. But she was too full of her own business to care that they had last parted on less than amicable terms.

"I happened to speak to McAllister this morning," she announced. There was a note of triumph in her voice. "We've discovered something that I think the chief inspector will want to know."

"That's wonderful, Miss Wellman," said Gibbons. "He should be in shortly and I'll let him know. Could you tell me what you've found out?"

"We now know when Annette left the house," she answered.

Gibbons's grip on the receiver tightened in sudden fear. "Yes?" he said. "And when was that?"

"I think it would be best if you came down and spoke to McAllister," she said firmly. "You can tell Chief Inspector Carmichael that my solicitor will be present."

"Yes, of course," said Gibbons, keeping his voice level with an effort. "The chief inspector will be very interested in this news. I expect he'll want to leave for Surrey right away."

"Very well, then. We'll expect you sometime in the course of the morning."

She rang off and Gibbons slowly replaced the receiver, stunned. If Maddie Wellman had discovered that Annette had left the house a minute or so after eleven, she would never by any chance offer up the information. She was too firmly convinced of Annette's guilt and too vicious in her hatred of the other woman. Therefore, she must believe she had uncovered evidence to show that Annette had left the house considerably later. But what on earth could she have discovered? Both he and Carmichael had spoken time and again to McAllister, who had staunchly maintained that he did not know what time it had been when he had seen Annette. Could he have simply been playing the loyal family retainer, his scruples now overcome by Maddie?

A sudden qualm came over Gibbons. For an instant he saw all of Annette's actions and conversations with himself as the ploy of a clever murderer. But his mind rejected the notion at once. The passion she felt for him was real, he was sure of that; no one was capable of counterfeiting such deep emotion.

Probably Maddie Wellman, in her zeal to have Annette arrested, was making a mountain out of a molehill. Gibbons glanced at the clock; Carmichael would already be on his way in so there was no point in ringing him. Instead Gibbons telephoned Bethancourt, but his friend was not home. He left an agitated message and then sat back to wait for his superior.

It was clear from the way she sat and the slight crease between her brows that Maddie Wellman's arthritis was troubling her this morning. But no pain could mask the excitement and defiance in her eyes.

In a chair drawn up beside her sat a rotund, balding man with wire-rimmed spectacles whom she introduced as her solicitor, Mr. Nailes. He regarded the police with a jaded and suspicious eye.

"Miss Wellman," he said, enunciating his words precisely, "wishes to make an additional statement about her actions on the morning of Mr. Geoffrey Berowne's murder."

Nailes had a very prim manner, thought Carmichael, taking an immediate dislike to the man.

"Yes," he said aloud, "we understood that." He turned a carefully bland face to Miss Wellman; though any break in the case would be heaven-sent, he had a natural suspicion of a sudden remembrance of important evidence. "If you would care to proceed, Miss Wellman? Sergeant Gibbons will take your statement down."

Maddie appeared to take no umbrage at Carmichael's attitude toward her solicitor. She leapt into the conversation eagerly.

"It's about when I saw McAllister from the window there," she said.

"Yes, I recall," said Carmichael, who had carefully reviewed her statement on the ride down. "You saw him working below in the tulip beds when you opened your window."

"That's right," she agreed. "I just called a 'good morning' down to him."

241

Carmichael frowned. "I don't believe you mentioned speaking to him."

Maddie shrugged. "I may not have," she admitted. "After all, whether or not I said 'good morning' seemed completely irrelevant at the time. The point is that McAllister remembers it, and after I'd opened the window, I sat down to write a letter and happened to notice the time. I keep a little clock there on the desk." Her eyes glittered. "It was eleven-fifteen."

Long experience kept any excitement from showing in Carmichael's face, and he was still suspicious, but this was certainly the sort of thing that might have been overlooked.

"And I expect," he said, "that McAllister saw Mrs. Berowne leaving the house after this incident?"

"That's right," said Maddie triumphantly.

"I'm very glad to have this information, Miss Wellman," said Carmichael. "Still, I would like to know why you never mentioned it before."

"Why should I?" she retorted. "What difference did it make what time I'd seen McAllister? We all knew he'd been working out there all morning. You never told me he'd seen Annette leaving."

"I see. Presumably you discovered that this morning?"

She was impatient now. "I woke early and went down to have a word with him about the vegetable garden. He was complaining about being pestered by you lot and that's how it came out that he had seen Annette leaving, but didn't know the time. Naturally, I asked if it had been before or after I had wished him good morning. He looked surprised and said he'd forgotten that and after thinking about it, he said it had been afterward."

"Very well," said Carmichael. "We'll want to speak to Mr. McAllister, of course, to confirm this. I take it he's working in the grounds?"

"Yes, in the rose garden, I believe. Mr. Nailes will show you."

"I'm sure we can find it ourselves," said Carmichael, who had no wish to be saddled with Nailes.

"Nonsense, Chief Inspector," said Maddie sharply. "You don't think, after what you put poor Paul through, that I'm going to let anyone speak to you without a solicitor present, do you? Except," she added vindictively, "Annette, of course. You can do what you like with her."

Carmichael clenched his jaw to prevent himself from replying to this. He nodded curtly, and left the room, trailed by Gibbons and Nailes. The silence as they went down the stairs and out into the gardens was tangible. Carmichael saw that Gibbons's blue eyes were blazing and thought that his sergeant was even more incensed than himself. But in Nailes's presence it was impossible to let off any steam.

Nailes proceeded at a slow, dignified pace, which did nothing to improve the detectives' tempers. Eventually they reached the rose garden, where McAllister was deadheading the early roses. It was apparent from the look he gave Nailes that he liked the solicitor no more than Carmichael did, and this for some reason raised the chief inspector's spirits.

"Good morning, Mr. McAllister," he said, jumping in before Nailes could say anything. "We've just come to confirm something Miss Wellman told us. It won't take long."

Heaving an exaggerated sigh, McAllister turned from the roses.

"It's just as she said," he said. "I was mulching the tulips when she called down to me, and it were after that I saw Mrs. Berowne leaving."

"How long afterward?"

McAllister shrugged. "Not long. Five minutes maybe."

"And was this before or after you had fetched the new bags of mulch?"

"After."

"How long after?"

McAllister looked unsure. "Don't know," he answered.

"Ten minutes? Fifteen?"

"Summat like that," agreed McAllister, but Carmichael had the impression that he would have agreed to virtually anything if by doing so he could shorten the interview and get back to his work.

"Perhaps more like half an hour?" suggested Carmichael.

McAllister scowled. "Don't think it was that long, but I don't really know. I never seen such a lot of fuss about the time before. You people must run your lives on stopwatches."

Carmichael took a breath to explain the importance of time in the investigation, but then let it out without bothering. He was sure McAllister wouldn't even listen. Already the man's eyes were straying back to the roses.

"That's very helpful, Mr. McAllister," he said instead. "Now, I've read your original statement over, as well as what you told me the other day. At neither time did you mention seeing Miss Wellman."

"I forgot it."

"I see. So the other day when we were going over exactly what you'd done, fetching the mulch and so forth, you didn't remember that Miss Wellman had called down to you?"

"I just said not," answered McAllister testily.

"But you remembered it when Miss Wellman reminded you?"

"That's right. She asked did I see Mrs. Berowne before or after she said good morning, and then I remembered her opening her window and waving at me, and that was *after* I fetched the mulch and *before* I saw Mrs. Berowne leaving."

He stared at Carmichael like a frustrated schoolteacher trying to impress a point on a dim-witted student.

"That's very clear," said Carmichael. "I don't think there's anything more I need from you just at the moment, Mr. McAllister. Thank you."

Nailes had said nothing during the entire interview, but as they left the rose garden, he announced he would see them back to their car.

"As you wish," said Carmichael cheerfully, and, remembering their stately walk through the gardens, he proceeded to set the fastest pace he could himself manage. Nailes was obviously displeased, but helpless to do anything about it. When he slowed down, the detectives simply drew ahead and he was forced to trot to catch them up. He bid them a truculent good morning at the edge of the drive and returned to the house. Carmichael watched him go with satisfaction mixed with a faint feeling of guilt at having behaved childishly.

"Thank God," muttered Gibbons and swung into the car. "Do you think any of it's true, sir?" he asked as Carmichael joined him.

"It could be," said Carmichael, settling the case file on his lap. "I'm always suspicious when witnesses start remembering things long after the fact, especially when it's something that indicts a person they're known to have a grudge against. But this is just the kind of thing that might get overlooked. Ah, here's Miss Wellman's original statement. Kitty Whitcomb came up to see her about nine-thirty, and stayed for perhaps an hour. Miss Wellman says she then began writing her letters. Asked by Commander Andrews if she stayed at her desk all the time until Kitty came to tell her about Mr. Berowne, she at first said yes, and then corrected herself and said she had gotten up once to open the window. Andrews asked if she saw anyone on the terrace, and she replied that the only person she had seen was McAllister, working just off the terrace in the tulip beds. No mention of the time, and Andrews didn't ask."

"He should have," said Gibbons bitterly.

"He probably saw no reason for it," answered Carmichael, "since McAllister freely admitted he'd been there the entire time. Now here's what McAllister told me the other day. Nothing, of course, about Miss Wellman. But McAllister's got no grudge against Mrs. Berowne—there's no reason for him to lie about having said good morning to Miss Wellman and seeing Mrs. Berowne after that."

"No, sir," said Gibbons, "but I'd be happier if we weren't depending entirely on Miss Wellman for the time. She's had it in for Mrs. Berowne from the start, and even if everything occurred just as she and McAllister say, there's nothing objective to show that it all didn't happen much earlier."

"True," sighed Carmichael. "Since she's so convinced Mrs. Berowne is the killer, I wouldn't put it past Miss Wellman to fudge a bit on the time." He frowned thoughtfully. "On the other hand, I doubt she knows exactly how much extra time Mrs. Berowne took getting to the village—we didn't know ourselves until you timed the walk with her. And this does fit in beautifully. If Miss Wellman is telling the truth, McAllister would have seen Mrs. Berowne leaving twenty minutes after she said she did, and twenty minutes is just the amount of time she can't account for. Plus there's Denford's testimony. If she left at eleven-twenty, that would put her on the path by the meadow at about eleven-forty, and he said it was past eleven-thirty when he saw her. And it accounts for the fact that he didn't see her earlier—she wasn't there."

Gibbons felt as if the noose was closing about his own throat. He was numb with panic and unable to say anything.

"I still don't like it, sir," he managed at last. "It's true that it all works out, but it's still completely dependent on Miss Wellman. If she'd said it was eleven when she saw McAllister, we'd be telling ourselves that Mrs. Berowne was definitely in the clear. Denford's statement isn't firm—he isn't certain whether or not he would have seen Mrs. Berowne the first time."

"That's the damnable part of it," agreed Carmichael. "They all have motive and opportunity. Still, this is the closest we've come to making a case, and I do think the coincidence of the timing is notable."

Gibbons swallowed. "Do you want to bring Mrs. Berowne in for questioning?" he asked.

"Let me just look over her statement," answered Carmichael, shuffling the papers in his lap.

While Carmichael read, Gibbons sat in agitated silence. He could not quite believe the turn things had taken and his mind was filled with the horror of entering the house and taking Annette in for questioning without any opportunity of reassurance. He glanced sideways at Carmichael who suddenly looked like an enemy, solemnly reading Annette's statement and weighing her guilt. It was as if he could see the logic falling into place in Carmichael's brain, tipping the scales against Annette.

"There's nothing here to get hold of," said Carmichael at last, frowning. "Her story's too simple to trip her up on any point. And unless I've lost my judgement of character altogether, she'll never confess. Still, I suppose there's nothing else for it. She might let out something. Yes, we'll take her in."

Gibbons felt as if there were a weight pressing on his chest. He said nothing, but climbed out of the car slowly and followed Carmichael back to the house. His mind seemed to have gone numb.

Carmichael rang the bell and they stood on the steps until Mrs. Simmons opened the door. She looked surprised to see them.

"Is Mrs. Berowne in?" asked Carmichael. "We'd like a word with her."

"No, sir," Mrs. Simmons replied and Gibbons breathed again. "She's gone shopping in Town. I don't expect her back until after lunch."

Carmichael frowned, disappointed, and glanced at his watch. "It's no good our waiting then," he said. "We'll call again later, or perhaps tomorrow. Thank you, Mrs. Simmons."

Gibbons was light-headed with relief as they returned to the car, but he knew it was only a temporary respite. His hands were shaking as he started the engine.

Carmichael decided to return to the local CID headquarters and see if Chief Constable Gorringe or Commander Andrews had any advice on the questioning of Mrs. Berowne. They had, after all, known her well. While Carmichael was closeted with Gorringe, Gibbons, feeling as if he would burst from the conflicting emotions roiling inside him, found a quiet corner and rang Bethancourt. This time his friend was at home.

"Jack!" he said. "I've been waiting about, hoping you'd ring back. What's happened?"

Rapidly, Gibbons gave him a precis of the morning's events. "The vindictive old bitch!" he said, referring to Maddie Wellman. "I'm sure she's lying about the time, Phillip. Either she never noticed it at all, or she's changed it to suit herself."

"That's possible, certainly," said Bethancourt slowly.

"And what am I going to do?" continued Gibbons frantically. "Any moment now, Carmichael will come out and we'll go off to pick her up. She'll think I betrayed her, Phillip."

"Nonsense," said Bethancourt. "She'll be confused, no doubt, but you can reassure her later. She'll see there was nothing else you could do—you can hardly be of any help to her if you give yourself away to Carmichael."

"That's true," said Gibbons. "But I'm still dreading it, Phillip. I don't think I can stand to face her and tell her she's wanted for questioning."

"It'll be all right," said Bethancourt soothingly. "Worse in the anticipation than in fact, I should say. Does Carmichael expect her to confess?"

"No. Which is just as well, since she's innocent."

"Of course," said Bethancourt, but apparently there was something false in his tone, for Gibbons burst out, "I know you always doubted her, but I tell you she's innocent. She loves me, Phillip, I *know* it. I've never been so certain of anything in my life."

"But, Jack," said Bethancourt gently, "you're not thinking clearly. Just because she loves you doesn't mean she's innocent. Even murderers can fall in love."

There was a long pause.

"No," said Gibbons at last. "You're wrong. I could never fall in love with a murderer."

"Not with someone you knew to be one, no."

"Oh, God," said Gibbons wildly, "you're just like everyone else. Why do you assume I think she's innocent because I'm in love with her? Why can't you understand that I fell in love with her because my instincts told me she was innocent? I don't know what to say to convince you."

"You don't have to convince me," said Bethancourt. "I am perfectly willing to entertain the idea that Annette is innocent. I'm just not as certain as you seem to be. Look, do you want me to do anything?"

"I can't think what to do," said Gibbons, appeased by this offer of help. "Maybe you can think of something. If you can, by all means do it."

"All right," said Bethancourt. "I'll put my mind to it. Ring me later, will you?"

"Yes, of course. God, I hope she stays out shopping till the evening. Carmichael won't want to start then."

"But he will in the morning."

"Yes, but by then I can ring her and warn her."

The was a startled silence at the other end of the phone.

"Do you really think you should, Jack?" said Bethancourt cautiously after a moment. "I mean, if she gives away that she's been warned, it'll all be up for both of you."

"I'll impress upon her that she must seem surprised. She'll be able to manage that. I'd better go, Phillip. Carmichael won't be much longer."

"Yes, of course. I'll talk to you later."

Bethancourt replaced the receiver slowly and stood staring at the phone. With this new information, he himself had no doubts that Annette Berowne was guilty, and he was relieved that it was over at last. Or he would have been, if Gibbons had shown the least doubt of her innocence. Once convinced of her guilt, he would get over this painful episode in time. But if he could not be convinced, he would never forget that the woman he loved was languishing in prison and that he had helped to put her there. It would certainly destroy his faith in his chosen calling; very likely he would end by quitting.

It could be even worse if she were acquitted, which was all too likely given the scant evidence against her. No one would ever believe her innocent, of course, and Gibbons would never forgive himself for not having solved the case successfully. Meanwhile, he would be married to a murderer.

Deeply disturbed, Bethancourt picked up the phone again to cancel the appointment he had made that afternoon with his broker. He did not think he could possibly concentrate on his finances.

A bar of sunlight lay across Chief Constable Gorringe's desk; he frowned thoughtfully at it while Carmichael explained what they'd found.

"So Annette did do it," said Gorringe solemnly when Carmichael had finished.

"It seems that way," agreed Carmichael. "At least it does if Miss Wellman's word is to be trusted."

Gorringe looked up, surprised. "Oh, I think you can trust whatever Maddie says," he answered. "Honest as the day is long, that's Maddie for you."

"She wasn't honest about the state of Paul Berowne's marriage," said Carmichael dryly. "And I would feel surer about what she told me today if she hadn't previously displayed such a vindictive attitude toward Mrs. Berowne."

"I suppose I expressed it poorly," said Gorringe. "It's not that she wouldn't stoop to lying. It's just that she couldn't possibly pull it off."

"She is a bad liar," admitted Carmichael, but he still harbored doubts. In this case, Maddie Wellman could be telling the truth with only the smallest variant—that of the time. Even the worst liar might be able to manage that. "But that's neither here nor there. What I really need your help with is Mrs. Berowne. Can you think of anything that might induce her to confess?"

Gorringe ran his fingers along the edge of a file laying open on his desk, frowning thoughtfully. "It's going to be difficult," he said. "My wife says she always knew Annette was self-centered—I never noticed that, myself. But if it's true, and if she murdered her husband for his money, then she must be one of those people whose worldview is completely warped, who believe absolutely nothing matters but themselves. I suppose all you can do is try to confuse her, or frighten her into making a mistake."

Carmichael was annoyed, though he did not show it. He was an old hand at interviewing suspects, and he rather resented this obvious advice. "Yes," he said. "What I want to know is what you think might frighten her."

But Gorringe only shook his head. "I don't know," he answered. "She's a charming woman, and I always liked her very much. But I haven't any insight into her character, especially not if she's a murderer. In that case, she's not the person I thought I knew."

༄ ༄ ༄

"It's remarkable," said Carmichael, settling into the car, "how virtually no one who supposedly knows her has any insight into Mrs. Berowne's character." He glanced back at the church from whence they had just emerged. "The vicar gave us a very clear account of Geoffrey Berowne's character the other day, but he has nothing to say about Mrs. Berowne. He thought she was charming. Ha!"

"It's very discouraging, sir," agreed Gibbons carefully. He was doing his level best to appear normal, and not as if he were particularly panicked about anything, and thus far Carmichael seemed to have noticed nothing.

"What about you, Sergeant?" asked Carmichael suddenly. "You've been spending the most time with her over this case. What do you think?"

The panic rose to new heights and Gibbons swallowed before answering while his thoughts raced.

"Well, I don't know, sir," he answered. "I have to admit, I'd about made up my mind that she was innocent. The more I saw of her, the more I thought so. Obviously, I didn't form a very correct opinion of her," he added, thinking he might have gone too far.

But his words did not appear to have rung any alarms in the chief inspector's mind. "If you say you thought she was charming, Gibbons," he growled, "I'm going to demote you on the spot."

Gibbons grinned. "Well, I did, sir. But aside from that, I thought she seemed very vulnerable, like a person who's lost their anchor. I never thought she was particularly devious, or even clever in that way. And as for being cold-blooded, frankly I found her just the opposite."

Carmichael sighed. "If Berowne was her anchor, she'd never have killed him," he said. "Not unless she had someone else ready to replace him. And there's no evidence of that at all—even those who think the worst of her don't seem to think she'd been having an affair." He sat silently for a space while Gibbons's throbbing pulse counted out the seconds. At last he drew a deep breath and said, "Well, let's get on, lad."

"Yes, sir. Where to?"

"Back to London. There's no one else we can talk to without risking their alerting Mrs. Berowne. It's a pity she's not back yet, but we'll pick her up first thing in the morning. And maybe it's for the best. I won't be sorry to have the extra time to think. We'll take the rest of the day off and come at her fresh in the morning."

Annette was waiting for him when Gibbons arrived home. It had briefly crossed his mind that her shopping excursion might be an excuse to see him, but since in the normal way of things she could not expect to find him home until long past dinnertime, he had discounted the suspicion.

Gibbons was so preoccupied with how he was going to tell her what had happened that for a moment when he saw her, he did not believe it.

"Annette!" he exclaimed. "You're here!"

He was torn between exhilaration and the impending doom of the news he had to break, but she seemed to notice nothing, coming forward to take his hands and kiss him lightly. His hand cupped her cheek as she stepped back and he gazed down into her warm eyes, hating himself for what was to come.

"Let's get inside," he said. "I have something to tell you."

Her eyes widened at his tone. "Has something happened?" she asked anxiously.

"I'm afraid it has," he answered, holding the door for her. "Come up to the flat."

She followed him silently up the stairs, but all pleasure had disappeared from her expression. Gibbons let them into the flat, shrugging out of his jacket, and moving first to the kitchen to put on the kettle. They would shortly, he felt, be in dire need of a cup of tea.

Annette stood a few feet within the door, her bearing marked by uncertainty.

"Jack?" she said. "What's wrong?"

Gibbons came back into the room and, taking her hand, led her to a chair. She kept tight hold of his hand as she sat, so he perched on the arm, reaching out to stroke her hair.

"It's bad news," he said. "But we'll get through it together, Annette—never doubt that."

"But what is it?"

"It's Maddie," said Gibbons, and he could not keep the anger out of his voice. "She rang Carmichael today and now claims that she has proof that you left the house after eleven-fifteen that morning."

Annette appeared altogether bewildered by this statement. "But it's not possible," she protested. "It was eleven when I left—both Kitty and I say the same. She had just brought in Geoffrey's coffee and she would never be late with it. Kitty's always very prompt about everything."

"I know," said Gibbons soothingly. "But McAllister was working in the tulip beds just off the terrace and he saw you leave. He hadn't any idea of what time it was, but he knows it was shortly after Maddie called good morning down to him from her window. Maddie now says that she looked at her clock then and that it was eleven-fifteen."

Annette was shaking her head. "It's not true," she said. Tears sprang into her eyes. "It's not true. I did leave at eleven. Maddie's lying."

"I know that," said Gibbons, cradling her head against him. "I know she's lying, but Carmichael's not so sure. I've done my best to plant doubts in his mind, but he's still going to pull you in for questioning tomorrow." He hesitated. "Annette," he said, "it's going to be bad, the interview. I can't help that. Carmichael's going to do his best to pull you apart like a puzzle and reassemble you more to his liking, and he's very good at what he does. Harrowing doesn't begin to describe it. But you've just got to be strong, no matter how awful it gets, and remember it will be over soon. Carmichael's got no evidence aside from Maddie's lie, and he won't charge you unless he can browbeat a confession out of you. You won't give him that, because we both know you didn't do it."

"Oh God," said Annette, her voice muffled against Gibbons's shirt. "I don't think I can stand it."

"Yes, you can," said Gibbons. "You're stronger than you know and you've already been through so much, you can take this little bit more. It'll be all right in the end, Annette. You've got to remember that."

She looked up at him through her tears. "Will you be there?"

"I can try to be, if you want me," he replied. "But it won't do any good. I won't be able to help you or even smile at you. If Carmichael ever suspects I'm in love with you, I'll lose any influence I have with him. He'll never believe another thing I say about you."

In truth, Gibbons did not want to be present for the interview. He did not want to watch Carmichael use his skills to break down the woman he loved, and he had already invented various excuses to give to his superior.

But Annette was shaking her head. "I don't care," she answered. "It'll be a help if you're there because I'll know there's one person in the room that knows I'm innocent."

"Then I'll ask Carmichael if I can sit in," said Gibbons, albeit reluctantly. "I can't promise, because if he's thought of an errand he wants me to run, I'll have to go, but I'll do my best."

"Thank you," she whispered.

Her tears were tapering off and Gibbons released her to lean back in the chair.

"There're two things you have to remember," he said, holding her eyes. "When we come to pick you up in the morning, you must act surprised. Carmichael mustn't know I've warned you. You can do that, can't you?"

She nodded, blotting her face with a handkerchief. "Yes, I'll remember," she promised. "I'll be surprised."

"The other thing is to demand your solicitor," continued Gibbons. "Carmichael may try to persuade you not to send for him, but don't give in. Refuse to answer anything until the solicitor arrives, and stick to it. No matter how reasonable Carmichael sounds, just keep asking for your lawyer."

"All right. I can do that." She reached up to touch his face. "It'll come right in the end. You say so and I believe you."

"You'll never have cause to doubt me," Gibbons promised.

CHAPTER

15

The morning dawned, bright and dazzling. Bethancourt did not feel at all in step with it. His first thought upon waking was of Gibbons taking the woman he loved in for questioning and standing by while Carmichael raked her over the coals. He had gone round to Gibbons's flat last night, after Annette had left, and spent his evening trying to cheer his friend. He had rashly promised to drive down to Hurtwood Hall this morning and do his own poking around, although he couldn't think what earthly good it would do. Nevertheless, he spent far less time over his coffee and newspaper than was usual, and was on the road an hour after waking.

When he arrived, he drove around to the service entrance, and knocked on the kitchen door with his mind firmly made up to be as objective as possible. If there was a reason to think Annette Berowne innocent, Bethancourt was determined to find it.

"Well, you're the day after the fair," said Kitty when she saw him.

"Excuse me?"

She waved impatiently. "They've been and gone, and taken Mrs. Berowne with them."

"Ah, yes, I know. Can I come in?"

"Yes, of course." She stood back to let him in and added, "Luckily it was only sandwiches for lunch."

"What?"

"I mean, I didn't have a lot of food waiting that would go to waste."

Bethancourt eyed her. There were circles under her eyes and her usual spirits appeared to be flagging.

"Sleep badly?" he asked sympathetically.

She pushed her hair back from her face. "I suppose I did. It's all very unsettling, you know. I mean, first Mr. Paul's a murderer, then he isn't and we're back where we started, and then it's Mrs. Berowne. I suppose you think you've got the right person this time?"

Bethancourt opened his mouth to say yes, and then closed it again as he remembered his resolution. "I don't know," he said at last. "It's a mess of a case."

Kitty sighed. "It is that. Well, sit down and have some coffee."

She joined him at the table, tucking one foot up on the chair and cradling her mug in both hands. Always before when Bethancourt had been in her kitchen, she had been a bundle of energy, tackling one job after another without pause, but now she had the air of being too weary to rise.

"You seem almost sorry that it's turned out to be Mrs. Berowne," he said.

"It's not that. It's the waiting to see if it is really her. I learned my lesson with Mr. Paul. The police took him in and I thought, 'Well, thank God it's over.' Only it wasn't. And let me tell you, Maddie gloating is no easier to put up with than Maddie furious about her nephew being suspected."

"She's been crowing, has she?"

"That's an understatement. She suggested we could have a bottle of champagne tonight with dinner. I don't feel like champagne."

"No, I don't expect you do. Tell me, Kitty, could she possibly be lying?"

Kitty looked surprised. "Maddie? You mean about the time she saw McAllister?"

"That's right." Bethancourt leaned back and reached out to scratch Cerberus's ears. "It's not that I firmly believe Annette to be innocent," he said, "but the timing does concern me. From the very first it was clear that Maddie loathed Annette and believed in her guilt more firmly than in God. Then the police come up with a motive for Paul Berowne and Maddie blows a gasket. The police have to release him, but Maddie had to know it wasn't over, and that Carmichael wasn't concentrating solely on Annette. And suddenly she remembers that it was eleven-fifteen when she said good morning to McAllister."

Kitty frowned and rubbed the tip of her nose. "Put like that," she said, "it does seem suspicious. But I honestly don't know, Phillip. Maddie's smart; it's not as though she couldn't think of it. But would she do it? I don't know. I guess I can't rule that out, though lying isn't like her."

Bethancourt nodded and sipped his coffee. "Tell me something else, then," he said. "Have you noticed any changes in Mrs. Berowne in the last few months, before her husband died?"

"Changes? Changes how?"

"I mean did she seem any different than she did when you first came to work here? Was she any less happy, or less bright and cheery? Did she drink more, or did she seem bored? Did she spend more time out shopping, or did she and Geoffrey have more frequent arguments?"

"They never had very many," Kitty answered. "And she certainly wasn't drinking more—I buy the liquor and I'd have noticed." She paused thoughtfully and looked off into space. At last she shook her head. "I don't think so," she said. "Certainly I never noticed a change in her. Why do you ask?"

"Because if she's guilty, one would rather expect some sign that she was tired of her husband, however small. On the other hand, perhaps she's just a superb actress and kept whatever she felt to herself."

Kitty was silent again, thinking this over. Then she sighed. "If there was any sign, I missed it," she said. "Even going over the past with that in mind, I can't pick out anything about her that seemed different."

Bethancourt was disappointed, though he kept it to himself. He had very much been hoping that Kitty, her memory jogged, would come up with something that would settle his conscience. Instead, all she had done was, in essence, to say that Gibbons's view of the case was perfectly possible.

Gibbons's nerves were on edge. Carmichael had determined that the best way to begin was to persuade Annette to admit that Berowne's money had been a factor in her decision to marry him. He had been leading up to this point gradually, and Gibbons had inwardly winced to see the wariness fade from Annette's face as the questions remained innocuous. But he knew, as she did not, that the interrogation would not remain innocuous for long.

It was dawning on her even now as Carmichael's questions became more pointed.

"So," the chief inspector was saying almost casually, "it was only four months after you began dating that Geoffrey Berowne proposed to you. And how long was it before you realized that he was a very wealthy man?"

Annette looked suddenly uncertain.

"I—I don't know," she faltered. "I suppose—I knew he was well-off by the places he'd take me. And, of course, when I saw the estate, I realized that he must have money."

"And that no doubt influenced your decision to marry him."

"No!" she answered, stung. "It did not. I would never marry a man I didn't love, no matter how rich he was."

"And yet you seem to only fall in love with wealthy men," said Carmichael evenly.

Her eyes pleaded with him, but she did not answer.

"It's rather curious, that. All three of your husbands were not only well-off, but many years older than yourself. Why is it, do you think, that you are only attracted to older men?"

Her eyes went to Gibbons involuntarily, but she looked away again at once.

"I don't know," she said softly. "It just happened that way."

"So if Geoffrey Berowne had been a younger man, a man your own age, for instance, do you think you would still have fallen in love with him?"

"I suppose so." She looked up. "It's what's inside a person that counts, isn't it?"

"Certainly," agreed Carmichael, "but in love, the outer package is generally assumed to play a role as well. Were you sexually attracted to Geoffrey Berowne?"

Annette flushed scarlet. "I loved him," she muttered.

"Yes, so you've said, but did you want to go to bed with him?"

"Of course I did."

"How long was it after your first date that you did sleep with him?"

She was obviously embarrassed, and answered in a low voice, her eyes on the table before her.

"It was the night he proposed. Six weeks before we were married."

"I see. So you dated him for two and a half months and although you lusted after him, you couldn't manage to get him into bed? I find that difficult to believe."

"He never asked me," she said desperately. "I never thought it strange—he had very conservative morals."

"Yes, a highly religious man, according to your vicar. So you never tried to seduce him because you were afraid of offending him?"

"I—I thought he would ask when he wanted to."

Gibbons clenched his fists and looked away. He knew it was only the beginning.

Bethancourt knocked on the door of Maddie Wellman's room with trepidation. He had not seen her since the day she had thrown him and Gibbons out, and he was unsure of what his reception might be. He was counting on the fact that she would probably be pleased at the opportunity to gloat over him and thus would tolerate his presence.

She looked surprised to see him, but immediately set aside the book she had been reading and motioned him in.

"I certainly didn't expect to see you," she said. "Come in and sit down."

"Shall Cerberus come in, too?" he asked. "I brought him up because you seemed to like him."

"Yes. Yes, of course."

She held out her hands to the great dog, who padded over to sniff them politely and allow his chest to be petted.

"Yes, you're a beautiful boy, aren't you?" she cooed.

Bethancourt lowered himself into a chair and reflected that the conversation might be all right after all.

"I came," he said, "to take my leave of you and Kitty, now that the case seems to be wrapped up."

"Ha!" she said, so sharply that Cerberus started. "And no thanks to you lot."

"No," admitted Bethancourt. "Thanks to you, as I understand it."

"Really," she said, "if the police would just tell a body things instead of endlessly asking impertinent questions, they might solve their cases sooner. I'd no idea that McAllister had seen Annette leaving the house that day. If I had, I could have solved the whole thing half an hour after that ass Gorringe got here."

She was obviously still greatly annoyed with the police performance, but she was equally obviously enjoying herself. Bethancourt began to relax a little.

"I'd no idea you didn't know," he said. "I suppose we all just assumed, since you'd seen McAllister out there, you would realize he had seen Annette."

"Never occurred to me," she said. "Usually McAllister's completely oblivious to anything other than the job at hand. And besides, he was nowhere near the side door when I saw him."

"But you knew the police had been questioning him?"

"Of course, I'm not blind. But I thought they were just trying to jog his memory, make sure he hadn't seen anything. I was rather amused," she admitted. "Having tried to have a conversation with McAllister myself, I could just imagine the grunts the police were getting instead of the information they wanted."

Bethancourt was exceedingly glad to hear that he and the police had apparently been separated in her mind.

"Gwenda was the only one he ever talked to," she added reminiscently. "I always thought he must have been a bit in love with her, the way he'd listen to whatever she said and run off and do it, while the rest of us could talk a blue streak and he'd just go along and do whatever he'd meant to in the first place." She sighed. "If I saw more of him, I might have known earlier what he'd seen. Apparently he'd complained to Kitty about the police, but she never realized I didn't know. When I came back from talking to him yesterday morning, I was all excited and I burst in on Kitty in the kitchen with the news that McAllister had seen Annette leaving. Quite a triumph, I thought it. And she just stared at me and said, 'Yes, I know.'" Maddie chuckled.

"How did he come to mention it to you?" asked Bethancourt.

"Well, it all started over these tomato seeds Kitty'd bought," said

Maddie, not at all displeased to be asked to tell the story again. "They're a different sort from the kind McAllister usually grows and I can't tell you why she's so keen on them, but she is. She'd given the packet to him and asked him to start them for her, and then discovered he'd never done it. She asked him again, and then they had an argument about it, and finally she came to me. So I went down yesterday morning early and said to him, 'Look here, McAllister, I know it's probably foolishness, but Kitty's got her heart set on these tomatoes. Can't you just indulge her?' And he started in on how he might be able to do extra things like planting extra tomatoes we didn't need if the police would stop pestering him about Mrs. Berowne, but as it was the apple trees were long overdue for spraying. So I said, rather sharply as I recollect, 'Really, McAllister, the police are hardly taking up all of your time. And why should they be bothering you about Mrs. Berowne anyway?' He said he didn't know, and if he'd realized they were going to hound him for the rest of his life, he'd never have told them he saw her leaving that day."

"You must have been very surprised," said Bethancourt.

"Completely taken aback," Maddie agreed. "I just stood there staring at him while he ranted on." She chuckled. "Of course, what he was really trying to do was divert me from Kitty's tomatoes, and it worked beautifully. We never mentioned them again—although I've promised her to have another go at him tomorrow."

Bethancourt grinned. "Good luck with it," he said.

"Oh, I think he'll give in eventually, especially since he won't be able to get me off the subject again so easily. I have to admit that when he said he'd seen Annette leaving, all thoughts of tomatoes fled my mind completely. At first I was furious, thinking the police were trying to cover up for her, and then I realized it was a matter of *when* he'd seen her leave. So almost at once I asked him whether it was before or after I'd called down to him, and he looked very surprised and said, 'That's right, you said good morning. I'd forgotten.'

Which," she added exasperatedly, "is just like him. It's a wonder he didn't forget seeing Annette as well."

"And of course you remembered perfectly well what time it was."

"I did. Because I recollect thinking it was taking me longer than I thought to answer those letters, and wondering if I'd have them done before lunch at the rate I was going."

If she was lying, Bethancourt could not tell. Her eyes met his without hesitation and he could see nothing in them beyond glee at having been proved right in the end.

"Well," he said, "whether McAllister ever plants them or not, Kitty's tomatoes have already served us all well."

Gibbons rubbed his hands down his pant legs. He could not remember ever having sweaty palms before, but then he had never felt so awful. The effort to keep his expression blank while emotions more powerful than any he had ever felt before raged inside him was coming near to breaking him.

Annette was crying now, answering Carmichael's questions in a choked voice while the tears streamed down her cheeks and her eyes held the hurt, bewildered look of a wounded animal.

Gibbons was not far from tears himself and he wondered how much more he could take before he, too, broke down. He looked at the clock and was appalled to find they had only been at it for two hours. It seemed an eternity.

Bethancourt stood at the edge of the terrace and stared across the expanse of the flagstones at the side door. He crouched down beside the tulips, riotous with color in the sunlight, and peered up between the balusters of the terrace railing. The door was still visible, but no one coming out of it would notice him here. He sighed and sat down abruptly in the grass. From what he could see, the story McAllister and Maddie told fit perfectly. Maddie had reason to lie about the time, and she might have done so. But she equally well might be telling the truth. There was no help here for Gibbons.

"Here!" McAllister's shout broke into Bethancourt's thoughts and he turned to see the gardener waving wildly at Cerberus, who was engaged in sniffing along the hedge. The dog's head jerked up and he cocked it to one side, apparently trying to make sense of McAllister's energetic gesticulations.

Bethancourt rose hastily and called his pet to heel.

"I'm terribly sorry, Mr. McAllister," he said, going to meet the gardener. "Was he bothering something? I should have kept a better eye on him."

McAllister was eyeing the dog suspiciously.

"Dogs don't belong in gardens," he said truculently. "They piss all over and kill the plants."

Bethancourt privately doubted that such a green and robust hedge would die quite so precipitously, but he merely reiterated his apology and said he would keep Cerberus close.

McAllister grunted and transferred his suspicious gaze to Bethancourt. "I remember you," he said. "You're one of them police. I suppose you've come to hear the whole thing again." He drew a deep and long-suffering sigh and, before Bethancourt could respond, strode over to the tulip bed, stopping not far from where Bethancourt had been sitting. "I was working here," said McAllister rapidly. He pointed up at the house. "That's Miss Wellman's window there. She opened it and called down good morning. I waved back and then finished spreading the last of a bag of mulch. I stood up to get another bag, which was lying handy, right there." He pointed again, this time to a spot on the grass. "As I turned around with it, I see Mrs. Berowne coming out of the door there and going off down those steps. And that was it," he finished, glaring at Bethancourt.

"That's what happened and that's all that happened and I'm sorrier than I can say that I ever mentioned it."

"It's all very clear," said Bethancourt soothingly. "Maddie waved to you and a few moments later you saw Annette leaving."

McAllister gave him a disgusted look. "Not her," he said witheringly. "It was t'other one."

For an instant, Bethancourt's mind failed to understand what McAllister had said, and he stared at him blankly. Then, "What did you say?" he demanded sharply. "The other one? You mean it was Marion Berowne you saw come out of the house and not Annette?"

"That's right. And that's what I've always said," he added stubbornly.

Bethancourt's mind fled back to that first interview with the gardener. He could not remember clearly, but he thought the man had simply said, "Mrs. Berowne." Kitty and Mary Simmons always said, "Mr. Paul" or "Mrs. Marion" to differentiate the younger Berownes from the older, but apparently McAllister did not bother, letting the context of his remarks make the distinction for him.

Bethancourt felt as though he were in a dream. It was totally impossible that a whole series of police detectives had simply assumed McAllister was referring to Annette. And yet, he had himself made the assumption because he knew that Annette had indeed left the house by that door.

"You're sure?" he said. "You're sure it was Marion Berowne, the dark-haired one who lives in Little House and is married to Paul?"

McAllister looked at him as if he had gone mad. "Of course I'm sure," he said indignantly. "There's nothing wrong with my sight. I need spectacles for reading, but not for anything else, and it's not as if those two look alike."

"No," agreed Bethancourt, still in a daze, "they don't."

McAllister was frowning. "Did Miss Wellman think I meant Mrs. Berowne?"

"Yes," said Bethancourt, abruptly recovering. "Yes, I believe she did. Thank you, Mr. McAllister—I've got to go. Come, Cerberus."

And he took off at a run, leaving the gardener staring after him.

It was an enormous relief to Gibbons when the constable came and beckoned him surreptitiously out of the interview room. Relief mixed with guilt that he must leave Annette to struggle on alone. He knew she was watching him as he left.

Outside, he passed his hand over his face and drew a deep breath.

"What is it?" he asked.

"A phone call, sir," said the constable, clearly a little nervous at having interrupted such an important interview. "I wouldn't have intruded, but he said it was urgent. A man named Bethancourt."

"All right," said Gibbons, pushing away from the wall. "I'll take it over there."

Bethancourt's voice was excited, but to Gibbons's weary brain it seemed to come from a great way off.

"Phillip?" he said. "I can't talk long—I have to get back there."

"What I've got changes everything," said Bethancourt. "McAllister never saw Annette leave the house at all."

"What?" said Gibbons, sounding only vaguely puzzled. "But he said he did, Phillip—he's said so from the very beginning."

"No, he didn't," insisted Bethancourt. "He only said he saw Mrs. Berowne. But he didn't mean Annette, Jack. He meant Marion Berowne. It was she he saw, not Annette at all."

There was a pause on the other end of the line.

"Jack? Did you hear me?"

"Marion Berowne?" repeated Gibbons. "Oh, my God. Where are you, Phillip?"

"At Hurtwood Hall. I'm calling from the car."

"Stay there."

Gibbons rang off abruptly and ran back to the interview room without even pausing to assimilate what he had been told. The news seemed hardly credible to him, but it was an excuse to stop the interview and by this time he would have taken any excuse at all to do so. He stuck his head in the door and said, "Sir? I'm afraid I need to see you a moment."

Everyone turned to stare at him, which told him that his emotions were plain to be read on his face, but he did not care.

Carmichael was surprised, but nevertheless said, "Of course, Sergeant," and suspended the interview verbally for the benefit of the recorder. Then he rose and came out into the hall, shutting the door firmly behind him, and looked at his sergeant curiously.

"What is it, lad?" he asked. "You seem all of-a-to-do."

"I suppose I am, sir," said Gibbons. "Phillip Bethancourt just rang. He went down to Hurtwood Hall this morning to say goodbye to Kitty Whitcomb and ran into McAllister. He says McAllister claims he never saw Annette Berowne leaving the house, that it was Marion Berowne he saw."

"Marion Berowne?" repeated Carmichael, thunderstruck. "Is Bethancourt sure?"

"He says he is, sir."

Carmichael frowned. "I remember talking to McAllister that first day. I could have sworn he just said 'Mrs. Berowne.' And I distinctly remember that all the other servants referred to her as 'Mrs. Marion' or 'Mrs. Paul.' "

"That's how I remember it, sir," agreed Gibbons. "I suppose McAllister could have meant Marion Berowne instead of Annette, but at the time all I remember thinking was that we had confirmation that Annette Berowne did leave the way she said she did at some point."

Carmichael's frown deepened. He re-entered the interview room and said, "Forgive me, Mrs. Berowne, but I've been called away. Constable, would you please escort Mrs. Berowne and her solicitor back to a holding cell?"

"Yes, sir," said the policewoman who had been brought in to witness the interview.

Annette looked confused, and her solicitor frowned, but Carmichael's attention was already on the case file lying open on the table. Gibbons smiled at Annette as she passed him, but dared give her no clearer sign, and then they were gone and Carmichael was beckoning him over.

"Here's McAllister's statement," he said as the WPC closed the door behind her. " 'I saw Mrs. Berowne leave the house and go down the terrace steps along the path.' That's what you wrote, Sergeant, and that's what I remember."

"Yes, sir, and I certainly thought he meant Annette Berowne at the time."

"But look here, lad. Just before that, McAllister said that Mr. Berowne came along quite early and spoke to him. I remember that, too, because I thought he meant Geoffrey Berowne and asked if he didn't mean Mr. Paul Berowne."

Gibbons was nodding excitedly. "That's true, sir. I remember it as well. What does Commander Andrews's report say?"

Carmichael turned back the pages until he came to the reports that had been given to them when they took over the case.

"The same thing," he said after a moment. "That James McAllister saw Annette Berowne leaving the house that morning, but of course that's just paraphrased from the actual interview." He leaned back. "I can't think why no one questioned this before. Even Maddie Wellman—she may have lied about the time, but I'm as certain as I can be that she wasn't concealing Marion Berowne's activities from us."

"I know why I didn't, sir," said Gibbons. "It was because that's what I was expecting to hear. Mrs. Berowne—I mean, Annette— had already told us she left the house that way and walked through the garden to the footpath and I knew from the case file that McAllister said he'd seen her do so. So when I heard him say it myself, it never occurred to me to question it."

"I suppose that's what was in my mind, as well," said Carmichael and he grimaced. "This is one case where great minds do not think alike. I wonder how Bethancourt came to discover it."

"I don't know, sir," said Gibbons. "I came to report to you as soon as he'd told me. But he's standing by the phone—I thought you'd want to speak to him yourself."

"So I do," said Carmichael, closing the case file and rising. "We've got a lot to do here, Gibbons, but let's take first things first. I'll talk to Bethancourt and then we'd best check with Gorringe and Andrews before we leave here to see McAllister. And while we're about it, we can be thinking about what motive Marion Berowne could possibly have to kill her father-in-law."

Bethancourt, after confirming to the chief inspector that he was absolutely certain of what McAllister had told him, punched the disconnect button and began turning the same problem over in his mind. He lit yet a third cigarette—oblivious to the one still burning in the ashtray—while he meditated, trying to wrap his mind around this new development. It was not that Marion Berowne had no motive at all; there was the £100,000 bequest and a loveless marriage to get out of. But Bethancourt could not see why she would have needed £100,000 so desperately and, as for her marriage, she had very little to lose by seeking a divorce. Any court would see to it that her alimony payments were adequate—unless, of course, she remarried. Could Marion Berowne have fallen in love with a poor man?

With that thought, he sat bolt upright and exclaimed, "What an idiot I've been!"

He reached again for the phone.

271

"I can't talk now, Phillip," said his sister when she came on the line. "I've got a meeting of the local garden club here in full swing."

"This will only take a moment, Margaret," Bethancourt promised. "Just tell me this: did Sir Rodney ever have an affair with Marion Berowne?"

"What? Really, Phillip, how can you ask such a question? Even if it was true, it's in the worst possible taste."

"Yes, but is it true? The sooner you tell me, the sooner you can get back to the garden club."

"How on earth should I know?" retorted Margaret. "I don't make a habit of prying into other people's affairs."

"You knew he'd slept with Claire Lyndhurst," said Bethancourt. "And I know, even if you don't, that Rosemary Chilton was having an affair with him. He tried it on with you, which only leaves Nancy Clarendon, Mildred Urqhart, and Marion Berowne from the orphan's committee. Nancy and Mildred are both over sixty, which really only leaves us with Marion. You can't tell me he didn't at least try."

"I don't know and I don't want to know," insisted Margaret.

"Margaret, please. It's terribly important."

There was a pause.

"Claire did say she thought Sir Rodney had broken it off with her because of Marion," said Margaret at last, unwillingly. "I don't know if she was right or not, and that is absolutely all I am prepared to say on the subject."

"That's enough," said Bethancourt happily. "Thank you, Margaret. You can go back to the garden club now."

"Good of you to give me permission," muttered Margaret and rang off.

The road spun away beneath the police car and Gibbons followed its curves effortlessly as it wove in and out of the sunshine. He was walking on air. He hardly cared that Marion Berowne had committed murder, so long as he could prove that Annette had not. Gorringe and Andrews had agreed that McAllister had referred to seeing "Mrs. Berowne" leave the house, and that they had never questioned the idea that he meant Annette. Moreover, in the notes Andrews's sergeant had taken during their interviews with McAllister, it was clear that Andrews himself had always referred to Annette as Mrs. Berowne while speaking with the gardener.

Gibbons had never been so happy to be wrong about something in his life. He turned into the estate's drive and gleefully stepped on the accelerator.

Carmichael was no less anxious to reach his new chief witness. "I won't truly believe it until I hear it for myself," he said. "I still can't believe I made such a mistake."

"But it's the right answer at last, sir," said Gibbons. "It has to be. Marion Berowne had no reason to lie about visiting her father-in-law if her visit was innocent. When Commander Andrews first spoke to her, no one even realized Geoffrey hadn't died a natural death."

"True," said Carmichael. "But I'd be happier if I could see a motive. Even if she was set on divorce, that doesn't give her anything like the kind of motive it gave her husband. He stood to lose everything if he divorced her, but she simply didn't have the same things at stake. Geoffrey Berowne couldn't prevent the courts from awarding her alimony, and if she remarried she wouldn't get alimony whether Geoffrey was alive or not."

"But she would have gotten a hundred thousand pounds."

"Yes," agreed Carmichael, "but that would hardly keep her in the style to which she was accustomed. Her lover must have been a very poor man indeed to make a hundred thousand pounds worth murdering for."

"Did she have a lover, sir?" asked Gibbons. "You looked into that, I thought."

"I did," affirmed Carmichael. "I didn't find anything, but that doesn't mean there was nothing there. Those things are the very devil to winkle out. Her friends all said she was faithful as the day is long, but then they would."

Ahead Gibbons could see the gray Jaguar parked along the curve of the drive with his friend leaning up against it. Bethancourt hailed them as they pulled up, coming over to open the car door.

"I've had a thought," he announced, pushing his glasses back up onto the bridge of his nose excitedly. "I do believe that Marion Berowne was having an affair with Rodney Randolph."

"Is he poor?" asked Carmichael, climbing out of the car.

"Poor?" Bethancourt looked startled. "Well, no. I wouldn't call him wealthy, but I should think he was reasonably well-off. Why?"

"Because," answered Gibbons, "she must have wanted that hundred thousand pounds for something. Geoffrey couldn't prevent her getting a divorce the way he could his son—if that's all she wanted, she had no reason to kill him."

"He might have had some other kind of hold over her we know nothing about."

"How sure are you about this affair?" asked Carmichael.

"Not positive," answered Bethancourt. "I'm only really sure he tried it on with her. If he did succeed, I should say he called it off after Geoffrey's death when Marion began talking about marriage. She must have been devastated."

"Why do you think that?" asked Carmichael. "Why shouldn't they have carried on?"

"Well, for one thing," said Bethancourt, looking disgusted, "Rodney would never have had any intention of marrying her. It's why he sticks to married women, so there's no risk of real involvement. But beyond that, it fits with what I've heard. I just never put it together before. Marion was one of the mainstays of the orphan's charity, even after Geoffrey was murdered. But then, just as the charity ball was coming up, she suddenly started missing meetings and generally not holding up her end."

Carmichael looked confused. "What do charities have to do with it?" he demanded.

"Oh, sorry, of course you wouldn't know. Marion Berowne is on the organizing committee for an orphan's charity whose guiding light is Sir Rodney Randolph. My sister is on the committee as well, which is how I come to know all about it. Rodney had an affair with another woman on the committee, who resigned when he broke it off, but she's a friend of my sister's and told her Rodney had dumped her for Marion Berowne."

"If it's true," mused Carmichael, leaning his elbows thoughtfully on the roof of the car, "it at least gives her a motive for wanting a divorce."

"He probably caught her at just the right psychological moment, too," said Bethancourt bitterly. "Here she is, estranged from her husband and becoming increasingly isolated from her father-in-law by virtue of his new wife. She must have been very lonely, and then along comes Rodney. I think he deserves to be shot."

"You don't think he could have had any hand in planning the murder with her?" asked Gibbons.

"No," answered Bethancourt, "much as I'd like to see him arrested. But the last thing he wanted was to have her free to marry him."

"It still doesn't quite add up in my mind," said Carmichael, "although God knows murders have been committed for even less reason. Well, let's get on and see McAllister."

The gardens were a blaze of color and scent and for the first time that day Bethancourt took note. Gibbons was grinning at him and he felt pleased that he had come through for his friend, even if it had been pure accident.

They found McAllister eventually beyond the gardens among the apple trees. He seemed unusually subdued and was going about his job with considerably less than his accustomed vigor. He did not even seem very upset to have the police come interrupting his work yet again.

"I always meant Mrs. Marion Berowne," he said in response to Carmichael's question. "I did think," he added, "that everybody knew that."

How they were all supposed to have divined his meaning he did not explain, and Carmichael was inclined to be magnanimous.

"Well, at least it's straightened out now," he said. "Didn't you think it odd, though, that Miss Wellman should be so excited over your having seen Marion Berowne rather than Annette?"

McAllister looked troubled. "She was going on about them silly tomatoes," he muttered. "I was just glad she stopped. I thought she was pleased to find out who killed him, and what would it matter who it was?"

"But surely you knew she believed it to be Annette Berowne."

"Did she? I wonder why that was."

The detectives all exchanged incredulous glances.

"Weren't you aware," said Carmichael, "that Miss Wellman didn't get on with Mrs. Berowne?"

McAllister clearly wasn't. "My job's on the grounds," he said. "I don't pay much mind to them in the house."

Still, he seemed upset to learn that he had sent the investigation—and Miss Wellman—off on the wrong path. After they took their leave of him, Carmichael looked worried.

"It's a fine time for him to suddenly start taking an interest in the case," he said, frowning. He glanced back in the direction of the apple orchard, though they had moved out of sight of the gardener. "I had thought," he said, "that we might interview this Randolph before we tackled Mrs. Berowne, but now I'm not so sure. I have a funny feeling that McAllister's conscience is bothering him, and that before day's end he might well be up at the house, baring his soul to Miss Wellman."

"And you think she would warn Marion, sir?" asked Gibbons.

"I don't know, Sergeant," said Carmichael thoughtfully. "She might. Her belief in Annette Berowne's guilt is absolute and she might go to Marion hoping she could explain away what McAllister saw. And I'd much prefer to spring the surprise on Marion Berowne myself and hope to startle something out of her. It's still circumstantial evidence, you see. We've no way even to prove that she knew lilies of the valley were poisonous. On the other hand, if I accuse her of having an affair with Randolph without having confirmed it and it turns out not to be true, it could ruin everything."

The two younger men watched him wrestle with this problem silently. At last he looked up and said, "I'll risk it. If I have to come back to her tomorrow having shown my hand today, at least I'll have had the opportunity to use surprise, and that might well be gone if I don't speak to her at once."

"It makes sense, sir," said Gibbons. "I think you're right."

"Then let's get over to Little House and hope she's home."

They were in luck. As they approached the house, Marion Berowne was plain to be seen sitting with another woman under the trees on the front lawn. A croquet set had been set up beyond the trees and three little boys were enthusiastically knocking the balls about without much regard for the rules of the game. Cerberus loped happily over to join them and they greeted his arrival with joyous squeals.

Marion rose when she caught sight of the police and came to meet them. There were dark circles under her eyes, and she still looked strained, but she smiled as she greeted them.

"Chief Inspector," she said. "I didn't expect to see you here today. I thought—that is, Maddie said you were questioning Annette."

"I have been," agreed Carmichael. "But something came up in

the interview that I wanted to check with you. Could we step inside for a moment?"

"Certainly. Linda will watch the children."

She led the way into the house and turned into the parlor, motioning them into chairs and taking a seat on the sofa herself.

"What can I do for you?" she asked.

"I wanted to ask about your movements the morning of the murder," said Carmichael. "According to your statement, you spent the morning in the schoolroom upstairs with your son."

"That's right," she answered. "We went up as soon as Mrs. Simmons was done."

"And you were still there when Miss Wellman rang to tell you what had happened."

"Yes."

"Then how is it Mr. McAllister claims to have seen you leaving the main house at about eleven-fifteen?"

There was a long, unbroken silence while she simply stared at him.

"Mrs. Berowne?"

"I'm sorry," she said, breaking off her gaze. "I was just so surprised. I can't imagine what McAllister means. He must have confused the days."

"I think not," said Carmichael. "He has always maintained he saw you leave the house by the side door—he told Commander Andrews that the first time the commander spoke to him."

She gave a brittle laugh. "This is incredible," she said. "It makes no sense. If McAllister thought he saw me, why hasn't anyone mentioned it till now?"

"Because he referred to you as 'Mrs. Berowne,'" answered Carmichael. "We all assumed he was talking about Annette, since everyone else here usually refers to you as 'Mrs. Marion.' It was only today that we discovered what he truly meant. There's not the slightest doubt about it. You were seen leaving the house and I would very much like to know why you've lied to us about your visit to your father-in-law."

There was a hunted look in her eyes now as she cast about for an answer.

"I—I did go to see him," she said. "I didn't tell you because I was afraid you'd think I'd killed him."

"Really?" Carmichael raised an eyebrow. "But you didn't tell Commander Andrews either, and when he spoke to you everyone still assumed Mr. Berowne had died naturally."

Her eyes were on her lap and she did not answer.

"What did you go to see him about?"

"What?" She looked up, confused and terrified.

"You must have had some reason to visit Mr. Berowne that morning. Some very specific reason, since you left your son here and couldn't be gone long. What did you wish to speak to him about?"

"I—I don't remember."

"I see."

Bethancourt was beginning to feel acutely uncomfortable and wondered why he had not thought to excuse himself from this scene. It was impossible not to pity this woman, murderer though she might be, and he felt a sudden urge to shake her and demand she tell the truth and have it end. Instead, he busied himself with lighting a cigarette and gazing out the window where the spring glory of the day made a mockery of the darkness inside.

"So," continued Carmichael, "you have no recollection of your conversation or your intent in seeking it, although it was important enough that you left your six-year-old son unattended in order to speak to Mr. Berowne in private. You must admit, Mrs. Berowne, that's not a very satisfactory statement."

She shook her head but did not reply.

"In fact, I think I can do better than that myself," said Carmichael, his voice harsh. "I think you were having an affair, Mrs.

Berowne, and wanted a divorce. You saw the lilies of the valley in Mr. Berowne's study and conceived a plot to be rid of him. You left your son alone and went to the study where you poisoned Geoffrey Berowne's coffee. But it didn't turn out to be worth it, did it? Your lover abandoned you."

Marion burst into tears and buried her face in her hands. She spoke, but her voice was unintelligible.

"What did you say?" asked Carmichael softly, his voice almost soothing now.

"I didn't mean it!" she sobbed. "I was so afraid—I didn't really think. And, oh God, then it was all for nothing! Rodney said he loved me, he said no woman had ever meant what I did to him. He wanted to take me away, to marry me—and it was all lies! Filthy lies! I killed Geoffrey for him, and he didn't love me at all!"

Carmichael rose and offered her his handkerchief. "I'll have to arrest you now," he said quietly. "Anything further you say may be taken down and used in evidence against you."

She was still weeping bitterly and gave no sign that she had heard him. Carmichael stepped back to have a word with his sergeant.

"Gibbons, you'd better bring the car around. And I don't know what we're to do about the boy."

"I'll go and fetch Kitty," volunteered Bethancourt. "She'll take care of Edwin, and she and I will pack Mrs. Berowne's guest off."

"Yes," said Carmichael. "That would be best. Thank you."

Bethancourt nodded and fled.

Kitty, who still believed that Annette was presently being charged for the murder of her husband, was shocked when Bethancourt arrived with the news.

"Good Lord," she said weakly, and leaned back against the kitchen counter where she had been preparing sandwiches. "Mrs. Marion did it? But why?"

"I'll explain on the way," said Bethancourt. "They're taking her away and you've got to come now and fetch Edwin."

Kitty's hands flew to her cheeks and her mouth made a silent O. "But whatever am I to tell him?" she said.

"Nothing," said Bethancourt firmly. "We tell him that his mother's been called away, that's all. Now come along, sweeting."

By the time they arrived back at Little House, Marion Berowne was gone. Apparently she had pulled herself together enough to take leave of her son with a vague promise of seeing him later, and to ask her guest to stay until Kitty arrived. The guest, a Linda Bancroft, was brimming over with curiosity which Bethancourt refused to satisfy.

"I'm terribly sorry to have interrupted your day this way," he said, "but something's come up down at the station that really calls for Mrs. Berowne's presence. I'm sure she'll tell you all about it later. We'd better be getting Edwin back to the house now for lunch."

"Oh, yes," she said, glancing toward her own sons. "Marion and I were just about to make some for the children."

"As I said, I'm sorry to interrupt your plans," said Bethancourt, edging away. "Delighted to have met you."

Marion had evidently put on a good show for her son. Edwin seemed a little confused, but not at all distressed, although Bethancourt could not help but feel sorry for him as he watched him romping with Cerberus on the way back to the house. His little world was about to come apart and there was nothing anyone could do to stop it.

He left the boy with Kitty in the kitchen and reluctantly climbed the stairs to Maddie Wellman's rooms. He had no obligation to break the news to her, but he would have felt ashamed leaving it to Kitty, who was grateful not to have to do it.

"You again?" she said. "I thought you'd left."

"I thought so, too," answered Bethancourt, taking a chair. "I'm afraid I have some bad news."

Maddie studied his face and began to look alarmed.

"What's happened?" she asked.

"I ran into McAllister after I left you," he said. "It was quite by accident, but, well, in the course of the conversation it turned out that when he said he'd seen Mrs. Berowne leaving the house after you waved to him, it was Marion and not Annette that he meant."

Maddie's eyes widened in surprise. "What?" she barked. "Marion? But Marion was at Little House with Edwin."

"So we all thought. I'm sorry, Miss Wellman, but Marion's confessed to poisoning Mr. Berowne."

"Marion?" Maddie repeated incredulously. "She's confessed?"

"Yes."

"But why on earth would she do such a thing? It makes no sense."

Bethancourt shrugged. "She was having an affair and wanted a divorce," he said. "It doesn't seem much of a motive, but she must have believed that Mr. Berowne would be able to stop her. And she'd been very unhappy for a very long time—I think she would have done almost anything for a chance to be happy at last."

"But to kill Geoffrey . . ." Maddie shook her head and then looked at him sharply. "Just how did this confession come about?" she asked suspiciously. "Without a solicitor, I'll be bound. That chief inspector of yours had a hand in it, didn't he? I always knew he fancied Annette. What did he do to get Marion to confess, threaten Edwin?"

"No, Miss Wellman. He simply confronted her with the fact that she had been seen leaving the house. I'm sorry, but it's true. Marion killed Geoffrey. I know you thought Annette did it—hell, so did I— but I heard Marion's confession and she didn't say it to protect Edwin or because Carmichael hammered it out of her. She confessed because she was caught and she's been wracked with guilt and regret ever since she did it."

Maddie heard the sincerity in his voice and all the combativeness drained out of her.

"If you say so, I believe you," she muttered. "But I still can't quite fathom it. Marion, of all people . . ."

"I know. It's difficult to accept." Bethancourt rose. "I have to be going. I just thought you should know."

"Yes. Thank you for coming to tell me."

She did not succeed in summoning up a smile for his departure and Bethancourt wished that his previous farewell to her could have stood, when she had smiled gaily at him and he had been able to respond in kind.

When they arrived back at the station, Gibbons was delighted to be given the errand of releasing Annette. She looked up as he entered, her eyes full of dread, and then frowned, puzzled by his air of good cheer.

"I'm very sorry for the delay, Mrs. Berowne," he said, nodding to her solicitor. "I'd like to thank you for your help with our inquiries today." The solicitor's eyes narrowed at this well-known phrase, but Annette merely looked confused. "You're free to go," Gibbons finished.

"That is certainly satisfactory," said the solicitor, rising. "Might I ask if you anticipate having to question my client at some later date?"

"I don't believe that will be necessary," said Gibbons. Annette was looking from one to the other of them in complete bewilderment, and Gibbons reflected that there was no reason they should not be told the truth. "We've arrested Mrs. Marion Berowne for the murder of your husband."

Annette's eyes widened in astonishment. The solicitor, better versed in the vagaries of police investigations, merely nodded. "That's very good indeed," he said. He turned to his client. "A difficult day, Mrs. Berowne, but at least it's ended well. Would you like me to drive you home?"

Annette was not listening. She was still staring at Gibbons, stunned.

"Marion?" she said incredulously. "Marion killed Geoffrey? But why?"

"She wanted a divorce," answered Gibbons. "I'm not sure why she thought Geoffrey would be able to prevent it, but apparently she did."

The solicitor, who did not care about motives so long as they were not ascribed to his client, said, "Ah," and glanced at his watch.

"But Geoffrey wouldn't—" began Annette. "I mean—I don't understand."

"I know it's a shock," said Gibbons sympathetically. "Perhaps you'd like a cup of tea?"

"I'm afraid I really must be going," said the solicitor firmly. "I'd be happy to drop you at home, Mrs. Berowne, but I can't wait."

"What?" asked Annette vaguely, aware of him for the first time since Gibbons's announcement. "Oh, of course. You go on, Ben. I'm sure the sergeant will phone a taxi for me. I just need a few moments to take this in."

"As you will. Don't hesitate to ring me if you need anything more. Good day, Sergeant."

Left alone, Annette stared at Gibbons as if willing an explanation out of him. With the solicitor gone, he came to sit beside her and took her hand.

"I was surprised, too," he said. "I knew, of course, that it wasn't you, but I had thought it much more likely that it was either Maddie or Paul. Marion just didn't seem to have a motive, and I still don't understand it."

"But are you sure?" asked Annette. "Perhaps there's some mistake, as there was with Paul."

Gibbons shook his head. "We're quite sure," he said. "Marion confessed."

"She confessed?" Annette shook her head. "I can't believe it.

What happened, Jack? I know the chief inspector was sure it was me this morning."

"I forgot you didn't know." Gibbons told her about Bethancourt's activities that morning and their results.

"Then that's it," said Annette rather emptily when he'd finished. "That's the end of it at last. I suppose I'm glad of that, but to know for certain that one of the family actually killed him . . . it's hard."

"I know," said Gibbons soothingly. "Let me get you that cup of tea."

"No." She drew a deep breath and managed a tremulous smile. "I'd really rather go home and have a stiff drink. And I'm sure you have things to do. Will I see you tonight?"

"Probably not," said Gibbons regretfully. "I imagine I'll be tied up here all evening. But I'll ring you in the morning and I don't see why we shouldn't have a celebratory dinner tomorrow."

She squeezed his hand. "I'll look forward to that," she said. She tilted her face up to be kissed, and then let him lead her from the room.

"So you were wrong about her," said Marla that night at dinner.

"I was wrong about her being a murderer," said Bethancourt, loosening an oyster from its shell. "I'm not so sure I was wrong about her making use of Gibbons."

"For what, in God's name?" asked Marla irritably. She had lost interest in the topic several minutes ago.

"As a port in a storm," answered Bethancourt. "But maybe I'm wrong about that, too," he added, reaching to refill her wineglass. "Let's hope so."

"Let's," agreed Marla, with the finality of one who had thoroughly exhausted a subject. "Phillip, did I tell you that horrible man has been ringing up the agency and leaving me messages?"

"What horrible man?" asked Bethancourt.

"You know—from the charity ball. Ronny Rotter or whatever his name is."

"Sir Rodney Randolph?" Bethancourt began to laugh.

"I doubt it'll come to trial," said Gibbons.

It was nearly a week later and he was comfortably sprawled in one of Bethancourt's armchairs with a glass of Lagavulin in his hand. Despite the intervening days, it was the first opportunity the friends had had to consult with each other since the arrest.

"Her solicitors seem more interested in talking us down from murder one," continued Gibbons. "And I think it likely they'll succeed. After all, they could work up a lot of sympathy for her among a jury—a husband who tried to leave her while she was pregnant and from whom she was subsequently estranged despite her best efforts to hold the marriage together, as well as being cut off from her father-in-law because of his remarriage."

"Unsound mind," agreed Bethancourt from the sofa. "But you haven't told me, Jack, why she did it. Did you ever find out?"

"Didn't I?" said Gibbons, surprised. "I thought I'd told you last week—it came to light quickly enough."

"No, you didn't," said Bethancourt, carefully restraining himself from pointing out that nearly all their telephone conversations had centered around Annette rather than the case.

"Oh. Well, it makes much more sense than her somehow believing that Geoffrey could prevent the divorce. She thought—and she may have been right—that he could take Edwin away from her."

"That's ironic," said Bethancourt grimly, "seeing as how she's now lost him anyway. How did she imagine Geoffrey would manage that?"

"She believed if she tried to break up her marriage, Geoffrey would see that as a sure sign that she was an unfit mother since no good parent would try to deny a child its father. I don't know whether he would have or not—Annette claims such a thing would never have occurred to him, but then she's never believed he really meant to disinherit Paul for his infidelity. Anyway, Marion had no doubts about it. She thought he'd accuse her of all sorts of things, starting with adultery and ending up with alcoholism and mental instability."

Bethancourt was startled. "She's not an alcoholic, is she?"

"No, of course not," answered Gibbons. "But the accusations could be enough, especially if Paul backed them up and Marion thought he might have, if Geoffrey brought pressure to bear. And with all of the high-priced legal talent Geoffrey could command, she didn't see how she could fight it. She knew Randolph couldn't afford a long, drawn-out battle in the courts." Gibbons frowned and sipped his drink. "That's the only bad thing about not going to trial," he added. "I was looking forward to seeing Randolph totally humiliated in court. You can't say the murder was his fault, since if he'd been completely sincere about wanting to marry her, she'd still have done the same thing, but on the other hand, if he hadn't seduced her, it would never have happened."

"Don't worry about Rodney," said Bethancourt. "I've got plans for him. What about the lilies of the valley? How did she know they were poisonous?"

Gibbons laughed. "That's the most incredible thing of all. Geoffrey told her himself. She brought Edwin by to visit him the day after Annette had put the flowers in the study and Marion remarked how pretty they were. So Geoffrey told her that they were deadly poison and even showed her the bit in his poison book about them. Marion says she had never considered killing him until that happened, and then it seemed almost like fate."

"Fate it was, at that," said Bethancourt. "I'll have to remember not to point murder weapons out to people."

"What did you mean about Randolph?" asked Gibbons suspiciously. "You're not planning to ambush him in a dark alley and hit him, are you? Because I would hate to have to arrest you for assault and battery."

"No, no," said Bethancourt, airily waving a hand. "Although I admit it did occur to me. But he'd recover all too quickly and meanwhile all his friends and associates would lavish sympathy on him. No, I've something more permanent in mind."

"Like what?"

Bethancourt smiled and sipped his drink. "I'll tell you if it comes off," he said. "How's Annette doing?"

"Better," said Gibbons. "She's been pretty devastated that Geoffrey was killed, as she sees it, by mistake. Since he would never have interfered in Marion's divorce, I mean, and since Randolph never wanted her to get one to begin with. I have to admit, sometimes it's made me a bit jealous, although of course I understand. But just lately she seems to be getting over it, and I've made plans for us to go off to Cornwall this weekend and have two whole days all to ourselves."

Gibbons had a positively dreamy look in his eyes, and Bethancourt repressed a sigh.

"That sounds just the thing," he said.

"Phillip," said Lord Ashcroft, "what's this my wife's been telling me about Rodney Randolph?"

Bethancourt quelled a desire to smile. He had never before enjoyed himself so much at one of his sister's dinner parties, which tended to be full of dull, well-meaning people, a great many of whom were involved in charity work. In fact, he had earlier been reflecting that the world of charities was a relatively small one and had a definite hierarchy, nearly all of whom seemed to be represented tonight. And Lady Ashcroft, by virtue of her title and her connections with the royal family, was very definitely as high up the ladder as he could reach.

"Rodney?" he said now in response to his lordship. "Oh, yes, a very sad affair, that. I always knew, of course, that he was a bit of a ladies' man, but I'd no idea he took things quite so far."

"Laura said he was mixed up in the Berowne murder," said Lord Ashcroft. "She said you told her so."

Bethancourt, with a sad face, related the facts of the case, stressing the ungentlemanly behavior of Sir Rodney in seducing a lonely and vulnerable woman with blandishments that made her believe he was, so to speak, offering her the golden apple of happiness when in fact he hadn't meant a word of it. Bethancourt waxed quite eloquent on the subject, and when he was done, Lord Ashcroft frowned.

"I'd heard something about Randolph being the reason Claire Lyndhurst resigned from the orphan's committee," he said. "I don't like to credit rumors, and we all know sometimes these things happen, but I'd no idea it was part of a pattern. At least, it seems that way to me." He cocked an inquiring eyebrow at Bethancourt.

"I don't know about Claire," said Bethancourt, "but—" and here he lowered his voice, "I do know Rodney made advances to my sister. She sent him packing, of course, probably with a flea in his ear, if I know Margaret. There's no nonsense about her."

"Certainly not," agreed Lord Ashcroft. "I'm glad we had this little chat, Phillip. I've found it very interesting. I take it you know of it from your friends at the Yard?"

"That's right," agreed Bethancourt. "Marion Berowne has confessed, so there won't be a trial, and they're very pleased over there to have wrapped it up so nicely."

"Yes," said Lord Ashcroft. "Good work, that. Excuse me a minute—I'd just like a word with Nancy Clarenden."

Bethancourt watched him wend his way toward another of the charity world's guiding lights with satisfaction.

"You're looking very pleased with yourself," said Margaret at his elbow.

Bethancourt raised his glass. "It's a wonderful party, Margaret."

She eyed him suspiciously, well aware of his usual attitude toward her soirees. "Thanks very much," she said. "We're about to go in to dinner. I've put you next to Mildred Urqhart, and I want you to pay particular attention to her. She's been in low spirits ever since her husband's stroke."

"I will do my utmost to cheer her," promised Bethancourt, reflecting that Mildred, too, was much involved with charities. It should be a lesson to him, he thought as he went to escort Mrs. Urqhart in to dinner, that even Margaret's social snobbery had its uses.

ML

10/16